The Redeemable Prince

The Star-Crossed Series

Volume Seven

Rachel Higginson

The Redeemable Prince

The Star-Crossed Series
Book Seven

By Rachel Higginson

Copy Editing by Carolyn Moon
Cover Design by Caedus Design Co.

Other Books Now Available by Rachel Higginson

Love and Decay, Season One, Episodes One-Twelve
Love and Decay, Season Two, Episodes One-Twelve
Love and Decay, Volume One (Episodes One-Six, Season One)
Love and Decay, Volume Two (Episodes Seven-Twelve, Season One)
Love and Decay, Volume Three (Episodes One-Four, Season Two)
Love and Decay, Volume Four (Episodes Five-Eight, Season Two)
Love and Decay, Volume Five (Episodes Nine-Twelve, Season Two)

Reckless Magic (The Star-Crossed Series, Book 1)
Hopeless Magic (The Star-Crossed Series, Book 2)
Fearless Magic (The Star-Crossed Series, Book 3)
Endless Magic (The Star-Crossed Series, Book 4)
The Reluctant King (The Star-Crossed Series, Book 5)
The Relentless Warrior (The Star-Crossed Series, Book 6)
Breathless Magic (The Star-Crossed Series, Book 6.5)
Fateful Magic (The Star-Crossed Series, Book 6.75)
The Redeemable Prince (The Star-Crossed Series, Book 7)

Heir of Skies (The Starbright Series, Book 1)
Heir of Darkness (The Starbright Series, Book 2)
Heir of Secrets (The Starbright Series, Book 3)

The Rush (The Siren Series, Book 1)
The Fall (The Siren Series, Book 2)

Bet in the Dark (An NA Contemporary Romance)

Striking (The Forged in Fire Series) This is a co-authored Contemporary NA
Brazing (The Forged in Fire Series) This is a co-authored Contemporary NA

To Angst.
To Love that doesn't give up.

Prologue

Seraphina
One year ago.

"Sera, we've been over this and over this. What don't you understand?"

Those words. That question.

As if I were stupid for wanting to talk about this, or a naïve child that couldn't grasp reality. *His* reality.

I swallowed back a hundred different snotty responses. I didn't like the taste of all that bitterness and resentment in my mouth. I loved this man, but I had never been angrier with someone in my life.

And once, I'd tried to impale the Queen with a thousand pieces of glass. So it wasn't like I was a stranger to anger.

But that was years ago. I wasn't that girl anymore.

I was reformed these days, and that meant keeping my vitriol at a low simmer instead of spitting acid all over this man like I wanted to.

"I don't understand why it's so easy for you to leave me," I answered calmly. My voice hardly trembled at all and I prayed that I was the only one that heard my weakness. I felt like curling into myself and hiding beneath the covers until this all blew over. My heart physically hurt from the pressure of this fight and the thoughts swirling around inside my head.

But I couldn't show him that. We'd been fighting for days about this and he was tired of my tears. Besides, they weren't helping me make any progress anyway. So what was the point? I could cry myself to sleep later.

He let out an aggravated groan from across the room. His hands scrubbed at his face and when he replied it was muffled through his palms. "I cannot say this a different way. I am not leaving *you*! I have to go. I have to fight for our people. I have a responsibility to Avalon and to the Kingdom. Sera, I cannot stay here and do *nothing*!"

My heart squeezed in my chest and my lungs stopped working. Why didn't he see how much his absence tore us apart? Why didn't he get it? Why didn't he feel this gaping hole opening in his chest, threatening to swallow him alive?

Didn't he feel the emptiness?

Didn't he feel the abandonment?

"I understand that." My shoulders shrugged forward and I felt myself shrink back into the warm, leather couch I'd collapsed onto a few minutes ago. I pulled my knees to my chest and wrapped my arms around them. I needed to hold onto something. I would have preferred it to be him, but I could tell the only comfort I would get tonight would be from myself. "Sebastian, I'm not asking you to do nothing. I'm asking you to do everything and anything you can, but from *here*. You don't have to be on the front lines to make a difference! You don't have to go after Terletov yourself! Let someone else do that. Stay here. Stay with me."

He looked at me for a long time. His body stilled and his hands fell heavily at his sides. His face remained expressionless, which grated against every last one of my nerves. These fights we'd been having lately were killing me, they were tearing me apart limb by limb and he couldn't even bother to look upset.

And when he spoke, the accent that I used to find so distinguished and sexy, resonated in this painfully hollow way. It sounded like an empty echo in my pounding head. I loved him, but I'd already lost him. His next few words weren't even a surprise.

Although they still hurt. *So much.*

"I can't," he said. His voice broke at the same time it held so much conviction.

He loved me, but he loved this Kingdom more.

I should have expected that. I should have seen it coming.

Sebastian would always do what was best for him first. He would always think about *his needs first*. That was just the way he was: A spoiled prince raised to think his wishes superseded everything else.

I had known that since the day I met him. In fact, at first I'd appreciated his self-centered attitude because I could relate.

But things were different now. We were at war again. Our lives and the lives of those we both loved were at risk.

We came together under a similar set of circumstances. We both fought for a better life for this Kingdom, for justice and the end of tyranny. We were on the same page and it was easy.

And since Lucan fell, our relationship had been relatively easy. Sure, we fought about silly things, but I thought all couples did that. We went through the normal stages and worked to get to know each other and build something substantial.

I put all of myself into these last three years. I did everything I could to make this a lasting, committed relationship. I thought Sebastian had too.

Now that we had something to really fight about though, I wasn't sure we'd done that great of a job. We were so similar in so many things. And when we didn't line up perfectly, I thought our opposites complimented each other.

I thought we had what it took to make it.

I pulled my knees tighter to my chest, so tight I found it hard to breathe. But I couldn't let them go. I couldn't give myself the luxury of breathing freely, not when every other part of my body and soul felt like it was crumbling apart.

"We've been talking about getting married, Sebastian. You told me you wanted to take this relationship to the next level. How can we do that if you're dead?"

His face scrunched with frustration. "Why is it that I am always the one getting offed in your imaginary scenarios? Why do I have to die? Why can't you choose Avalon or Kiran? Both would be better targets than me! I'm not even royalty anymore!"

"It's not about who Terletov chooses to kill, Sebastian! It's about what could happen to anyone that goes after him! And Kiran wouldn't leave Eden to go run after bad guys. He's not signing up for missions and offering up his life. He's playing it safe for the Kingdom and for the people that count on him!"

"So I should just do whatever Kiran does? He knows best, is that right? My cousin, the perfect King. Do you still hate Eden for stealing your boyfriend after all of these years?"

I sucked in a sharp breath. It felt as though he'd taken a dull knife and gutted me with it. I felt my heart hemorrhaging the last remnants of hope and my spirit shrivel into a hard, lifeless ball.

This was how shrews were made. Hags. Old Maids. This was the point in my life I would be so very broken I would never be able to put myself back together.

In a hundred years, I would look back at this moment and know this was the exact point in time I became destined to own sixty cats.

Because after this, I was done with men. I would never put up with this again.

He'd managed to strip away my self-confidence and good faith while shattering my heart at the same time. That took both skill and a pure ruthlessness I had not known he was capable of.

"This has nothing to do with Kiran," I rasped with a voice that could only just be heard. "Whether you want to believe it or not, you're still a prince. The entire Kingdom thinks of you as royalty. You have a prominent position in Avalon's cabinet and you're Kiran's closest confidant. You can lie to yourself or feel sorry for yourself or whatever, but you will be a target out there. Terletov will see you and know he can use you. So maybe you're right. Maybe he won't kill you. Maybe he'll just conduct all those sick experiments on you or steal your magic. And maybe that somehow justifies this stupid, save-the-world attitude, but you're leaving me and you don't seem to care. And that is my problem! That is my biggest issue."

"You are being unnecessarily dramatic about this. Stop acting so crazy."

He probably could have said anything else but that. That one phrase, that one word, actually did make me crazy. It was like a trigger for my temper and he knew that.

We'd had plenty of fights over this before.

I was fine with being labeled high-maintenance. I *was* high-maintenance. And if he wanted to call me difficult or habitually late or temperamental or even bitchy, I would be fine with any of those.

But crazy was too far.

When I didn't immediately respond, Sebastian went on, "Seraphina, I don't want to leave you, but I have to do this. I need you to understand. If you force me to choose between you or the Kingdom, you won't like the outcome."

I felt like he'd slapped me in the face. I never said he had to choose. He said that. And then he simply informed me that I would be the loser.

"What if I do like the outcome?" My voice shook again, but this time it was from anger, not from hurt.

He let out a gruff laugh. "What do you mean? You're saying you *want* to break up with me?"

"It sounds more like you want to break up with me."

He took three steps toward me and his entire body radiated with some emotion I couldn't understand. I was too wrapped up in my own world of pain.

I watched his tall frame move toward me and admired him in the way I always did. I couldn't help but notice the muscle packed tightly all over his body, his broad shoulders that pulled his t-shirts tight or his long legs that sent all kinds of memories heating my body.

I couldn't help but take in the perfect angles of his face. The strong Kendrick nose, the lips that were almost too pretty for a man. His dark blonde hair that he'd let grow out a little more recently. It piled on his head in a tussled, rebellious way that hinted at his devil-may-care personality.

I loved his hair. My fingers tingled with the memory of running through it, of holding on tight, of pulling it. I stared into his hazel eyes and saw myself reflected there. Not literally, of course, but figuratively. I felt myself in the endless depths, in the soul that sat so closely to their surface. I belonged to this man and he belonged to me. So why was he hurting so irreversibly me now?

"You want to end what we have over this?"

"I want you to make me a priority in your life." My chin tilted defiantly, but I felt none of the confidence I pretended.

There was a part of me begging to get down on my knees and tell him I didn't care about any of this. I just wanted him and I would take him however he would give himself to me.

I'd been brushed aside in the past for his cousin or Kingdom duties, and I'd let it all slide off my back. But this felt different and I knew I couldn't give in or I would be second place for the rest of my life.

I had already been that in a relationship. I'd already been promised to a man and thrown aside for another woman.

Sebastian wasn't technically cheating on me, but he had chosen something else over me. He was willing to leave me for a crusade that could easily get him killed. And I hated feeling this way. Again. I hated being second choice *again*.

He loomed over me. His hands clenched into fists, his magic coiled tight with irritation and simmering fury. "Sera, I love you. And when I go to take out this sick monster, I will still love you. This entire discussion is ridiculous!"

Tears welled in my eyes and slipped unforgivably down my cheeks. I didn't want him to see how much this tore me apart. I didn't want him to see me shatter.

It might have been silly and maybe pointless, but he chose this. I couldn't say my feelings any clearer. He knew how much his decision hurt me and he was willing to make it anyway.

"I love you too, Sebastian. But this is it for me. I cannot just wait for you to come back, hoping you'll survive."

He dropped to his knees in front of me and I felt it through his magic how hard it was for him to humble himself like this. His hands rested on top of my kneecaps and pressed into my skin. It was this version of him that nearly broke me.

I could take him angry and annoyed. I could not resist him broken in front of me.

"Sera, please think this through. Think about everything we've been through. I do want to marry you. I do want to give you a commitment. This will all be over soon and then we'll get onto the good stuff."

I clenched my jaw and held back my questions. We'd been dating for three years. Why did I have to wait until after he got back from his suicidal testosterone-fest?

"You gave me an ultimatum. I don't want this any more than you do."

His eyes flashed with that same emotion I didn't want to see. "Fine," he bit out and backed away from me. "If it has to be this way, then fine. But you remember that I did not want this. *You* chose this. *You* ended us. I'm not going to come crawling back to you, begging for you to take me back. And I sure as hell am not giving up this mission or any other future missions. You're going to have to live with this. Not me. I didn't do anything wrong."

I turned away from him and stared out at my room. It was the room I always stayed at when I visited the Citadel. There were so many years wrapped up in this place, memories and thoughts and stolen moments with this same man who was now tarnishing everything we had.

"Fine," I echoed in a whisper. "I'll take the blame. This is on me." As if I didn't already know that.

As if I didn't also know that if I could just get over this damn need for validation in our relationship, this obsession with my need for him to pick me above all else, that we wouldn't have a problem.

I hated how damaged I felt, how irrevocably screwed up I knew I was. God, if I could just hold myself together, then Sebastian wouldn't have to suffer from my crippling insecurity.

"This is on you," he repeated. He stepped back and stared at me for a long time. I couldn't look at him. I couldn't face him. I was ashamed and guilty, but at the same time I felt the conviction burn through me.

His magic pulled itself free of mine and I felt it the hardest. I was bereft. Lost without him. My soul felt split in half and my magic immediately grieved his departure.

No.

But it was too late. He turned and fled the room. He didn't look at me again. I didn't have to watch him to know that was true. I felt his distance, I felt it widen and deepen and crack into a gaping canyon.

Sebastian and I were finished.

The love of my life left me to fight for our Kingdom while I wept his absence, my decision and the brokenness inside of me that always seemed to ruin everything.

He was right. I did this. I destroyed us.

I destroyed everything I touched.

That had been true about me for as long as I could remember. He was my one shot at happiness and I didn't just destroy him, I annihilated him.

And myself in the process.

Chapter One

Sebastian

This goddamn wedding.

Sure, I was happy enough for the couple, but their eternal bliss really churned my stomach. How could anyone stand this much happiness? Or love? Or... happiness?

"Don't like the champagne, Cousin?" Kiran asked with that frustrating smirk plastered on his stupid face.

"The wine is fine. Why do you ask?"

"You look ready to murder someone. I hoped it was simply bad bubbly."

I let out an exaggerated sigh and mentally pulled myself together. "It's not the booze, your royal highness. It's the celebration. It's contrived and so desperately sweet, my teeth hurt."

Kiran sounded nearly angry when he replied, "It's neither of those things. It's been a beautiful day and it's bloody well time these two shared some something sweet. After all Talbott and Lilly have been through-"

I held up a lazy hand. "Stop. I know I'm being an arse."

"Yes, you are." He pulled up a chair next to me and chuckled. "But I suppose you have good reason to be one."

"And what does that mean?"

Instead of answering my question, he simply grinned at me. "I'm happy to see Seraphina with someone again. It's been almost a year since she tossed you out. It's good to see she's finally moved on."

I swallowed back an ugly growl. "Right."

"I never thought she'd go for a Russian though. He's just so much bigger than you."

For an entire minute, I seriously considered assassinating my king before Avalon slunk down next to us and opened his mouth. Then I considered murdering both of my kings.

"Seraphina is smiling again. She must be into that whole giant thing." Avalon sounded truly interested in her love life, which was disturbing.

"What are you talking about?"

Avalon sat forward and rested his elbows on his knees. "Seraphina's date. He looks like Dolph Lundgren."

"Dolph Lundgren is old," I pointed out.

"Not today's Dolph Lundgren. But you know, Dolph Lundgren in his prime."

"It sounds like *you* have a crush on him, Avalon. Why don't you see if Seraphina will let you cut in?"

Kiran clasped my shoulder with his hand. "And it sounds like *you* are jealous."

"Of the commy boxer? Not on your life." I ran a hand over my eyes. I suddenly had a headache.

"It has to be kind of rough, though," Avalon continued. "The girl you're still in love with is happy and dancing with someone twice your size in more ways than one. And you're sitting against the wall, miserable, lonely and pathetic."

I was definitely going to kill them both. Terletov could send me a thank you note. I couldn't take this anymore.

"Didn't your date cancel on you at the last minute?" Kiran goaded.

"Her sister had a baby." I breathed in slowly and out even slower. I fought bad guys on a daily basis, surely I could put up with these two nitwits for a few more minutes.

"Oh, right," Kiran sympathized. "The old, her-sister-had-a-baby bit. It's alright if you couldn't find another date on such short notice. No one thinks any less of you."

"*Her sister had a baby*." Her sister had a baby! Not that I had been terribly upset when Jessica called to cancel... but they didn't need to know that.

And I hadn't known Sera would show up with a date of her own and rub it in my face.

"Sure, she did." Avalon slapped me on the back. "We believe you. Don't we Kiran? Sure, we believe you."

I stood up. I couldn't take this anymore. "You're all a bunch of wankers, you know that?"

I left the heckling hyenas to make jokes to each other while I wandered toward the bar. Lilly and Talbott's wedding had been quiet and intimate. While we all celebrated their nuptials, the occasion was more than a little somber.

They had been through so much over the years. Under Lucan's reign, while the Kingdom adjusted to accepting Shifters and now with Terletov's terrorism, they had suffered more than any couple should. To make the event even more difficult, Gabriel had not been present to perform the ceremony.

Everyone in attendance mourned Gabriel and Silas all over again. While Avalon officiated and made everything legal, at least according to our laws, he could not replace the priest.

Avalon had a pretty enough face, but the reality that my dear friends were gone forever hit harder than I thought possible. It had been four months since I watched them die. Four months since they were murdered at Terletov's hands. I had moved on as much as possible. I had grieved and attended their memorials and I had found closure.

But to have something like this, such a momentous and historic occasion, without them felt so... wrong. And in the wake of that, I had to watch Lilly drag herself up the aisle to her husband.

She went happily and with the biggest smile I'd ever seen her wear, but her body was still deep in the healing process. She looked tiny standing next to Talbott. Her body had become frail during her long coma and Terletov's captivity. She always looked small and delicate, but these days she looked downright fragile.

Having such a small gathering, with all the people I cared about, yet while missing some of the most important and watching the bride struggle to stand for the entirety of her wedding, put things into sharp perspective for me.

I didn't normally like moments like this. Ones of poignant clarity or deep, internal speculation. I preferred to ignore everything that caused feelings to happen inside of my bitter, cynical soul. I preferred indifference and sarcasm.

Those were my safe places. My happy places.

But these things and emotions happened to me anyway. It was rather frustrating to find out that I couldn't stop them.

And when I found myself wallowing in grief and self-pity, I also found myself looking at the one person I had sworn I was finished with forever.

Seraphina.

I thought she might understand what was happening inside. Or I'd hoped that maybe she felt the same sadness sweeping through her that I felt in me. I'd wanted someone to commiserate with.

Or at the very least, someone to help me forget how depressing life had become lately.

We broke up a year ago, but that didn't mean we hadn't occasionally taken a night off from loathing each other with the passion of a thousand suns.

Alright, we still hated each other; we just focused that passion toward more... mutually satisfying endeavors.

But that hadn't happened this time. Instead, she'd been sitting next to her Russian ogre, happily enjoying the vows. She hadn't even noticed I had been seated directly across the aisle from her. She'd been too busy with the pale troll.

I had turned back to Lilly and Talbott and decided those two fools were making the biggest mistake of their lives. Sure, they'd both been through hell and worse over the last four years, but marital bliss had to be much worse than anything they'd gone through yet.

How could they willingly commit themselves to an eternity of pain and suffering? Did they enjoy arguing with each other every single day from now until the end of time?

Maybe they did. Maybe Lilly could be all quiet in front of us but hot and passionate behind closed doors.

No. That was wrong. And now it was weird that I was thinking about Lilly like that. She was like a sister to me.

Before I could make it all the way to the bar and lose my troubles at the bottom of about six highballs of great bourbon, a very gorgeous, very pregnant, very married woman intercepted my path.

"Dance with me," Eden ordered.

"I'm not sure there's room for me." I gestured at her rather large stomach.

She glared at me. "I'll make room."

I couldn't help but laugh. She did that to me in a way her arse of a husband never could. And her idiot brother was even worse. But this woman made me smile. Always.

I took her hand and led her to the small dance floor in the middle of rows and rows of grape vines. The wedding had taken place in a quaint, little church that bespoke romance, tradition, and secrecy.

Immediately after the nuptials, we'd moved to this remote vineyard, where the wedding guests danced under a millions stars, drank bottle after bottle of wine and breathed in the balmy June air that seemed to sing along with the music.

It was a very nice night to get married. Kudos to the bride and groom for rushing this shindig.

I dropped my hand to Eden's large waist and then jumped when I got kicked. "Apparently, they don't think I belong here."

It was her turn to laugh. "Don't worry, they do that to everyone. They love me the most and yet I am kicked *all of the time*."

"Nasty already? Just wait till they pop out."

"I love that your idea of childbirth involves children just popping out. That sounds much nicer than what I'm envisioning." We laughed together while we moved seamlessly around the dance floor.

Okay, that wasn't entirely true, but I didn't want to draw attention to the fact that Eden, one of the most beautiful women I'd ever met, was waddling like an overweight penguin.

"Nervous?" I raised my eyebrows at her.

She stared me down with those glittering black eyes of hers and I could practically feel the hairs on her arms rise with challenge. Her black hair floated around her shoulders in the night breeze and pretty lips tilted into a small smile.

"Not any more than usual," she replied.

In Eden-speak, that meant she was nervous as bloody hell, but planned on jumping in feet first and with all the gusto she usually reserved for storming castles or killing tyrants.

These children were in good hands with her as their mother.

We had danced in silence for a little longer before she said, "The love of your life is on a date with someone that isn't you."

"Titus?" I glanced over my shoulder. I didn't think this was technically a date for him, but he'd been rather interested in Ophelia ever since her sister and Jericho started sucking face. I thought for a while he would go after Roxie, but O seemed to have caught his full attention, where Roxie managed to only catch most of it. "I think he has a thing for her. I'm trying to control my jealous rage."

"I meant Seraphina."

"Ah. So you also meant *former*-love of my life."

Her intelligent onyx eyes narrowed further. "You should know I think it's adorable you're in such strong denial. It reminds me of me once upon a time."

I snorted. "You were in denial, my pretty Queen. I am firmly in reality. Seraphina and I are over. I moved on. She moved on. With Sven apparently."

"Sven?"

"The Russian."

"I think his name is Andrei."

I snorted again.

"See?" She pinched my side until I squirmed. "You still love her."

"No, I still love myself, which is why I've decided to steer clear of her and any other females that want the two L's."

"The two L's?" She cocked her head back and made a guess. "Love and... licorice?"

"My last name and a large diamond ring."

Her head fell back further and she looked up at the starry night desperately. "So it's not love you're afraid of, but matrimony?"

I nodded. "I'm not afraid of love. I *love* love. What I don't love is a lifetime of having to answer to someone else or incessant nagging."

"I know you think you're funny, but Seraphina was never like that to you and you know that."

I shrugged. "I didn't say she was."

"You should dance with her," Eden ordered. And this was not a question or suggestion, this was her queenly edict that she would not let me ignore.

"You should probably dance with your husband and forget all about me."

She tried to lean in, but her protruding stomach prohibited her from getting too close. She made a growly sound in the back of her throat before she settled for patting my waist with her dainty hand. "I think you better stop being stubborn and go after the girl that actually makes you happy."

"You make me happy. Can I go after you?"

"Sure," she grinned. "I bet you can't wait to be a father. I bet you're so excited to stay up all night and help me feed the babies and watch me give birth and learn to change diapers and-"

"That's enough," I said quickly. "You don't have to turn me off kids forever. Let's keep some of the mystery."

Eden smiled at me and her eyes softened. "I just want to see you happy and settled."

"I *am* happy and settled," I promised.

"No, you're bloodthirsty and vengeful. And those aren't attractive qualities."

I made an incredulous sound in the back of my throat. "You're those things too! And you're with child! The bastard took the Citadel, Eden, of course, I'm vengeful. He killed some of the best men I've ever known and experiments on innocents. *Of course,* I'm bloodthirsty."

She slapped my bicep. "I wasn't talking about Terletov, Bastian. I was talking about Sven."

And then she shoved me. The Queen of the Immortals, the Queen currently pregnant with twins, shoved me.

I was too surprised to catch myself right away. I stumbled backward and bumped into someone else, which wasn't a surprise since I was already in the middle of a busy dance floor.

I spun around and caught the person I was in the process of knocking over. One hand grabbed for her slender waist and the other managed to get hold of her arm. She let out a soft squeal before I pulled her upright and met that wide ice-blue gaze.

Seraphina.

Eden had terrible timing. Although, I suspected she was quite proud of herself at the moment.

I had two options. I could drop Seraphina and flee. My brain told me that was an excellent idea and ordered my feet to move posthaste. They did not listen because they were on board with option two: Pull her closer and dance with her.

Most of the time, my brain controlled my body. But there were the few occasions when my body took over that no amount of rationale or reasoning could intercede. Seraphina fell into arms as comfortably as she always did. I pulled her against my chest and something inside of me clicked into place. I hadn't felt like this in a while. She hadn't let me feel like this in a while.

I swore to myself I would get the small fix my entire body craved and then I would release her back to her Russian.

But first I needed her familiarity, her memorable body touching as much of me as she would allow.

God, this girl could infuriate me beyond anything else in this world, but I couldn't ignore the perfect way she felt in my arms.

Deftly, I slid my hand down her forearm and grabbed her hand so I could lead her around. She was too stunned at first to make any protest and then it was too late. Other people had noticed us dancing together and Seraphina would dance with me for the rest of the night before she caused a scene. I had never appreciated that quality about her until this moment.

"Hello," I grinned at her.

"What are you doing?" she hissed.

"It isn't obvious?"

She narrowed her eyes. "It isn't."

"I'm dancing with you."

"That part is obvious. I want to know *why*?" She stepped into me and I inhaled her signature perfume. She smelled like flowers and home and I wanted to dip my nose into her neck and become intoxicated by her.

And then I wanted to push her down and run as far away from here as fast as I could. These were the kind of insane thoughts this woman made me feel. She turned me mad, *actually mad*. I couldn't tell up from down when I was near her, right from left or sane from insane.

Toxic. She was toxic for me.

I pulled my damnable Magic back from hers as quickly as I could. Our Magics were often tricky when we got together. I would often catch mine sneaking off to join hers. The Magic hadn't gotten the memo that we were over. And no matter what I did to interest it in another woman, he seemed intently devoted to this one harpy and this one harpy alone.

"Before your active imagination runs off with you, I should blame this on Eden. She practically commanded me to dance with you." Alright, so that wasn't the smoothest way to lull her into dancing with me, but I thought probably the safest.

Sera wrinkled her nose. "Ever the slave to the crown."

I slid my hand to the small of her back and pushed her forward so that we pressed against each other. The slow string ensemble played something melodic and I slowed us down to an intimate pace.

"Mmm." This was an old argument between us and now was not the time to rehash how I wronged her or what I could have done differently. I was tired of that conversation. So, very tired of it. "You look lovely tonight, Sera."

Most girls would have blushed beneath my concentrated compliment. Not, Seraphina Van Curen. This one knew my number.

Her expression grew warier and her entire body tensed. "Thank you."

"Who's the KGB?"

She looked around. "The who? Oh, you mean Andrei."

"I mean Andrei." Something sizzled through me, bitter and furious. I struggled to take a deep breath. I needed air. *No, we were already outside.* I needed... something.

"When's the last time we saw each other?"

"The Citadel," I answered immediately. How could she not remember that? I couldn't stop thinking about that day. Terletov took our home, our most sacred place. And after we'd escaped...

"Oh, right." She cleared her throat nervously. Good. I wanted her unsettled when she thought about that night. "Andrei and I started shortly after that."

I took a moment to digest those words. "Shortly after that?"

"Actually, almost right after," she confirmed.

I stepped into her and closed whatever space had remained between us. I burned with anger and an adolescent need to punch something hard. I wanted bloody, broken knuckles and a blinding pain that would sear these words from my consciousness. I wanted to hurt something. I wanted to demolish it.

It being Andrei.

Despite the volcano raging inside of me, my nose traced the shell of her ear and I let my breath out in the slow, measured way that used to drive her crazy. "That night must have meant nothing to you then."

Her voice trembled when she replied, "I told you that it wouldn't."

I stepped back and dropped my arms to my sides. I hadn't believed her then and I wasn't sure I believed her now. We'd spent the night wrapped in each other's embrace in a hotel room in Budapest because neither one of us could let the other go after such a traumatic day.

I'd been halfway around the world, bailing out Jericho in the morning and then forced to rush back to the Citadel, hoping and praying the entire time that Seraphina would still be alive when I got there. Out of everything, I should have been worried about or every person I should have been concerned for, including my King and my cousin, or my little sister, or anyone else, it was Seraphina consuming every one of my thoughts.

I had practically kidnapped her in order to get her to stay with me, but once we were alone, she was there. She was present. She had no more wish to leave that room than I did. And save for a few stolen kisses, the night had been spent in nothing but innocence.

I just wanted to breathe her. I just wanted to feel her heart beat. I just wanted her and nothing else.

But in the morning she had left before I ever woke.

And now, here we were months later.

"Don't cause a scene," she warned me.

"Afraid I'll embarrass you?"

"I'm afraid you're going to make something out of nothing. I started dating someone else. So what? You've been dating a string of someone elses for months now. You didn't pee on me, Sebastian. Other men are still interested in me, even if you think of me as your property."

"I don't think of you as my property-"

"Which is painfully ironic, don't you think? Since you don't want me. And now you're upset because I'm here with someone else?" She started to storm by me. "How cliché can you-"

I grabbed her wrist and stopped her escape. "I'm not upset because I think you're mine. I'm angry because you're not."

I didn't know why I said those stupid words, or what prompted me to confess something I'd been in denial about ever since she dumped me. I immediately wanted to take them back. If I could have snatched them from the air and swallowed them back down I would have.

My confession seemed to paralyze her. She neither moved nor tried to rip her arm from my grasp. And that turned out to be a small miracle. Because while I internally berated myself for my stupidity and she struggled to wrap her head around my insane confession, a light flared overhead.

I had been constantly in the field for a year now and if it wasn't for my experience, I didn't think I would have moved as quickly as I did. Instinct led the way and I yanked on Sera's arm. In two seconds, I had tossed her over a table and thrown my body on top of hers. I screamed something in way of warning, but most of the other guests had seen the flash of light as well.

The explosion hit the ground a second later. Rock, glass and other debris rained down on my head, slicing open my tuxedo and cutting into my back, neck, and legs. I held Seraphina in my arms tightly, trying my best to shield her from the gruesome attack.

My ears rang with a muffled, high-pitched sound. I used my magic to dispel it quickly and by the time I could hear again, the hazy silence was replaced with screaming and shouting.

I pulled myself away from Seraphina and stared down into her cold blue eyes. "It's a good thing we were standing so close."

She choked a little on the smoke. "Let me guess, you've wanted to throw me across the room for a while?"

I grinned at her because, well, she was right. "That, and now I can save you."

"You're not saving me! I'm here on a date!" Whom apparently she just remembered, because she tried to sit up and look for him. I didn't let her get very far. Andrei the Giant could take care of himself. "Also, I don't need saving!"

I couldn't stop grinning at her. "You do need saving because your date is officially over."

I scrambled to my feet, pulled her up to hers and then tossed her over my shoulder. She screamed and hollered at me. Her fists beat on my back, but she didn't put up any real fight.

Which was a good thing because we would have enough of a fight trying to get out of here. Terletov's men didn't swoop in to murder us or anything, but I had a feeling they'd already accomplished their first goal. If we didn't get out of here right this second, we wouldn't have time to fight with each other, we'd be too busy fighting everyone else.

And that wasn't nearly as fun.

I glanced around the room and finally caught Avalon's steely gaze from across the crater in the now empty dance floor.

I tilted my head.

"Go!" he mouthed wildly.

"Everyone else?" I mouthed back.

"Go!" he repeated.

I took one more glance around the vineyard and saw that almost everyone had a partner and was on their way out of here. It was a small reception to begin with and that made it possible to count heads and find all of my friends still alive and kicking.

I also saw Andrei stalking toward us with a concerned look on his face. *Imbecile*. We didn't have time for him to worry about Seraphina's safety. We had to get out of here. There was time to lick our wounds later. But not right now when they would most likely launch another attack on us.

I spun around and took off. Seraphina bounced on my shoulder and screeched at me the entire time. When I finally reached my rental, I tossed Sera into the backseat, locked the door with Magic and jumped in the driver's seat.

I joined the rest of the cars fleeing the reception and nodded at Talbott and Lilly at the fork in the road that would lead back to the nearest coastal town or deeper into the Italian countryside the other way. Talbott and I drove opposite directions, he on his way to his honeymoon with his lovely bride, me on the way to anywhere-but-here with my kidnapped ex-girlfriend.

I would have paid a lot of money to trade places with him.

I glanced back at Seraphina, who had righted herself and glared at me from the backseat. Her short, black dress inched up her shapely thighs and her long blonde hair tangled around her face. She looked livid.

I turned back around. I didn't want to mess with that just yet.

There would be bloody hell to pay for my actions, but I needed to make sure she was safe. And only *I* could keep her safe. Not her stupid new boyfriend Andrei and not her stubborn self.

Me.

Just me.

"Where are you taking me?" she demanded in a low voice.

I bit back a smile and said, "I was thinking Budapest."

She sucked in a sharp breath but then seemed to level out some. "It won't matter."

She sounded so positive and self-assured, I couldn't help but ask, "Why not?"

"Because the first chance I get, I plan on killing you."

I couldn't hold back the grin any longer. I might be a dead man, but at least I was a satisfied dead man. It probably would have killed me anyway to watch Andrei fumble his way around rescuing her. She didn't have time for that.

But I wasn't so sure I had time for her, either.

Chapter Two

Seraphina

Eight hours later and I still wanted to kill him. Badly. So badly my fingers tingled and my blood burned.

He had me holed up in a cheap motel in northern Italy. He said nobody would find us here, but I suspected he knew there would be no way for me to call anyone to come get me.

My purse had been lost during the attack. It held the keys to my father's beautiful Lambo, my cell phone and my makeup.

That's right, I was trapped in a dingy motel room with my ex-boyfriend and no makeup. I didn't even have emergency toothpaste.

God, Sebastian. It was like he loved to make my life miserable. I swear, he *loved* it. The second I started to feel anything other than completely wretched, he swooped in, created World War Three kind of havoc and then disappeared into the night. He couldn't just once stick around and clean up his mess. Oh, no. That would be far too mature and decent of him. He much preferred to watch me suffer from a distance.

He was like a child. He didn't necessarily want to play with me. He just wanted to make sure none of the other boys on the playground got to touch me.

Selfish. That's what he was. For as long as I could remember he had been the most selfish person I knew. At one time, it had been sort of endearing. Well... up until the point that his selfishness imploded our relationship.

"I don't like the look on your face," the man I was silently contemplating murdering commented from across the room.

"And why's that?" I asked innocently. He was technically stronger than me and his powers manifested a bit more tangibly than mine did. If I wanted to get the upper hand with him, I had to trick him, lull him into a false sense of security and then pounce.

"It's the look you get right before you destroy something."

I dropped the act. It wasn't worth it. He should know I was going after him. He should have to suffer through the anxiety. "And what have you seen me destroy, Sebastian?"

"My hopes and dreams. My faith in humanity. My manhood."

I rolled my eyes and threw my body back on the tiny bed that creaked every time I shifted my weight. "What are we doing here?"

I was at my wit's end. He seemed perfectly adjusted. I should have expected that though. He thrived in situations like this. His sarcastic nature and laid-back personality made it possible for him to adapt to any scenario easily. I was so much more high-strung than he was, so days like today were especially difficult for me.

A normal boyfriend would have felt bad for his neurotic girlfriend and taken steps to pamper her or at the very least help her also adapt. Sebastian was not a normal boyfriend though and when we dated before he seemed to relish throwing me into situations where I would flop around like a fish out of water and make a fool of myself.

Just once, I wanted him to put my needs above his own. Just once. It didn't even matter that we weren't a couple anymore and that I could hardly stand the sight of him. I just wanted for him to think of anyone other than himself for thirty seconds.

Was that asking too much?

He replied to my question, "That idiot you brought to the wedding would have gotten you killed trying to escape in that stupid orange clown car you drove. I did what was necessary to ensure your safety. You should be thanking me."

Definitely asking too much.

"You assume I would have let Andrei drive us out of there."

"No, I know you would have insisted that you drive. Which is also how I know you would have ended up dead. I saved your life, Seraphina. Face it."

"You didn't. And I won't."

He groaned. "You're going to make this as difficult as possible, aren't you?"

"*You're* making this as difficult as possible. Let me go, Sebastian. Nobody is out there looking for me. I'm not in danger anymore. You did whatever it was you set out to do; now mandatory visitation is over. You need to let me go home now."

He gave me a sideways look before peeking through the front blinds. "I'm just waiting for a phone call from Avalon and then we'll be on our way. Yeah?"

"Separately?"

He didn't answer. Instead, he walked over to the other side of the room and rummaged around on a small desk. There wasn't much to look through and neither one of us had brought a suitcase in.

"You could have at least let me grab my luggage! Then I could get out of this ridiculous dress. And these shoes!"

"We could walk around the market," he suggested. "I saw some shops when we drove into town. They would have something for you to change into."

"I don't have any money!" I growled at him. "How can I purchase clothes, when I don't have any money?"

He didn't respond. He just kept moving some embossed letterhead around the table as if he were putting together a puzzle. When his eyes finally did lift and meet mine, I sucked in a sharp breath.

Anger simmered in his hazel depths. Bright, hot and heavy. I had to be aggravating him, but I couldn't seem to stop my verbal poison spewing all over him.

He brought out the worst in me. I was almost positive he always had. I wanted to be anywhere but here. I wanted to be with anyone else but him. Andrei and I had started something good. He wasn't exactly my type and there were times I wondered if his huge muscles used up all of his brainpower, but he was sweet. And kind. And he went out of his way for me.

We weren't exactly exclusive like I'd told Sebastian earlier, but it was headed that direction.

Bringing him to Lilly's wedding had been a huge step in our relationship. I felt like we made this major progress. I was even willing to have some kind of determine-the-relationship conversation with him after the party was over.

Instead, I'd been tricked into dancing with my ex-boyfriend, nearly blown to pieces and then kidnapped by that same ex-boyfriend. Andrei had to be worried sick.

And instead of the progress I hoped to make, this had to be one giant step back.

"Can I at least borrow your cell phone?" I asked in a more humble tone.

I could fight with Sebastian for hours. And that wasn't a lie. That used to be one of my favorite activities, especially right after we broke up. But so often, arguing with him just turned into some weird, unhealthy version of foreplay and I ended up exactly in the place I didn't want to be.

It would be better for my sanity if I kept my calm and not antagonize Sebastian into a fight. If I were completely honest with myself, he was better at the bickering thing than me. He had this controlled calm that drove me absolutely crazy. While I screeched at him like a deranged banshee, he just sat back and used his sarcastic wit to push me over the edge.

I knew that. I'd watched him do this to me more times than I could count. But I didn't have enough self-control to stop it from happening.

And I hated that.

He regarded me levelly. "Why?"

I forced my face to stay neutral. I wanted to bite back that it wasn't any of his damn business, but that seemed counterproductive.

"I want to let my mom know that I'm okay. Just in case she heard about the attack." And I wanted to let Andrei know that I was safe too. My parents probably didn't care one way or the other, but Andrei had to be searching everywhere for me. I wanted to ease his mind.

Sebastian pulled his cell from his pocket and walked over to me. I raised myself into sitting and looked up at him while he loomed over me.

He held out the phone but when I went to take it, he didn't immediately let go. "I did what I had to do, Sera. I won't apologize for it."

I nodded, ignoring the pang in my chest when he called me by my nickname. I loved his accent. That I couldn't deny. His sexy clipped tones, his rolling vowels. I loved how my name came out of his mouth, especially when he used to be sweet to me.

That was how he sounded now. He sounded like he cared, like he loved me still.

But I couldn't think thoughts like that and hope to walk out of this room with my heart in one piece, so I said, "I know you think you did what you had to. But we really should have worked something else out. Then you wouldn't be in this mess with me right now, holed up in some Italian version of a Motel Six."

"He's not your type." As usual, Sebastian ignored everything he should hear and focused entirely on listening to himself talk.

"I'm fine with that. Actually, that makes him sound better to me." I tugged at the phone until he let go.

"You have good instincts. You should listen to them."

Well, that wasn't going to happen. I smiled and waved him off dismissively. He did take the hint and wander off to the opposite side of the small room.

I played with the phone in my hands and thought about his suggestion. Listen to my instincts? Yeah, they wanted me to tackle Sebastian to the bed and make up for all the time spent apart.

My magic played just on the edges of his and no matter how much power I asserted, I couldn't pull it back completely. I felt him everywhere. I felt him all around me, inside me, a part of me. He filled up the room and my lungs and my chest. He infiltrated everything, the air, the molecules, the oxygen burning through me and once he grabbed hold, he did not let go.

I wanted to believe he did it on purpose and that my awareness of him was somehow his fault. He did this to me. He made me fall in love with him and then he refused to let go. Or let me let him go.

I didn't even have those feelings for him anymore. I loved him in a way that I would always love him, that echoed with the feelings of a first love. But I wasn't in love with him.

I couldn't be.

It wasn't healthy. We had taken something beautiful and destroyed it. Whatever bristled in the air between us wasn't love or affection, but unhealthy and toxic.

And I knew he felt the same way.

Besides, it was impossible for him to be in love with me. He loved someone else.

He loved himself.

I would always be second place to that kind of all-consuming, unquestionable love.

Ugh, selfish bastard.

I swiped the phone screen and guessed at Sebastian's numerical passcode. I got it right on the first try. I smiled to myself and considered stealing his identity and wiping out his bank account.

All of his bank accounts.

The silly boy used the same codes and passwords for everything depending on the length and requirement.

Some things never changed.

I dialed my parents and got their housekeeper. Mom and dad were off on safari apparently. I left a message with Marta that I was fine.

She told me she'd pass the message along. I noticed she didn't offer to give me a number where they could be reached.

Don't even get me started on why I didn't have my parent's current number. Basically, it started and ended with the fact that they were terrible parents. And I had moved on with my life.

I called Andrei next.

I listened to the ringtone for a long time before he answered in a hesitant voice.

I had exaggerated a little bit when I told Sebastian that Andrei and I were a thing. We'd been on a few dates, but nothing serious. I thought he might have been surprised that I asked him to go to the wedding with me.

I tried to make it seem as though I thought we had something special and I wanted to pursue our connection. But really, if I were completely honest, I couldn't face Sebastian alone.

If I didn't love Lilly so much, I would have blown off the wedding completely.

"Seraphina, where are you?" He sounded practically angry with me.

As if it were my fault Sebastian kidnapped me!

"I'm fine," I tried to placate him. "In the chaos of the explosion a friend of mine thought I was in trouble. He helped me get to somewhere safe."

Andrei huffed in his thick Russian accent. "It must be nice to have friends concerned about your safety."

I cocked my head to the side. "Are you mad I didn't help save *you*?"

Sebastian snorted a surprised laugh and I instantly regretted my question. I should have kept my mouth shut. I should usually keep my mouth shut.

It was always getting me into trouble.

Andrei grumbled something in Russian that I didn't catch before saying, "I can obviously take care of myself. But it would have been nice for you to have thought of me at the moment."

I cleared my throat delicately. What I really wanted to do was hang up the phone and move on with my life. I had no time for men who needed women to save them. Call me old fashioned, but I wanted the kind of guy that would swoop in on a white horse, pick me up with one arm and plant my ass in the saddle as we rode off into the sunset.

I didn't even know if those men existed anymore. Really, Paula Cole, where *had* all the cowboys gone?

My eyes drifted unwilling to Sebastian. Had he acted white-knightish back at the vineyard?

Did it matter?

Nope.

I sighed noisily and then laid it out on my wedding date, "Listen, Andrei, I'm sorry I didn't stick around to make sure you survived. I didn't mean to leave you in my dust. It just happened. It sounds like you got out just fine though. So yay for being alive still! Looks like we have another thing in common."

"Seraphina, I didn't mean-"

"Save it, Kid. I'll call you later." I clicked off and rolled my shoulders. I had originally felt guilty for leaving him behind. He could have easily died or been a target for one of Terletov's disgusting experiments. But the fact that he survived and blamed me for leaving him rankled me in all kinds of ways.

I avoided Sebastian's white-hot gaze as I dialed another number. Two calls down and I had yet to find someone that cared I was still alive.

Poor me.

I rolled my eyes and stamped the inner-bitch down. I had been raised with all the privilege in the world and spoon fed from solid silver since the day I was born. Spoiled and bratty were my default settings. Sometimes I wondered if I knew how to behave any differently.

During my relationship with Sebastian, I had fought diligently to be somebody else... to be the girl he could fall in love with and live his life with. But my entitled beast of a personality always hovered just beneath my shiny surface. There were times I let her slip out. There were times I thought I would lose my mind if I didn't scream at the top of my lungs!

I had struggled for the last four or five years to let go of all those snobbish mindsets and release my prejudices back to the hell they'd crawled out of. It wasn't easy. Honestly, hating and bitching were so much more comfortable for me. But I wanted to be better. I wanted to be genuine and authentic.

I just didn't always succeed.

When I was with Sebastian, I lived with this constant fear that he would see those ugly parts of me. I was terrified the real me would slip through my polished, pretty façade and he would be horrified by the picture of truth he managed to glimpse.

I sometimes wondered if that was why he could never commit to me in the end. Maybe it was me that sabotaged our relationship and led him on for three years. I hated myself for the person I couldn't be. And even more for ruining something that should have been beautiful.

But then I would hate Sebastian even more for being unable to love the girl that I was instead of the girl we both wanted me to be.

"Hello?"

"Eden," I breathed out in relief. "Thank God."

"Sera? Where are you? Gosh, I was so worried! Are you okay? Are you hurt? I saw Andrei on the way out, but he didn't have any idea where you went. I thought you... I thought Terletov might have-"

"I'm fine," I rushed to assure her. My spirit instantly lightened at my friend's concern. It was people like Eden that made me want to be better and understood when I wasn't. She handled our friendship with love and respect, no matter how snobby I could be. I felt freer with her than with anybody else.

Sure, I could still be cruel and unthinking, but because she would love me no matter how I behaved, it took the unwanted pressure off my behavior. It was easy to be good and loving and kind around Eden because she was all of those things and especially to me. "Sebastian kidnapped me and stashed me away in some roach motel. But we're both alive."

She didn't say anything for a long time.

"Stop it," I growled at her. "I can feel you gloating from here."

"I'm not gloating!" She was totally gloating. "I'm just surprised Sebastian thought about saving someone other than himself. That's all."

I snickered. "Believe me; nobody's more surprised than me."

"What's the plan then? You guys want in on some of the impending action? Or are you running off to Paris to elope?"

"E, give it up. Not everyone in the world is destined to be as happy in wedded bliss as you."

"Not true," she argued.

"We want in on the action." I needed to cut her off before she started waxing philosophical on all the benefits of a happy marriage. There was only so much till-death-do-us-part I could take in one day. "We're ready and willing. Tell us when and where and we'll be there."

"Meet us in Geneva," she said. "We'll reconvene and go from there."

"See you in twenty-four hours."

We clicked off and I finally met Sebastian's stoic gaze. He stood with feet apart and arms crossed over his broad chest. I tried to remember if he'd moved since we walked in this dingy room. He was like a statue over there, cold, unmoving and made out of stone.

"What did we just agree to?" he clipped out with all of those perfect British syllables.

"We're meeting our beloved King and Queen in Geneva. Should I not have agreed to go? I figured when the Monarchs ask you to be somewhere, you're always the first in line."

He narrowed his eyes at me. "It's fine. I planned to call Kiran anyway and find out where they needed us."

"You," I clarified. "Where they needed *you*. You don't get to take orders for me or include me in yours. We're not partners anymore."

"I'm not sure we ever were."

His words hurt me more than he meant to. At least I thought it was unintentional. I could have been wrong. Maybe he wanted to rip me apart with every cruel comeback. Maybe he saved my life so he could be the one to torture and kill me.

If that were true, only a few more eviscerating remarks like that and I would be weeping at his mercy.

"Are you ready?" I asked him neutrally.

"Do you need a few hours of rest? You've been awake for a while."

I ignored the softer tone in his voice. I didn't want to believe he could be capable of any kind of kindness.

But he was right.

I had taken an overnight flight to get to Italy from the States and hadn't been able to sleep the entire flight thanks to my ricocheting nerves about seeing Sebastian for the first time in months. Then, I'd spent all of yesterday helping get the venue and the bride ready. We'd driven through the night and now I faced more travel.

I needed to be in top form if I were accepting missions.

And some new clothes.

"I probably should sleep for a bit," I relented through a yawn.

"I'll wake you in a few hours then."

"Give me an extra thirty minutes to take a shower?" I scooted back on the bed and flopped down on the pillow. This might be a grungy place to stay the night, but it was perfect for a morning nap.

My eyes fluttered closed and I felt my breath deepen immediately. A little embarrassed about my exhaustion, I fought sleep and tried to give Sebastian a steady smile. Through the haze of sleep I saw him still standing in that same spot, arms still crossed, feet still spread.

His expression was different this time though. He seemed to be lost as he stared at me... completely confused. I didn't even bother to analyze him though, or what he was thinking.

I was much too tired and so I let sleep carry me away. I didn't have a good feeling about this mission. Or about spending anymore alone time with Sebastian.

Call it Psychic intuition, but I knew without a doubt this would be some of the last moments of peace I would have for a long time.

Chapter Three

Sebastian

I woke Seraphina up four hours later. I had been careful not to touch her while I called her from her deep sleep.

She had always been impossible to wake, and I'd usually had to physically shake her to get her attention. Today was no different, but I didn't relish the idea of moving her body with my hands.

She had scraped me raw by just a few hours in her presence. I didn't know how she did this to me every time we found ourselves together.

She brought the absolute worst out of me. I was never proud of myself when we were near.

And this morning had been no different.

While I still believed I did the right thing by helping her escape, I had acted deploringly ever since. She was right to hate me. And most of the time I knew that I was right to hate her.

But I didn't have to be such a bloody bastard about it.

I'd watched her fall asleep with more conflicting feelings warring inside of me than I knew what to do with. The familiar, habitual side of me had wanted to crawl into bed with her and press my chest to her back. I'd wanted nothing more than my arms wrapped around her tiny waist and my hands free to wander. But the rational, thinking side of my brain and body had known better.

Aside from the fact she would have probably attacked me or called the police, it was only the memory of our combined Magic that lulled me into that fantasy.

We weren't those people anymore.

I needed to always remember that.

After I'd stared at her for an inappropriate amount of time, feeling like an obsessive stalker, I went out into the village in search of different clothes for her.

I had plenty of choices stashed away in my suitcases, but her luggage had been left behind.

I had no doubt that Seraphina could wage any war in the skyscraper-length heels she wore and the too-short skirt, but I wanted her to be more comfortable.

And less distracting.

Besides, I felt guilty for all of my cruel remarks. This was my way of making some of it up to her.

I'd found a decent little shop and went to work selecting jeans, workout pants, and comfortable shirts that I knew would pass her fashion standards.

Nothing had a designer label on it or cost more than an average amount of Euros, but everything was in her size and would fit her.

She seemed pleased with the selection I presented her with and even stooped so low as to thank me before taking off for the shower. I had already used the bathroom and done the necessary straightening of my appearance.

She got ready as quickly as she could and then we gathered what little of our things had made it to the hotel room and carried them with us to the rental car.

As soon as we sat down I could feel the shift in her demeanor. She had been uncharacteristically quiet since she woke up, but now something seemed to bother her. No, not bother, that was too light of a word... this thing, whatever it was, had afflicted her as if with plague.

"What's wrong," I asked as I pulled onto the main road.

She glanced at me for a moment before flinching and pressing three fingers to her temple. "I don't know. I dreamt... I dreamt something. When I woke up, I couldn't remember exactly what it was, but now it's coming back in bits and pieces."

"A vision?" I asked in a low voice.

Seraphina was a Psychic and a pretty damn good one. While arguably, my family and Eden's were more powerfully clairvoyant than hers, she held her own easily. I had never truly had a vision. My powers favored the Witch side of my Immortality. But Sera was purebred Medium and often felt twinges of something that would take her a while to decipher.

That might not sound like much, but in the version of watered-down Magic my people lived with during the Kendrick reign, it was a hell of a lot more than most.

She gave me another sideways glance. "Go through Vienna."

I adjusted my direction and followed her orders without questioning. If she felt something, I didn't want to argue with her. Although, it was a bit risky following Seraphina's whims. She could be leading us straight to Terletov or to a major sale in the middle of Vienna's shopping district.

Still, until she knew better herself, I wouldn't dissuade her from following her vision.

"It's not Terletov," she said after a long silence. "I've had a feeler out for him for a long time now. I would know if it was him."

"But it's something, right?" I asked gently.

"It is something."

"Then we follow it," I told her. "Even if we have to drive twelve hours out of the way."

She made a wincing sound but didn't argue. I pulled out my phone and plugged it into the car charger. After a quick text to Kiran, I set out for the six-hour drive to Vienna.

We were mostly quiet on the way. Seraphina fiddled with radio stations and stared out of the window a lot. I tried to think of something to talk about that wouldn't get us into a fight.

I thought about bringing up that cretin she brought to the wedding but decided against it. She hadn't seemed thrilled with her conversation with him and I couldn't blame her. What kind of idiot goes on a date with a goddess like Seraphina and then worries about his own safety? I didn't even like her and knew better than to let her save herself during the attack.

I wanted to strangle this guy! I hoped he was well on his way back to Moscow by now or there would be an altercation between us.

I almost relished the idea. I would love to hurt something that deserved it.

I checked my simmering rage and navigated the outskirts of the beautiful Austrian city Seraphina had led us to.

"Where to now?"

"St. Stephens," she replied simply.

I frowned but obeyed her command. The famous cathedral? This should be interesting.

I parked the rental in a paid parking garage and we hit the old-world streets of Vienna with purpose. Seraphina seemed to know the way without needing a map, so I let her lead.

"We don't have any weapons," she suddenly noted.

"Are we going to need them?"

She shot me a glance over her shoulder that promised we would. A nervous feeling settled in my gut and unnerved me. Not for the first time did I wish I had the Titan power of feeling out other's Magic. Without it, we were walking into this blind.

We weaved through the crowded city on high alert. The early evening light spilled over the weathered stucco siding and cobbled streets. The air was hot and stifling this late in the summer, but it felt good after blasting the air conditioning in the car for the past six and a half hours.

Seraphina was a master of moving through crowds undetected. I had always admired her stealth and sly quickness. She shot me a taunting smile when I clumsily bumped into an elderly gentleman who veered right in front of me.

I made my apologies and then hurried to catch up to her. She hadn't bothered to wait around for me and I shouldn't have been surprised.

She led us straight to the other side of the street from St. Stephens. I peered up at the massive stone structure and swore I could feel the Magic bubbling around the place.

There was a legend in our Kingdom that one of the old Kings had hidden a well of Magic here. Much like India, Peru and Morocco, this place held a secret only Immortals knew. Except this place was quite a bit more cryptic than the others and held firmly in the human realm.

I tried to remember what exactly lay beneath the church, but couldn't remember. The place had been abandoned when humanity had firmly taken over and made it a hub of their activity.

The rest of our Magic strongholds were maintained in rather mysterious locations. And at least two of them had been completely abolished since Eden's arrival.

Ahem, India and the well beneath the Romanian prisons.

"You're sure, Sera?"

She met my gaze and her blue eyes flashed with purpose. "I'm positive."

"What's the plan? Storm the church? Burn the building to the ground? Crawl through the catacombs?"

She made a face at me. "Have you never heard of subtlety?"

"I can't seem to remember what that word means."

"I didn't expect you to."

She took a step closer to me and slipped her arm through mine. I felt the hot press of her body and my Magic flared to life at her simple touch. I narrowed my eyes and dared her to say something.

She didn't call me out on my embarrassing overreaction and I silently thanked her for that. Her Magic had just as hard of a time as mine did staying under control. Old habits die hard and all that.

"We're pretending to be tourists," she whispered. "Two lovers admiring the pretty church."

I nuzzled my nose along the shell of her ear. I inhaled the hotel shampoo and the intoxicating scent of her skin. "Mmm," I murmured. "How far are we going to take this ruse?"

She slapped my chest. "Straight into a lover's quarrel."

I couldn't help but chuckle as she pulled me across the street. It was too fun to mess with her. I sobered quickly once we were through the massive arched doors.

I had seen many beautiful things in my life, but this cathedral could very well have been the grandest. Ornate pews sat over glistening tiles in diamond patterns. Every structure seemed to be carved straight from stone and appear in every style, from functional to delicately detailed statues and figurines. The gilded ceilings reflected the many golden accents shining throughout. Tourists took on a quiet reverence once entering the church, demanded from them by the breathtaking house of worship.

This place was spectacular.

I could have gotten lost in here for hours. I would have loved to read all of the historical plaques and lit a candle for my loved ones. The tourists seemed equally transfixed. This place called to a deeper part of us, a holy place buried inside the depths of our souls we hadn't known existed until we stepped through those doors.

"Look for suspicious behavior," Seraphina whispered in my ear, bringing me out of my reverie.

I snapped into focus and stopped admiring the incredible details of middle-ages architecture in favor of hunting the bad guys we detoured for.

I wondered at the significance of their presence here. We'd caught them in Peru last fall and in Omaha not long after that. They'd taken the Citadel over the winter, which had been another hotbed of Magic for us. India would have been as useless to them as it was to us.

There were stores of Magic in Russia, but they had also been abandoned. And Africa held more mysteries for us than even we had time to discover.

We had chased them to Morocco before but had not found them. And now we were here, in another well of Magic.

Although this one had remained untapped for at least a thousand years.

So, why? Why here and why now?

"Where are we going?" I whispered to Sera as she pulled me toward the far wall and to the back of the cathedral.

We continued to wander through tourists, keeping our arms casually linked and our bodies turned into each other. She would sometimes pause and lay her head on my shoulder. The gesture reminded me of what my life could have been like if things with her had worked out.

If we had managed to stay together. Which of course... we couldn't do.

"Weren't you the one that suggested the catacombs?"

I looked at her sharply. "You're not serious."

"My vision suggests..." She pointed one finger at the floor. "Down."

"No."

She cocked her head to the side and gave me an assessing look. "What do you mean, no? *Yes.*"

"No," I said firmer. "We can't break into the catacombs in the middle of the day."

"Use your Magic. Make these people turn their heads."

"I don't want to."

"Why not? It's simple Magic. If you won't, then I'll do it psychically."

"Sera, no," I argued.

"Bastian, why not? Oh."

"No, oh. There is no *oh*. There's just no. Get the thought out of your head because I'm not going down there."

"They dead bodies are not what you have to worry about you big chicken! There are live people down there that may or may not be causing serious harm to someone we know and love! Or even someone we don't know and love! What if it's your aunt down there? What if it's Analisa or Jericho's mom? Or, worse! What if there's a whole bunch of people down there and Terletov has solved the mystery of how to transfer Magic and keep people alive?"

"I hate that you're making sense right now," I grumbled. I felt goose bumps prickle over all of my skin and I steeled myself for the chilling foreboding that there was no way out of this.

"Well, I hate you, so I guess that makes us even."

"Yes, you might hate me! But that doesn't mean you're inherently afraid of me! Or that you have nightmares of being buried alive with me! Or that something down there, something that has been dead for centuries upon centuries will reach out and grab you and pull you into its skeletal grave where you'll be forced to give it your corporeal body so that it can raise an army of undead and take over the world!"

She scrunched her eyebrows together and shook her head at me. "It's basically the same."

I let out a steadying breath. "This is a real fear, Sera. I cannot go down those steps." Especially now that I could see how far down they went. An iron gate and rail blocked our easy entrance to crumbling stone steps that lead to a lower part of the church. I could feel the cool air as it rushed up from the crypt. Torches lighted the way, but that did not make it any more welcoming.

The locked gate that kept people out seemed to be a temporary fix. Usually, tourists were allowed to explore the upper part of the tombs and see all the buried priests, bishops, and one Spanish prince, that long preceded them. Experience and a love of history and culture promised that once we walked through the main antechambers of the crypt, we would come to secret stairs leading deeper into the bowels of the church. Eventually, we would find the oldest of catacombs, holes dug into the walls stuffed with bones of ancient bodies.

That was the place I dreaded most in life. I had an unnatural fear of dead things. And I always had. I wasn't supposed to die. My people weren't supposed to die. Therefore, death freaked me out more than anything else.

Seraphina clicked her nails on the iron gate and waited for me to make a move. When I didn't, she used her own powers to keep heads turned away while she started shaking the gate loudly.

I sighed with resignation and Magically unlocked the padlock so that I didn't have to make a fool out of myself.

"You could have done that five minutes ago," she complained.

"I could have."

"You're just mad I'm making you go down here."

"I am," I confirmed. "You could have warned me back in Italy that I would have to do this. Then at least I could have mentally prepared myself."

"And you could let me go down here alone if you want to. I'm sure I'll be fine."

A punch of anger hit me in the kidneys and I wanted to wrap my arms around her and hold her to my chest. How could she think I could do that? Did she really know nothing about me? I would never make her do this alone, especially when her powers weren't exactly useful in a situation like this.

Not for the first time, I wondered what we were going to do when we actually found this trouble we had come looking for. We had no weapons and a limited supply of Magic.

What if Seraphina was right? What if we stumbled right into Analisa, or even Terletov? Then what? Would I sarcasm them to death?

Would that even work?

My constant wit seemed to torture Seraphina well enough. Or at least make her want to kill herself.

Maybe the same approach would work with the bad guys.

I kept my eyes trained on my surroundings without really taking too much in. I didn't want to memorize the details of the carved tombs or embellished coffins. I just wanted to find the big bad and get the bloody hell out of here.

We had to be creative with our Magic to continue our journey to the lowest catacomb. We made it a point not to damage any of the history or artifacts, which became increasingly difficult as we went.

The air became bitingly frigid the further down we traveled. It smelled like musty, cold earth. Our bodies were forced together in the cramped hallways and corridors, but I practically worshiped the feel of Sera's warm, living body against mine.

It at least beat the sensation that dead hands were going to start clawing through the packed dirt walls at any second.

A light in the distance pulled me away from the horror movie replaying in my head and we quickened our pace. The hallway widened out into a large circular room with smooth walls and a sloping center. In the middle of that space stood four hooded men chanting around a blue orb of light.

Magic.

The old school kind.

Their presence felt shifty and odd. I hated the sensation Terletov's goons brought with them. I might not have been a Titan, but I could feel this. I could feel how wrong it was. My skin crawled and my internal organs itched uncomfortably.

But we'd found the right place. Seraphina's vision had been spot on.

"Well, well, well," I grinned, still trying to come up with a plan to break up this party of evil. "Look, Sera, we're not too late after all."

Chapter Four

Seraphina

I decided right after we took care of these jackasses, I needed to kill Sebastian.

Could he do anything without sarcasm?

It might be physically impossible for him to speak without infusing some kind of inane jokey-joke into every single word.

The four men that had been hovering over the blue orb of Magic looked up at us from under their dark cloaks and scowled.

"What's the plan?" I whispered to Sebastian out of the corner of my mouth. I felt pinpricks of fear work over my body as I realized we had no escape plan... no way to get out of this one.

"You were supposed to come back with something about how you're always late and then I was going to say something about how you're on time for the important things."

I pushed his shoulder. "Are you kidding? You're working out a bit? Like we're comedians!"

He smirked at me. I nearly told the group of Terletov's men they could have him.

"I'm stalling for time. You were supposed to realize that!"

"No need to hesitate," one of the burlier men announced. "We're ready when you are."

The blue orb continued to spark and sizzle with super-heated Magic. It actually reminded me a lot of Eden. I had seen her Magic more than once and this was a very good representation of it.

I knew it was old, but not much more than that. Eden was the only Immortal I knew that had dealt with any of the Magical hotspots up close and personal. And she'd never learned to wield the power in its Source form. She always ended up fighting it, until she beat it into submission.

In India, she'd basically stolen the healing Magic from the Cave of Winds. And in Romania she'd wrestled some kind of tornado and destroyed the holding powers of the dungeons.

These men seemed to be trying to harness the power somehow, but their methodology didn't make sense to me. Also, I didn't see Terletov around anywhere and I highly doubted he would let his henchmen absorb whatever superpower the orb had for him or the others. If there was something to be gained from this place, he would be here himself.

That meant this was a suicide mission. Or at the very least, Terletov had sent them to test it for him.

Sebastian must have had the same thought.

One of the men pulled out a gun while his friends yelled at him to be careful of the orb. Sebastian took a leaping jump and crashed into the goon closest to him. Sebastian didn't hesitate to shove the man straight into the orb of Magic.

I jumped back as the circle of electrified light expanded and contracted to encompass the entirety of the man. He screamed out in absolute agony while the crackle of lightning grew to a deafening volume.

I tried to look away, but I couldn't. The vision of the man getting fried to death while his cloak turned to flames around him was too much. I had to see it through. I had to know what happened to him.

His screams echoed in the small, rounded chamber and chased each other down the narrow corridor. His body seemed to convulse for eternity. The Magic took its sweet time killing him and all the while his skin became blacker and blacker.

By the time the blue orb released him by dropping him on the compacted dirt floor, every inch of his body had turned black and ashy. I felt like I could blow hard in his direction, and he would crumble to dust and blow away.

My stomach churned at the horrific sight and I finally ripped my eyes from the gruesome scene. I looked back at the orb and noted that it was noticeably bigger. Now, mixed in with the blue, faint strands of puke green could be seen that weren't there before.

The dead guy's Magic.

The orb had taken it and absorbed it into its own.

How strange.

There had been a marked silence while the man electrocuted to death and for long moments after as we all comprehended what happened.

And then, as if an alarm had been sounded or a starting gun let off, we moved into action at once.

Sebastian jumped for his next victim and I did the same. Without weapons, I had to put myself in a position where I couldn't be shot or shoved into the orb of Magic that would incinerate me.

That was the last thing I needed or wanted.

I dove for his waist and tried to tackle him to the ground. I had hoped to catch him off balance and force him to throw his gun away.

That didn't happen.

First, I threw my arms around his waist but couldn't get him to move. Apparently, I wasn't as strong as I liked to believe I was. Second, he swatted me away like a fly.

I felt the punch come at my ribs and knock me five feet into the curved wall. I hit my back first and then my head. My bones seemed to crack with the impact and black dots danced in my vision.

I reached back to find a thick trickle of blood on the crown of my head.

Bastard.

My body would heal quickly, but as he lifted his gun with a sadistic chuckle, I realized not quickly enough.

I could barely see through the pain, but if I didn't do something fast, I would never get the chance again.

I fumbled around for a weapon of some kind with my fingertips. I managed to find a rock that would do the job. I lifted it quickly and used Magic to aim for me.

The rock sailed out of my hand and hit his right arm in the wrist. That was the hand he'd been holding the gun with and the rock managed to hit him just right. He dropped the gun when it went limp in his hand. And he stared at me with a mixture of undisguised rage and surprise.

I dove for the gun at the same time he did and we became a mess of tangled limbs and flying fists.

I was used to men behaving like gentleman. This was the first time a man hadn't cared at all that I was female. Even Lucan had treated me with a certain amount of respect. This guy fought me like he hoped he could kill me in this fight.

And he so easily could have.

We rolled around on the floor while Sebastian fought off the two remaining guys nearby. The searing hot orb crackled overhead. I could feel the heat and electricity of it bouncing around in the air just above my face.

The man fighting me tried to push me toward it. I struggled desperately and just managed to hold my face back from the charged field that surrounded the meaty part of the Magic.

I wiggled my knees up to my chest and leveraged my feet against his torso. I pushed hard and tried to kick him into the Magic. I had grimaced for all of one second before I realized that was what he had been trying to do to me.

I kicked harder.

I tried to push my Magic into him, but he had all kinds of mental blockers up and running. I swirled my Magic around and turned on the persuasion. Mediums didn't have the coolest, violent powers that the rest of the Immortals had, but we did have the ability to bend others to our will.

If I could slip by his mental defenses, I could persuade him to push himself into the Magic. Or at the very least not hurt us. But I couldn't. I came up against a solid, impenetrable wall.

He pulled back an inch and then threw himself on me. His hands went around my neck and he maneuvered me so that my back was now to the pulsing Magic. I felt the heat of it press against my skin and the finality of death hang over me.

Geez! Was this really how I was going to die? Single, dirty from rolling around on the dirt and in the basement of a church where my body would turn to ash?

No way. I had always imagined my death as some kind of *Sleeping Beauty* scenario. After a long, prosperous, fulfilling life, I would simply lie down on a handmade trellis bed carved by my handsome lover and close my eyes. My hair would be laid out perfectly, my hands primly folded over my stomach and my shoes would be designer, not the cheap tennis shoes Sebastian picked up for me earlier today.

A gun went off and echoed loudly in the small chamber. I screeched and faltered for a second. The man I was trying not to let kill me pushed me with more force and I almost rolled into the orb's reach. A body slumped to the ground and then I heard the telltale sound of searing skin. The orb had claimed another and I was terrified that it was Sebastian.

My heart lurched in my chest and a hundred confusing emotions swirled around me, but most of all fear gripped me tightly. That couldn't have been Sebastian. He couldn't die. Heartache bellowed in my chest and I thought for a moment, that if he died, I would follow after him. I couldn't lose-

"Duck, Sera!" the man himself called out.

Oh, whew. He was still alive. I could stop being so dramatic.

For once in my life, I didn't question him. I dove to the side while he came barreling at me. The guy fighting me didn't have time to adjust with me when Sebastian rammed into him from behind.

We had been on our knees fighting, and when Sebastian's body pushed into his, it sent the traitor flying forward. The Magical orb scooped up his body immediately and expanded to cover both his and the other guy recently shot. Sebastian grabbed me by both arms and pulled me with him as we scrambled back to press ourselves against the wall and away from the sparking electricity.

The two men were nothing but charred bodies layered in ash and dead flesh. I stared at them for only a second before I dove for the abandoned gun just two feet away. I staggered to my feet and held my finger steadily over the trigger.

By the time I stood up, the remaining guy had his gun pointed at Sebastian. His hood had dropped back to reveal a sickly looking man with putrid yellow skin and sunken eyes. His hair had come away in clumps all over his scalp and left scabbed over patches of bloody skin.

From here, I could smell him, rotting death that reeked of evil.

This was how all of the other victims had smelled right before death. When Terletov tried to exchange their Magic and failed, this was what happened to their body.

This man was about to die.

A warning flared in my gut. I didn't understand it though. I didn't understand what I should stop him from doing.

I pointed my gun at him and growled, "I will shoot you. I will kill you if I have to."

His lips twisted into a cruel smile. "You'll kill me? Maybe I want you to."

Sebastian took a step towards him with raised hands. "You don't have to work for him. We can help you. We can... fix you."

The man shook his head, still sadistically amused. "You can't fix me. I don't want to be fixed."

"He's lied to you," Sebastian went on. "Whatever he's promised you, he can't deliver. This Kingdom belongs to one family and if it's not in their hands, those who seek to control it die. It happened with the Kendrick line and it will happen with Terletov's as. And all those that stand with him. That's the way our Magic works."

He cocked his head to the side and looked closely at Sebastian. I held my breath and pressed my finger more firmly on the trigger. I wouldn't shoot unless I absolutely had to, but if I did, I hoped I was the fastest gun.

"But what if you could change the Magic?" the man asked slowly. "And what if the Magic changed its loyalty?" His expression evolved from scary and cold to purpose-driven. His focus shifted too. He had been staring at Sebastian, watching him closely. When his attention moved to the orb, I had a split second to realize his intentions before he carried them through.

"What are you talking-"

"No!" I gasped as the man dropped his gun and jumped straight into the orb of Magic. It exploded with that sickly green energy. Sebastian and I dove out of the way, but not before I felt the searing burns of that super-heated light lick up the back of my legs and torso.

I screamed out in agony. I couldn't think beyond the pain of that Magical touch, even as the orb tried to pull me back into it.

Sebastian caught my arms and pulled with all his might. He braced his legs on either side of the corridor entrance and refused to let go of me. I was sure that my arms were close to ripping out of my body, and I knew Sebastian would let them before he let me go.

The Magic continued to expand as it consumed the final body. My own Magic raced to heal my burning skin and the two forces warred with each other for control over my fate.

Finally, the Magical orb seemed pacified with the four sacrifices it had already claimed. My body released suddenly and Sebastian's pull sprang me forward. I knocked him over and landed directly on top of his torso.

And there I stayed.

I couldn't make myself leave the comfort of his chest. His arms wrapped around me immediately as if he were just as reluctant to let me go. My Magic worked quickly and wherever there had been burns before became new, freshly healed skin.

I breathed shuddering breaths and trembled against Sebastian. I had never been more afraid in my life. I could have sworn those were my final moments. I could have sworn the Magic had been seconds from claiming another victim.

Sebastian pushed up suddenly and our gazes clashed together. I could only imagine what I looked like, filthy, terrified and so relieved that tears filled my eyes.

He looked painfully handsome as he stared back at me with aching care. His face had been smudged with dirt and his hair deliciously disheveled. His body was a hard, but hot surface that pressed into mine in heart-warming familiarity.

As I stared into his eyes, my breathing leveled out and my shaking subsided. He centered me in a way that I hated to admit. I didn't want to believe I still had any kind of feelings left for him, but our bond from the past was too strong. He still had the ability to soothe me, to comfort me in the most persuasive ways.

"Are you alright?" he breathed and I closed my eyes at the anguish in his tone.

There were parts of him that still cared for me too. He might hate me in the day-to-day but at least he didn't want me to die.

"I'm fine," I told him.

He shifted so that I was cradled in his arms. "I thought I was going to lose you."

"I thought I was going to lose you too."

Our words were forbidden whispers in a place where nobody would hear us and we could choose not to remember. This was our barest honesty, our most truthful pieces ripped from our souls. We shared more emotions in those few moments than we had in maybe our entire relationship.

Sebastian's head dipped and I thought he might kiss me. His eyes had that half-lidded look that used to do all kinds of crazy things to my willpower. His tongue swept across his lower lip as if in preparation.

My stomach flipped suddenly and my entire body tuned into his motions.

And then... I panicked. I couldn't let him kiss me!

Was I completely out of my mind?

Obviously. Obviously I was out of mind.

One heroic gesture and a full minute without sarcasm and I'd completely forgotten that I hated him.

And I did hate him.

Really, I did.

I mean... right? No. Yes. I definitely hated him.

I felt stripped naked in front of him with my heart on display. If he kissed me know I would give him everything, every last bit of me and I would be lost to him forever.

And he would leave me.

Maybe not immediately... but eventually. And this time when he left... I would die.

I wouldn't be able to take it.

I turned my head away from his lips and felt his entire body stiffen. It was like a wave of cold, hardened energy passed over him. One second his body molded to mine, pliable and giving. The next, he stiffened into granite and completely shut down.

I knew I'd rejected him, so I shouldn't feel as miserable as I did. But the coldness in his touch and the hardness in his eyes cut to the bone.

"We need to go," he said as he disentangled his body from mine. He jumped to his feet and held out a hand to help me up too.

"Right."

He looked back at the dead, Magic-less bodies and shook his head. "I don't think we stopped them from accomplishing their goal. I think they came here to die."

"Which would solve the Where-in-the-world-is-Terletov question," I mumbled.

Sebastian did a double take. "Is that a Carmen Sandiego reference?"

I couldn't look at him. It was more than a little embarrassing that I knew what that computer game was and loved playing it as a child. So I gave a careless shrug instead. "Ever since we started the Terletov missions, it's felt very much like that game. We're running all over the world and can't seem to catch him."

"It's just funny," he said. "I thought that last winter."

I didn't know what to say. I was so used to Sebastian's sarcasm that I didn't know if he was sincere or not. Part of me was waiting for him to come in with his punch line. But he simply moved on, leaving me to wonder what other computer games he'd played as a kid. Somehow we managed to avoid conversations like this during our relationship.

Weird.

"Are you okay with leaving this place like... this?" I gestured at the bodies.

"What choice do we have? I'll call Kiran on the way and see if I can't get some Titans stationed here until we figure out what to do. I doubt killing four of his men was Terletov's entire purpose."

"No kidding," I snorted.

"Ready for more of this?" He raised his eyebrows at me and jerked his chin toward the way back to the surface.

"You mean Geneva?"

"I mean all of this. It feels like we're finally getting close, Sera. I'm ready to end this."

I agreed completely. "Me, too."

"So, yes. Geneva then."

I let Sebastian lead the way to the surface. My mind spun in all kinds of different directions. I felt the same way Sebastian did. The Terletov conflict was headed for climax. One way or another everything was about to change.

I felt that truth as clearly as I felt that we were supposed to be here, to see and witness whatever that was. I knew something big loomed on the horizon.

I just didn't know what yet.

And that scared me in every possible way. I didn't know if I was prepared.

I didn't know if I was ready.

Sebastian glanced at me over his shoulder in the dark corridor and shot me a reassuring smile.

I held my breath until he looked away.

I suddenly felt unprepared for a lot of things in life. Terletov was just one of them.

Chapter Five

Sebastian

We arrived in Geneva near dawn the next day. The streets were still warmly lit with plenty of artistic, outdoor sconces and streetlamps. The city seemed to glow under the soft yellow light.

I liked Geneva.

It was one of my favorite cities in Europe. It held a charming class that I felt comfortable enjoying without feeling snobbish or needlessly pretentious.

The hotel that Kiran always chose to stay at felt very well like home. I'd spent a large portion of my childhood there. It being an old Kendrick palace, my parents felt like they still owned the place.

I woke Seraphina just as I handed the rental off to the valet. She blinked up at me with sleepy eyes and a small pout. Without her defenses raised and rearing, she looked lovely. Breathtaking even. I shook that thought away quickly and led her inside. We stopped by the front desk to pick up our room keys and then walked side-by-side up the endless flight of stairs to Kiran's suite.

I texted him once we arrived in the city so that he knew to expect us. I had called ahead to book my room and a room for Seraphina on the way. I doubted she was pleased with my handling of her accommodations, but I decided not to worry about that. She needed my help whether she wanted it or not.

She'd fallen asleep almost as soon as we'd left Vienna. Her body needed some major healing. The fight at St. Stephens had been brutal and especially rough on her. I hadn't disturbed her until we arrived. She slept the entire ten-hour drive.

While I spent the long car ride trying to process what it had felt like to nearly lose her.

We'd been in plenty of dangerous situations before, but she'd always managed to keep her neck out of danger. This time had been different.

I couldn't explain the feelings of almost losing her, not even to myself. I felt nothing but a deep, possessive need to take care of her now. I wanted to hold her, wrap my arms around her and never let her go.

I couldn't make sense of that.

Because at the same time, I wanted to shove her out of my life and never hear from her again. The woman was positively infuriating. And she just didn't see it.

Nearly kissing her had also been a mistake. We had been so close, physically that is. And her body had felt alarmingly right in my arms. I had wanted to roll her over and cover her with my body while I ravished her mouth with mine.

Of course, she'd seen right through me and done the wise thing by turning away.

Still, the anger I'd felt at being denied what my body wanted most on this earth was a nearly painful thing. Followed shortly by the irritation that she'd rejected me.

Again.

Bitterness and hatred settled inside me, only unseated when I would remember the look on her face as she nearly toppled backward into that horrible Magic. Or the swelling pride in my chest when I remembered how courageously she'd fought. My emotions were on a constant cycle, flipping through all of these different thoughts and feelings until I thought I would go mad.

Or at the very least, spontaneously turn into a woman.

We'd been quiet on our walk to Kiran's suite and I couldn't help but wonder what went on in that frustrating head of hers. I was also curious to see how she would spin the entire debacle into my fault.

I knew it was coming. I was somehow to blame for... for whatever we'd seen and been through, at least in her eyes.

Kiran had opened the door before we had a chance to knock. He spoke through a yawn when he explained, "Eden felt you coming." He walked back into the suite, leaving me to catch the closing door.

I held it open for Seraphina and then followed behind into the massive penthouse. The central room had only one lamp turned on and left the rest of the rooms in complete darkness. Eden was nowhere to be seen, so I had to assume Kiran planned to run this one solo and let his very pregnant wife get her rest.

He gestured to a couch and then waved at us, in his very kingly way, to proceed.

"I had a vision," Seraphina explained through her own yawn. "Well, of sorts. Anyway, it took us to Vienna as you know."

"Yes, Sebastian explained this earlier," Kiran said. He sat forward and rested his elbows on his knees. Seraphina hadn't had many visions until the last part of our relationship.

Some people believed that with the Magic restored thanks to Eden and Avalon, the entirety of the Kingdom's powers would be enhanced. Immortality had never been a real thing before, but in the three years the twins had taken the throne, not one Immortal had died from natural causes. And the King's Curse had been completely eradicated.

Seraphina's increase in psychic visions could very well be a manifestation of this theory.

"We followed my instinct to the catacombs of St. Stephens," she continued. "Well, beyond the catacombs, really." She put a comforting hand on my kneecap. I almost smiled. I had been rather afraid of going down there. She went on to explain the altercation with the Terletov's men and how they all came to die.

"We think they had always planned to die," I finished for her. "Some kind of suicide mission, perhaps."

"But why?" Kiran's expression darkened with fury. He was as anxious to get rid of Terletov as anyone. He wanted his home back, his Kingdom safe again and his wife and children out of danger. He wanted his mother safe again. I knew losing her weighed heavily on his shoulders.

"The orb..." I used my hands to give an example of the massive size of it. "It started out blue. Almost the same color as Eden and Avalon's Magic, if not exactly that same blue. By the time the fourth man had thrown his body into the light, the color had shifted to a dull, sickly green. It started to match the men's Magic. It had also grown substantially in size."

Kiran threw his back against the couch and let out a weary sigh. "They're trying to corrupt the Magic," he decided. "They're trying to destroy it."

"But why the old kind? We haven't been drawn to Vienna in a thousand years. Why would Terletov want to destroy it now?"

We sat silently for several minutes before Seraphina perked up and slid forward. "What if he's not trying to corrupt it or destroy it? What if he's trying to control it?"

My exhausted brain snapped back to life with her theory. Kiran seemed to come alive too. He sat forward and gave her a concentrated look. "Explain."

"So, we've always known that Eden has had this weird connection with the Magical hotspots. In India, she basically shut down the entire operation. And in Romania, she destroyed the holding power of that particular Magic, the dungeons. And tell me if this is a coincidence. Her Magic manifests as blue, or it used to before you and her, er, consummated your relationship. But before you, she always had that bright blue Magic. Then that weird smoke she has is also blue. Okay? It cannot be chance that the Magic beneath St. Stephens was blue. Maybe it's... maybe it's like the natural color of Magic. Maybe that's the Magic in its purest form. Eden and Avalon were born with that Magic after thousands of years of the Magic diluting through segregation and whatnot. So, we've always known their Magic is stronger and more powerful. But, they've also been able to control these Source-spots too. It's like those original Magics respond to them, bend to their will because they hold the same kind."

Kiran and I nodded along, waiting for her to get to the point. "So?" I pressed when she took a break to suck in a breath. "What does that have to do with Terletov's corruption?"

"What if he's not corrupting it?" She pushed my shoulder with the proudest look on her face. "What if he's changing the Magic to respond to him? What if he's infusing his tainted Magic into the original Magic so that he has unlimited access to it? He sent his guys primarily to infect the orb with what was in them and now it's green and huge and seemingly stronger than ever. And Terletov controls that now. He's bonded to it."

Kiran shook his head, wanting to discredit that theory. "But controlling the Magic doesn't do anything unless the Magic is willing to cooperate. In India, Eden basically absorbed the Magic and yes, she can now use it, but the Romanian Magic didn't turn out the same. She had to fight to control it. It did not go willingly. She almost died. And she had plenty of experience absorbing Magics. Terletov has been without any kind of real power for a very long time now. I saw him in Romania. There is no he is strong enough to control something as powerful as a Source Magic. It would kill him."

I grunted a bitter laugh. "I don't think we're going to get that lucky."

"I agree with Sebastian," Seraphina chimed in immediately. Well, that was a first. "I'm not saying it would be an easy process for him. Or that it's even possible. But my gut is telling me that's his plan. He's turning the wells of Magic against us and he hopes to control them."

Kiran's eyebrows drew together and he ran a hand through his hair, his tell that he was wrestling with something important. "What do you think, Cousin?"

Without hesitating, I said, "I think Seraphina is on to something. I think it makes sense. And you should have seen these goons, Mate. You should have seen how willing they were to throw themselves into that thing. And that was no pleasant death. They watched each other suffer and die one at a time. I mean, it was gruesome. And still, especially that last guy, it was like he was taunting us, like he knew he got one over on us."

"Then why fight you?" Kiran pressed. "Why not just throw themselves into it as soon as you showed up?"

"Who knows? Maybe they had to do it one at a time? Or, maybe they thought they could take us with them."

Seraphina sat up straighter, "Or maybe they knew we would do our best to keep them away from there. We hadn't gone in with the intention of killing them all. In fact, if we had our way, we would have brought them back here for questioning. Maybe they had to make sure they got in that orb, even if it meant killing us first."

Kiran thought that over for another couple of minutes. While he was silent, I studied the dark room we sat in. With my Magic, I could see far past the circumference of light from the one lit lamp. I moved my eyes around the lavish suit and tried not to think about the girl sitting next to me.

When had she ever shown such intellect? When had she ever been so surprisingly bright and involved?

When we started dating, there was a shallowness to her... a vacancy. We fell in love, but there had always been a surface level quality to it. After had broken up, I swore to myself I'd been in love with her body but not her personality.

I was still in love with her body. Seraphina Van Curen was breathtaking. She had the kind of beauty and grace that legends were made from. Helen of Troy. Juliet. Bathsheba.

I had been a panting teenager when I'd drooled after her. And she'd let me; she'd led me along with the tip of her finger.

I had hated myself for a long time after we broke up for letting her have so much control over me. Directly after she'd ended things with me, aka, shattered my soul, I'd decided that she had only been with me because of my bloodline.

Immortals were supposed to bond for life, even before marriage. Our Magics tended to wrap up in each other and refuse to let go.

Ours might struggle today to stay separated, but we'd managed the initial separation without much issue. I had braced myself for death or worse, a lifetime of wishing for death. But I'd faced no such horrors.

Instead, I'd come to this conclusion; Seraphina had never held true feelings for me. She'd allowed a relationship with me for my bloodline, for the crown I should have had and for the title that died when the St. Andrews took the royal seat. She'd dated me because I had once been a prince and still held that reputation.

My family had given up our titles. And I'd given up the right to be heir to a throne I never wanted. When that became clear to her, she left.

I wasn't the prince she wanted. I was just another man foolish enough to fall for her pretty looks.

"You sent a Titan unit to check out St. Stephens?" Kiran's voice brought me back to the present conversation.

"I did," I confirmed. "And asked them to guard it until I sent further instructions."

Kiran frowned. "I gave Talbott and Lilly leave to take a honeymoon." He gave me an unreadable look and then said, "For as long as they'd like. They've been through enough. This time for them has been a long time coming and Lilly... Lilly just isn't ready to fight yet."

"Ah." I didn't know what else to say. I understood that Talbott's primary responsibility was Lilly and always would be. But, going into this without Talbott was a huge risk on our part. As the lead Titan and commander of Kiran's personal guard, he held incredible responsibility.

My cousin the King pushed forward in his seat and I could feel the weight of his request before he ever asked it. "I would like you to take over during the interim."

I cocked my head back and processed his words. "I'm not a Titan," I reminded him.

"But you are in line for the throne. And it's your place-"

"*Am* I in line for the throne? If somehow Eden and Avalon, the unkillable Immortals, managed to die, and you *and* my sister. Oh, and your children. Then I suppose it falls to me, but I'm hardly the likely survivor in this scenario."

"Sebastian, I cannot ask Avalon, obviously. You're the only one that I trust well enough to take over this position."

"Jericho."

Kiran snorted.

"Titus," I suggested. "I trust him. He's who I would choose."

"We've made progress over the last three years, Cousin. But I can't charge a Shifter with the entirety of the Guard. Especially when I can't be sure my Guard hasn't been compromised."

"They will not listen to me any more than they would a Shifter."

He narrowed his eyes on me. "I am not asking, Bastian. I am decreeing."

Seraphina let out a surprised laugh next to me and I shot her a glare. When I turned back to Kiran, I had to struggle to swallow the bitter taste that coated my tongue. "As you wish, Your Highness."

He sat back with a satisfied smirk. "Good. Your first order of business is to investigate all of the other Magical wells and decide which ones are the most at risk."

"Yes, Sir."

He stood up, ignoring my blatant disgust with my new position. "And your second order of business is to get out of my hotel room so I can go back to sleep. We'll talk more over breakfast."

Kiran disappeared into his bedroom and Seraphina dissolved in laughter. She threw her body back against the sofa and held her belly while she laughed.

"What is so hilarious?"

She twirled a finger at me. "You and your new position. The man who chooses every death-defying mission and opportunity to throw himself in harm's way but has run from responsibility since birth. That's what I'm laughing at. Head of the Titan Guard. Lord, help us!"

I crossed my arms and tried not to pout. "You know, I had already come up with the decision to investigate all of those hotspots, right? Kiran's going to get all of the credit, but I had the idea at least twenty minutes ago."

She started laughing again, so I decided it was time to leave. She could laugh at me all she wanted, but I didn't need her approval.

Besides, I hadn't run from responsibility before. I'd just never been entrusted with it.

There was a huge difference in that.

Chapter Six

Seraphina

Five days later, I found myself at home. And peacefully alone. I couldn't have been further from the Kingdom drama or my narcissistic ex if I'd tried.

I owned a condo in Seattle. It was kind of a random place to set up a life as I had no family near or even friends in the area. But I supposed that was what appealed to me most.

After a long year of being the center of attention as Kiran's betrothed, and then the following years in just as much spotlight as Sebastian's girlfriend, I needed space.

Eden, Mimi, and Lilly knew about my home, but I wasn't close enough friends with any others for them to care. I didn't even think my parents knew about this place.

I'd bought it shortly after Sebastian and I had broken up.

At twenty-two, I'd been waiting to start a life with my longtime boyfriend. After high school, I lived in hotels and crashed at my parent's various homes around the globe. I had been waiting for Sebastian to propose, to take our relationship seriously and marry me. I had been waiting for Sebastian to tell me when my life could start.

But he hadn't.

So when all of my hopes and dreams with Sebastian dissolved into nothing, I decided I didn't need to wait for someone else to start the life I wanted. I could start it anytime I wanted.

I could start it now.

And so I did.

My seaside condo wasn't anything extravagant, just a two-bedroom apartment with a view of the volatile North Pacific. I'd decorated to my taste and enjoyed the silence and solitude.

I knew I had the reputation of a socialite, but honestly I preferred being alone.

I'd spent too much of my life around people that expected the worst behavior from me and didn't think for themselves. My current friends were awesome, but they were all busy with their lives and families.

I had a few human friends I went out with sometimes, but I always felt like I couldn't get too close or they would discover my secret.

Or at least have the EPA come sweep me away for alien-related testing.

I sat down on my comfortable pale suede couch with my steaming cup of coffee and stared out of my floor-to-ceiling windows at the stormy day. The sea tossed and turned through the glass. The waves rose high, cresting with foaming white bubbles before crashing back to the rocky surface and swirling in pockets of unrest.

I couldn't help but feel oddly connected to the mood of the ocean. I had been restless since I got back, anxious and uncomfortably uneasy.

I thought back to my weekend abroad and shuddered with the foreboding feeling that it wasn't over for me.

With the wedding, Sebastian's kidnapping and Vienna, I had enough of Terletov and his games.

Ever since I went back to Romania for Eden and Kiran's coming home party over a year ago, I'd been trapped with the rest of the Monarchs in an endless cycle of worthless missions. But it had been easy to stay with them when our home base had been the Citadel.

Now, with Romania firmly in Terletov's greedy hands, we were spread out across the globe, struggling for a place to settle down until we could regroup and fight back.

Kiran and Eden had moved to Kiran's family palace in England. Avalon and Mimi had set up in Paris near Mimi's parents. Who knew where Lilly and Talbott had run off? And Jericho had been staying with his new girlfriend wherever she went to school.

At the same time our Kingdom was under attack, my friends had been marrying off and settling down. I wondered if it was the war that spurred their domestic inclinations. Did they finally see how short life could be even for Immortals? Did they finally understand the importance of finding someone to love and share this life with?

I had seen that too. And then when I asked Sebastian to do something about it, he chose the mission.

I sighed. I really hated all the pity-parties lately. I had mostly gotten over him, especially in the last few months when I hadn't been forced to see him. But fresh from several days with him in a row, I couldn't seem to think about anything else.

As soon as he'd stumbled off to bed in Geneva, I took off. I'd used the hotel phone to call my parent's valet. He sent the charter to fly me home. As soon as I landed, I'd gotten to work replacing all of the things I'd lost during the explosion, like my phone and credit cards.

I glanced down at my new phone, the military-grade smart contraption that was now chirping at me with an annoying beep.

I swiped my finger across the screen and answered warily, "Hello?"

"Sera," Eden breathed heavily. She seemed perpetually out of breath these days. But the babies were due in a month, so I didn't really blame her. They were like sitting on her lungs or something. And apparently her bladder if I listened to her complain about them. "I didn't think you were going to answer."

I didn't confirm that I had been thinking about ignoring her call. "Why not?"

"Because I know you're hiding from us. You only go home when you're trying to avoid us."

"That's not true! I go home because... well, because it's home."

"Yeah right. Seattle is such a hotbed of Kingdom activity. You're completely surrounded by friends and family and-"

"Does this phone call have a point?"

She grumbled something very crass about my questionable virtue, but I chose to ignore her. "We saw Ileana."

Her words held a profundity I didn't understand. The Gypsy Queen rarely brought good news and so I couldn't help the flutters of anxiety at Eden's declaration. "Where?"

"Uh, we're in Romania."

"I'm sorry, what?"

"I, er, wanted to visit her before we headed back to London."

"She's too close to the Citadel. Where are you now?"

"Timisoara. We're flying back to England. We're fine. I haven't detected a single Immortal since we arrived. Well, you know, other than the Gypsy."

I didn't like that. I didn't like that she was there at all. "I can't believe Kiran let you go there. Is he crazy?"

"Mostly, Ileana called us and told us we needed to get our asses over here."

"So what was so important?"

"She, um, well... It was mostly about you."

"Me?"

"You."

"E, you're *killing* me."

"She said that you need to pay attention tonight. And that the powers are coming, so you should be prepared."

"Oh, geez."

"I know."

"Anymore words of advice?"

"She said," Eden paused to laugh at some joke I didn't get. "She said that when your powers expand, so will your Magic."

"Okay..."

"And you should love how your Magic feels."

"Son of a bitch."

"Hey! Not in front of the babies!"

It was my turn to laugh. "I don't think my potty mouth will affect them in vitro. Now, when I babysit... that will be a different story."

"I stopped listening after 'when I babysit.'"

My heart squeezed. I missed my friend.

"Get back to London, Your Royal Highness," I ordered. "And then call me the very second you go into labor so I can be there to see those little princesses."

"Will you still love them if they're little princes?"

"As long as they don't look like the Kendrick side, I can love anything."

"Not according to Ileana," she taunted.

"That old Witch doesn't know anything."

"First comes the vision, then comes marriage, then comes the baby in a baby carriage."

"Oh, my god."

"Her words! Not mine!"

"I'm hanging up on you now."

"Sera!"

But it was too late. I swiped off the phone and threw it to the other end of the couch. I couldn't even. Visions were bad enough, draining and disorienting. I got nervous just thinking about what this one could be about.

Mostly though, I hoped it never happened. I didn't want to start down this rabbit hole. And I wasn't too stupid to realize that Ileana hadn't prophesied anything about Sebastian. My Magic could expand to the moon and my feelings for him along with it. But that would never mean he had to return them. He would never commit to anything he didn't want to.

Except maybe an interim position in the Titan Guard.

But I hadn't been worth his time when he actually loved me. I wouldn't be worth his time now.

I spent the rest of the day in a funk. A Sebastian-slash-impending-vision-induced funk. And I hated it.

There were times I loved my willful isolation on the West Coast. And there were times I wanted the distraction of people and my friends that could make me laugh out of any weird mood.

I probably should have gone to bed early, but I was afraid of that stupid vision. So, instead, I binge-watched *Supernatural* on Netflix until I passed out on the couch. Also, I ordered Chinese for dinner and I could have sworn there was something off in the Kung Pao Chicken.

Those two reasons together followed me into my subconscious and made things a little confusing.

I woke in a dream. I knew it was a dream because the sky had darkened into a deep purple, the kind of purple that didn't exist in real life. The air gusted past me with a chilling bite and seemed to nip at my skin as if it were alive. The ground stretched out around me in a barren wasteland of cracked, red earth.

There was no life in sight. Not even a tree or a bush.

Green Magic swirled at my feet and around my ankles. My stomach felt sick with loss and my mind whirled with the possibilities.

What happened here?

Who did this?

"Seraphina?"

I whirled around and came face-to-face with the very last person I expected to see. "Sebastian? What are you doing here?"

He looked around. "What is this place?"

"My vision."

"What am I doing in your vision?"

I raised my eyebrows at him. How was I supposed to know? "Are you real?"

He looked down at his body and then turned in a circle. "I think so. I feel real."

"Hmm, but that's what the vision-version of you would say."

"What vision?"

"*This* vision."

"You've never had a vision like this before. Are you sure this is a vision?"

"Oh, my gosh. If you say vision again, I'm going to castrate you. Then we'll figure out if you're real or not."

He gave me a condescending look. "Someone's cranky tonight."

I pressed my lips together and prayed for patience. I knew I didn't call him here. I hadn't Dream-Walked with Sebastian for years, not since the beginning stages of our relationship when it was exciting to be together and we couldn't get enough of each other.

"Okay, so really, where are we?"

I looked around again and felt the slithering feeling of being watched glide over my body. "Your guess is as good as mine."

He started walking away from me and I hurried to catch up with him. He glanced over his shoulder at me and gave me a tight smile.

I let out a resigned sigh and followed him. This was my vision, but he seemed to be the only one with any initiative.

We stumbled over uneven terrain where rocks and dead branches seemed to jump out of the earth just in time to trip us. The Magic on the ground turned into a fog that made visibility practically zero.

He reached out his hand and grabbed mine to help lead me forward.

"Maybe we should go back," I suggested.

"Is that where your vision wants you to go?"

"No," I sighed. "We're going in the right direction." Of course, I had no concrete confirmation that was true, but my gut told me to press on. And that was the thing with visions, they were mostly about all the feels that came with them and less to do with what actually happened inside of them.

Nothing more was said as we traveled onward. He never let go of my hand and I never asked him to. Visions could be scary but were rarely harmful to my corporeal body. In a Dream Walk, however, my life was totally up for grabs and I really wanted to avoid dying via dream.

Eventually, we came to a crumbling stone wall. Or rather, Sebastian walked straight into it. The fog had become so thick that we couldn't see anything in front of us and had been forced to stare at the ground to avoid tripping.

He stumbled back a few steps and the fog seemed to clear in front of us. The heavy-bricked wall stretched on and on in either direction. We looked up at the same time. The stone bricks were built so that we could probably climb up it, but we couldn't see how far of a climb that would be. The wall seemed to rise forever.

"Pick a direction," Sebastian suggested.

"This way." I pulled him to the right and we walked along the wall for a long time.

The world was eerily silent. The wind didn't make any sound and nothing else was alive to offer a soundtrack. Our footsteps seemed to scream through the quiet.

After a while, the wall gave way to a gate. The ironwork had been ripped from the hinges and left to dangle haphazardly. It also began to look familiar.

We stepped through the gate and looked out at the Citadel. Or what was left of it. The buildings had all crumbled to nothing but scattered debris and ruins. The Immortal fountain had been bashed to pieces. And the castle that lay in the distance looked charred, blackened by fire and death.

"What happened?" Sebastian asked. "Is this what will happen if we attack Terletov?"

I walked to the shattered remains of the fountain. I put my hands on the broken stone and the mangled statues that once depicted our equality and history. The remnants whispered through my skin. They brought my Magic to life and jump-started my heart. They spoke to me.

"This is what will happen if we don't bring war to Terletov," I told him. "This is what he will do to us. To the world."

I felt Sebastian's entire body tense next to me. "He can't... How?"

"The Magic. It's in harmony with the planet. But if he... if he infects it like he plans to, then this will happen."

Sebastian spun in a circle and stared back through the gate. In this vision, we were in one very specific place, but I knew instinctively that this destruction would spread to every corner of the earth. There would be no place left untouched.

We were spoiled as Immortals. We thought our small Kingdom could live apart from humanity and remain untouched. We wouldn't bother them and they wouldn't bother us.

But nobody was safe from Dmitri Terletov.

His evil would infect the entire planet, killing Immortal and Mortal alike.

"We have to stop him, Sebastian."

He turned to me, his hazel eyes sparkling with purpose. "We will, Sera. I swear to you, we will."

I reached out my hand to him and... fell off my couch.

Oh, shit!

What a vision.

I scrambled to find my phone underneath me. I struggled with the tangle of blankets and the remote to my TV. Finally, I dug it out and peered at it through bleary eyes. Once I pulled up the numbers, I realized I hadn't added Sebastian's number to my new phone.

I was just about to call it up in my Magical memory when the damn thing started buzzing in my hands. I screamed at the top of my lungs before I settled down and forced myself to answer the unknown number.

"Hello?" I asked breathlessly.

"Seraphina?"

"Were you there, Sebastian? Was that real?"

"Yes," he agreed solemnly. "Yes, it was real."

Several moments beat between us. Neither of us knew what to say or where to begin. There was too much. The task at hand felt too heavy, too important.

"Have you called Kiran?" I asked him after a long while.

"Only to get your new number from Eden."

"You should call him."

"I will."

More silence. I didn't know where to begin or what to say. I didn't even know if there was anything to say. But I didn't want to hang up. I didn't want to lose him to his busy life where I didn't know what he was doing or if he was in danger or not.

As if he read my mind, he said, "I want you with me."

"You do?" I sounded spitefully skeptical and I wanted to eat my words.

"For the, uh, for your visions. It would be easier if you were with my team and me."

"A bunch of Titans? No thanks."

He snorted a derisive laugh. "Bloody hell, Woman! I'll call in the old team for this one. Obviously."

"Sebastian, we don't work well together. We can't stand to be around each other. And you basically hate me. If I have another vision, I'll just call you."

"Please, Sera. I need you."

He should have started with that. I had no defense against "please."

"Where are you?" I whispered.

"Where are *you*? I'll send a plane."

"Seattle."

More weighted silence before he said, "What's in Seattle?"

"Um, my house."

In a clipped, impatient tone, he snapped, "Keep your phone nearby. I'll text you an airport and departure time."

And that was that. He hung up on me.

I set my phone down on the coffee table like it had just bit me. Holy hades. Sebastian and I working together? What had I just gotten myself into?

Chapter Seven

Sebastian

I paced in front of the fireplace anxiously. What had I done? What the hell had I done?

I'd gone on one trippy doomsday subconscious walk-about with Seraphina and impulsively invited her along? *On this mission?*

I couldn't decide what bothered me more. Bringing her with me and placing her in all kinds of danger? Or putting myself in close proximity to her for the foreseeable future?

Was I a complete idiot?

I was a complete and utter idiot.

I looked around at the small hotel room I'd rented for the week. We were near Gabriel's old place, but I couldn't bring myself to stay there.

Not after...

God, I wanted to murder Terletov. More than anything.

Titans littered every sitting space in the small suite. I wanted them out of here, but that didn't seem very leader-like. Especially since we were in the middle of plotting our next move. They needed my guidance and I needed their experience.

I didn't want to do this whole interim thing, but it looked like I would be strapped with it for a while.

Damn you, Talbott and all your wedded bliss.

Someone opened the door and loud, boisterous conversations died into nothing in a second. I blew out a breath of relief. I had expected Seraphina to show up first. I couldn't have been more thrilled that she hadn't.

Xander, Xavier, Titus and Jericho walked into sight, followed by Olivia, Ophelia, and Roxie. My team. My real team. Not these Titan imposters.

I mean, sure Titans were trained since birth to fight and go on missions, but they had nothing on these guys. The Titans took an oath and lived in special training camps. But how could that compete with the Resistance?

Obviously, it couldn't.

"Look who decided to finally show up."

"And look who took a step up in the world," Xander called back.

Nobody looked impressed with my "promotion." Not even the new girls. And they didn't know better! They were supposed to be impressed by default.

Of course, one of them was dating Jericho, so clearly she had questionable standards.

"I'll be requiring your utmost respect and unquestionable obedience moving forward. You may now refer to me as Sir."

Crickets. Nobody said anything.

Best to lose the people I actually led before this became truly embarrassing. "Guard, you're relieved for now. We'll reconvene in three hours to hammer out tomorrow's details."

The robot army stood freakishly in sync and departed silently from my room.

"They've always creeped me out," Titus announced.

Xavier pushed him. "Because when they look at you, all they want to do is stab you straight through your animal heart."

Titus shoved him back. "That's the exact same feeling I get when I look at *you*."

"They're not like that anymore," I defended them. Bloody hell, one week with the Titans and I already felt loyal. No wonder Talbott was such a hardass; it came with the job description.

The entire group gave me a look that said they knew better. I just let it go. No use in arguing with this lot.

"So what's up?" Jericho asked casually, as if we were discussing the weather. He had his arm around his girlfriend, Olivia. A twinge of jealousy pinched in my chest, but I brushed it away.

It wasn't Olivia in particular I felt envious of. Although, she was lovely and he was a very lucky man. It was more the ease and comfort in their relationship that I coveted.

I wanted that.

I could admit that.

My friends had all settled down and I wanted to as well. I had lived a lifetime of volatility and uncertainty. I wanted to enter into the next phase of my life- the calmer, more stable phase. And I wanted a girl by my side and plans of a future together, of a family.

I wanted everything Seraphina and I had talked about but never acted on.

Only, I wanted it with someone else.

Someone who didn't hate me.

I cleared my head of those thoughts and went on to explain what Seraphina and I had been up to of late. I filled them in on St. Stephens in Vienna and then the Dream Walk vision I'd shared with her.

This of course, brought on a bevy of crude comments that I laughed off.

"So, tell us again how you ended up in bed with the ice queen?" Titus laughed. "I thought all future dealings with Seraphina were *null and void*?" He looked around the room. "Those were his exact words, I kid you not."

More laughter at my expense.

"We ended up in a dream together, hardly the roll in the hay you're painting."

"But it was so hot. So, unbearably *scorching* hot." Seraphina's voice cut through the room and we all jumped at the sound. "Sebastian couldn't keep his hands off me in between the prophesy about the end of the world and the death and decay all around us. I have never been more turned on in my life."

I hung my head. No way could I get out of this one. She'd walked in at the worst moment. The very worst moment. This was always how things tended to work out for me.

Was bad timing a talent? Because I had it in spades.

"Seraphina, I-"

"Don't bother," she sighed. "I'm too tired to go to battle."

She flopped down on one of the couches next to Roxie. They shared one of those silent girl conversations with just their eyes and frowns. I wanted to know what went through both of their heads! It felt like they were gossiping about me, but they hadn't said anything.

Impossible women.

"So what's the plan, Boss?" Jericho pulled us back to the task at hand.

"We are headed to the City of Kings at dawn. We're going to investigate the ruins and decide if there's anything there for us. Obviously, we know there is a source of Magic somewhere near the ruins, but it has yet to be determined if it's hidden on the mountain or somewhere nearby."

"Machu Picchu," Jericho explained to Olivia and I watched her pale a little.

The mountain was where we'd found her sister and her. I wondered if being back here freaked her out at all or if she had adjusted enough into her newly Immortal skin to be able to funnel all that anger and vengeance into something useful.

Probably the latter, Olivia was a fighter.

"And if it's not there?" Roxie asked.

"Then we keep looking. We are working under the assumption that Terletov has not found it yet. We have no evidence to support this, but we do have hope. And we have a determination to find it. Once we do, we will leave Titans to protect it while this particular team moves on to the next source. After a conversation with Angelica, Ileana, and the Monarchs, we have decided there are precisely seven Sources of Magic around the globe. India and Romania are taken care of as Eden now holds those Magics. Vienna is now in Terletov's control presumably. That leaves this place, Morocco, Siberia and Mali."

"Mali?" Ophelia spoke for the first time.

"More specifically, Timbuktu." Her eyes grew especially wide with that declaration. I suppressed a smile. If this girl hadn't traveled much, she was about to get a crash course in the Immortal jet-set lifestyle. Which meant, flying around the world nonstop and trying to find bad guys.

It wasn't exactly glamorous.

"There could possibly be another in North America and a ninth option in Indonesia. But we are saving those for last resorts as nobody knows the exact location of either."

"This sounds impossible," Roxie grumbled. "And how are you going to protect every spot with Titans. You're going to run out at some point. You don't exactly have an unlimited supply." Roxie's tough expression hardened even further as she spoke. She was right. And we all knew it.

"We have to try, Rox. We have to do something. And maybe while we're doing something, we'll run into these guys and stop them."

She pursed her lips and nodded. "Yeah, maybe."

"Listen, this has to stop. Countless Immortals have died and now humans are becoming victims as well. Our friends are dying. Our friends and family aren't safe anymore. We have to put a stop to Terletov and his nefarious plans. And we have to do it soon."

"We need a leg up," Jericho said. "We need something that's going to put us a step ahead of them instead of the other way around."

I shared a look with Seraphina. "Well... it looks like we might have one actually. Seraphina's vision of the end of the world wasn't her first. She's been getting them more frequently. I've asked her along in case another one has as prodigious timing as the first two. She's the reason we knew to go to Vienna in the first place. She's the reason we know any of this stuff."

"Why the visions now, though?" Xander asked. "What's changed?"

I opened my mouth to give my theory, but Seraphina spoke before I could. "I think it's the Magic. Maybe it's finally trickled down to me or whatever, but I've been having more and more visions of late. My powers come easier and I have no problem accomplishing mindless tasks that used to take up not only time, but energy."

"I've noticed this too," Jericho put in. "But I thought it had something to do with Liv. Maybe it doesn't. Or maybe it's both."

"I've felt it too!" Titus exclaimed. "I mean, nothing really happened. Bu the other day I swore I could have turned into a polar bear if I wanted to." When we all just stared at him, he said, "Guys, I'm a grizzly! That's a big deal. A really big freaking deal."

"So, anyway." Everyone looked back to me and I tried to move us beyond whatever... that was. "This is all fantastic news. We're in a good place. We just have to keep pushing forward, keep doing what we know how to do. This bastard is going down. And we're going to be the team to take him down."

They smiled at me, completely bloodthirsty and murderous. God, I loved them.

"Assignment for tonight?" Xavier asked.

"Just get some rest. We're leaving at precisely five in the morning. Be ready."

They nodded their agreement and ambled off to find their respective rooms. Seraphina lingered behind and while the rest of our team said goodbye to me and tried to talk my ear off, I worked up an apology in my head.

Only, I had way too much to apologize for. I didn't know whether I should start with asking her on this mission? Or the conversation she'd walked into.

And then I remembered that she'd bought a house. In Seattle. And a flood of irrational anger filled me from top to bottom.

I wanted to pick a fight with her and watch her squirm. I wanted to make her hurt like I hurt. I wanted her chest to split open and ache like mine.

Finally, the two of us were the only ones left. She played with her purse straps and glanced at the door several times before finding the courage to meet my eyes.

"So, I'm here," she said timidly.

Everything I wanted to say dissolved into ashes and cowardice. My mouth opened to say something, but nothing came out.

She waited patiently while I pulled a thought together. "Thanks for coming. We need you on this one."

"Because you needed me on all the ones before this one?"

I swallowed against rocks that had suddenly been shoved down my throat. How to go from here?

I took a step toward her and lowered my voice. "Sera, you have to know I wanted to protect you. I'm not all wickedness and misery."

She turned her head away and lifted her chin. Defiance personified.

My heart kicked to life in my chest. Such a firecracker. She intimidated most men. Hell, she intimidated all men. Even my once betrothed cousin. Kiran was the King these days, but he had no idea what to do with Seraphina when they'd shared their brief engagement.

Fire and brimstone, this one. She knew what she wanted and went after it with unwavering resolve. She also didn't give up on anything.

Well, almost anything.

There'd been that brief interlude when she'd left me. But other than that, this woman fought for those things she believed in and didn't stop until she had what she wanted.

While other men felt intimidated, I felt nothing but alive. She brought something out of me that would naturally stay buried. She spoke to my spirit in ways no other person could. And not just because of our Magical connection. No, Seraphina could look at me and I would feel the call of her challenge.

At times, I found her infuriating. We did nothing but bicker and fight until our claws were bloodied and gorged with each other's flesh. Metaphorically speaking of course.

But then there were times when the challenge between us turned to passion and I thought I would drown in this woman. Happily. I would give up breathing air to breathe her. Give up living alone to stand by her side for the rest of eternity. I would do anything for her. Even if she hated me.

Even if she destroyed me.

"You're not," she agreed with me. "Sometimes your selfishness and thoughtlessness too."

I looked at my feet and tried not to smile, although I did not quite succeed. "Stop before you make me blush."

She cut her eyes to me in an unamused glare. "We're never going to get through this, Bastian. One of us is going to kill the other before we ever get close to Terletov."

"I promise it won't be me that kills you."

"And you're okay with me killing you?"

You already have.

"If I thought you could really hurt me, I wouldn't have asked you here."

"I'll try to play nice."

Her words rippled over my skin like an electric charge. Fissions of lightning and energy licked at my bones like live wires. I didn't want her to play nice.

I wanted her to play rough and a little bit dirty.

Maybe a lot dirty.

"Only do the best you can," I taunted her. I shouldn't want her to be angry and worked up. I should let her be. I should give her a chance to move on. I should give myself a chance to move on.

But as I watched her stand in the middle of my suite, with the late summer light spilling over her hair and shoulders, her skin aglow from the sweet, warm sun, I knew I couldn't do that. I couldn't let her be. It wasn't in me. I would push her, fight her, and antagonize her until she fought back.

Until she gave me what I wanted.

Even if I didn't fully realize what that was yet.

"And you don't think I have it in me to be nice to you?"

"I don't think you have it in you to be nice to anybody. It's not specifically me you have an issue with. You hate everything."

Her eyes flashed with fury. A brewing storm panted beneath her carefully constructed mask of posh snobbery and refinement. She might have all the manners in the world, but she stood at the edge of a precipice, her storm gathering strength and volatility. She would explode soon.

And when she did, I would stand in the path of her destruction and let her annihilate me.

"I'm a different person than you dated. You don't know me anymore." Her voice sounded sharp and cutting, but her eyes flashed with something pained.

I instantly regretted baiting her. I wanted to draw her into heated banter, not hurt her. I was a bastard.

Yet, she wasn't completely innocent in this. And she was wrong. I did know her. I knew her better than anyone else on this planet.

I couldn't let her forget that.

"You're different now? You own a house? You moved to the remotest place you could find and now you're journey to self-discovery has revealed someone I have never met?"

I hadn't realized I'd moved until I stood over her, our bodies just a breath apart. She gazed up at me and blinked away the tears that pooled at the lashes.

"Seattle is hardly remote," she sniped, but it lacked the heat from earlier.

"Maybe it's not isolated in terms of people, but from this Kingdom? It is. You're running. You're in self-imposed exile."

Her eyes grew big, as if she just realized how close we'd become. She took a step back and sucked in a steadying breath. "I need space."

"You said that already. A year ago. Have you had enough space? Have you had enough time to grow? Mature? Spread your wings?"

"You're being cruel."

"I'm being curious."

"I should go."

Stay. My chest screamed in pain and my Magic reared in protest.

"I need to find my room," she continued with a glance at the door.

"You could..." *Stay here. Stay with me. You could stay in my room*. I glanced at the door that led to my bedroom and stifled the urge to toss her inside and lock the door so she couldn't leave until I allowed her to. "You could have done that before you found me. You didn't have to rush straight here."

I struggled to pull myself together and had to turn away from her in order to do so. I felt her eyes on my back, the intensity of their gaze searing through my starched oxford and burning me down to the bone.

She shrugged but didn't say anything. She made her way to the door where her abandoned luggage sat against the wall. I thought about offering to carry it for her, but recognized her retreat for what it was. An effort to get the hell away from me.

"Seraphina," I called after her. She turned around halfway through the door and raised her eyebrows. "If you'd like to see me tonight, no need to pull me into the apocalypse. Just knock."

"*If* I want to see you tonight, I'll remember that."

She disappeared down the hallway and slammed the door shut with her Magic. I sunk down into the nearest chair and let my face fall into my hands.

Her departure felt like the abrupt but familiar sting of rejection. I tried to sort through the multitude of thoughts in my head and tried to decide if I wanted to be okay with that or not.

I wanted her.

I didn't want her.

I loved her.

I didn't love her.

I wanted to kill her.

I wanted to make love to her.

I couldn't untangle my thoughts long enough to pull one strand from the other. They muddled together in an indecipherable soup of unwanted memories, nightmares, hopes and fears.

I took a deep breath and purposed to move on once and for all. My confusion regarding my ex was hardly comparable to the mission at hand. I needed to focus on capturing Terletov.

Capturing and then killing him.

Seraphina could wait. At least until we'd secured the fate of the world and doomsday didn't loom on the horizon. The four horsemen of the apocalypse weren't currently planning their first holiday to earth; this was not the right time to have girl problems.

At the very least, I could wait until Mimi called me back with the information I truly wanted- how much real estate in Seattle I could purchase without looking suspicious.

Chapter Eight

Seraphina

A knock at my door had me jumping from my lazy position at the end of my bed. I closed my eyes and tried to send out my Magic ahead of my body. My heart hammered in my chest, but my Magic didn't feel him, so I hoped I could answer the door without stabbing whoever stood on the other side.

Namely Sebastian.

If he'd come to taunt me some more, I definitely planned to teach him a lesson.

With a knife.

I was so tired of his bullshit. Hot and then cold, friendly and unfriendly, hero and nemesis. The guy had major personality problems.

Like schizophrenia.

"Open the door, Sera! We know you're in there."

Roxie. Thank God.

I gave a lazy flick of my wrist and the door pulled open. Roxie practically tumbled in with the two blonde girls close on her heels. My spicy Latina friend jumped back to her feet with a fierce glare.

I just smiled and showed off my pageant wave.

"You could have warned me," she growled.

I nodded, agreeing. "I could have."

The sisters shared a look of scared bewilderment. Oh, brother. I wasn't *that* scary.

Most of the time.

One of them shut the door and Roxie gestured for them to follow her closer to me. Roxie and I had been through enough of these together that we'd developed an easy friendship.

We didn't have all that much in common in our non-mission lives and so we weren't exactly best friends. But I would die for this girl. Without a second's hesitation.

And I knew she would do the same thing for me.

Sometimes I wondered if the bond of battle was heavier than any friendship. Friendship was nice and comfortable. But there were things that went deeper, things that bled thicker. There were Immortals I would do anything for and the closest to a real conversation we'd ever gotten was helpful tips on how to kill whoever was attacking us.

Roxie jumped onto the bed next to me and shoved my thigh. "You know Liv and O?"

"We've met."

"So you don't want to be here or what?" Liv asked with all that sharp-tongue-feistiness Jericho routinely bragged about.

I raised my eyebrows at her and wondered if there were a way for her to possibly understand the complexities of my hatred for Sebastian. "My ex-boyfriend is the lead on this mission. I'm less than thrilled to be part of a team he doesn't want me on."

Roxie snorted. "I'm pretty sure he wants you on something... Maybe not his team... but, ahem, something."

"You're so dirty," I said through a laugh.

"Sebastian?" O, the younger sister seemed to need clarification.

"Yes."

"You guys dated?"

I bit my tongue to keep from lashing out unnecessarily. I didn't like the flash of interest in her pretty face or the familiar tone she said his name with.

I didn't have to want him or like him, but that didn't mean I wanted other people to be interested in him.

And I wasn't foolish enough to think he hadn't moved on from me in every way.

But I didn't want to see the evidence standing in front of me. Or future evidence.

Sebastian wouldn't turn a girl like Ophelia down. She was gorgeous with her choppy blonde bob and bright orange eyes. She'd also recently come into the fullness of her Immortality.

Her association to Jericho's lady love made her a very interesting target for the single men in my circle. And there were so many of them.

She probably had her pick of Friday night dates.

I wondered if she had her sister's weird hang up on Immortals or if she'd acclimated better. I found myself hoping she despised Immortals as much as Olivia once had. That would keep my forbidden thoughts pacified.

But I doubted it.

With Olivia fully on board the Immortal-train, Ophelia was sure to follow.

Roxie pushed my leg again and I realized I had never answered her question. I'd been too busy plotting a subtle way to get rid of her.

Ahem.

Not as in murder, obviously. But... in other ways.

Not that I would. I didn't even care that she seemed interested in Sebastian. I didn't want him, so why couldn't she have him?

Obviously, she could.

I wasn't going to stand in her way.

I wasn't.

"We did date. A long time ago."

"Not that long ago," Roxie cut in. "They've only been broken up for a few months."

"*A year.* And a lot has happened since then. I can hardly remember being with him at all." *Liar.* I was a big, fat liar.

Roxie snorted again, calling me on it. I shrugged one shoulder and gave her a "what?" look. She just shook her head and stretched out her short legs.

"Why did you break up?" O pressed.

I wanted to snap at her to mind her own business, but I realized that might look like I still harbored feelings for him. So instead, I cooled down my raging inferno of a heart and took a deep breath.

"We fought all the time," I explained. "Neither of us was happy in the relationship. We both wanted... different things."

I wanted marriage. He wanted to be a hero for this Kingdom.

I wanted him to want me to be a part of his future. He wanted to leave me behind while he "found himself" on the battlefield.

People told me I couldn't blame him for wanting to make a name for himself, but they were wrong. I could blame him.

I did blame him.

"That doesn't seem like Sebastian," Ophelia mumbled thoughtfully.

My eyes bugged out a little bit and I wanted to turn back into the bitch I fought so diligently to bury. Was she serious? Roxie pinched my kneecap to get my attention.

When I looked at her she shook her head in warning. I barely bit back a scream, and fought to see things from their perspective.

To a girl like Ophelia, I was sure that Sebastian appeared in all his laid-back, sarcastic glory and the underwear just melted off her body.

However, to someone that knew him as intimately as I did, I could have told her, fighting with me was his favorite pastime. Even more so than Fifa for PlayStation.

Which was a major accomplishment on my part.

"Date him for three years and then tell me how he seems." Ophelia's eyes flashed with regret and I immediately felt bad for the bitterness lacing my tone. I sighed and admitted, "I shouldn't have said that. That makes him sound like he was a terrible boyfriend for all that time. He wasn't. We loved each other. Things just didn't work out in the end."

"Are you friends at least?" Ophelia asked carefully.

I glanced at Roxie. "We're working together on this mission. That has to count for something."

"So you loved each other a lot," Olivia concluded. No question. No doubt. She looked at the facts I gave her and announced judgment.

"It was serious," I confirmed. "And if Terletov wouldn't have shown up when he did, we might be married by now. So, at least we were saved from making that monumental mistake."

Liv's brows furrowed over her expressive eyes and she shook out her blonde bob. "Relationships are hard. All of them. Even the happy couples have to work their asses off to stay happy. It doesn't mean the work isn't worth it. Or the pain and heartache."

I chewed on my bottom lip and thought over those words. Her relationship with Jericho seemed perfect. They were always nothing but smiles and goo-goo eyes for each other. And they couldn't keep their hands to themselves.

When I said as much, she frowned again and announced, "We need wine for this!"

Ophelia ran off to find us some and Olivia continued. "I love Jericho. And a lot of the time our relationship is easy and fun. But there are other times when we have to work hard just to like each other. Our relationship can definitely be a huge struggle. It's not always the pretty destiny I want it to be. And, I mean, you could tell me that if I have to force myself to be with Jericho than I shouldn't be. But I don't believe that. I chose him. He's it for me forever. That means, yeah, sometimes I'm going to want to be selfish or detached or give up or whatever and there are times that he feels that way too. But we're it for each other. That's the decision we made and we're going to work as hard as we can and do everything possible to make sure we stay together. To make sure we stay happy. So it might not always be the perfect fairytale relationship that only exists in fiction. But, it's exactly the place I want to be in forever and he will always be the man I want to spend it with."

"I get that." Kind of. "But our issues were deeper than that too. I wanted to get married. He wanted to go run off on some crazy mission and risk his life." I felt the anger bubble up inside of me again. I swore up and down that I'd gotten over this and that I'd moved on. But this still made me so angry. His actions. His abandonment. I just couldn't get over it. "And you know what? It wasn't even about marriage. He could have put that off for however long he wanted. I just wanted some outward show of commitment. I wanted to be considered with the rest of the plans he made for his life. You know?"

"You told him that?" Olivia asked with a serious expression making her look older... wiser.

I nodded while feeling the opposite. I felt young, immature and so not ready for any kind of curveball Sebastian would bring to my settled life if I had to be around him much longer.

Olivia's frown deepened. "I don't know Sebastian that well. But it sounds like you were right to break up with him. He has to know that."

I shook my head. "I don't know what he knows. He acts like I betrayed him. Like I gave up on him. And maybe I did."

Roxie patted my back awkwardly. She wasn't known for her gentle affection and the gesture made me smile. I shot her a look over my shoulder and she scowled at me.

"What? I feel bad for you," she laughed.

I laughed too. A real laugh from the brittle corroded places inside of me I thought had withered when Sebastian left me for this. "That's so compassionate of you."

Roxie's smile spread and transformed her bitchy-resting-face into a shockingly pretty expression. "I'm a very compassionate person." She looked up at Olivia. "What? I am."

And then we all dissolved into laughter.

Ophelia came back a few minutes later carrying four bottles of wine-one for each of us. Of course, we tried to be ladies like about it and only open one at a time. But by the time I waved a drunken goodbye to the girls sometime in the middle of the night, all four bottles had been emptied and I had laughed more than I ever had in my life.

I wanted to feel threatened by Ophelia's potential interest in Sebastian, but after dissecting every man on the mission, talking about the guys they'd dealt with in the human world and picking apart my ex-boyfriend to the bone over Malbecs and Cab Francs, I couldn't.

I stumbled to the bathroom and giggled at my purple teeth and red lips. Laughter felt easier after all of that wine. My chest seemed less rusty, less... atrophied. That felt really good. Very cathartic.

Sebastian and I broke up and then my entire world spun into depressed-survival. With Terletov on the loose and friends missing or dying, there was hardly time to heal before I would be faced with more unthinkable grief.

Things weren't over by any means, but they were getting better.

If we could just stop Terletov first.

I tried to brush my teeth and scrub off the wine stains, but I wasn't entirely successful. I stumbled to bed and threw myself on the handmade quilt and feather pillows. My fuzzy brain spun around and around as Sebastian's face danced in my mind's eye.

A night of rehashing our relationship and all of the reasons we went wrong brought him to the front of my thoughts. I wanted to send him back to the nameless place I dumped all of my unwanted emotions, but he was stubborn.

In real life and in my subconscious.

My body felt weightless on the comforter, detached from reality and consequences. I was too tired and drunk to fight the memories and the aching loneliness that burned through my body like wildfire whenever I thought about Sebastian.

In this place where I couldn't remember why I shouldn't think about Sebastian, I didn't bother to mourn the future that died in our breakup or the reasons I left him to begin with. No, in this place, I only remembered what I loved about him.

His laugh.

His smile.

The way he could bring me out of myself and remind me I could be fun and funny. I wasn't those things without him. He was everything in life and happiness bottled into one gorgeous body. I was the Debbie Downer to his Party-Boy lifestyle.

Except when I was with him.

He made me better. He made me whole.

The way his arms wrapped around me like he never wanted to let me go.

How we could stay in bed for hours, all day long, how we never wanted to leave.

His legs tangled in mine.

His fingers stroking sensual paths over my bare stomach.

His lips on my neck and in my hair and on my mouth.

And how we connected.

How we could talk through the pain of our pasts and heal each other. How we told each other everything. There were no secrets, no reasons for secrets.

Sometimes I wondered if he knew me at all during that time. I had been so careful to hide the unpleasant parts of me. I didn't want him to see me at my worst, at my ugliest.

But as I lay there, watching the ceiling fan flap in lazy circles over my head, I realized I only made sure to tuck those embarrassing pieces away when we were with other people. I had always been honest with him. Our time together had always been open and raw.

My heart squeezed painfully in my chest and I felt sick to my stomach. The wine swirled through my blood and made the clear, rational thoughts fizzle out into more confusion.

He still chose the battle over me. And if I were honest, if I were truly real, I chose the easy, less vulnerable path over him.

I didn't want to be hurt again and again as he chose mission after mission over me. I didn't want to face the possibility of losing someone I loved so deeply. I didn't want to have to face my intense feelings for him and give up myself and what I wanted, so that he could go after what he wanted.

I was the one that had been selfish.

But, despite all of my unworthiness, there was a stubborn emotion inside of me that would never go away.

Love.

I would always love him. Always.

And it seemed stupid that I would realize this now… a year later.

We were beyond salvaging at this point.

I might hurt for him for the rest of my life, but there was nothing I could do about it.

There was nothing I wanted to do about it.

My eyelids eventually fluttered closed and the hazy shroud of drunken sleep found me. I dreamed about crosses and women dressed as nuns. I dreamed about a square of white and a hand that held mine so tightly I couldn't let go.

I didn't want to let go.

Chapter Nine

Sebastian

The silence of the mountain echoed in the fuzzy gray of early morning. The absence of sound screamed through the night louder than I could imagine it would. My ears felt stuffed with cotton. The sheer pressure of quiet pressed down on my shoulders and head and I thought my brain would explode from it.

Something had changed on the mountain.

Something vile and terrible had seeped into the ground and destroyed the good, vibrant Magic that ran these hills.

I looked around for signs of life or peace, but only the ancient stone stared back.

Machu Picchu. City of Kings.

We hardly used this place, except it seemed, as a meeting ground. Silas's people had lived nearby in a settlement that would never acclimate to the human world. They were Shifters and wild in their human forms. Which made them completely untamable in their animal.

They ran these mountains with uninhibited abandon. Silas had cultivated this in his people and I couldn't help but be jealous. I wanted that. I wanted to run free, in the spiritual sense. I wanted to run free of myself.

I wondered where they were today though or if they were even still in these mountains. It was possible that after Silas's death, they had moved elsewhere.

Or maybe Terletov had found them.

A renewed sense of responsibility coursed through me. I no longer associated myself with the Monarchy, but I felt tied to these people, to this Kingdom. Kiran and Eden could no longer fight on the frontline. Avalon and Amelia had to stay put and run the ruling.

This mission could go to no one else.

I was the answer.

I had to be.

My team scattered through the ruins. The tourist section didn't officially open for a couple more hours. We had the run of things, but I didn't know where to start.

"I don't think there's anything here," Titus decided. He'd come up to stand next to me and looked out at the tumbling of stone steps and what remained of an ancient, proud civilization.

This moment felt symbolic for some reason.

Would this be us one day?

A legacy of bad Kings and a powerful people that wasted their gifts on greed and prejudice? We stood at the forefront of a new age for our Immortal Kingdom. We had the potential to be great. To make a difference in this world and in each other.

But we were immature in our newness, untried and untested. Would we survive this conflict? Could we defeat Terletov and become the people I knew we were supposed to be?

Or would Seraphina's vision become our reality?

Would we destroy the world we should be protecting?

"Can you feel the change?"

"Like swallowing soap. It's bitter and wrong." Titus's power rippled in the air around him. I couldn't feel all the Magic, but he and I were especially close. It felt like his bear shivered his great length and shook the evil air off of him, like water after he'd emerged from a lake.

The Titans I'd dispatched scoured the grounds dutifully. They were efficient and smart, and they could sense the Magic that I couldn't. I didn't love being charged with the interim, but I did enjoy the skill and perspective they brought with them.

Jericho walked over to us. The Gypsy Queen had called him the general. And the Titans treated him in that way.

Kiran had given me this position, but I knew what it meant. I was the Royal mouthpiece, the blood relation that they were supposed to look to. Jericho was the talent.

"There's nothing here," he declared. "This can't be the well. I think the Magic would be stronger and not just... off."

"So where to, then? We've narrowed the well down to this country, but that can't be it. We have to find this quickly. Terletov has it. Obviously. We have to do something."

Seraphina and Olivia approached us with their eyes searching and appalled. We all felt the change. It grated against our skin and sickened our insides. It was easy to see that this Magic could destroy everything. Its very definition was destruction.

"Sera, have anything?"

She looked at me, seeming surprised that I'd spoken to her. She brushed her blonde hair out of her eyes and leveled me with a confused look.

"I had a dream last night," she said. But then she stopped talking and shot Liv a "help me" look.

"What?" Liv laughed. "I don't know what you dreamed about!"

"I can't remember!" Seraphina cried. She looked horrified for only a second before she put her hands over her face and started laughing.

She laughed so hard that her shoulders shook and she doubled over. Olivia started laughing too and clutched at her stomach as if it hurt her to laugh so hard.

Jericho, Titus and I just watched them, so completely confused. How was it funny that she couldn't remember her dream? And since when had Seraphina decided to become friends with the former-humans. That didn't seem like her style at all.

"So it wasn't a vision?" I asked when the girls tried to settle down.

"It was the wine!" Seraphina laughed.

"What wine?"

"All the wine!" Liv giggled.

"They've gone mad," I groaned. "The girls have gone mad."

"Do you think it's the bad Magic?" Titus asked seriously.

Roxie and Ophelia joined us with Xander and Xavier. The brothers gave the giggling girls a once over before they looked to us for explanation.

"What's so funny?" Roxie asked while trying to suppress her own laughter.

I didn't understand. Was giggling contagious? We were on a mission! Did no one remember this?

"Something about wine," Jericho explained. "And a vision?"

Ophelia's surprised laugh popped in the silent moment. She tipped her head back and became as wild and out of control as the other two.

Even Roxie wiped away tears of hilarity.

"We had wine last night," she explained. "Lots of wine."

"Is that why you can't remember your vision?" I scowled at Seraphina. How could she be so reckless? Careless? Didn't she realize what was at stake?

We had to be sharp. Always.

Abruptly, Seraphina's head snapped upright and her vision cleared. "Gabriel," she whispered. "The church."

"Let's go." I didn't hesitate. I didn't question her. I called in the Titans and we left.

It made sense. It made perfect sense.

Bloody hell, why hadn't I thought of it?

Why had Gabriel exiled himself from the Kingdom to run a small church that had zero congregation? The church itself was a poor excuse for a house of worship and the nuns that ran the grounds did nothing to improve the situation. Yet, they stayed relentlessly devoted to the building.

The church itself had been attacked before by Terletov's men.

And Gabriel had always returned here.

He had refused to stay on with Avalon.

He left the Kingdom in supposed hiding; yet everyone knew where to find him.

The church.

I was an idiot.

We piled into the various rentals we'd caravanned out here in and sped our way to the small little village where Gabriel had lived the majority of his life.

We were silent as we went. It took a couple hours to arrive, but we were wired with anticipation and relief.

There would be battle ahead of us; our nerves wound tight and ready as we counted the seconds until that looming moment. But we had a direction. We knew where to go.

And even more than that, I had been right to involve Seraphina in this mission.

We arrived at the church and flooded the small sanctuary. I could have given instructions, but nobody needed them. These were vetted soldiers. The mission could only go one way.

We had to win.

We had to win every battle from now on.

The Magic felt thicker than ever inside the small, disheveled space. I had been here before but never had I felt the pulsing energy beat in the air.

I felt it now and wished I couldn't.

It scraped against my skin and screamed inside my head.

The Titans spread out in protective formations and we made our way over the crushed pews and shattered glass. The room was shrouded in darkness, not even the light from the early morning could penetrate the oppressive gloom.

The cross at the front of the room had been pulled down and broken over the pulpit. Candles in red glass looked to have been thrown on the ground and shattered on purpose. The only thing not broken in this room was the dingy stained-glass windows that remained untouched.

We moved beyond the sanctuary and through the door to the left of where the cross used to hang. Down narrow hallways and beyond nun's dormitories that were as torn apart and destroyed as the front of the building.

The Magic grew stronger and my sense of it as well.

The Titans started tearing apart rooms, looking for anything that would give us a clue as where to go next. I led the rest of our group deeper into the maze of living quarters.

I had never been back here before and was a little shocked by the primitiveness in which Gabriel and his nuns lived. Even the kitchen was sparsely furnished, not even containing a refrigerator. The building itself had no electricity and all of the lamps and candles had been destroyed.

Towards the back of the house, the Magic grew immensely stronger. I felt the physical pressure of it against my skin, as though it pushed back at me, trying to keep me from finding the Source.

My gut churned with indecision. I needed to get to the bottom of this, but I didn't want to put my friends' lives at stake.

I knew they signed up for this. And I knew they were aware of exactly what they risked when they'd answered my phone call. But still. I could not... *would not* be responsible for their deaths or worse.

"You have to go through that door," Jericho encouraged.

We stood in front of a door that would presumably lead outside. We'd been through all of the rooms and there didn't seem to be an upstairs or a downstairs. The only place left was out, but every instinct inside of me flared to life with warning.

"Tell the girls to stay put," I told him over my shoulder.

And then I pushed against the building force of Magic and walked through the door.

Nothing happened right away and I allowed myself a small breath of relief. I didn't know what I expected, but something along the lines of total and complete annihilation had run through my head a few thousand times.

The door opened to a courtyard with stucco buildings all around. The ground was cobbled stone and spread out in a rough octagon. Not one of the other buildings had a backdoor, nor was there another way to leave the courtyard except by scaling the tall windowless buildings or through the door I'd just walked through.

In the center of the courtyard was an old-fashioned well. It had a thatched roof over weathered wood supports; a rusted pale hanging on a hook and the stone that made the actual well portion had been worn and rounded. Grooves in the ledge pulled me forward.

A rusted ladder lay against the inside wall of the well.

"Well, that's not ominous," Titus sighed next to me.

"No kidding." I ran my fingers over the distorted metal rungs. The tainted Magic in the air pressed against me forcefully, nearly stealing the air from my lungs. "It doesn't want us down there."

Titus leaned forward. "To be fair, I don't really want to go down there either."

We turned and shared a meaningful look. What choice did we have? In fact, this was exactly the lead we were looking for.

I dropped the pack I'd been carrying and swung my leg over the cold stone. I started to descend the ladder into the utter darkness of the well.

"Bastian!"

I heard the voice and instinctively raised my head. Seraphina stood in the doorway watching me go. Her blonde hair whipped around her face from a wind that came out of nowhere. The morning had suddenly grown grim and cloudy, but she stood in the doorway burning brighter than any gloomy darkness.

Her pretty face was pinched in concern and her hand stretched out to me as if she wanted me to stop.

I glanced down into the obscure abyss beneath me and then back at her. I let this memory of her sear into my memory, promising myself I would keep it with me forever.

She was beautiful. Staggeringly so. She was the air in my lungs and the blood in my veins.

I didn't want to admit that. Bloody hell, I didn't even want it to be true. But there it was. She was the loveliest thing that existed for me. And I'd pissed away her trust and loyalty without understanding the consequences of my actions.

"Am I going to die, Sera?" I asked her confidently.

She gave a quick shake and tried to suppress her smile. "I don't think so."

I winked at her. "Don't follow me."

"I wouldn't."

"This is why I fell in love with you."

She actually tripped after I said that. She wasn't even walking or moving in any way. But my words seemed to startle her so completely she nearly tipped over.

I hurried down the ladder, enjoying this game I had started to play with her.

Well, it wasn't so much a game, more like a gamble. A gamble with my life, my future, my legacy.

I just didn't know which way I was betting yet.

I eventually found solid earth again. The air was compressed and cold. It sunk in me with all the weighted destiny of death.

At the bottom of the well, a tunnel opened up to my left. I turned toward it and used my own Magic to see through the curtain of darkness.

More footsteps landed behind me. Titus and Jericho had followed. I didn't want to acknowledge the comfort I felt with their presence. I could pretend to be as courageous as I wanted, but this shit scared the hell out of me.

I was glad not to be alone.

"What was that?" Titus asked in a whispered tone.

"What was what?"

"That exchange with Seraphina?"

I glanced at him over my shoulder. "I think I made a colossal mistake with her."

"Breaking up with her or realizing you're still in love with her."

"Both," I admitted.

He flashed a toothy grin at me in the dark. "Another one bites the dust. Another one bites the dust. Another one gone and another one gone, another one bites the dust!"

"Oh, god. Stop singing."

And now he'd added dancing. We were likely on our way to meet our doom and the Shifter, who could turn into a grizzly bear, was moonwalking behind me whilst singing Queen.

"Hey, I'm gonna get to you, too! Another one bites the dust!"

"Jericho?" I spun around and stared at the General as he finished off the chorus. "You're all mad. All of you."

The two idiots that were supposed to have my back smiled at each other and gave a discreet fist bump. I tried to force my mind back to the task at hand, but the atmosphere had been sufficiently calmed.

I turned back around and continued to lead the way down the dark tunnel. "Funny they kept this such a secret from us."

"You would think something like this would have come up in the last three years," Titus agreed.

"Not even Kiran knows about this?" Jericho asked in a serious voice. Glad to know he had given up the song and dance routine.

I shook my head. "He seemed as baffled as I did when I told him about St. Stephens."

"But that thing with Eden in India, nobody knew she could do that, right?" Titus asked.

That was true. We'd all been as surprised as she was that the Magic had basically jumped inside of her. So maybe these places were as much of a mystery to the previous line of Kings as they now were to us now.

But Amory should have known. Amory should have said something.

And clearly Gabriel had been tasked with protecting this place. So what was it?

The tunnel opened into a wide chamber, similar to the one beneath the cathedral in Vienna. The walls were rounded and smooth. Gray light poured from an electrified whirlpool in the center of the floor. The pool looked liquid, but I did not trust it to be so.

I stayed near the wall and scooted my way around the edge. Titus and Jericho followed me in, equally as wary of what lay in the middle of the dirt floor.

White bones picked clean of flesh and blood lay all around the edge of the pool. So many of them. In every size.

"How many men?" I couldn't get beyond my fear of dead things to count them.

"At least four," Jericho confirmed. "Same thing as in Vienna?"

"It has to be, doesn't it?"

"What color do you think the pool was before they went for a swim?" Titus asked.

"Blue," I said without a doubt.

"What makes you think that?" Titus took a tentative step toward the pool and the liquid snapped and sizzled in response to his closeness. Lightning flashed across the surface and forced ripples to spread from one end to the other.

"It wants to eat you, Dude," Jericho observed. "Be careful."

"Eden and Avalon have that blue Magic. It's got to be the original. I know we've said that before, but it's all I can conclude. Eden's smoke is blue as well. The orb under the cathedral was blue. Blue is the color we want. Green is the intruder."

"Green is Terletov," Jericho agreed.

Titus dragged one of the bones to him with the toe of his foot. I held my breath until I was sure nothing would jump out of the pool and grab him. He picked it up with two fingers and then tossed it at the pool. The bone bounced off the surface and skittered to the other side of the room.

It didn't trail liquid with it or leave a wet spot on the hard-packed dirt. The bone was dry. The pool rejected it completely.

"Think I can walk across it?" Titus asked with a lift of one eyebrow.

I shook my head, even though I knew he was being facetious. "I think you won't get a foot near it before it pulls you inside. It wants your Magic. Even before it turned green, it would have swallowed you whole."

Jericho frowned and crouched low so he could get a better look at the surface. "So how do we get it to go back to blue?"

"Eden's the only one who's ever been able to do anything when it comes to these," Titus said quietly.

"She's pregnant." Jericho ran a hand over his hair and sighed. "Obviously, she can't do anything about this now."

A thought started to gather momentum in the center of my head and build speed. I leaned back against the wall and let the kernel of something interesting grow into something substantial.

"Maybe she doesn't need to," I said. "She could control the Magic when it matched hers in color. Maybe she would have no power over a Magic that's been changed at a molecular level."

"Then who can control it? Who has this color of green Magic?" Titus asked while Jericho stood up again and looked at me thoughtfully.

I stared at the pool just as lost in thought. "I'd bet my old crown that Terletov's Magic is a near match."

"Eden has his Magic," Jericho reminded me.

I groaned, a little frustrated with them for not getting this right away. "But he's been operating with something over the last several years. His brother as well. Every one of his goons has the same color Magic. It's all tied to something. It all has to be the same in some way."

Jericho looked just as frustrated with me. "So if Terletov's Magic is green, essentially he'll be able to control all the Sources that he finds and manipulates. How does this help us?"

"I think it will work both ways. Each time Eden grappled control of a source, she had to fight for it. She's one of two truly immortal Immortals. Terletov doesn't even have his original Magic."

"You think the source would kill him?" Titus asked with a bloodthirsty grin.

"I have a feeling it will do more than just kill him."

"You think it will restore the original Magic," Jericho concluded.

"I do."

Chapter Ten

Seraphina

I had just decided to go down after him when his golden brown head surfaced over the ledge of the well. I stared several seconds too long which was why he caught me waiting for him.

Damn it.

I had wanted to watch through a window, but there was none that looked back here. So, I had stayed in my place in the doorway and waited for Sebastian to climb out of *The Ring*-inspired well.

Gosh, that thing gave me the creeps! I'd seen the movie. I knew how it ended.

Next, Sebastian would be crawling out of my TV and there would be nothing I could do about it, except pass the video along to the next unknowing person.

I meant to hurry into the house as soon as I saw the first glimpse of evidence that he was alive and well, but I'd gotten snared on the incredible bicep muscles that wrapped around the stone ledge and pulled him to solid-ground-freedom.

I'd also gotten distracted by the smirk on his arrogant face and the twinkle in his hazel eyes.

When had he gotten so hot?

Had he always been like this?

Or was this some trick of the non-existent light?

He caught me staring. *Bastard.* His smirk grew into a cocky smile and I rolled my eyes just to piss him off.

Jericho and Titus followed him out of the well and I looked to them when I asked, "What did you find? Anything interesting?"

"Only if you consider a bunch of dead bodies and a broken source interesting."

Bad news. "So, he got here before us."

"In a big way," Jericho confirmed.

"Big way!" Titus confirmed, stretching out his hands to emphasize his point.

They scooted past me into the house, not minding that they pressed me against the wall and blocked my retreat.

I shoved at Titus's shoulder as he passed, but he just chuckled at my weak attempt to manhandle him. I scowled after him and my distraction cost me.

When I turned my head again, Sebastian was there in my face. His hand rested on the doorframe behind me and put us in a frustratingly intimate position.

My stomach flipped and my throat felt dry all of a sudden, but I refused to acknowledge that he could do that to me.

"Worried about me?" he asked with his clipped accent and hooded eyes.

Yes. "No."

"No?"

"Well, yes. I was worried about all of you. Nobody else seemed to care though." I forced my gaze to glance around the empty courtyard. Apparently nobody had been concerned that these guys were headed to death.

Ugh.

Since when did *I* become the sentimental one?

"Hmm," Sebastian considered.

I poked the fleshy part of his shoulder. "Well, someone had to listen for the screaming and crying."

His mouth split into a wide grin. "I'm glad it was you."

What? *What?* "You are?"

"I am."

I cleared my throat and sidled back into the building. "Did something happen to you down there? Did you hit your head? Are you possessed? Body snatched? What's going on?"

His smile softened and he looked at me with something that could be considered close to... affection. Like maybe the distant cousin or a great, great aunt. "I don't think so," he said seriously. "But I suppose if I were possessed or body-snatched I wouldn't exactly be aware."

A shiver slid over my spin at the low tone to his sexy accent. I closed my eyes to help forget the reaction my body had to his body. Or that my Magic had found the edges of his and breathed a big, old sigh of relief.

We had barely connected in that Magical way. But his was so open to mine. I felt the pulses of his energy, the fractures of excited electricity that surged through my Magic and reached my body, my blood, my fragile, embittered heart.

"Well, do you feel different?" I asked him while trying to keep my tone light and playful.

He took a step toward me. His fingers brushed against mine, once, twice, and then just the tips of his fingers slid between the tips of mine. "I feel different about a lot of things."

My voice was a pathetic croak. "About bodysnatching?"

"I don't have any feelings about bodysnatching," he chuckled.

"Good. That probably means your fine." My lips were dry, so I swiped my tongue across the bottom one in order to find some relief.

His eyes dropped to that unintentionally slow movement and his gaze heated while he tracked every moment of movement.

I pressed my lips together in an effort to halt whatever had begun between us, but Sebastian didn't seem bothered by my attempts to pull back.

When his gaze lifted back to mine, his eyelids had dropped to hang hooded over his burning gaze. There was promise in his expression, wicked whispers of his intentions.

Where was this coming from?

"Seraphina, I-"

"You hurt me, Sebastian." I swallowed back the pressing tears and forced myself to be brave. "You ruined me."

"And I-"

A resounding crash obliterated the trance he'd put me in. Both of our attention swung toward the front of the church and we took off, racing to get there. The sounds of fighting reached us as we pushed through the scattered debris and narrow hallways.

Sebastian's hand on my back urged me forward even when part of me didn't want to know what lay ahead of us.

The Magic in the air seemed to stir with the conflict we couldn't see yet. The oxygen pulled from my lungs and the atmosphere pressed against me with a sickeningly evil pressure. My eyes blurred against the pain and violence that beat around me.

"Stay close to me, Sera," Sebastian demanded in a growly tone. "I'll keep you safe."

"I can take care of-"

He glared at me. "No you can't. Don't try."

Bastard.

But there was no reason to argue since he was right. A few Titans had engaged Terletov's men near the bedrooms. They fought with swords on either side. Gunshots punctured the sounds of clashing metal and grunting men. They ripped through the building deadly and silencing.

Sebastian reached out and yanked me so close to his body that my entire front plastered against his back. I straightened out our tangled feet and glowered at the back of his head.

Okay, I was pretty useless during physical combat, but he didn't need to be such a bully about it.

We ran by a fallen Titan laid out over an equally injured bad guy. I swept down and picked up his discarded gun. I didn't know how the Titan had managed to put the other guy out of commission and end up shot himself, but it wasn't like I could ask many questions right now.

I felt a little less helpless with a gun in my hand.

Avalon had made gun training mandatory when Terletov first came on the scene. I'd taken the required courses just like everybody else, but I'd never gotten around to carrying a weapon.

I decided not to let this one go. I would sleep next to it from this moment on.

I checked the chamber to make sure it still had something inside and then readied it in my hands.

I knew what I was doing, but the weapon still felt awkward and foreign in my grasp. I swallowed my fear and let Sebastian lead me into the sanctuary.

What was once a place of worship was now a gore-filled, communal grave. Men littered the ground, sprawled out over broken pews or on beds of broken glass. Blood mingled with dirt and dust. The air seemed thick with a greenish fog that felt icy against my skin.

Every one of my friends fought, engaged with some crazy, fanatic psycho that would steal Magic from my kind.

I had no respect for these people. They made me sick to my stomach with their cruelty and sadistic plots.

There weren't as many as I expected there to be. But I wondered if this was a small group of them. They had most likely been left behind to watch the church. When we showed up, they came to stop us or find out what we were up to and had been left with no choice but to fight us.

Terletov or his maniac brother, Alexi were nowhere in sight. Which was a bummer, since I had glamorous plans of murdering both of them.

Sebastian ducked to the right and took me with him. He lashed out immediately with his Magic. Black energy burst out of him in a deadly stream of undiluted power. The man that shot at us flew backward. His arms flailed wide and he lost control of his gun.

Sebastian jumped on him before he even hit the ground. Bastian's fist came back and then pummeled forward again and again and again.

I watched his knuckles become bloodier and bloodier with each hit. And when he'd had enough of that, he turned his Magic on him. He knew better than to drain the enemy. We didn't want their sick Magic. So instead, he pulled out a dagger from his boot and stabbed the guy right in the heart.

The green Magic that had been entombed in the traitor exploded forward and mingled with the tainted Source Magic in the air.

I had been so intently watching Sebastian's struggle, I forgot about my own safety. How I heard the creaking floorboard behind me will always be a mystery. If I had had time, I would have wondered if it weren't my psychic senses that tipped me off.

Maybe it was just my paranoia. Or residual battle instincts.

It didn't matter. The only thing that mattered was that I turned around in time. I didn't think. I didn't have time to think. I raised my gun and fired before the other guy had a chance to shoot first.

I nailed him in the gut and he dropped to the ground immediately. I let out the breath that had frozen in my lungs and ran over to him.

This was probably the opposite thing I should have done, but I needed to figure out if I'd killed him or merely maimed him.

These bullets put normal Immortals into deep comas, unless you were Eden, Avalon or one of their soul mates. They seemed the only people able to wake up from the damaging bullets. Even still, a coma was infinitely better than dead.

Terletov's men were not so lucky. Their Magic was stronger in some ways, but weaker in others. These bullets killed them. Immediately.

The guy at my feet bled out from his waist. His eyes stayed open but unseeing. His mouth twisted into an agonized frown and his hands clenched at the wound that I'd put there.

Guilt assaulted me as quickly as our showdown had ended, but I pushed the remorseful feelings away. He would have done that to me.

That and worse.

I scooped up his discarded gun too and tucked it into the back of my jeans. It wasn't exactly comfortable, but I didn't have eight arms so...

I hurried back to Sebastian's side. He had engaged another bad guy but seemed to have the upper hand.

I turned around and happened to bump into Ophelia. We both jumped and nearly attacked each other.

"I'm not used to this yet." Her eyes were wide and terrified.

I handed her my extra gun. "Me either." She grabbed it gingerly and stared at it for a moment. "Do you know how to use that?"

"I know the basics."

I checked it over for her and then said, "Point and shoot. Don't miss."

"That's all I needed to know."

By some unspoken decision, we moved forward side-by-side. Apparently we were going on the defensive.

Someone burst through the church doors and both of us whirled around. The instinct that I did not know this person was strong enough to encourage me to pull the trigger. Ophelia followed suit and we emptied both of our guns into the newcomer.

I knew not all of our bullets found purchase in his evil body, but enough did. He fell forward and I knew, I just knew, he was dead before he hit the ground.

He never had a chance to close the door behind him, and now his lifeless body barricaded it open. Mid-morning light streamed into the darkened, bloodied sanctuary, washing our deeds in clarity.

Holy cow, there were more of them than I thought.

He might have been the last though. Or the rest of the guys had decided fighting us and consequently dying, was not worth it.

The dead guy in the doorway brought us back to the human world and our conflict abruptly ended. People walking by peeked through the doorway at the bloodshed and body count we'd left for their eyes. I heard the blaring South American police sirens in the distance.

I looked around the room and quickly counted my friends.

All here.

All alive and conscious.

Thank God.

"Collect our men," Sebastian barked at the Titans gathering guns and anything that could draw us into the human legal system. "Meet us in Omaha. Keep the authorities out of this church and especially away from that well."

I tried not to express how surprised I was by Sebastian's quick thinking. It would be best for us to split up and reconvene elsewhere, but I hadn't been able to think that quickly.

Anyone of us could use Magic on the humans to divert their attention elsewhere, but it was always easier to avoid any confrontation to begin with.

Sebastian walked back to me with a grim expression on his face. "Are you alright?"

"I'm fine," I answered curtly. When his lips twitched, I narrowed my eyes and glared at him. "What?"

"Aren't you going to ask if I'm alright?"

I cleared my throat and tried not to be embarrassed that I hadn't thought to ask how he was. I was also embarrassed to admit that I'd watched him nearly the entire battle, and so I knew he was fine. I hadn't been able to take my eyes off him.

He was more than fine.

He had gone from a boy proficient in battle to a man that dominated any struggle. Sebastian was no longer the lean, practiced warrior I'd known him as before. His body, mind, and skill had matured into a skilled fighter with natural grace and intuition that stole my breath.

"I can see that you're fine," I said subtly.

His hazel eyes danced with amusement. "Shall we go?"

I rolled my eyes and stomped around him. I had almost made it to the busyness of the crowded street. I just had to step over the man I'd shot down in the doorway.

Just as I lifted my foot to move over him, his cold hand reached out and grabbed my ankle. I let out a startled scream and tried to wrench my foot away.

I felt Sebastian at my back reaching down for his dagger.

It was only a matter of seconds before I could get this corpse off me, but it wasn't soon enough. He garbled something at me with a mouth full of blood.

I looked down at him in disgust and held my tongue from screaming obscenities at him. He hadn't killed any of my friends today, but he or his friends could have so easily. We lost plenty of Titans. And I didn't know if they were dead or unconscious. And if they were unconscious, I didn't know if Eden was strong enough to heal them. At least not until after the babies were born.

Not to mention, he was a part of a movement that tried over and over to destroy everything I worked to build. Everything I believed in.

"He's killing the Queen," the man grinned up at me.

"What?"

His cold eyes lit with laughter and he choked through the pooling blood in his mouth. "She will die. He's going to take his time with her and make sure she feels every moment of it!"

A hundred questions sat on my tongue. I prepared myself to wrap my hands around his neck and shake him until an explanation coughed out of him. But Sebastian beat me to it.

With savage efficiency, he bent low and used his dagger to slice across the man's throat. The enemy gurgled and sputtered for a few more agonizing moments before his head dropped back on the ground and his rotten green Magic left him completely.

I stared at the dead man and then my ex-boyfriend and tried to make sense of everything that just happened.

"What the hell, Sebastian? Why did you kill him?"

Sebastian lifted his eyes to mine and I stumbled back a step from the ferocity that glared back at me. "He tells you our Queen is going to die and you want to keep him *alive*?"

I threw my hands up in the air. "For questions! I wanted to ask him more questions!"

"And I'm sure he would have been very accommodating, except that he was about to die anyway! At least I had some satisfaction with his death!"

"I was the one that shot him in the first place."

"And then had a change of heart!"

"I didn't have a change of heart! I wanted to know what he meant. I wanted to know if he meant that literally or if it was a threat about the future!"

"You are an impossible woman! I did what had to be done and somehow that makes me the bad guy! Not the guy that actually is bad!"

"I didn't say you were the bad guy. I said-"

"Hey, Bonnie and Clyde!" Titus called from the passenger's side of a rented van. He waved his cell at us. "Eden and Amelia are both alive and well. I just called to check. Can we go now?"

Satisfied with that answer, I took a step away from the dead body and kicked his grip off of my ankle. My clothes were covered in dirt and blood and all I wanted to do was check into a nice hotel and step under a scalding hot spray of water and stay there until my fingers pruned and my body forgot the feel of other people's blood on my skin.

Sebastian grabbed my hand before I could get through the door though. I shot him a furious look over my shoulder and snapped, "What now?"

"Analisa," he said quietly. "If there is a Queen that Terletov is currently killing, it would be Analisa."

I forgot my next step or any plans I had of finding clean water. I stepped back into Sebastian's space and wrapped my arms around him. He buried his face in the curve of my neck and pulled me tightly against him.

Analisa, his aunt.

I knew I could be heartless and cruel, but this was too much for even me. I felt the fear and grief vibrate through his Magic. I felt the man I had just deemed so capable and dominant become vulnerable and afraid.

"What do you want to do?" I whispered close to his ear.

"Omaha," he decided. "I want to go to your place in Omaha."

I knew that was a bad idea. Actually, a terrible idea. But I couldn't say no to him like this. So I simply nodded instead and pulled him toward the van.

My mind argued with my heart, but my heart was stubborn. Apparently it didn't mind being sacrificed in order to give this man I no longer wanted to love everything he needed in his time of grief.

And I would. Whatever Sebastian needed, I wanted to give to him.

Even if that meant destroying all of the healing I'd been through over the last year.

Chapter Eleven

Sebastian

Omaha.

It felt like coming back to the start.

The start of everything.

This was where my transformation happened- from racist prick to the upstanding gentleman I was today. You're welcome world.

This was where my attraction for Seraphina first began. All of the time I spent with Kiran and her while I knew my cousin loved someone else. This was where I made time for her. This was where I started to see that she wasn't the girl everyone thought she was.

And in way of the Kingdom, Omaha was where everything started as well. This was where Eden and Avalon plotted with Amory to take over the Monarchy. This was where the Resistance was born. This was where Lucan lost his foothold. This city was the catalyst that eventually brought about his ruin.

And this was where Terletov attacked last fall and set us into violent motion once again.

It seemed the majority of the most important points of my life could be traced back to this city.

Sure, there were certain things that belonged to other places, such as Lucan's death, the first time I'd kissed Seraphina or told her I loved her. But so much of my maturity had happened right here.

And last summer.

A year ago.

Before Terletov, before we were summoned back to the Citadel, before any of this happened, Seraphina had stayed in the condo she owned here. We'd spent a lazy summer traveling to rustic parts of Canada and exploring Mexican beaches, but we'd grown tired of living out of suitcases and wanted a permanent place to crash for a while.

We set up residence in the posh, but small one bedroom flat she'd stayed in during high school. We'd hardly left the entire time. Instead, we spent our days lounging around the pool or experimenting with our cooking skills in the apartment. We'd talked of our future and planned out lives together.

At the time, it felt like all the times before. We'd been together for so long, I was used to the marriage conversation and the idealistic future we could paint whenever we were alone.

But then the fall had come. We'd been swept up in the drama of the Citadel and castle life and then suddenly Terletov had invaded our world and we were tossed into the middle of hell.

When I looked back at last fall, I could see how selfish I'd been and how obtuse. I had thought Seraphina was asking me to give up my position in the Kingdom completely. I'd already given up my crown; I couldn't believe she'd asked me to give up more.

But now that I looked back, I realized that she simply wanted more from me, not for me to do less. She wanted to be a priority in my life. She wanted a commitment. She wanted the commitment I could so easily give my cousin and the Kingdom, but not her.

I should have taken her that night and married her. I should have demanded that she marry me and follow me wherever my orders took me.

And I believed she would have gone. Willingly.

Instead, I'd managed to muck it all up and push her away instead.

We arrived in Omaha near midnight. The Titans had taken an alternate route and an alternate jet. They would meet us at dawn in the old clubhouse. Kiran had it restored over the winter and we would be the first to use the new facility as a meeting place.

But we were trying to get some sleep rest before we had to be down there. We used the private airstrip we always used and then the cars that were kept on site. I was thankful there were enough of them to take us all where we needed to go.

Jericho had a place here, so he took Olivia and her sister with him. Titus, Xander, Xavier, and Roxie headed to the farm. Angelica had fixed it up since Lucan's destruction, although she was rarely there. She had stayed close to Kiran and Eden, ever since the babies were announced.

I had somehow managed to convince Sera to let me stay at her flat with her. I'd used the excuse that I had plenty of belongings still there, including a toothbrush.

I even told her I'd forgotten my other one and that I was tired of borrowing Titus's.

It was still unclear if she believed me or not, but she'd agreed to let me tag along.

After the excruciating morning and the long flight here, nobody was in a mood to argue. Not even her.

The drive to her downtown building was quiet and still. I drove while she leaned against the window and pretended to sleep.

I parked in a designated spot below ground and we walked to the elevator in silence.

Once inside, she gave me a sideways glance and said, "You're sleeping on the couch tonight."

I was too tired to argue. "Where else would I sleep?"

The question hung in the air. I watched her work to swallow out of the corner of my eye and decided I liked her squirming.

"I mean it, Sebastian," she warned in a shaky voice.

"I'm not arguing with you, Seraphina."

She didn't respond to that.

We made it to the top floor of the building in silence. She led the way down the hall and opened the door with Magic. I had a feeling her keys were in her pack, but she was too tired to pull them out.

The air conditioning hit me as soon as the door opened and I stood in the dark while she fumbled around for lights. The cold air felt foreign against my skin after the day I'd had.

"My housekeeper," Seraphina explained. "I pay her to clean the place once a month and she must have forgotten to turn off the air after she left."

"That would explain why it's so cold." The place probably got pretty hot during the weeks the housekeeper didn't come. She probably blasted the thing to cool it down quickly while she worked.

Seraphina walked over to the kitchen and straight for the refrigerator. She rummaged around inside for a minute but only came back with bottled waters.

She held one out to me with an apologetic smile. "This is all I have."

"It's fine," I assured her. "I mostly just want a shower."

"Ugh," she groaned. "Me too. What a day, huh?"

I nodded with my eyes transfixed to the long lines of her throat as her head tipped back. She unscrewed the top from the water bottle and took a long sip. My gaze stayed on her lips and the small drop of water that escaped them and trailed down her chin.

I stepped up to her and brushed it away with my thumb before I even registered my move. She jumped back a step, startled.

I took a step back too. "Sorry. You just had... you had a little something on your chin."

She cleared her throat and disappeared into the bedroom. I thought she meant to run away from me and so I sunk down on the leather sofa and dropped my head into my hands. I was messing this up.

Big time.

I needed to pull myself together and figure out how to move forward.

The door opened again and she returned with arms full of my clothes and an old toothbrush sitting on top. My things.

She set them down on the coffee table in front of me and then joined them. She sat just to my left, with her long legs pressed together in front of her and her elbows resting primly on top of them.

"Did you talk to Kiran?" she asked and the events of the day rushed back at me with savage force.

I shook my head sadly. "I want indisputable proof before I put him through that." I rubbed my hands over my face and tried to comprehend how I would tell Kiran that his mum might not last much longer. Maybe she was already dead. It was impossible to tell at this point.

"I'm sorry, Bastian. I hate that you have to be the one to investigate this."

I couldn't look at her. I hated it too. I hated that my aunt was going through so much. And I really hated that Terletov may have managed to take someone else I cared about.

I needed to call my mum. I just needed to know she was okay. After that... I didn't know where to go from there.

I was already on a mission. There were Titans already looking for Analisa and for Jericho's mom, Katja. But I couldn't trust them to do the job anymore. I would have to make this not only my responsibility, but also a priority.

And it wasn't going to be easy.

I basically had the entire world to search. Her body... she could be anywhere.

Bloody hell.

"I don't even know where to begin," I groaned. I rested my elbows heavily on my bent knees. "I don't know how to solve this problem."

Seraphina laid a tentative hand on my shoulder and gave it a squeeze. Even though her contact was nervous and a little awkward, I still relished the willing touch from her. She gave me more comfort than I could have expected from such a simple touch.

I reached across my chest and put my own hand on top of hers. I didn't want her to pull away, so I removed the option. I hadn't realized how deprived my spirit felt until that moment, until she showed me.

I longed for her touch. I needed her security. I wanted *her*.

And I was in a place, where I'd do just about anything to have her.

"I'll help you," she whispered. "We will find her. He won't keep her from us, no matter what's happened to her."

I lifted my focus and finally met those sapphire blue eyes of hers. "Thank you."

She shrugged one shoulder shyly. "I care about Analisa too. And Kiran and Eden. This is the wrong time for something to go wrong with Kiran's mom. With the twins on the way... Kiran would be devastated. This should be a happy time for them. And Eden shouldn't have to mourn while she's so close to the end of her pregnancy."

My gut squeezed. I honestly hadn't even taken any of that into consideration. I'd wallowed in my own impending pain and forgotten all about my cousin and his temporarily fragile wife.

Seraphina chuckled, apparently reading my facial expressions. "That's why I'm here. Someone has to stop you from putting your foot in your mouth."

"That sounds like full-time job. I don't think I'm paying you enough."

"That's because you're not paying me at all! This is all pro bono, Baby!" She shot me a happy grin, but before I could really admire her relaxed expression, it was cut off by a giant yawn.

"We should go to bed," I said obviously.

She nodded and then looked at where I still covered her hand on my shoulder. I jerked a little since I'd forgotten it was there as well.

She retracted her hand and stood up. I jumped up quickly to follow.

Seraphina was tall for a girl, but I was taller. I towered over her, covering her body in the shadow of mine. When we dated, she loved that she had to look up to me and I loved that she had significant height, so I didn't have to bend in half to kiss her.

It was convenient now too.

I stepped into her and put my hands on her waist for a long moment before sliding them around her waist. "I need a hug," I told her.

She didn't immediately hug me back as I'd hoped. "*You* need a hug?"

I wasn't imagining the skepticism in her voice. I wanted to laugh, but held it in. "I do."

I ignored the sound she made in the back of her throat and pulled her closer. Slowly her arms wrapped around my neck and she melted against me.

Our Magics flared with life around us. They lit up and tangled together in a sudden burst of light and electricity. The explosion of our energies propelled us tighter together.

Her chest pressed into mine and I breathed her in as deeply as I could.

We hadn't been this close in more than a year, not like this. Not willingly and with such strong emotion bouncing back and forth between us. I suddenly felt like a starving, dying man. She was water in the desert. She was manna when there was no other food. She was shade when I was burning alive. She was life when I was lost in the catacombs.

And she had no idea.

I hadn't told her. I'd let her walk away and believe that I didn't want her and that I didn't want to put her before everything else.

"Sebastian." My name sounded like a warning on her lips.

"Seraphina," I countered, whispering her name like a prayer.

"I should go to bed," she finally said. "Or take a shower. Or, er, go to bed."

I pressed my smile into her throat. "You already said that."

"I need to go." She pulled away this time and I let her.

"I miss that," I said honestly.

She didn't respond verbally. Instead, she looked out of the large, picture windows and then at the kitchen in the other direction. Basically, she looked anywhere but at me.

I heard her sharp breath and braced myself for a reply. I thought she would cut me down or remind me of all of the things that had gone wrong between us.

But she didn't.

"Goodnight, Sebastian," she said instead. She walked to her bedroom, slipped inside and closed the door.

I smiled to myself in the emptiness of the room, embarrassed and confused. Last summer, things had been so simple here. I was the one that complicated them. I was the one that kept complicating things even when it was obvious she wanted nothing to do with me.

I cared about Seraphina, but there had been a reason I pushed away before. There was a reason I still felt compelled to push her away.

I cared about her and would always care about her. But I couldn't keep doing this to her. Or to me.

Especially when I should be completely focused on the mission and finding Terletov.

Honestly, we didn't have time for each other or to wade through the thick tangle of hurt and love that seemed synonymous with us.

I lay down on the couch that took up an entire side of the room and toed my Pumas off. I grabbed a throw from the armrest and made myself comfortable.

Or tried to.

The couch didn't feel right. Not when I remembered what it was like to sleep on her luxurious bed. We had occasionally fallen asleep together on this couch after watching a movie or consuming copious bottles of wine. But I remembered always waking up sometime during the night and carrying her to the bedroom where we would both be more comfortable.

I couldn't do that now. She was already in the bedroom and I had been abandoned to the lumpy exile of the tan sofa.

I didn't know how much time passed as I lay there and stared at the ceiling. I talked myself in circles and tried to come up with however many reasons it took to keep from doing what I wanted to do most.

I'd already talked myself out of following her in there a hundred times. I reasoned that she was familiar, and that's why I wanted to go in there. I told myself it was her feistiness. I swore it was because she had pulled away more than ever before and I was nothing but a petulant child that wanted what he couldn't have.

In the end, the reason that made my feet plant on the floor again and my legs push myself into standing and move toward that shut door was sleep.

I needed sleep.

And I couldn't get it on the couch.

I opened the door as silently as I could and used every ounce of stealth I possessed to creep across her floor like the stalker I was.

She lay on her usual side, perfectly poised for me to crawl into bed and wrap my arms around her. I felt a little mad as I did just that.

I pulled back at the last second and forced myself to be content with simply lying beside her. I wanted nothing more than to touch her... hold her. But I knew waking her up would be a huge mistake. This moment was beautiful for me. Familiar.

I felt like I'd come home after the longest journey away.

And waking her would shatter every peaceful second. She would undoubtedly kick me back to the couch and probably file a restraining order.

I watched for a while longer. She was always beautiful, but in sleep, when her defenses were down and her carefully built mask put away for the night, she was magnificent.

I had never seen anything lovelier.

Soon, the restlessness that plagued me in the other room receded into a drugging tranquility and my eyelids began to drift close.

I gave one last mental effort to move back to the living room, but quickly dismissed the idea when she moved closer to me.

There would be hell to pay in the morning, but sometimes the journey to hell was sweet enough to make the price worth the penance.

This was confirmed several hours later when Seraphina's shrieking jolted me awake. I had only a moment to react before she kicked me out of bed with enough Magcially reinforced strength to push me into the far wall and leave a Sebastian-sized dent.

While I groaned on the floor, holding my manhood and Seraphina's point of contact, she flew out of bed in her deliciously skimpy pajamas and raced to the bathroom.

I only had a few blissful seconds to stare after her impossibly long legs before the bathroom door slammed shut. I blew out a breath of relief that my suffering was over and lay back against the cold wood floor.

I had just started smirking at the ceiling, deciding last night's reward was well worth all of the trouble, when Seraphina reemerged from the bathroom in a knee-length robe. She carried a decorative pitcher full of something steaming.

My mind registered scalding hot water just a second before she dumped it on me.

I squirmed and screamed like a girl while she gloated above me.

"Never again, Sebastian! I only let men into my bed that I've invited! And you are not one of them!"

And then she disappeared again.

My skin cooled and my smile reappeared.

Worth it.

Chapter Twelve

Seraphina

"I know what you're trying to do and I should tell you, it's not working."

I glared at the idiot that dared to speak to me after I woke up with his chest pressed into my back and his arms snaked around my body, one hand tightly splayed across my belly, the other cupping my breast.

Was he serious?

"What am I trying to do?" I seethed.

"Murder me with your Psychic thoughts." He turned around on his barstool and grinned at me. "As you can see I'm rather impervious to that particular method of homicide."

I stood up. He was right. Glaring at him was definitely ineffective. Wrapping my hands around his neck until I stopped his airflow however…

Roxie grabbed my wrist and yanked me back into my seat.

"Not so fast, Killer. We need him."

I made a growly sound in my throat.

"You need me." Sebastian pointed at me condescendingly.

"*I* don't need you." I gestured at the rest of our small group. "*They* need you. I'm fine if you jump out of this plane and try to fly. That would be fine with me."

"Try to fly." He chuckled as if I'd said the funniest thing ever.

I looked around at the rest of the cabin filled with my supposed friends. They all tried to hide their own smiles. Apparently we were entertaining to them.

Or I was.

"I can't believe you all!" I hissed at them. "Your fearless leader is a pervert and you find it hilarious!"

Titus threw his head back and barked out a laugh. "You say that like it's news! We've always known he's a pervert. Always."

I nearly choked. "What!"

"Well, er, at least perverted," Titus amended.

I slammed my arms across my chest and tried not to scream. With no help from anyone else on this stupidly small plane, I turned my attention to the Atlantic Ocean.

Miles and miles below the luxury jet, the water appeared in a solid blue streak of paint. Clouds in puffy bursts of wispy white and gray were the only things to interrupt that sapphire brushstroke.

We'd met at the Omaha clubhouse earlier this morning only to decide to leave for Morocco right away.

Sebastian had argued that our biggest priority had to be securing all of the Sources. Terletov had managed to get two under his control. Eden controlled two. That left three Sources up for grabs. I worried that even if we managed to beat Terletov to the remaining three, the Kingdom would forever be wounded because of what he'd taken. We still had to try.

And out of the three Sources left, Morocco appeared to be the biggest threat.

I just hoped Terletov hadn't already gotten to this one too. So far, our mission was zero for two.

Not the best average.

We needed to shut this down and fast.

My mind kept jumping back to that ominous vision I'd had of the world completely falling apart. I wanted to be a part of this mission about as much as I wanted to rip my own toenails off with a pair of pliers. And I wanted to be near Sebastian even less than that. But that vision...

I couldn't let that happen.

And because I was the one to see the end, I felt a strong sense of responsibility to take down Terletov. Whether that was a rational feeling or not, it was mine.

I needed to be there. I needed to see it happen. I needed to make sure this world, my Kingdom, my friends weren't in danger any more from this monster's sadistic plans.

"He's just trying to get a rise out of you," Roxie comforted me a few minutes later.

I shot her a look. "Listen, I got a rise out of him this morning. I doubt he's simply trying to return the favor."

She nearly choked on her laughter. "What do you think he wants? Does he want you back?"

I looked over the seats in front of me toward where Sebastian sat with his back to me. He still talked with Titus in an obnoxiously animated conversation that I had a feeling was about me.

I shook my head. "I don't know what he wants. But I'm sure it's not me. Especially not after all this time."

She studied my profile while I watched Sebastian. I could tell she wanted to say something, but held back for some reason. She didn't really need to. Roxie and I had always been painfully honest with each other. It was one of the reasons I knew we could always trust each other, but we'd never be the closest friends.

Everyone had a limit to how much honesty he or she could handle. Eventually, it stopped being refreshing and got rather annoying.

That's how Roxie and I functioned together. We looked out for each other completely, but there was always a hint of irritation when we interacted.

Sebastian turned around and caught me staring at him. He didn't seem surprised and I wanted to verbally defend myself, but I held my tongue.

Everyone here already thought I was a little crazy. No need to confirm their suspicions.

He held my gaze until I looked away, back out of the window and away from whatever it was I saw reflecting back at me.

I needed to banish all thoughts and feelings for Sebastian Cartier. And I needed to do so quickly.

Two hours later, the plane descended into a remote airstrip in the Moroccan desert. There was no official Immortal outpost in Morocco. Unlike Romania and India, a palace had not been erected over the top of it.

Legend said that this was because Morocco was a wild place when early Immortal civilization spread its first explorations. It also said that our Magic was looked on as a threat to the early culture of this country. Where both India and Romania embraced our differences, Morocco sought to burn us at the stake and grind our bones to dust.

That's right, we were the original Salem. Those poser witches had nothing on us.

Xander landed the plane with all the expertise his cheating Magic gave him. He had used the airstrip that the Kingdom always used, and up until this moment, had seemed so random sitting in the middle of the desert.

Soon, I had stepped from the cool cabin of the plane to the dusty heat of the desert. The hot sun beat overhead with an unforgiving light and a hot wind blew sand over me with vicious intent.

I pulled my billowy, cotton scarf over the top of my head and then tossed one end over my shoulder so it covered my mouth and nose. I slipped on my oversized sunglasses and adjusted my turquoise Henley. I used Magic to erase all of the disorientation jetlag gave me. We'd been traveling so much over the last few days, I needed my energy to ground me.

I was slightly irritated with our detour through Omaha. Especially because of the trauma I'd woken up to this morning.

However, I was glad for access to some more of my practical clothes. I'd only packed what I had in Seattle and since I hadn't been on a long-term mission in a while, my Seattle wardrobe was severely lacking. Omaha housed all of my more utilitarian clothing options.

My khaki cargo pants and this long-sleeved shirt were light and cool, easy to move in and nearly indestructible. Everything I needed for this sandy mission.

Maybe they weren't the cutest clothes I owned, but it wasn't like I was trying to impress anyone on this trip.

I felt the Magic in the earth almost immediately. It started as a faint buzzing that tripped over the edges of my consciousness. The longer I stood with my boots in the sand, the more I became aware that something was trying to get my attention.

My Magic responded with its own vibration and soon my heart pounded in tandem with the energy in the air around me, in the earth beneath my feet and with my own force.

It wasn't a physical thing. I wasn't a Titan and didn't possess the skill to actually "feel" Magic, but I could experience this. I could sense it. I could close my eyes and get lost in it.

The Magic belonged here.

And this Magic was still healthy and whole.

I breathed in deep and let the Magic take hold of me. There was healing power in this. Not the kind of healing that Eden could whip out with her blue smoke, but something more intrinsic, something deep down and hidden. Wounded, broken places inside of my soul, the damaged pieces of my heart, the bitter, exhausted parts of my mind… they felt the soothing caress of this Magic.

It was honestly remarkable.

I looked around as my team stretched and explored the endless sand. A second plane circled overhead and we moved out of the way for the Titan transportation.

Once the second plane landed and the armed Titans disembarked we gathered around Sebastian and Jericho. They gave us our designated coordinates and we took off.

There was supposed to be a sandstone altar or something out here. The runway had been here for as long as any of us could remember. The Kingdom used it whenever necessary, but honestly, nothing of necessity brought us to the middle of the desert.

The altar was supposed to be a landmark of some kind. Similar to the Immortal Fountain in the Citadel, it was supposed to be a shrine to the original Oracles.

Nobody had seen it in centuries though. We thought it might be covered in sand by now or torn down by Berbers.

We spread out, rather isolated from each other, as we followed nothing but instinct and Magic. I wandered away from the evening sun and made footprints in the sand that were quickly wiped away with the wind.

I had nothing to go on but the pull of something greater than me. I could feel the humming beneath my feet, the buzz over my skin, the whisper of greatness just beyond my immediate awareness.

The wind picked up and the flying sand obscured my vision. I pulled the scarf tighter around my face and squinted through my dark shades. They were more of a visor against getting sand in my eyes than anything else and without my Magic, they would have made it difficult to see.

I crested a particularly high dune and looked out over the vastness of the desert. There was nothing but sand for miles and miles and miles. When I spun around, my teammates and the Titans with us spotted the rich orange sand, but other than that, there was nothing but sky and sand in every direction.

I sucked in a dusty breath and felt despair pit in my stomach. How could we find something ancient out here? It was probably covered in centuries of sand, buried in a place we would never discover.

Something tugged at my spirit, pulling me deep into the folds of sand and desolate isolation.

I was a little nervous to walk out of sight from the rest of my group, afraid they would never hear from me again. But we all carried GPS devices to help us return to the plane. Besides, the Magic called strongly and I couldn't help but respond.

I thought about calling to Olivia and Jericho, who were to my right, but I didn't. I had started to enjoy my alone time out here. It helped me think. Breathe.

My thoughts became clearer and the voice of the Magic became more audible.

I felt my own Magic swirl around me, energized by something I couldn't see. I had this strong sense of purpose and direction. I felt it swelling inside of me, electrifying my blood, pounding against my chest, inhaling and exhaling with every breath into this epic, climactic moment.

And then I tripped.

And then I epically tripped.

I managed to face-plant in the dune. Even through my scarf, I inhaled way more gritty sand than I ever wanted to. And it didn't stop there.

The dune was steep enough that when my body flew forward, the momentum followed me and I just kept falling. I tumbled in somersaults down the massive incline in an unforgivably clumsy way. Head first and then my ass would follow. I couldn't manage to find a foothold or grip on anything because as soon as I reached out for something, the sand would shift away from me and I would pick up speed.

My Magic seemed useless against the sand-snowball my body created. There was no slowing me down. I felt my cheeks heat from an embarrassed burn and I swore to myself that once I reached the bottom of this dune I would leave Morocco and never come back.

Finally, I bounced to a stop at the bottom of an immense mountain out of sand. I rubbed sand out of my eyes and choked on the same filthy stuff until I could breathe again. The sky swirled in a dusky blue overhead and the wind rushed against my ears.

It took me a while to get my bearings and even then I felt stuffed with sand in all of the important places. I couldn't hear right, my tongue was disgustingly dry and dirty and my eyes stung from the residual grains I hadn't managed to extract with my equally grubby hands.

Damn it. So much for professional.

So much for purpose-driven.

I pushed myself up on my elbows and surveyed my new surroundings.

I rolled over so I could crawl to my feet, but my disastrous gymnastics routine down the dune wasn't enough for fate.

My body landed on something seemingly solid. Instantly I realized there was something beneath the sand, right before the ominous crack boomed through the air around me.

It was a roof, I realized a little too late. A roof to something thirty feet beneath me.

And it collapsed with my weight.

I crashed to the ground in a pile of splintered, weakened wood and sand. My landing created a haze of dust that puffed up like a mushroom cloud above me. I choked and sputtered from the fall and lack of clean oxygen. Hazy light filtered through the speckled air and I looked up at the sky again praying there was nowhere else to fall.

A face appeared above me and I groaned in protest.

"Sera!" Sebastian hollered. He threw himself over the broken ledge and jumped the long distance. He landed on his feet like a cat and before I could blink he was at my side. "Are you dead?"

"Yes," I croaked. I sent my Magic spiraling through my body. I needed to heal. And fast. That shit hurt.

"What happened?" I tried to glare at him, but my body hurt too badly. I could hear the bastard's laughter in his voice and when I finally faced him, he wasn't even trying to hide his smile!

"Ow!"

"Right." He wiped at his mouth as if he could physically remove that stupid grin. "You're hurt."

"I'm hurt!"

"Badly?" He let out another chuckle as if he just couldn't help himself.

"Very badly!"

His tone was frighteningly calm and reserved when he asked, "If I tell you your left leg is severed completely off, will that make things better or worse?"

I snapped to sitting and grabbed my completely intact left leg. "You bastard!" I swung to punch him in the face, but he caught my wrist with his annoying hand and held me still.

"You're fine, Sera," he promised in a low voice, not at all bothered by my fists of fury. I opened my mouth to scream obscenities at him when he leaned in and place an affectionate kiss on my nose. "Now, let me help you up and you can tell me what you found."

In stunned silence, I let him pull me to my feet. Both legs worked, which surprised me all over again after the scare he'd given me. But by the time I stood on my own, I was completely healed and there was really nothing left to complain about.

Except all of the falling.

But that wasn't exactly Sebastian's fault.

We spun around in a synchronized circle to inspect whatever kind of hole I'd fallen into. The leftover light of the day cascaded around us through the crater my body had created and glittered off of the polished sandstone all around us. It appeared to be some kind of pavilion. A temple maybe? Some kind of communal open-aired building that had been buried beneath centuries of sandstorms.

"If I didn't know better, I'd think you were trying to prove me right."

I chanced a glance at Sebastian before the words slipped out. "Prove you right about what?"

"That it was brilliant of me to insist you come along. Between the visions and your clumsiness, you might single-handedly bring Terletov to his knees."

I noticed something then that I hadn't noticed before, the Magic. It was spectacularly strong down here. It zinged through the air, bouncing off walls and wrapping around my skin. It had an intensified aura like I had never felt before. I couldn't decide if it was a trick of the dim light or if the air was actually shaded in blue. It didn't really matter either way because I could feel how pure and wholesome this Magic was.

Terletov or any outside forces did not taint this. This was our Magic in its purest, most raw form.

"This is the Source?" I asked with a voice no louder than a whisper.

"I believe so." Sebastian took a step forward toward a rounded building with a domed top.

The shrine looked like a turret off of a Persian palace. Like a giant plucked it from the rooftop of Jasmine's castle. The domed top glittered in what had to be solid gold and the sides of the shrine glistened in pretty sandstone.

Each side was carved with intricate patterns and symbols. The doorway into the shrine had figures etched into the perfect arch. The path to the door started just in front of us and led the way in more shaped gold.

I sucked in a breath and mourned that the Immortals that created this weren't still with us. That was the whole point of being Immortal that we would stick around forever.

I was honestly moved by such a pretty place, even more so because it seemed lost forever in the vast and lonely desert.

I couldn't let Terletov find this place. And I really couldn't let him control it.

He didn't deserve something so beautiful.

He didn't deserve something so worthy.

He was the antithesis of this place and I would die before I gave it up to him.

"What now?" I stepped onto the golden path and felt the Magic under my feet like a current straight to my heart.

"Do you think Eden's up to making the journey?" His tone was just dry enough that I could tell he was joking.

I gave him a look. "Not Eden, but she can't be the only one that can tame Magic."

Sebastian frowned. "Avalon's never done what she can."

I flashed a cheeky smile. "It's never too late to start trying."

Chapter Thirteen

Sebastian

By the time Avalon and my sister arrived five hours later, we'd all had enough of the desert.

I called for help using my satellite phone and a bit of Magic to make it connect. Jericho and all of the reinforcements had come to check out the lost Source. Someone had gone back to one of the jets for an emergency rope ladder and I'd put the Titans to task making sure it was safe to use.

I wasn't really worried about anyone getting hurt, but it would be simpler and more efficient if the rope stayed in place.

We had come to the desert prepared. There were plenty of battery-operated torches to illuminate the space after the sun set. There was also enough camping gear for us to set up for the night and meals to cook over an open flame.

We all had Magic of course, but these tangible items would mean we could focus our energy wholly on the task at hand.

We hadn't known how long we would have to stay in the desert, but we had planned not to leave until we found what we came for. It was sheer luck, or divine providence, that Seraphina had stumbled onto the Source so quickly. We'd hardly been here twenty minutes before I watched her cartwheel down the hill straight into the hidden ruin.

I had been out of my mind with fear for her. I raced after her, but not fast enough before she collapsed the roof and dropped to the bottom.

I thought I would be sick watching her disappear into the unknown.

I hadn't known what she fell through or where she would end up. My mind had envisioned all kinds of hellish scenarios. I leaped through the hole without a second thought.

The worst of my fears, an endless abyss that would swallow her whole, proved to be false when my feet landed awkwardly on the splintered debris.

And then she'd been so still. Her body hadn't moved as I rushed to her side.

I didn't think the short fall could seriously injure her, but my body couldn't seem to process that she was okay or going to be okay.

And then when it finally caught up to me, there was this huge surge of adrenaline that came out as... well, as laughter.

It wasn't exactly on purpose. I hadn't meant to trivialize her trauma, but honestly, I thought I had lost her forever.

And then she was fine.

Elated. I had been *elated*.

Now, I watched her speak to my sister in the corner of the spacious cavern. They whispered together like when they were younger. I wasn't sure if they ever grew out of the habit of whispering secrets to each other or giggling about them behind an open palm.

I used to adore how close they were. I loved that my sister cared about the woman I loved so completely. I respected their trust for each other and their immovable friendship. Those two women had meant more to me than anything else in the world at one time.

One of them still did.

Okay, maybe both of them still did.

But now that bond seemed to bite me in the arse more often than not. Mimi couldn't forgive me for what happened between Seraphina and me. And Seraphina would forever be a part of my life simply because she adored my sister.

Their friendship was now a curse upon my life meant to smite me with fire and brimstone.

However, I couldn't deny my heart-wrenching reaction when I watched Seraphina disappear the way she did. Or the way I'd held her last night.

I had to start being honest with myself. I needed to face the obnoxiousness of my inconvenient feelings for her and decide what to do with them.

I was beyond ignoring them and pretending they didn't exist.

Obviously, I still cared for that stubborn woman.

But now what?

I could clearly see that what I felt between us had disappeared, but how did she feel about me?

She didn't seem nearly as in love with me as she used to be.

Which seemed impossible, but still relevant.

"Stop staring at my wife, Sebastian. She's your *sister*."

I cocked my head back, surprised by the words spoken at me. I blinked twice before I recognized Avalon and forced myself back to the present.

Avalon grinned at me. "I heard you've been accused of being a pervert. I'm not sure anyone is safe from your depraved ways."

I wrinkled my nose. "You're disgusting."

"No, *you're* disgusting. I'm just looking out for my wife."

"I was not looking at my sister, you prick. I was looking at... Just never mind."

"Oh, oh, oh!" Avalon sing-songed. "Who exactly had your attention?"

I scowled at him.

It didn't work.

"T, has Sebastian been a little distracted lately? Kiran put him in charge thinking he had stellar focus. Could his Royal Doucheyness be wrong about that?"

This Kingdom was so messed up. I supposed that's what happened when you put a bunch of twenty-something idiots in charge of an entire Kingdom of Immortals. We had forever to become mature. Why start now?

Titus shot me a shit-eating grin and ambled over to us. "He has been a little distracted lately." Titus cupped his jaw and narrowed his eyes in dramatic thoughtfulness. "I think he's been thinking about his sister though. Which is weird, right?"

"Bastards. Both of you are bastards."

They howled with laughter at my lame insult and drew the attention of everyone down here. Seraphina gave me a scalding look, apparently blaming me for the King's poor behavior. I tried to look innocent, but that tactic hadn't worked with her in ages.

"Ready to get started?" she asked Avalon.

"Sure, sure." He rolled his shoulders and faced the shrine. Nothing happened.

I wasn't surprised.

Rumor had it that when Eden walked into the Cave of Winds the Source of Magic attacked her. Avalon had been in those caves dozens of times before that and not so much as a whisper had floated by him.

The same was said to be true about beneath the prisons. Eden warred with some kind of Magical tornado. Avalon spent the better part of two years wandering aimlessly down there and never ran into something as simple as a light gust of wind.

Eden was clearly the better half of the St. Andrew family line.

However, Eden, thanks to those tiny little Immortals bumming around in her stomach, was currently unavailable.

So we had to use the second string.

Seraphina stepped up behind Avalon and cleared her throat. "I have a theory about why Eden picked up two Source Magics early on."

Everyone swiveled to look at her. I was more than intrigued. I hadn't heard this before.

When she had everyone's attention, she continued, "Terletov was a threat even back then. We just didn't know it yet. Couldn't it be possible that the Source Magic was looking for protection?"

Avalon looked skeptical. "You're saying, the Magic jumped into Eden to save itself because of Dmitri Terletov?"

Seraphina shrugged. "I mean, maybe? Doesn't it seem a little coincidental that Terletov made his debut at the same time Eden started collecting Magics?"

"Maybe it happened because Eden had never been inside before. Maybe it had nothing to do with Terletov." Titus looked just as unbelieving as I felt.

Seraphina shrugged a shoulder, agreeing with him. "True. The Magic was under as much of an attack back then as it is now. But either way, the Magic *is* under attack. I think it will do whatever it takes to remain untainted."

Avalon looked at me. "What do you think, Bastian? You on board with this?"

I huffed. Obviously. "I wouldn't have called you out here if I didn't think it would work. Sera's right. The Magic is under attack. If you don't figure out how to protect it, it's going to end up like the others. Besides, she's the Psychic. Best to do what she says."

Avalon frowned. He looked to his wife who gave him an imperceptible nod. He mouthed his "I love you" to her and then turned back to the shrine. Looked like he was ready to get on with it.

"Everyone should get out," Avalon ordered. "The Magic can be rather... violent through this process."

That seemed wise.

The room emptied as each Immortal took turns up the rope ladder. My sister stood in the corner, nervously chewing her bottom lip.

"Come, Mims," I coaxed her. "He'll be fine."

She tilted her chin defiantly. "I'll be fine as well."

Why were women always so stubborn? Couldn't I just meet one female that was easy to convince? I decided I would marry her. The second I ran into a woman that did what I wanted her to do the first time I asked her I would toss her over my shoulder and carry her to the church and make her marry me.

"But will Avalon? If he's worried about you, he won't be as focused."

Her expression turned mulish and I could feel the desire to fight me. It was some sibling instinct born from a childhood of bickering.

Queendom seemed to agree with Mimi though because other than a puff of frustrated breath, she complied with me.

"I suppose," she grumbled.

Up the ladder she went while I moved aside for Seraphina. She had just started the climb when I reached out and patted her bum affectionately.

She jumped three inches and glared down at me. "Sebastian," she growled.

"Just wanted to say, great work with Avalon. You made some excellent points." She seemed a little dumbstruck by my compliment, but not at all appeased. "You also have an excellent arse. I couldn't resist."

The rest of her climb seemed a bit aggressive, but that could have been my imagination.

Out in the open again, the expansive desert seemed to shrink into a tight black box. The standing torches that had been staked into the ground around the buried Source's perimeter made the golden sand glitter in their soft light, but their radius only reached so far. Beyond the faint circle of light, the desert became black oblivion.

The sky above hid its stars behind thick clouds. The moon that should be full tonight had shrouded itself as well. My Magic reached my vision into the wall of night, but the darkness made everything a hazy gray.

I felt exposed out here. The lanterns and torches aided our cause, but also shined a spotlight directly on our activity. Anyone could find us out here if they knew the general direction to look. And that made us vulnerable.

Which was never a good position to be in.

"You look spooked," Seraphina said gently from where she stood at my side.

Below us, through the collapsed roof, Avalon's Magic began to go to war with the Source. Or that was how it seemed. The ground beneath my feet rocked and surged from the power struggle. Sand cascaded from level ground to the hole below.

I took Seraphina's arm and moved her further from Avalon and the Source. "I'm wondering if we're secure enough."

"There are Titans patrolling the area. Do you think Terletov knows we're here?"

"You tell me."

She huffed. "I'm not a Magic Eight Ball, Bastian."

"But you *are* Psychic, Sera. I trust your instinct. You should too."

She gave me a sideways glance and then narrowed her eyes on the perimeter. "We're safe here."

"Why do you sound so uncertain?"

"Because we won't be for long."

Her eyes flashed to mine and I instinctively took a step forward. A sick feeling churned in my gut and our Magics collided with startling force. It was as though they clung together for safety. I felt her energy surge through mine, and the same feeling she had just put into words fused itself with my blood.

I felt the same thing.

We would be fine here, but it was only a matter of time.

As soon as the thought had settled in my mind as truth, I questioned her power all over again. I searched frantically for my sister, but couldn't find her through the crowd of Immortals congregating around the hole in the ground.

Dread clutched at my chest and I shouted out for everyone to *get down* just as Avalon's Magic exploded from the cavern and burst through the night sky.

I lost my grip on Sera when the Magical eruption threw me thirty yards and buried me in the desert sand. Unconsciousness swirled around my mind and my Magic seemed to stutter and then come to a complete stop.

I unwillingly dropped my head back on the bed of sand and blinked up at the starless sky. I gave into the blackness just as Avalon's raging shouts penetrated the eerily quiet night.

Something was wrong.

Something was very wrong.

My eyes shot open and I jumped to my feet. Sand gushed down my body, sifting through my collar and waistband and digging into places sand didn't belong. I brushed it off of my face and spit it out of my mouth.

My chest heaved with anxious breaths, but I blinked at pure darkness. My mind told me not much time had passed since I'd fallen asleep, but fear raced through my veins.

An explosion.

Avalon shouting.

Unconsciousness.

Something had happened.

Magic pulsed through my veins and I pushed it harder, faster, surging it through my body, bringing life back to my confused senses.

With the aid of my Magic, I could see clearly again. I took off in a sprint toward the crater-sized hole that had once been a hidden temple. I sent my energy out to search for Seraphina. It had taken thirty seconds before I found her just as I had been, half-buried in the sand and out of it.

I knelt at her side. Unlike when I found her at the bottom of the hole she'd fallen through, I was not amused. I picked up her upper body and cradled her in my arms.

I could feel her heart beating steadily and her Magic readily clinging to mine. I tried to temper my smile as I enjoyed the willingness of her Magic to connect with mine even when she seemed to run from me every chance she got.

Her eyes opened slower than mine had. She blinked up at me with brows furrowed in confusion and her pretty lips pursed against the sand.

I gently brushed the sand away, letting my fingers graze over the perfection of her mouth.

Her expression softened some and she said, "I didn't give you permission to touch me."

I let out a frustrated groan. "I wanted to make sure you were all right. I wasn't molesting you. Stop making it sound perverted."

She pushed away from me and struggled to her feet. Immortals popped out of the sand all around us. The amount of sand falling from standing bodies made a whooshing sound in the quiet night.

I watched Seraphina cringe and brush sand from her body. She stomped her feet and then shook them out. I wanted to reassure her that there was no amount of Magic that would dislodge the sand form all of her crevices, but I thought this was probably not the right time.

Oh, shite. Avalon!

I turned from Seraphina, admonishing myself for letting her become such a distraction and raced for the Source.

The structure that had been built around the ancient temple had been completely demolished from whatever happened. Splintered wood and crumbled stone filled the hole nearly to the top.

"Avalon!" I called down.

I jumped off of the ledge and started to pick my way over the bigger pieces of stone in order to uncover where he'd been buried.

I told myself not to worry about his physical state. He would be fine. He had to be. There was almost nothing in this world that could destroy his Immortal life.

Except for maybe a persnickety Source Magic that might not have been so pleased with his effort to control it.

"Avalon!"

Stone shifted in front of me and I hurried my pace. An ashy hand popped through the debris and reached out for help.

"Could you be more dramatic?" I snorted.

Muffled grumbling answered me.

By the time I'd reached his hand, Titus, Xander and Xavier had joined me. We moved the heavy stones out of the way quickly and pulled Avalon to his feet. His entire body was gray with dust and grit. His green eyes seemed to glow from his ashy body.

"Did you get it?" Titus demanded.

When Avalon spoke, a puff of dust burst in a cloud from his mouth. "Yes," he wheezed. "But damn..."

"You own the Source?" Xander clarified.

"I do," Avalon agreed. "I made that Magic my bitch."

We all chuckled in relief. Our shoulders relaxed and for the first time in a long time, I felt some hope.

"Well done, Mate." I clasped my hand on his shoulder, truly proud of my friend. "We can check this off the list then."

"What are we going to do with it?" Xander raised his eyebrows expectantly.

Avalon and I shared a look.

"Keep it the hell away from Terletov," Avalon finally said.

"And figure out what it does," I added. Maybe it had healing properties like Eden's smoke. Or made someone invisible.

I would like to be invisible for a day.

"Where is my wife?" demanded Avalon.

"Here," Mimi said.

I whirled around to take inventory of her. Between Seraphina and Avalon, she hadn't exactly been a priority on my mind. But she seemed well enough, standing at the top of the hole. I breathed out my relief, but it was short lived.

"Son of a bitch," Avalon shouted suddenly. He bent over so fast his forehead collided with my shoulder and knocked me back. He let out another god-awful scream and his entire body went tight with pain and tension.

"Is it the Magic?" I demanded.

His answering shout did nothing to solve my question, except confirm that something was wrong.

Very wrong.

I realized then that these were the exact sounds I'd heard before I blacked out. But he didn't mention being in pain before.

Had that been a vision? A residual effect from being so close with Sera right before the explosion?

"What's wrong?" I growled at him.

Through gritted teeth, he ground out, "I think I'm in labor."
"*What*?"
"I'm in labor," he repeated. "I mean, *Eden*. Eden is in labor!"

Chapter Fourteen

Seraphina

It took us forever to get to London. The plane ride was only a few hours, but knowing one of my best friends was in labor and I wasn't there to offer moral support killed me.

It didn't help that Avalon couldn't sit still and kept shooting Mimi anxious looks. Sebastian had asked him if everything was alright several times, but Avalon had been tight-lipped. That left the rest of us in confused limbo.

Was labor more difficult than they expected?

Was it too soon?

The babies were Immortal, more so than any of the rest of us, but what did that mean for them? They were only babies? Could they survive premature birth and complications?

Surely.

But still, we were all on edge.

By the time we reached the London palace, my hands shook with anxiety and I had to push a massive headache away with Magic. I needed sleep and food, but my friends were infinitely more important than my own needs.

We raced inside the opulent mansion only to be stopped by security. Avalon was with us so the hang-up only lasted a minute, but everything that stopped me from getting upstairs felt like it dragged time through mud.

Sebastian and I had hitched a ride with Avalon and Mimi and left the rest of our entourage to bring the other two planes. Avalon and Mimi always traveled with a few Titans that made up their personal guard, but as far as us storming the castle, we were hardly a threat.

Still, in a reluctant part of my mind, I was glad the Guard was being as cautious as possible.

I had been to the London palace multiple times in my life, but I had never quite been able to take in all of the intricate details. It wasn't exactly a palace, although the entire Kingdom referred to it as one.

It was more of a ginormous house with a towering stone wall that fenced the property. Titans patrolled the grounds and whenever the Kings and Queens felt the whim, they held court here.

This was the home Kiran was raised in. Lucan had rarely visited the Romanian Citadel, except for holidays and festivals until Eden and the

Resistance became a threat, and then he'd moved his family there in an effort to prove his strength and authority over the Kingdom.

Obviously, it hadn't worked.

I hadn't met Kiran until he came to Omaha. We had already been engaged at that point. And we were only engaged for a short while. During that time, I had never been invited here.

It wasn't until after Lucan fell and Kiran and Eden had taken over the Kingdom that I'd entered the London Palace and understood why everyone continued to call this place a palace when it was technically not one.

White marble gleamed from ceiling to floor, up an extravagant centered staircase with detailed balusters. Golden accents shined from every surface and railing while the second story balcony wrapped around the foyer. The house boasted thirty-seven bedrooms, a ballroom, a massive dining room, indoor and outdoor swimming pools, tennis courts, and a soccer pitch. Apartments had been built beneath the basement of the house to house the Titan Guard on duty. There were forty bathrooms.

Forty.

The house was more than enough to accommodate the two Royal families and their Guards and attendants and whoever else they wanted to join them in London. And if for whatever reason they ran out of rooms, there were three separate guest houses toward the back of the property.

We sprinted the distance of the house to the Kendrick apartments. Guards stood watch at the door and milled about the hallway. Angelica waited in a chair that had been pulled into the hallway for her. She looked frail and exhausted as she rested her forehead in her hand. She perked up a little bit when she saw the four of us barreling down the hallway, but not by much.

"It was sudden." Angelica's greeting was hardly that, but it was the information we needed.

"It was because of me," Avalon confirmed. "The shock of new Magic to her system. Am I right?"

Angelica nodded. Avalon rubbed his hands over his face and looked completely defeated. His shoulders sagged and the frustration and humiliation rolled off of him in waves.

"I should have thought of that. I should have realized it didn't matter which of us faced the Source, we would both feel the effects."

"That's not true." I snapped from my own exhaustion and frustration. "You didn't know about India. And you don't have easy access to that Magic either. We had no idea this would happen." Nobody said anything to that because there wasn't anything to say. "She was due in two weeks." I looked at Angelica for confirmation. "It's not as though they're too early."

Angelica sighed. "Sylvia isn't worried about the timing. She has full faith that if Eden can get through this, then the babies will be fine."

"So what's the problem?"

"Labor is extremely difficult for some reason. I haven't heard of another Immortal having problems like this before. The babies won't come. And Sylvia doesn't know what to do. A C-section might have to happen before the end of the night."

Eden's wrenched scream resounded through the hallway and our anxiety level ratcheted up significantly.

"She's also in pain," Angelica continued. "Magic isn't helping."

"I can feel it," Avalon confirmed. "I can shut it off, but obviously, Eden can't."

The next three hours were spent with our butts on the ground and our backs to the wall. The Titans brought chairs out for us, but I felt more comfortable with my knees pulled to my chest and my head buried between them.

Eden continued to suffer in a way she shouldn't. It wasn't as though Immortals had completely painless childbirths, but our Magic made it possible to ignore the pain. And rarely were there complications.

Eden, of all people, should not be having complications.

I had hoped that Avalon would give us updates through the afternoon and evening, but he stayed pretty tight-lipped. Amelia pressed herself close to his side and let him slip into silence as we all waited for something good to happen.

Eventually, the other planes arrived in London. Titus, Xander, Xavier, Roxie, Olivia, Ophelia and Jericho joined our waiting game in the hallway. The cooks brought up food for us, but nobody made a move to eat anything.

I felt sick with worry. My Magic buzzed around inside of me like angry wasps. I felt jolted and stung by the ferocity of it. I tried to use my Psychic powers to predict the outcome of today, but I couldn't see anything beyond a severe warning of upcoming danger.

The instinct that the worst was yet to come was strong enough to make me panic. I wanted to warn everyone, but I didn't know what to say. I couldn't see what was coming or why I felt such a strong urge to lock us all in the basement bomb shelter.

Sebastian sat next to me in the expansive hall and had been as quiet and stressed out as the rest of us since we left Morocco. I hadn't even noticed that our Magics had been opened to each other since before the explosion in the desert. It had been second nature once upon a time and sometimes I forgot to restrain my stubborn energy.

I must have looked like a deer caught in headlights when I met his melancholy gaze and yanked my Magic away from his.

Sometimes I felt like my Magic was a disobedient child that I had to constantly control and discipline. One day, I would figure out how to attach one of those backpack-leash things to it so it couldn't go anywhere without my express permission.

Sebastian didn't say anything about my dramatic reaction and I was eternally grateful for that. I didn't have the patience to deal with *us* right now.

"She's going to be fine," he told me quietly. "The twins will be fine."

I swallowed down my objection. "I hope you're right."

"It feels like we should be preparing for something though, doesn't it?"

I nodded. Looking down the hallway filled with my friends, teammates and highly trained Guard, and second-guessed all of my Psychic instincts.

Sebastian's hand slid over the gleaming floor to rest over mine. I twitched at the hot contact of his skin but didn't pull back.

It took everything inside of me to keep my Magic separated from his, but I was thankful for the distraction. I didn't want to think through the myriad of terrible possibilities and reasons for my negative feelings.

"We should talk, Sera," Sebastian said in a low voice so that only I could hear. "There are things I would like to say."

I pursed my lips and tried to figure out how to respond to that. Thankfully, I was saved by Kiran's exhausted frame in the open doorway. His hair was more than disheveled; it looked practically yanked from his head. His eyes were bright and filled with equal parts excitement and terror. But his mouth... his smile... he was giving us good news.

I immediately relaxed.

"A boy and a girl," Kiran panted with a heaving chest. "A healthy baby boy and the most beautiful baby girl that has ever been."

My smile hurt it was so big. Tears filled my eyes and slipped down my cheeks before I could hold back all of my emotion. I pulled myself to my feet and waited my turn to hug the new father.

Kiran stood next to the open door after the congratulations were finished and gestured for us to go in.

Soon, Eden's "hospital" room was filled with all of the people that loved her and would treat these children as if they were each of our favorite niece and nephew. She looked exhausted in her bed and so did Syl as they each held a baby, one wrapped in a pink blanket, one wrapped in blue.

Kiran walked over and took his daughter from Syl's hands. He pressed the sweetest kiss to her forehead and nuzzled his nose along her pink skin. He lifted his head to share a look with Eden and I swear I melted at the look of pure adoration the two shared, not just for their new babies, but for each other as well.

My heart swelled and emptied at the same time. On one side of my soul, I couldn't have been happier for my friend. I felt full with how much joy I shared with her. On the other side, I felt completely hollowed, like I was missing the most important thing. My heart hurt with the sensation and my spirit seemed to drain.

I recognized my need for this.

I wanted *this*.

I wanted the kind of epic love Eden and Kiran had. I wanted to be safe and secure in a relationship that was actively working to build a life together. I wanted commitment. The permanent kind.

And I wanted my own babies.

I could be honest with myself, just as long as nobody asked me to admit that out loud. I wanted to settle down. I wanted a house full of children biting my ankles and yanking on my clothes. I wanted a husband that would look at his children as if they were the greatest miracle ever created and gaze at me as if he wanted to tear my clothes off every second of every day and then hold me in his arms until the world ended or time stopped.

I was jealous of my friends. Not because of who they were. I'd never really had feelings for Kiran and whatever had been was long over. I was jealous of everything the represented.

They'd been through hell together, but had managed to figure it out.

And now they had this.

"Sera, come see," Eden beckoned me.

I moved to her side and sat down on the edge of the bed. I looked down at the squishy newborn face of her son and felt the tears start all over again.

"He's gorgeous, Mama. You did a good job."

"Mmm, I have never been more exhausted in my life."

"Do you know why it was so hard?"

She held up the little bundle and I took him from her. He was so very tiny in my arms that I was terrified I would break him. I held him snuggly in the crook of my arm and felt my womb weep with longing.

Alright, that was a little dramatic.

But I definitely felt the pangs of baby-envy.

I wanted this.

So much.

"We think it was the Magic," Eden answered in a croaky voice. "They started to come early and the Magic knew it wasn't exactly time yet. It was doing everything it could to protect their little lives."

"So you had to fight it?" She nodded. "That sucks."

"I would do it again," she whispered. "I will do anything to protect these little nuggets."

I smiled at her affectionate nickname but knew without a doubt how serious she was. Of course, she would. So would I, and they weren't even my children.

"So, names? I'm dying! What did you decide to call them?"

She brushed her fingers over the little guy's face and answered with a proud smile in her voice, "This guy is Gavriel Justice."

More hot tears slipped from the corners of my eyes and I sniffled quickly, trying to hold back the pressure of emotion. "After Gabriel and your dad?"

She nodded. "His name means freedom and justice."

Now she was crying too. We were just a mess of tears and emotion.

"And the little lady?"

Her voice was a broken whisper when she said, "Amari Delia."

I swear the whole room burst into tears at the sound of her name. I felt a comforting hand squeeze my shoulder. I looked up at Sebastian and felt my heart thump in my chest. I didn't understand my reaction to him, but I almost swayed from the force of it.

He stood closely behind me with his chest pressed against my back and his hand resting on my shoulder. He looked down at baby Gavriel and me with a proud smile on his face and eyes red from his refusal to cry.

My Magic surged with something I couldn't quite grasp. It almost felt like a vision had fused with my present and I could somehow see the present and the future at the same time.

Only they were the same.

Well, the same and different.

A premonition?

No. It couldn't be.

"I didn't expect him to be so... ugly," Sebastian said, effectively breaking me out of whatever weirdness I'd slipped into.

"What?" Eden gasped.

"He's so... squishy. Is his face supposed to look like that?"

"Sebastian, he is the most beautiful baby in the entire world," Eden growled. "Take that back right now or I'm going to throw you in prison."

He tsked at her and wagged his finger. "Now, now, my Queen, don't waste my time with idle threats. You destroyed the prisons. Remember?"

"Sebastian," she hissed.

"It's really a compliment," he tried to explain. "It's just that you're so lovely. Clearly he favors his father's side."

"You're on his father's side!"

"But obviously, I favor *my* father's side. There's nothing to worry about. He'll grow into that nose." Sebastian cut a look at me. "I hope."

I pressed my lips together to keep from bursting into laughter. Kiran hadn't been so successful. He laughed at his cousin's jokes as if it was perfectly fine that Sebastian thought his child was ugly.

"I'm only teasing, Eden. He's very handsome. You'll have your hands full once he's grown. Possibly before then. Now you'll get the pleasure of every mother in the Kingdom shoving their infant daughter his direction, hoping they develop some sort of infant bond so you can betroth them as soon as possible."

Eden wrinkled her nose. "This is all new to me. Obviously. I have no idea how to raise a prince."

Sebastian leaned forward and ruffled her tangled black hear. "I'll help. I know all there is to know about raising princes. I was once one, you know."

Kiran let out a scoffing sound from the back of his throat. "Don't take his advice, Love. Just look at how he turned out. In fact, I wonder if we shouldn't ask Bastian to leave now before any lasting damage is done."

"I'm practically this child's uncle!" Sebastian protested. "And that one's too!"

Avalon stepped up to the bed and took Amari from Kiran. I stood and handed Mimi Gavriel. I stepped out of the way so Mimi could sit down.

"I'm actually this child's uncle," Avalon crooned sweetly to the little girl in his arms. "You don't need Sebastian, little one, not when you have me."

Eden and Kiran shared a terrified look. "We should rethink our circle of friends and family," Kiran murmured to her. "These people were fine before the babies were born. But maybe we shouldn't associate with the riffraff now." He looked up at all of us, clustered close by. "Except for their birthdays, of course. You'll still be expected to spoil them rotten."

Eden laughed lightly and gave everyone an apologetic look. "We don't really think you're riffraff. You'll be able to see the children whenever you'd like one day a year."

We all burst into laughter, not expecting Eden's humor after hours of labor and pain and suffering.

"They're beautiful, E," I told her. "You did a great job."

Eden smiled and passed baby Gavriel from Mimi to Angelica. "I did, didn't I?"

The room fell into comfortable conversation after that. In hushed tones we admired the new babies and spent as much time with Eden and Kiran as we could until they kicked us from the room so that they could get some sleep and feed the two little ones.

I left the Royal wing to find the room I usually stayed in here feeling happier than I had in a long time. But at the same time, I had this loneliness inside of me that seemed to open up like a great cavern in my soul. Or the mouth of a beast. It was hungry and desperate for something permanent. My heart ached from the intensity of my singleness and lack of baby-making prospects.

"Sera!" Sebastian caught up to me just as I reached my door.

I dropped my head back and I felt more sand losing from my massive hair. I realized then how dirty I was. Kudos to Eden for not being the neat-freak mom that scolded us all for coming straight from the desert. We had all scrubbed our hands and arms, but I needed a shower.

Pronto.

"I just want to go to sleep."

"I would like to talk to you," he pleaded softly. "It will only take a moment."

I turned my head and regarded him carefully. His eyes were soft and beseeching. They searched mine, waiting for my answer with hope I didn't want to believe was still there. His strong body towered over mine and his hand reached out for me as if he expected me to take it.

No.

No.

"I can't talk to you tonight."

"You can't? Or won't."

My chest ached with the desires that had made themselves so clear upstairs with Eden and her new babies. I knew the answer. And I knew what would happen if he got me alone tonight.

I would fall back into whatever we had before and that was very bad news. He would never give me what Eden had. And I didn't even want exactly that. But I wanted the idea of it. I wanted the concept.

I wanted a man that would look at me like I was his everything. I wanted a man that would fight for me.

Most of all, I wanted a man that would fight for me.

"Tonight, of all nights, I *can't* talk to you."

His jaw ticked as he bit back whatever it was he wanted to say, but knew he shouldn't. I took that opportunity to slip into my room and shut the door quickly behind me. I locked the handle for some reason.

Not that it would really keep him out. And not that I felt like I needed to.

More like, I needed to keep myself inside.

I had wanted to break. So much. I wanted nothing more than to yank the door open and drag Sebastian into my room. I wanted to spend the night with him and forget everything I ached for, longed for and just let him ease the pain for a few hours.

I was lonely and I wanted arms around me. No matter who they belonged to.

But I couldn't do it.

I couldn't.

I had to respect myself. And I had to stay strong. Sebastian and I were over.

Forever.

I left the door in favor of a shower. Someone had dropped off my things earlier and so I stripped out of my filthy clothes and stepped beneath the scalding stream of water.

I spent as much time as I could scrubbing my hair and skin clean before I was too exhausted to stand. By the time I crawled into the massive bed and sunk down onto silky sheets and glorious pillows, I had washed away all of the regrets that involved Sebastian and banished the clinging desire to call him back in here.

I had moved on.

I could keep moving on.

And I could be happy for my friends without making stupid mistakes that would only break whatever was left of the heart that stopped being whole a year ago.

The morning would be easier, I promised myself.

And besides, right now, I was just too tired to care.

Chapter Fifteen

Sebastian

Who knows how long I stood outside her door waiting for her to come back to me. I stood there like a fool, hoping she would realize I wasn't the same man that had let her leave a year ago. I hadn't been thinking then. I hadn't been prepared for her willingness to leave or for her determination to stay away.

We had been in plenty of disagreements before that final one. I had expected that one to end like all of the others. I had expected to scream at each other, to get pissed at each other and then to make-up just as aggressively.

I loved making-up.

It was one of my favorite physical activities.

But it wasn't as though I expected to get that lucky tonight, or rather, lucky at all. I had started to see some of my own fault in our demise. And after all we'd been through lately, and the help Seraphina had so kindly given, I felt I owed her an apology.

I was disappointed she didn't want to hear it. I decided there was no reason we couldn't be friends. We'd been friends before we'd been in a relationship.

For the sake of the rest of our friends and the Kingdom, and out of respect for the feelings we once had for each other, we needed to try friendship on for size.

I just needed to get her to agree first. Luckily, I was very charming. She would see things my way in no time.

I wandered down the hall to a room I'd declared mine after Sera and I stopped sharing sleeping accommodations. My things were laid out on the bed and there were fresh linens on the bed.

I washed the grit of the day and the filth of the desert off of my exhausted body and climbed into bed, still thinking of Sera and how it felt to be thrown away from her this afternoon.

There was something gnawing at the inside of my chest and it seemed to get worse the more I replayed those frightful moments in my head. I clenched my hand into a fist and tried to ignore the memory of her hand being torn from mine.

I closed my eyes and felt sand all over me and an emptiness of my side where Sera should be.

I finally used Magic to push those traumatic thoughts away and fall asleep. Thinking of nearly losing her today did the opposite of what I needed my brain to do in order rest. Magic turned out to be the best sleep aid though and soon, I had stopped thinking of Seraphina and merely started dreaming of her.

Well, I didn't know if "dreaming" was the right word. More like having a horrific nightmare that I couldn't wake up from. I was stuck in a spinning vortex of sand and Sera stood just on the other side, but she wasn't safe. For some reason, I was the one that was safe, even in the midst of a cyclone. I reached out my hand, but she couldn't reach me. I did everything I could to get to her even though she merely stood there, watching me. No matter how hard I fought she always remained out of reach. I was panicked and hysterical. And then, I was jolted awake by another explosion.

My eyes popped open and for a long minute I lay there wondering why I was awake and what had awakened me. Slowly my sleep-addled brain came to life and the distant sound of screaming penetrated my hazy brain.

Then the entire house seemed to explode. Well, not exactly. I was apparently far removed from wherever the explosion took place, but I still felt the residual effects. The bed rocked beneath me and plaster rained down from the ceiling.

I shot up to sitting and listened for a moment longer. A door down the hall opened and then slammed shut. I heard footsteps sprinting down the hall and then a male voice- Xander's maybe?- shouted back down our secluded corridor, "We're under attack!"

Just as he finished his warning, another explosion bombarded the building, this time much closer to me.

A vase shifted to the end of a priceless, antique vanity and tipped over the edge, shattering all over the floor. The sound of it shattering snapped me into action and I jumped to my feet. I yanked on jeans and shoved my feet into shoes while I stumbled around the room searching out a shirt.

I finally found one at the bottom of my suitcase and grabbed it as I sprinted from the room. I stopped at Sera's door just as she pulled it open, looking adorably disheveled with her blonde hair in a wild ponytail and silk pajama pants twisted around her waist.

"What's wrong?" she croaked. Her eyes stopped at my bare chest and her eyebrows scrunched in confusion. "Why are you naked?"

I would have laughed except another explosion pulsed through the building and we both fell to our arses. I landed awkwardly on her sprawled out legs and tried to untangle myself, but somehow ended up on top of her, my length covering her.

"What's going on?" she whispered.

"We need to find out."

I put my hands on her waist, feeling the longing of familiarity in our positioning. God, this woman could infuriate me beyond measure, but all it took was this. This touch. Her body. Her against me. And I was a lost man.

I helped her to her feet and then reached down for my shirt. We avoided eye contact as we moved over debris and broken glass from various antiques that had met there end.

"It has to be-"

"Put your shirt on," she whispered fiercely at me.

"I will."

"Now, Sebastian. Put it on *now*."

I tried not to smile as I wrestled the t-shirt on. The smile quickly disappeared when we rounded the corner and came upon some of Terletov's goons.

They probably would have had the upper hand had we not caught them by just as much surprise. They were in the middle of kicking a door open and searching the inside.

Seraphina and I immediately jumped into action. I took out the first goon quietly. I wrapped my arm around his neck and drove him to the ground. He let out a strangled cry for help, but his gun dislodged from his hand and clattered away.

I used my Magic against his as we fought to take each other out. Seraphina must have retrieved the gun because I heard it fire several times while I wrestled around on the floor.

The bastard managed to get a painful hit in my kidneys. I flinched and he landed another punch on my jaw. My head jerked back from the impact, but I blocked his next hit with my Magic. I bore down on him with as much energy as I could, strangling him with my energy.

He made gurgling sounds as he struggled to fight my superior hold. His Magic fought back, but while physically he might have been superior in strength, my Magic was by far the more admirable competitor.

I had just about knocked him out when I felt a searing pain slice over my ribs. I sucked in a breath and held it, hoping to stay the pain.

No luck.

My side lit up with fiery pain. I refused to release my grip on this idiot, but black dots danced in front of my vision as I struggled against the pain. I couldn't think outside of the pain.

And because of the pain, I started to become extremely weak.

In fact, I felt more than extremely weak. I felt unbearably weak. Before I could sort out what happened, I was on the ground, my face smashed into the marble floor and the hot flow of blood soaking through my clothes.

"Sebastian!" Seraphina screamed.

I watched her out of one eye, from a sideways position, slide across the dust-coated floor in bare feet. She lunged for the man who'd stabbed me and shot him in the face with the deadly gun.

Not only did she destroy the man's ugly face, she shot him with his own weapon. I hope the bastard died on the spot.

Because it seemed I was going to as well.

I pressed my hand against my side and it came away sticky and drenched with my own blood.

It also came away coated in my Magic.

He'd stabbed me with the killing kind of sword.

Damn.

I flopped to my back and stared into Sera's cerulean eyes. "Sera-"

"Shut up," she hissed furiously. "You're not dying. Don't even think you can get out of this so easily."

"Get out of what?"

"*Shut up,* Sebastian!" She sounded so serious that I felt like I had no choice. One of us needed to figure out what to do. It sure as hell wasn't me. So I might as well listen to the boss-lady. "Stand up," she ordered.

Except for that.

"I can't." My voice was a pathetic groan that I was embarrassed of.

I had no intentions of dying this way. If I had to go, I wanted it to be in the heat of battle, I wanted it to be with a sword across my throat and not a second to ponder my departure from this world. I wanted it to be epic and memorable.

I wanted it to be so momentous that they turned the day into a holiday.

I did not want it to be whilst I rolled around on the parquet floor in my Manchester United t-shirt.

However, my wishes didn't seem to line up with what was actually happening. And even though I *wanted* to stand up and obey the cruel tyrant shouting orders at me from her lovely mouth, I couldn't.

No matter how much Magic I pushed into my bones and muscles, my body simply didn't want to move.

"I'm going to get help," Seraphina informed me. "You're useless."

I would have argued with her if that wasn't true. Besides she sounded terrified. And if I had to die, I at least had the satisfaction that she cared enough to want me to live.

"Hurry," I told her.

She looked down at me for a second longer. "If someone comes by, just play dead. They'll probably believe you."

Then she was gone.

Probably? *They'll probably believe me?*

She could have at least given me a gun!

As it happened though, nobody ventured down this hallway. This wing we were staying in was pretty secluded from the rest of the palace. The Royals lived on the second floor and on opposite sides of the house. Seraphina and I stayed in what could be considered converted servant's quarters.

The current regime had long ago done away with servants, in favor of paying their employees generously. They also allowed them to live off premises, except for the Titan Guard, but their quarters were underground.

Since I knew now that Terletov was behind the attack, I could safely assume that he was after the Royals.

I listened to the sound of boots stomping and guns firing, as I lay helpless and waiting. The world around me came in and out of focus and my hazy gray Magic danced in the air around me. I tried to grasp it. I tried to shove it back inside of me.

But it would not go.

Stubborn Magic.

Difficult Magic.

Magic like a woman I knew.

I must have lost consciousness completely because the next thing I knew my entire body ached from head to toe. It felt like I'd been slammed in the back with a semi and my head screamed from a pain I was confident would never go away.

"You didn't have to drop him!" a familiar voice shrieked loudly.

"I didn't mean to."

"Let me see him," a different voice said. "We don't have any time. I need to do this quickly."

I started to black out again, but I felt better about it. My body started to warm and buzz pleasantly. A sense of peace settled over me and I couldn't help but want to smile.

I had no idea if I actually smiled because soon I was drifting in a different world, only I knew, instinctively, that it was a world I was supposed to be in, a world that I wanted to be in.

The next time I woke up was to shouting.

Lots of whispered-shouting.

And I didn't wake slowly.

I jerked awake in the middle of cramped bodies in a very dark place. It took a while for my Magic to adjust. Every part of me felt sluggish and slow. My side especially felt very tender.

I looked around in the dark and made out the faces of my friends and family. We were in a large cupboard in the kitchen. I recognized it after a few moments of staring blankly at the food stored along the shelves.

Kiran's strong hand on my shoulder helped bring me out of a daze. "Good to have you back, Cousin."

"Good to be back," I whispered. That was when my memory decided to return. I'd been stabbed, nearly to death. Someone had healed me... A voice. A few voices?

Eden.

I turned to my cousin-in-law, who sat huddled in the corner with a baby held tightly against her chest. "Thank you."

She pursed her lips and shook her head. "As if there was any other option."

"What's the plan?" My voice stayed a near-silent whisper.

"We need to get to the backyard," Kiran whispered. He also held a sleeping baby in his arms. "Eden apparently knows of a tunnel that will lead us out of here." There was a sarcastic edge to his voice and I almost smiled.

Eden trying to kill Kiran... those were the good old days.

"Terletov," Avalon growled.

"He knows about the babes?"

Avalon nodded gruffly. "He won't get them."

I nodded. Of course, he wouldn't. There was not a scenario in this world in which anyone in this pantry would let that demonic monster take these precious infants.

I looked to my left at Seraphina, who sat with her back to the shelves and her fingers tapping nervously on her bent knees. Terletov would get none of these people. Not one of them.

But just as I'd had those thoughts, the man himself came bursting into the kitchen with raucous behavior and what sounded like at least ten men. They filled the large room with fast precision and started tearing it apart in the next second.

I could hear Terletov bark orders and his men's boots stomp around and rip open cupboards and drawers and wherever else they imagined we could be found.

Shite.

Not one of us moved as they continued to search the room. We had an advantage of being somewhat hidden away. We were really stashed away in a pantry within a pantry. And nobody had dared use our Magic to even quiet our movements for fear they would sense it.

There was a half window at the back of this room. I could just barely make it out between the top of a shelf and the ceiling. I tapped Avalon's shoulder and pointed to our only hope. He nodded, moving stealthily to open it. I held my breath while he silently swung the pane down.

He gestured at Titus, the biggest man in our group, and helped him jump up and squeeze through the window. Titus couldn't manage to do this entirely without sound and my head felt close to exploding while we waited for him to clear the space. Xander and Xavier crawled through next, so they could provide cover for the women and children. I knew they used Magic to muffle their movements and I just had to hope Terletov's men couldn't pick up on it.

This was too much stress. Even for me.

When a goon searched the front pantry, I had to close my eyes to keep myself in check. Every instinct inside of me screamed to bust through this wall and kill the man that would dare come after innocent babies or my friends.

But that was the thing.

The infants were in the room, as well as both Kings and Queens, and Sylvia and Anjelica, who did not stand a chance against Terletov and his forces.

Roxie and Seraphina were also in here. Jericho and the human Immortal sisters were nowhere to be found, but I decided that might be a good thing.

My heart pounded in my chest and I swore it would give us away. I struggled to labor out my breathing, but I was beyond rational thinking at this point. Fight or flight had kicked in and I would do anything to fight for the survival of these people that I loved. Seraphina, my sister and the babies were at the top of that list, but everyone in here meant something tremendous to me.

"Move on," Terletov called out in a thin, reedy voice.

Whoever was searching the cupboard didn't hesitate. I heard him immediately pull back and rejoin Terletov.

But just as their boots cleared out, and their voices started to drift down the hallway, Gavriel let out a bleat of unhappiness. Kiran immediately turned him in his arm and offered him the tip of his father's finger, but the little guy was too hungry to be tricked.

He made just one more small sound before a pacifier could be shoved in his mouth.

It was too late.

As if in one, synchronized movement, the retreat on the outside of the pantry stopped. Completely.

Silence screamed at us from the other side of the false wall. I swear I could hear Terletov mulling over what he thought he might have heard. I felt it crawl over my skin and sink into my nerves.

I didn't know how many of them would be on the other side if they were to discover us in here, but I did know we would be rounded up for capture.

Or worse.

We had practically gift-wrapped ourselves for them.

And I would not let that happen.

Sylvia and Amelia had made it out the window. Eden was halfway through and passing Amari off to someone on the other side. Kiran stood with Gavriel in his arms while he shared meaningful looks with Avalon. Angelica had yet to make it through the window. And Seraphina sat next to me, shaking with nerves.

Shite.

I stood up on still-shaking legs and moved to the exit. I heard Kiran whisper something from behind me, but I was too focused on my goal to bother listening to his reprimand. A hand clutched my knee, but I shook it free by soundlessly sliding the door to the side. I slipped into the dark pantry and shot one last glance back at my cousin. I gave Kiran a cheeky wave and then darted into the kitchen.

Terletov had been staring in the direction of the pantry, but the doorway had obscured me until I came directly into view.

"Oh, I thought you'd gone."

"Where did you come from?" His thick Russian accent sounded more slurred than I remembered from before. His color had significantly paled as well.

He was a weak, monstrous version of himself and I nearly smiled at his obvious misery.

"I just popped down here for a midnight snack. Didn't expect to run into another houseguest." My tone sounded flippant, but my heart hammered violently in my chest.

Seraphina suddenly stumbled out behind me, stretching seductively and blinking at Terletov with wide-eyed confusion.

"Bastian?" she murmured with all the sex-kitten sultriness I knew she was capable of. She rested her hands on my shoulder and pressed her body against my back. "I wondered where you went to."

"My men searched that room," Terletov pointed out.

I shared a smug look with Seraphina and murmured, "Not very well."

Terletov growled out a very unhappy sound. "Take them," he ordered his men. "This is the prince."

"I'm not a prince," I argued out of principle.

I wasn't a prince.

Why didn't anyone ever get that I had given that title up? I gave it up!

"It doesn't matter," Terletov grinned at me. "You're coming with us."

"Thank you, but we'll decline."

"You don't have an option." He raised a gun that trembled in his hands and I raised my hands in submission. I did not want to go through the pain of death again.

I would do almost anything to avoid it actually.

"We'd rather not."

"Bag them," he ordered. "But don't hurt them too badly. Yet."

"That sounds ominous," I mumbled to Seraphina. She clutched me tightly and breathed in my ear. I could feel her Magic trembling around me. I glared at her. She should have stayed inside the hiding place. I had this covered!

I was the only one that was supposed to go!

What had she been thinking?

"And then search the cupboard again," he went on. "Make sure we didn't miss-"

Another explosion detonated painfully close. I wrapped my arms around Seraphina's waist and clutched her to me. I needed this as much as she did right now.

I glanced around frantically for a weapon or something to fight these people off with, but the gun pointed at Sera happened to be incentive enough for me to behave.

One of Terletov's men popped his head in the kitchen looking completely insane with pinpricks for pupils and wild hair. "Boss, they're coming."

"How many?"

The guy shrugged. "At least twelve. They have explosives too."

"The King? The Queen? Where are they?"

Nobody answered. Nobody knew.

Except Seraphina and me.

Another explosion. Closer.

"Move!" Terletov screamed. "Now!"

His violent tone propelled his men into action. Seraphina and I were suddenly swept up in their departure-chaos. We clung to each other, reaching for each other's hands and staying pressed against one another.

I didn't want to do this. It was guaranteed torture and general awfulness.

But I didn't see a way out or a way to leave Sera here and out of this. She was in this now, whether she wanted to be or not.

Whether I wanted her to be or not.

Chapter Sixteen

Seraphina

Hours later, *many* hours later, I crawled to the middle of my "cell" and dropped to the floor in agony.

My prison cell, a converted room in the castle, had been completely emptied out. No drapes hung over the large windows, no furniture adorned the now-cold space and no rugs covered the hard stone floor.

We were back in the Citadel, but I could hardly recognize this once vibrant star of the Kingdom.

Not even under Lucan's tyranny had this place felt so stark and purely evil.

Every inch of my body ached and thrummed with pain. I felt my heartbeat all over. It pulsed and throbbed as if the very beats pounded too harshly for my sensitive body. My blood seared with fiery agony and my brain wanted nothing more than to shut down completely.

They hadn't taken my Magic or infused me with anything else, but they had tortured me until I couldn't have told them the truth if I wanted to. The torture made me delirious and my thoughts confused and jumbled.

A body landed next to me, limp and hardly breathing.

I lifted my head just long enough to make out Sebastian's unconscious body crumpled in an awkward position.

Although I wanted to help him, but it took a very long time before I could summon the strength and convince my body to cooperate. I pulled on his shoulder until his body flopped to his back. I kicked out his legs so that he could be semi-comfortable.

Or as comfortable as possible on a stone floor with nothing to soften the hard rock.

I heaved my body the rest of the way and collapsed on top of him. It hurt to touch him, to touch anything really. But I needed something to hold me together. I needed to grab onto the fragile pieces of myself that threatened to shatter into a million broken fragments after what I just went through.

And I hoped the closeness would be good for Sebastian too. I had followed him deliberately. I couldn't let him go through this alone. I couldn't let him suffer for all of us alone. I couldn't let him take the brunt of Terletov's wrath or give that monster a reason to keep searching.

But I probably should have taken some more time to think this through.

Like thirty more seconds.

Then I would have realized what I signed up for and what a colossal mistake it would be.

Instead, I'd seen Sebastian throw himself through the false door and panic. Since when did he get so martyr-ish?

And why had my heart stopped beating completely when his body disappeared?

He groaned next to me and I shifted my body so he could stretch out more comfortably, although that was its own personal joke. There was no way we would feel "comfortable" while we were here.

Not on the unforgiving floor and not when Terletov felt the desire to ask us more questions.

His methods of interrogation weren't exactly hospitable.

"Sera?" Sebastian croaked.

"I'm here," I whispered through tears. I would not let this psychopath break me. I was strong. Or, maybe not. But I could *be strong*.

I would be strong for this Kingdom and for the man next to me.

"Are you alive?"

I would have laughed if my lungs didn't burn so intensely. "As alive as you are."

Sebastian squirmed under me and managed to wrap his arm around my waist. His fingers slid beneath my tattered silk cami and held me tightly to him.

Word of advice, if you're going to be kidnapped, and then tortured *for hours*, try to wear something that is not silk pajamas.

"I have to say, this little adventure is living up to all of my expectations."

This time I did snort. "I would love to be as cavalier about this as you are."

His arm tightened around my waist and he shifted again so that we lay facing each other. "You shouldn't have come, Sera. You should have stayed with Eden and Kiran."

"You should have too. You were an idiot to do what you did."

"And you were an idiot to follow me."

"Fine, I accept that."

His face was bloodied and bruised. Eventually, our Magic would work its way through our battered bodies, but this kind of damage would take time to heal. And there were parts of us that might not ever heal; spiritual, emotional parts that would recall these hours until the day we died.

Terletov and his crazy brother, Alexi, had abused us until we were useless. And then he locked us away for our bodies to piece back together, just so he could start all over again later. He wanted to know where Eden and Kiran were; more specifically he wanted as much information on the babies as possible.

Clearly, he had a spy at the London palace. And he really, *really* wanted those babies.

Which scared the ever-living hell out of me.

"Sera, we're going to make it out of here alive. I won't let him... let him..."

"Kill me."

"Yeah, that."

My lips pushed up into a soft smile, despite my belief that I might not ever smile again. "It's alright, Sebastian. I'm not asking you to protect me."

"You don't have to ask. I will protect you whether you want me to or not. I've always wanted to Sera, that won't change now. Especially not now."

I hummed something that sounded like disbelief. "I can't believe we're here. We were supposed to catch him, not the other way around."

"I'm sorry I dragged you into this."

"Don't be." My hands rested on his chest and I felt his heart beat more normally beneath my open palms. The feeling was comforting, *so comforting*. I wanted to keep it beating. I wanted to be the very reason it beat to begin with. But that was silly. That part of my life was over. I wasn't Sebastian's reason for anything anymore. And he wasn't mine either. Lying in his arms while I went through a life and death experience might just ruin me forever.

But what could I do?

Nothing could make me leave this place until, well, until something actually made me leave it. Like Terletov and his merry band of insurgents.

And nothing could have kept me from following after Sebastian when I knew he was going to kill himself.

"I like you here with me," Sebastian said on a raw whisper. "I should have realized this sooner."

My breath caught and my stomach flipped. "What do you mean?"

"I was afraid of this, Sera. I was afraid I'd drag you into something we couldn't fight our way out of. I was afraid you'd get hurt. I was afraid I wouldn't be able to protect you from everything you needed to be protected from."

"You mean something like this?"

"I mean something exactly like this."

"I'm not breakable, Bastian. I'm stronger than you think." My words came out in a shaky whisper that contradicted them completely. But I meant it. I wasn't fragile or weak or incapable. I had trained for circumstances like these as long as Sebastian had and I had always known I could end up somewhere just like this or worse. Even when Lucan was in charge.

"I can see that," he murmured. "And now that we're in this bloody place, I realize how nice it is to have you with me."

A sound came out of me that would have been laughter if my lungs didn't feel bruised and beaten. "Oh, this is *so* nice."

"I'm not alone though." The arm that held me around my waist squeezed weakly. "And I like that I'm not alone. This would have been hell to go through all by myself. And I have this nice, warm, body to comfort and console me. I should have thought of that before."

"Mmm."

He dipped his head and nestled in the curve of my neck. "You know, this might be our last night alive." I felt the slow burn of a trail of kisses across my collarbone. Even in this much pain, my skin tingled and my heartbeat picked up. "We don't want to waste it."

"Are you hitting on me?"

"I'm making the most of an opportunistic moment."

I should have pushed him away. I really, truly should have. But he had started kissing up my neck and I knew we were physically not capable of taking this further than these sweet, but oh, so hot, kisses.

His mouth was warm as it marked a sizzling path along my throat. My breath hitched again and my head swam with fuzzy thoughts and nostalgic memories.

I found my hands gripping his biceps with what little strength I had left. His body moved closer to mine until we were pressed chest against chest, hips against hips. His teeth nibbled at my earlobe and then tenderly bit down on the curve of my jaw.

His playful nipping turned to more kisses as he seared his mouth along my jaw. I licked my lips and prepared for his next move. He would kiss me on the mouth. I had this routine memorized. Our physical relationship had *never* been boring, but after so many years together, I had come to know what to expect... what to anticipate.

His lips hovered over mine, but he did not seal them together. He stayed there, so close but not touching. I felt every inch of his hard body as we lay there length to length. I felt his damaged, tortured Magic revived with purpose to pulse and surge and wrap around mine with tight, inseparable union. And yet he didn't kiss me.

Wouldn't kiss me.

"Sebastian?"

"Sera, I want to..."

"But?"

"No, but," he said quickly. "I want to kiss you and I will. And when I do, you should know that it means-"

The door slammed open and both of us jumped and held tighter to each other. Angry, sick men filled the doorway with guns raised. They filed into the room and surrounded us.

I didn't exactly feel embarrassed to be caught in Sebastian's arms. None of these men really knew us and I could care less if they used this opportunity to judge me. Although, I didn't really think they would. They could probably equally care less about my ex-boyfriend drama.

However, it was still an uncomfortable feeling to be caught like this. We were vulnerable. *I* was vulnerable, more so than I had ever been before in my life.

And also, I felt stupid.

What did it mean to Sebastian to kiss me? Nothing? Everything? Nothing?

God, what timing these assholes had!

"The girl," the sniveling, heavily accented voice called from the doorway.

I tore my eyes off of the men surrounding us and turned them to Dmitri Terletov. And immediately recoiled. He looked like death personified. His pasty skin glistened with sweat and grease. His shoulders sagged and forced him to hunch over and his hair looked stringy and thinner than the last time I saw him- a half hour ago.

This man was not well.

And yet, he'd captured the Citadel and commanded an unknown number of men who killed for him, who tortured for him, who sacrificed their own lives at his whim.

One of his men made a move toward me. My Magic had only just started to gain strength again and my body was broken. The thought of going through his interrogation made me want to... not go through it again... do whatever it took to *never ever ever* go through it again.

"Too much of a coward to get her yourself?"

I looked up at those words and shot Sebastian a sharp look. His attention was focused on Terletov though, so he didn't see it.

What was he doing?

He was going to get us both killed!

"Coward?" Terletov snorted. "Hardly."

"But you are one, aren't you? Only a coward would command other men to die for him without any sacrifice to himself."

Terletov shot off the doorframe. His stolen Magic swelled with his anger and I felt it push against mine. He was furious and crazed in his fury. Spittle pooled in the corners of his mouth, making him appear rabid and deranged.

"Those men died for a cause, not for me. A cause we all believe in."

Sebastian threw his head back and mocked Terletov's conviction with a laugh. I wondered where Bastian had gotten the energy to move like that. I could barely lift my head.

"A cause? This is a cause? Killing people? *Torturing* people? That's your *cause*?"

"Cleansing the Kingdom," Terletov spat. "*That's* my cause."

Sebastian tipped his head down and leveled Terletov with a look that would kill him if it could. "This Kingdom doesn't need to be cleansed. The rightful King and Queen rule our people. It was their bloodline that was intended to rule from the beginning. The Magic is free because of them. We are Immortal because of Eden and Avalon. And the only thing your insignificant little cause is cleaning is the dust off the Kingdom's loyalty to them. No true Immortal would ever listen to what you have to say or follow you. No true Immortal would waste their eternal time on an imposter."

Terletov's gray eyes flashed with sinister fury. "We are the only true Immortals, you sycophantic dog."

"True Immortals don't have to *steal* Magic in order to do something as simple as breathe."

I sucked in a silent gasp, but then let out a scream when Terletov's booted foot swung out and landed in Sebastian's side.

Sebastian arched off the ground from the impact, holding in every sound. He didn't even grunt. His back settled back on the ground and his arm flopped uselessly to his side. He was as weak as I was, maybe weaker since his pain was fresher.

I wanted to yell at him for making Terletov so angry, especially since it was apparently my turn to go get tortured. I didn't know why Sebastian was provoking this evil man. It would only mean evil things for both of us.

I thought it was over though. I assumed they would pick me up and drag me back to their torture chambers.

I thought wrong.

Sebastian looked up at Terletov, and with a cocky brow raised, he started laughing. "So defensive," Sebastian chuckled. "Tell me, how much does it bother you that the Queen has your Magic. She has it at her fingertips and she knows how to give it back to you and she won't. She could do it from where she is now. She could do it with the flick of her fingers or a passing thought. She could make you whole again. And yet... she doesn't. And even better, she doesn't have to. Because she is the rightful heir to the throne and you are just a poser. You *will always be* a poser."

Terletov didn't stop with kicking this time. He threw his Magic at Sebastian with violent force. He knocked him around the room. He beat Sebastian's head against the ground. Terletov didn't stop until Sebastian coughed up blood and his breaths rattled and wheezed.

"I've changed my mind," the monster said to his minions. "Take the prince first. I have something special for his royal highness."

"No," I whispered.

Sebastian reached out quicker than I thought was possible in his current state and squeezed my wrist hard. I looked at him, eyes wide and desperate. I would take this for him. He couldn't go like this because he would die.

He would.

Terletov would kill him for everything he said.

I started to volunteer, "Take-"

"Something special?" Sebastian rasped out. "So you've felt it too?"

Terletov stilled for a long moment before taking the bait. "Felt what?"

"The heat between us."

"The heat?"

"The attraction. The sizzling chemistry. The white-hot sexual tension. I feel it too, Dmitri."

Terletov's eyes flashed with understanding and apparently he did *not* feel the sexual tension between them.

Oh, geez, Sebastian. Could he not take anything seriously?

"Pick him up," Terletov snapped in a low voice. "Now!" he screamed.

His men quickly obeyed. Two of them jumped forward and grabbed him roughly. They picked him up by his arms, one on each side of him, so that his body from the waist down dragged on the ground. He didn't even put up a fight. In fact, I swore I saw him smother a grin.

What the hell was he up to?

Terletov marched from the room without giving me a backward glance. His men followed obediently behind him. The last to leave the room dragged Sebastian with him.

I pushed into sitting and stared at him leaving, unable to reconcile what just happened. Terletov had already promised to hurt us, to *not stop hurting* us! So why had Sebastian gone to such lengths to piss him off even more?

I couldn't catch my breath as I watched him go. I didn't know if I would ever see him again. I didn't know what would happen to him. There was a very good chance Terletov would kill him!

I didn't have any strength or energy, every muscle, bone and blood vessel in my body screamed with pain. But I still scrambled to kneeling. I would follow after him. I would fight. I would do whatever it took to keep Terletov from hurting him.

"Seraphina!" Sebastian barked from the doorway. He'd finally started to put up a fight. The guards looked annoyed.

My eyes flew to his and I begged him to keep fighting, to refuse to go.

Instead, he said, "Stay. *Please*."

The breath whooshed out of me and I felt helpless. Why was he doing this?

He relaxed as soon as I stopped struggling to stand up. The guards resumed dragging him from the room. And then just before he was through the door, he looked over his shoulder and winked at me.

The door slammed behind him and I heard locks click into place. I was alone again.

And it wasn't until I was alone that I realized what Sebastian had done.

He'd done that for me.

He'd stopped Terletov from having me taken to be tortured.

Sebastian did all of that for me.

Chapter Seventeen

Sebastian

Alright. This could be over now.

And if the bloke screaming at the top of his lungs would keep it down a pinch, that would be fantastic.

Oh, I was the bloke screaming at the top of his lungs.

I hadn't meant to scream, or make any sound, really.

I felt a little like a pansy. Until the next electroshock of misery shot through my Magic and wrung another pained holler at out of me.

My stomach churned with sickness. The pain was so intense my body shook and shivered from it. But it wasn't just the agonizing torture that got to me, it was the way Terletov went about inflicting pain.

Everything inside of me screamed that this was wrong, unnatural. Nothing should be able to touch my Magic like this. Nothing should be able to worm inside my very essence and twist and destroy and change what made me. This was my *life*. This Magic inside of me defined my very atoms and DNA. And Terletov had the power to scrape away at it until I knew that it would never be the same again.

He could turn my Magic into something ugly and less than what it should be.

And I hated him for that.

But not just for me. I hated him for all of the others he'd done this to already. I hated him for the humans that he'd kidnapped to experiment on and for turning them something that was unnatural and wrong for them.

And I really, truly, utterly hated him for touching Seraphina, for planning this despicable thing for her and her beautiful Magic.

I would not let that happen. I would not let him get near her and carry through with his sadistic methods of interrogation.

I would also never reveal Eden and Kiran's whereabouts.

Which probably meant I would die.

I didn't bother to follow that thought trail any further. I opted to start screaming again instead. That seemed a much more prudent use of my time.

My Magic seared through my body. But it didn't stop there. My aura, the Magic that hovered around me, and could be used to manipulate the physical world, ached as well. I could feel pain everywhere. I breathed pain. My heart beat with pain. My thoughts were wholly consumed with pain. And I knew it would never end.

Terletov wouldn't take my Magic because he wanted to keep me alive. Turning me into an empty husk that would wither and die would serve no purpose for him. He would keep me alive, but just barely. He would use me to leverage something he wanted.

Or maybe not.

Maybe he would continue to torture me without ever offering a trade. He probably believed he could eventually break me if he put on the right amount of pressure.

This fun little spa treatment he gave me today would never end. My future would be filled with days like this, all to get me to give him information that I could not.

Where was Eden and Kiran?

Truthfully, I had no idea.

Where were the babies?

Again... no clue.

What was my name again?

I'd forgotten that hours ago.

It would be useless to torture me. I had nothing to give him.

Then again, maybe he didn't want anything. Maybe he simply liked to be a cruel bastard and torturing me gave him the sick thrill to go on living.

Which clearly he could barely do on his own. He wasn't exactly a shining picture of health.

"Had enough, Prince?"

I grunted through the agony. The punishing feeling of something blazing through me had eased for the moment, but my body felt broken on the table. Only my skin held together the fragmented pieces that had shattered inside of me.

My Magic stuttered and stumbled as it tried to get to work healing my body. But it was just as broken. I couldn't make anything function properly, not my limbs, not my Magic and most certainly not my thoughts.

"The artist formerly known as." My words came out as a hoarse jumble.

"What was that?" Terletov took a step forward so his rodent-like face intruded my hazy vision.

"I go by the artist formerly known as. I'm no longer a prince. So you can stop referring to me as one."

A sneer turned his thin lips and his empty eyes regarded me with contempt. "The Kendrick's are still the royal family du jour, are they not?"

I didn't say anything, for the obvious reason that I'd used all my speaking abilities on sarcasm.

"They are," he answered for me. "That liar of a Queen promised that she would destroy them. *All of them*. And yet, the Kendrick heir still wears the crown and now his bloodline has been extended."

I was wrong. I managed to find more energy to speak. "Weren't Lucan and you buddies?"

His lip curled in disgust. "I did what I had to in order to survive."

I made a sound. I hoped it sounded like mocking laughter. "How's that working out for you?"

Alexi cut in, "You're awfully cavalier for the position you're in. I would be more frightened if I were you." Dmitri's brother looked just as sickly and near-death as the older Terletov. Only Alexi was still spry. He was the one that had been put in charge of carrying out the torture. Terletov bellowed out a command and Alexi jumped obediently.

I couldn't wait to kill them both.

"You're not the first person to tell me that." I pushed up with one elbow so I could look them both in the eyes. I tried not to wince or groan, but I didn't entirely succeed. "It doesn't matter what you do to me, or the lengths you go to survive, you will not win. You will not control this Kingdom. And you will not touch our Kings or Queens. You've already lost. And by the looks of it, you're both already on the way to the afterlife. I'm not frightened of anything because *there is nothing to be frightened of*."

The lines around Terletov's mouth pulled tight as he puckered his lips and scowled at me. Fury radiated off of him and his murderous look promised more pain.

I used the last ounces of energy to sweep the room and search for a way out. There was only one door to this room. This used to be the Titan Guard quarters before Terletov moved in.

I had grown up in this castle, I knew every in and out, every nook and cranny. I also had a vague idea of an escape plan piecing together in my splintered mind. I would need to save my strength though. Somehow I would need to gather some mobility and kick my Magic into gear.

I could easily figure out how to get out of here, but unless I could find the energy to run, we wouldn't make it very far.

I hoped that Seraphina was in a better position than me. If she could run or even walk quickly, we might be able to make it out of here alive.

"We have the Citadel," Alexi snarled.

Terletov grunted a sound of agreement and said, "I have men with unprecedented strength and the means and prominence to bend this Kingdom to my will."

I collapsed back on the steel table and resigned myself to another monologue. "But you don't have the loyalty of the people."

"I don't need the loyalty of the people when I have their fear!" His voice roared through the room and only added to the splitting headache that threatened to rip my skull in half.

I turned my head slightly so I could look him directly in the eyes and say, "Tell that to Lucan. Oh, right. You can't because he's dead. Loyalty means more to these people than fear ever will. And you'll only ever have fear. You'll never be the kind of leader that rules the people in a way that makes them *want* to respond. You can take over the Citadel, but when Eden is not here, or Avalon or Amelia or Kiran, this place is just empty buildings to them. This Kingdom has never been a people tied to one specific place and you should know that. This Kingdom exists outside of the realm of time and place and war. They no more recognize you as their leader than they would me. You are not their chosen King. The Magic did not anoint you. And the Magic does not bow down to you. If you come to terms with that now, you might just be able to live through this."

Terletov glowered at me with the hatred of a man that truly knew how to hate. I watched the wheels click and turn in his head; I watched his features sharpen into harsh lines and unforgiving angles. I watched him decide how to murder me.

He was tired of my truth and my perspective.

That was fine with me since I was very much tired of his ugly face glaring down at me.

However, I wasn't quite ready to die just yet.

I at least had to find a way for Seraphina to be rid of all this. And then find a way for her to fall back in love with me.

And after that, I needed to figure out a way to get her to agree to marry me.

Then there would be the babies.

And the happily ever after.

I smiled despite my circumstances. Seraphina had felt bloody wonderful pressed against me on the floor. She had been sweet, warm and pliable next to me.

I knew how her mind worked. She would chalk those moments up to life or death experiences and an uncertain future. But I'd also felt the pull of her Magic and the delicious familiarity of her hands exploring my chest.

She wasn't as over me as she'd like me to believe. And at this moment, I didn't care what brought us back together. I didn't care that this war was the reason we'd split to begin with or that we had to be tortured- literally- to realize how much we still cared for each other.

I was just happy to have finally come to terms with the fact that I would never be over her. I would never stop caring for her, stop loving her. It was time to give up trying and start working to win her back.

She would have reservations, those were natural. She would also have fears and doubts and the natural inclination to muck things up.

But she also had feelings and hormones and a heart that once beat in sync with mine and Magic that pulsed together with mine.

She was welcome to resist me, to resist us. But I would win her over in the end.

She really didn't stand a chance.

Terletov's look soured at my expression. I had to look half-deranged. My entire body bent at weird angles, my face bloodied and uncomfortably swollen. And yet I smiled.

That was the thing about love. It was strange.

It made all men half-mad.

"I'm going to kill you now," Terletov promised.

"Do your worst," I grinned at him.

He grinned back. "I plan to."

And then he did.

The next few hours faded into ugliness. I lost consciousness more than once as pain overrode every sense and thought.

Terletov did his worst. He had not lied about that.

Unbearable misery became my reality. Terletov enjoyed hurting me, watching me suffer and writhe in agony. He laughed while he tortured me. Sometimes short, amused giggles. Sometimes long, psychotic cackles. His eyes practically twinkled as he used his evil skillset to destroy me.

Sometimes he would ask about Eden and Kiran. But for the most part I understood that this was sport for him, his hobby.

And his men didn't need an excuse from him. By their immediate obedience and constant silence, I saw how afraid of him they truly were. They maybe believed in his cause, but the man himself frightened even them.

Even Alexi cowered from his brother, afraid to set Dmitri off and have his anger turned the wrong direction.

The only thing that kept me grounded were thoughts of her. If I hadn't had Seraphina to focus on, to concentrate on, to remember and hope for, I would have given up and faded away.

Nobody should be able to withstand this amount of pain. Or be expected to come back from it a sane and rational Immortal.

But the entire time I kept our imagined future at the forefront of my wild thoughts. I pictured her by my side and in my bed. I envisioned our life together as we added children and a permanent place to live.

Maybe it would be in Seattle where she'd already chosen. Or maybe we'd spin a globe and see where our fingers landed.

I remembered her kisses from earlier this day and fantasized about kissing her again.

My body writhed in agony, but mind focused on what it would take to win her back.

A knock came at the door, but it took me a long time to process what it was. The torture eased some, but my mind swam with confusion. Blonde hair and blue eyes danced in front of me. I moved out of my body to catch the fragmented beauty dancing out of reach.

"This is unfortunate," a voice bemoaned.

I didn't listen. I couldn't.

"We'll have to pick this up later," the voice went on. It moved away from me and said, "Throw him back with the girl. No one touches him but me. Is that clear?"

I didn't hear another word until pain hit my back again. I came to and realized that I was in a different position. My muscles screamed and my bones threatened to turn to ash. I tried to move, but nothing in my body responded when I asked it to.

My thoughts started to drift again until I heard the sweetest sound in the world, "Sebastian."

I told my eyes to open, but they refused to obey. Something touched me and I wanted to scream out from this new pain, but no sound came out of me. The pain moved over me until I was in another new position.

That felt better.

The pressure came back and touched my face. That felt worse, but somehow better at the same time.

Hands, I realized.

I was back in our room and Seraphina was cradling my face.

I felt her warmth as she leaned over me and then the gentleness of her kiss when she pressed it to my forehead.

"Don't die, Bastian," she whispered on a sob. "Please don't die."

I felt myself smile. Maybe not on the outside, but on the inside. She might not love me like I could now admit I loved her, but she didn't want me to die. That was something.

At least a start.

I let myself relax in the cradle of her arms and the blackness came again.

The next time I came to, I was more coherent. Seraphina still held me in her lap. It was her whispered words that pulled me from the depths of the abyss.

I tried to move something belonging to my body and this time managed to shift my head.

She stilled immediately and gasped. "Sebastian? Are you awake?"

I groaned.

"I thought you were going to die," she hiccupped. I felt something wet hit my face before I realized she must be crying.

I groaned again to reassure her. It didn't seem to reassure her.

More wetness followed and she dropped down to lie next to me. Her warm, soft arms wrapped around me and she continued to whisper quickly. Too quickly for me to understand.

Purpose suffused my thoughts as I realized again where we were and what would happen to me if I didn't get my arse in gear.

I formed my words carefully and tried to shift my body without much success. She felt my wiggling and stopped the incessant mumbling, I was sure hadn't stopped since I left her here.

"Kiss me," I rasped.

"What?"

"Kiss me."

It was her turn to groan. "Sebastian, this is hardly the time or the place to be coming onto me. And you're not really-"

"Magic. I need your Magic."

"I don't really think-"

I willed my fingers to move until they tugged on her shirt. She stilled again. "Fuse them together and I can heal."

She didn't argue with me this time; however she didn't immediately attack my face either. She seemed to take in my solution and weigh it against every other possibility. If I would have been able to spar with her on equal footing, I would have reminded her that we had kissed fairly passionately not that long ago and this was a matter of life and death so she should probably get over her pompous pride and get to work making sure I didn't die.

Unfortunately, at this time I could only commit to one or two words at a time.

After long, stubborn moments, I finally felt the soft press of her lips against mine. They were warm and soft and felt like heaven. Slowly, she worked up her courage to give me more. And as she kissed me, her Magic released into mine.

It wasn't an easy connection. Mine felt nearly beyond repair. But slowly, with the help of her affectionate, attentive kisses, her Magic began to bring mine back to life.

My bones fused back together and my Magic was revived again. I felt energy enough to open my eyes and see this beauty in front of me.

At this moment, she saved me. But her salvation went beyond this near-death tragedy. So far beyond.

And she had no idea.

When my hands could grip her hips with some strength and I finally returned this life-saving kiss, she pulled back but left her Magic wrapped up with mine.

She stared into my eyes intently for stretched moments, her icy blue eyes dewy with emotion. "You'll live?"

I felt my lips turn up. "Not if we don't get out of here. He'll kill me if he gets a chance." A look of utter despair changed her relieved expression. "Don't worry, Sera. I have a plan."

She pulled back to survey my body. "Sebastian-"

I grinned at her. "When have I ever let you down before? Come on, this is the fun part."

Chapter Eighteen

Seraphina

I watched Sebastian pull himself to his feet and wondered how in the world he planned to get us out of this one.

He staggered over to the door and leaned heavily against it. I felt much better after the long hours I'd had to recuperate and especially after our little experiment in Magical making-out. However, he still looked like death. I had no idea what he thought he could accomplish in this state.

"The door is locked." I thought maybe he forgot.

He looked at me over his shoulder. "The door *handle* is locked with Magic."

"Right. That's what I just told you."

His drawn face lit with a cocky smile. "Do you know why Eden makes such a great Queen?"

Ten snarky comments sat on my tongue, but I swallowed them all except this one, "She's the only one that's been able to tolerate Kiran?"

He chuckled, but barely. "She constantly thinks like a human."

"And usually that gets her into trouble."

"But sometimes it gets her out of trouble." He fiddled with the doorjamb until the hinge popped apart in his hand. Then he moved to the middle one and then the top. I expected them to be stuck tight after centuries of Immortal staff ignoring them, but the pins were surprisingly slick and well-oiled.

I helped him with the last one, admiring the very old hinge-system I had never paid attention to, despite all of the time I spent in the castle. The door angled precariously, so I righted it by sticking my fingers through the crack in the bottom and holding it in place. As soon as he'd pushed the pin through the hinge, the door swung open.

We were free.

"That was disgustingly easy," I murmured.

Sebastian stuck his head into the hallway and looked from side-to-side. "That was disgustingly human, which is why they didn't expect it."

He reached for my hand and pulled me out into the hall. We crept along the cold, stone walls and moved slowly. I resisted the urge to push him. I knew we needed to hurry, any second they would discover we were gone, but I also knew he had to last longer than getting out of his castle. Sebastian had to save his energy or we were both dead.

The hallways were empty. I knew Terletov had an army, but it was still unclear exactly how many men he had at his disposal. Plus, I knew that we were not the only prisoners being held. Apparently, he kept enough men handy for terrorist attacks, but not enough to control his castle. Interesting.

"You can be clever when you want to be."

He looked back at me over his shoulder and his hazel eyes lit with something dark and enigmatic. I sucked in a breath and tried to ignore whatever emotion danced in those familiar depths.

"You have no idea."

I leaned forward and tried to lighten the mood. "I have *some* idea. I know you better than anyone."

The corner of his mouth pulled up, "I'm going to enjoy this, Sera. I can't believe it's taken me this long."

"What's taken you this long?"

"Shh," he ordered while seeming to switch gears. "You're going to get us caught."

Panic flared low in my belly and I ignored his warning. "What are you going to enjoy, Sebastian? What are you talking about?"

He pushed a finger to his lips and scowled at me, but his eyes brightened with amusement. I wanted to punch him. And I would have. Except I was afraid I would kill the poor guy.

There was something I didn't like about his tone though or his smug expression. Or his mysterious words. Or the heated look in his eyes. Or... just everything about him in general.

My mind spun with possibilities and continued to land on our healing kiss. Had that been more to him than the desperate act of fixing his broken Magic? Did he misread my intent?

I tried to shake those thoughts away and save them for when my life wasn't so dangerously on the line, but it wasn't possible. Sebastian headlined every single one of my thoughts. *The bastard.*

He knew his way around the castle better than I did. And even though the halls were darkened and the layout a maze of sharp turns and long corridors, he knew exactly where he wanted to go.

A few times I tugged on his sleeve to pull him back. One of Terletov's men would walk by seconds later and we would press ourselves against the wall and hope they didn't see us.

It had to be my psychic skills. I had never been this in-tuned with them before, but now they almost assaulted my senses. Instinct mingled with Magic, premonitions blended seamlessly with the innate ability to sense what was to come.

I needed confidence and experience though. I found it hard to trust myself. I wanted more control over my thoughts and feelings. This ability felt very much out of my control. It happened to me and I was forced to react and most of the time, I had to react quickly.

Whether this new intensity of ability was driven by circumstance or necessity, I wished I could have had some more time to figure it out before it was thrust upon me.

Although, it clearly kept saving our lives, so I couldn't complain too much.

Just as I had that thought, something sharp and blinding seared through my head. The pain came so quickly that I bent over at my waist and grabbed my knees. I thought for sure I would puke, and I was in too much pain to care or worry about it.

The pain in my head pulsed through the rest of my body. Blinding white light filled my vision behind closed eyelids. I heard myself whimper and then cringe at the added pain agony voice brought.

But then I saw it. My Magic was at work again and this time in a very important way.

When the pain passed and the nausea receded, I slowly pulled myself into standing again and registered Sebastian's firm grip on my shoulders. He moved to stand in front of me and brought my body to within an inch of his.

His hands rubbed a soothing path over my shoulders, up my neck and across my jaw until he cradled my face with his two big hands. "Sera?"

His words were a whisper, but I felt his deep concern all the way to my toes. "A vision," I whispered. "Analisa's not dead. She's here. Terletov's keeping her here."

His expression turned from worry to rage in a half-second. He dropped his hands and shot a furious glare in every direction. I reminded myself that she wasn't just Kiran's mother, but his aunt as well. She was family to Sebastian, and after what we'd just been through at Terletov's hands, I could understand his fury.

"Where?" he growled. "Where is she?"

"Not far."

"Then let's get her and get the hell out of here."

"Great idea."

I took the lead and moved as fast as I could. I gave in a little more to my stronger instincts with each passing moment. My Magic seemed to step up with the level of danger we were in.

Or maybe it had something to do with Sebastian's Magic still wrapped up with mine.

We hadn't been this free with our energies in over a year. We went from constantly a part of each other to nothing. When I pulled my Magic out of Sebastian's for good, I thought I would ache forever from the separation.

I thought not being with him would leave my Magic a diluted version of itself and I would never recover.

But my heart had felt that way too. Now that we were working together again and I had the unlimited resources of combined Magic, I wondered if my Magic had been waiting for this moment ever since we broke up.

Once I fought through the heartache and disappointment of losing the man I thought I would love forever, I assumed that my Magic had fought to restore itself too. Sure, I'd never felt absolutely perfect again or even vaguely like myself. But I had been a kid before Sebastian and I started anything. I was just eighteen and had gone through a different kind of heartbreak when I lost Kiran.

How was I supposed to know better?

How was I supposed to know I was supposed *to feel better*?

It was as we ran through the silent halls of the castle, toward the elderly Queen, that I realized I would have to go through that all over again. My heart might be more protected this time. And by that, I meant calloused and scarred, so it would be easier to recover. But my Magic would suffer just like before.

Only this time I would know the difference.

That thought alone was almost enough to make me separate from Sebastian. I could make the clean break now and save myself some pain later.

Except I couldn't.

If I wanted to get out of this alive and bring Sebastian and Analisa out of this intact too, I would have to suck it up and keep us connected. We did so much better together. We had energy. We had resources.

We had a chance in hell.

And that was all I could ask for right now.

I jumped back when our corridor came to a T. We could go right or left although instinct told me to go right. It also told me that the door hiding Analisa was heavily guarded.

"Down that way," I whispered as quietly as I could.

Sebastian's face flickered in the soft lighting that came from lit torches that lined the wall. The Citadel was equipped with electricity and every contemporary convenience, but it was a complicated system since everything modern had been added longer after the structure was built.

Magic could easily run any of the lights, fixtures or amenities, but I got the feeling that these people didn't have a lot of Magic to waste. So Terletov had reverted back to the old ways of torches and candles. Most of the windows had been draped with heavy, black curtains.

I hated the Citadel like this.

Of course, I would hate it no matter how Terletov kept it. But the bad lighting and constant scent of smoke and tinder made the atmosphere revert to the Dark Ages. This felt archaic even for Terletov.

Sebastian pulled me out of my lighting debate when he put two hands on my shoulders and backed me against the wall. Cold stone pressed into the thin fabric of my silk shirt and pants. His fingers dug into my shoulder blades and his palms rested over my collarbone. His thumb traced the hollow of my throat. I struggled to swallow and then struggled again when his thumb reached up and drew a delicate line over the movement.

"I need you to be quiet," he whispered just loud enough for me to make out.

He left me pressed against the wall as if I could do anything else but what he said. He seriously needed to tone down the charm or I wasn't going to make it through this little adventure of ours alive.

Next time he touched me like that or looked at me like that or spoke to me with such absolute command, I seriously worried that I might spontaneously combust.

Right there on the spot.

Damn him.

He leaned over me to see around the corner. When he pulled back and met my confused gaze, his expression was bleak.

"There's six of them."

And two of us with hardly any energy to spare and no weapons. Shoot.

He didn't say it, but I saw the concern written all over his face. *How were we going to get out of this?*

"I'll create a diversion," he whispered to me. "You get Analisa and meet me near the ballroom."

"The ballroom?"

"I know a way out."

My stomach tied itself into knots. I bit down on my bottom lip and struggled to come up with a different plan.

Any other plan.

"You're going to meet me in the ballroom?"

"Near the balcony doors," he continued to explain. "We'll run through the maze. There's a back door."

"I don't think it's a good idea to split up."

"Sera," he intoned. "None of this is a good idea. But it's the only idea we have. So, are you ready?"

"No."

A slow smile pulled at his full mouth. "Too bad."

"Sebastian-"

"You're the one that wanted to prove herself on missions. Am I wrong?" I pressed my lips together and refused to answer. I wanted to go on real missions, not willful attempts at suicide. Sebastian didn't need my response in order to make the rest of his argument. "I'm not wrong. You wanted to go. You knew you could be something that I didn't want you to have to be. Well, here's your chance. I'm going to go over there, create a diversion and you're going to sneak in that room by any means necessary and extract my aunt from it. Then you're going to keep running down this hallway until you get to the main staircase. You should be able to find your way to the ballroom from there."

"And if I get caught?"

He breathed out slowly. "Seraphina, listen to me, you are the most beautiful woman I have ever laid eyes on. You know how to smooth talk just about anything that can speak back to you. You know what to do if you get caught. But more importantly, don't get caught."

"Wise words."

He chucked me under the chin. "You've got three seconds until I leave you. I suggest you mentally prepare."

I winced an ugly, needy sound and immediately wanted to take it back, shove it in my mouth and swallow it completely. I sounded so weak.

And I wasn't weak.

Sebastian was right. I wanted this opportunity. I wanted to be treated as a real member of the original Resistance teams. But more, I wanted Sebastian to see me as valuable and important.

I wanted to be his peer, not just his trophy.

I had always wanted that.

This was my chance.

I wouldn't let him down.

I nodded just in time for him to give me a confident smile and then slink across the hallway. It was just dark enough that he managed to get into the long part of the T without being seen.

I realized what he planned and pressed myself against the wall as tightly as I could. My heart beat in my throat as I watched him across the way.

I wasn't just worried about myself or Analisa. I was worried about him too!

So very worried.

I couldn't think about that though. We had to do this right and fast or we would be back in our prison cell with only endless hours of torture to look forward to before our unfortunate deaths.

I jumped when Sebastian slammed into the wall nearest him. He stumbled forward and pulled a tapestry off the wall. It knocked a torch down in the destruction. I watched it until the flame died.

Then I looked back to Sebastian, who I could tell was trying not to smile.

I thought maybe he wanted to start a fire and that his plan had died. But he didn't seem fazed at all that his fire went out.

Instead, he looked down the hall in the direction of Analisa's room and at all of the men guarding it and said, "Who's going to clean this mess up? It sure as hell isn't going to be me."

He sounded inebriated. I thought he might have been going for delusional, but it just came out sloppy and drunk. Still, his plan worked.

I heard several of the guards yell, "Hey!" before they took off after him.

He shot me one more wink that I wouldn't have been able to see if I would have closed my eyes with panic like I wanted to. And if I hadn't felt his action through our still-shared Magic.

He turned around swiftly and took off down the hall.

I counted the men as they went. I breathed a sigh of relief that all six of them pursued Sebastian and then waited thirty seconds more to make sure Sebastian had counted them correctly in the first place.

When I was sure everyone had gone after Sebastian, I slid around the corner and stayed against to the wall. As I got closer to the room I thought was Analisa's, I picked up my pace and then sprinted the last few feet.

I let my Magic feel the door and the energy that locked her in. I wouldn't know how to get inside without a trial and error process, but hopefully Sebastian had bought us some time.

I walked over to the door and twisted the door handle.

Locked.

Grr. I shouldn't have been surprised, but I wanted this to be easy.

I looked around the hallway and couldn't find anything to help me. I racked my brain and tried to think like a human and did everything that I could think of. But nothing helped.

The door remained locked. I remained on the outside of it. And Analisa was still trapped on the inside.

Minutes ticked by and I started to fumble through things. I was too nervous to concentrate. Sweat dotted my brow and my lower back. I should know this. I should be able to figure it out!

I searched my vast resources of Magic, but no answers popped into my head. My Psychic instinct didn't lead me in any other directions.

I was basically stuck.

Just stuck.

"And what do you think you're doing?"

The voice came from behind me. It was cold, calculating and American. Not that I had anything against Americans. In fact, if pushed, I could admit that I was an American. It was the fact that we were both Americans and supposed to be bonded in solidarity and the Pledge of Allegiance and bald eagles and instead he'd traded in our mutual patriotism to work for Terletov the Douche Bag.

It bothered me.

A lot.

"I need in this room," I replied honestly.

He stood at my back with the hard barrel of his gun digging into me. I wanted to squirm from the fear of having that dangerous bullet lodged into my spinal cord. And then I had to quell the urge to spin around and kick this guy in the face.

"You can go in that room if you really want to." He chuckled sinisterly and I would have sworn he threw his head back and wiggled his fingertips together if we were in a cartoon.

"Really?" Maybe after he heard my accent, we would bond after all!

"Really," he deadpanned. "Just until my friends catch up with your boyfriend, then we'll take you right back to Mr. Terletov, so he can decide what he wants to do with you."

Well, there went the matching-accent theory. Bummer.

"*Mr.* Terletov," I snorted.

"Get in the room." He shoved the gun into my shoulder blade until I bowed backward at an awkward angle.

I didn't hesitate when he reached around my waist and infused the handle with his sickly Magic. The locked clicked open and I tripped forward into the room.

I took in as much of the room as I could in two seconds. There was a body laid out across a bed. A small electric lantern flickered on a nightstand next to it, but it was the only light. There were no windows and the large fireplace in the center of the room was untouched. The room had been emptied of all other furniture except for a chair near the bed with something slumped over on top of it.

I steadied myself and whirled around to face my captor. He was a young guy, younger than me. Probably not even twenty yet. His gun pointed at my mid-section and his eyes scanned the room nervously.

I felt him take in the scene as quickly as I did. He was alone right now. And even though he had a gun to protect himself and subdue us, there were potentially more prisoners than guards.

Except that most of the prisoners were unconscious and incapacitated and not one of us had a weapon.

Still. He had reason to be nervous.

"Do you think he'll kill me?" I made my eyes as big as I could and made sure my bottom lip jutted out in a trembling pout.

This never worked with Sebastian, but he knew me better than this kid. Plus, Sebastian had called me beautiful- the most beautiful woman he'd ever seen. Surely, that meant something to this kid, trapped in a stone castle with only men and zero lights.

And my pajamas.

The kid took in my skimpy silk top and the pants that had started out loose but now clung to me from blood and sweat- *super hot, I know*. This kid apparently hadn't been around a woman in a while. His hand dropped half an inch and his Adam's apple bobbed in his throat. "I'm not sure," he answered.

"I'm scared," I whispered. I took a step forward and the kid didn't even have enough sense to step back. "I don't want to die."

"I'm, um, sure that you, er, won't."

We were just inches apart now. His gun pointed at my feet and his eyes now firmly fixed on my face. He swallowed again and gulped with it.

I let a tear slip out of the corner of my eye. I had always been able to make myself cry on command. It was something that got me my way with my daddy, something that irritated the ever-living hell out of Kiran and something that Sebastian never acknowledged.

Not once.

This guy didn't know any better though.

His expression blanched with wild-eyed panic and his free arm twitched at his side as if he'd almost moved to wipe my tear away and then thought better of it.

I suppressed my triumphant smile and made my move.

Faster than I thought possible, I swatted the hand that held his gun to the side. This arm swung wide and I pulled my right arm back and punched him in the face.

Granted, it wasn't the best hit in the world, but my Magic supported me enough to cause blood to burst like a geyser out of his nose.

I shook my hand out and then made a mad grab for the gun. He tried to shove me off of him while aiming at me, but I attacked with the ferocity of a rabid beast.

I pulled at his hair and threw my whole body at the arm that held his gun. I even bit him! I wasn't going to let him shoot me. And I didn't feel bad about biting him.

Okay, I felt a little bad when he yelped in my ear. But I couldn't let that stop me.

My Magic pushed against his Magic until I could hardly breathe through the struggle. The entire time I knew he was going to win the upper hand and shoot me. He was younger than me but bigger, tougher and had that stupid, super-strength his Magic transplant gave him.

Plus, if I were honest with myself, Sebastian had reason to want to keep me out of battle. I'd been in skirmishes and used my Magic forcefully, but it had been a long time.

I was used to decent Immortals that didn't want to kill anyone, even if they had differing views.

I let a frustrated scream when he elbowed me in the jaw. My head snapped back and my tangled hair flew in my face and obstructed my view.

I retaliated by kneeing him in the groin, but it hardly had any effect on him. Either he was determined to fight through the pain or Terletov had removed his manhood along with his Magic.

That was a definite possibility.

The metallic taste of blood coated my mouth and my Magic surged with long pulses of dwindling energy.

I needed to end this.

And I did.

Although, I would never be able to recall exactly how it happened. One moment he was just a move away from gaining control of me, and the next, I'd somehow turned the gun on him.

I threw every last bit of strength I had into maneuvering his hand to point away from me. It was only by luck that I managed to point it at him just at the same time he pulled the trigger.

The shot rang loud and poignant through the room. I didn't believe that it didn't hit me. It took long moments of holding my breath before his body grew too heavy for me to hold and I realized our fighting had come to an end.

I took a step back, away from him, and his body dropped to the ground immediately. The muffled thump he made when he hit the floor seemed to echo for eternity and mingle with the ringing sound of the gunshot.

Hysterical urgency surged through me. I knew someone would have heard our struggle and especially the gunshot. Reinforcements would be on their way.

I needed to grab Analisa and get out of here. Fast.

Plus, I had no idea where Sebastian was and if he was already to the ballroom or if he'd managed to get captured again like I almost had.

What a mess!

I ran over to Analisa and immediately put my fingers to her pulse. I breathed a short breath of relief when I felt her faint heartbeat and the warmth of her skin.

She was alive, if barely.

Sebastian clearly hadn't thought his plan all the way through because I had no idea how to get her out of here. Was I supposed to carry her?

Not happening.

She was basically the same size as me and I didn't have enough Magic to sustain us the entire way.

Besides, me carrying Analisa was about as opposite as inconspicuous as possible.

I looked around the room frantically, but I didn't come up with any solutions. I stared at the lump of something that took up the entire chair next to her bed and wondered if it was a dead body.

It was definitely body-shaped and it hadn't moved since I walked in the room.

I didn't think it even acknowledged the tussle I had. Which was really too bad because I wanted some accolades for kicking that guy's ass!

It didn't look like I was going to get it.

I pushed on Analisa's shoulder and when she didn't stir, I pushed her over so she lay on her back with her head drooping off the bead. Whoever had tossed her here had done exactly that: tossed her.

She moaned with the movement, but her eyelids didn't even flutter.

Suddenly the lump moved and then all at once it shot into sitting.

So I was right about the body-shaped hunch. However, not dead. I really hoped that was a positive thing.

Something wild and uncivilized appeared before me. His long, scraggly beard was an impossible tangle of bristled hair. His dark eyes glistened like onyx in the dim light and he licked at his dry lips as if he could repair some of the massive damage done to them with just his sandpaper-like tongue.

It was not a pretty sight.

"Don't touch her," the beast-man growled at me. He leaned forward but started coughing violently almost as soon as he'd moved.

I wanted to yell at him to be quiet, but that probably would have been counterproductive.

"I'm here to help her," I snarled back. "Can you help me lift her?"

"Help her?" His voice was just a whisper as he gaped at me with disbelief.

"Yes. I swear."

"Do I... Do I know you?"

I took a step towards him and tried to peer at him through his mangy hair and Sasquatch-styled look.

"I am Jedrec." He continued to whisper, but this time I could tell he was less sensitive to the people around us.

"Oh, my gosh!" I squealed quietly. "I'm Seraphina. We've met a few times before."

He nodded like he could finally place me. "You're really here to help her?"

I gave him a confident smile. "Yes! And you, if you'd like help. We're trying to get out of here."

"We?" His eyes narrowed in quick suspicion.

"Sebastian's here with me."

"Sebastian?"

"Sebastian Cartier."

Jedrec's eyes got even bigger. "The prince! You brought the prince to help rescue us!"

I cleared my throat. "Actually he brought me here." I thought back to our recent arrest.

He shoved his body onto shaky legs, wobbling for a while, but eventually steadying out. "I can walk," he declared.

I bit back my naturally sarcastic response and decided to smile patiently at him instead. I wondered when he had walked anywhere was and if he had been unconscious when I walked in or playing dead until he knew what to make of me. "That is fantastic news. How do you feel about weight-lifting?"

His face betrayed none of his emotions when he asked, "Weight-lifting?"

"Your Queen," I told him. I nodded in the direction of Analisa. "I don't think she's walking out of here and I'm too short to manage her."

And by short, I obviously meant not Hercules.

Jedrec ambled over to the bedside and ran the backs of his fingers over her slender, but filthy, neck. "I can help her."

Despite his obvious weakness, he swooped her up into his arms and swung around to face the door.

"Are you sure you're strong enough?"

He gave me a determined look and grunted at the open door. "I'm fine. Let's go before someone else finds us."

He had a point.

All of this would be in vain if Terletov's henchmen caught us before we even got down the hallway.

Thankfully, no one did.

We moved as quickly as we could in our pathetic states. We pushed our bodies to their limits and sprinted, or ran with much gusto, down the hallway.

Sebastian had been right. As soon as I got to the staircase, everything started to look familiar. I relaxed just a pinch and said another prayer for Sebastian.

I hoped he was well enough to outrun all of the men chasing us. I hoped he was fast enough and tricky enough to get to the ballroom.

Footsteps pounding against the stone floor and the shuffle of pants and belts and men broke into our quiet getaway. I grabbed Jedrec by the back of his shirt and steered him behind some drapes. It felt very *Tom and Jerry* of us to hide in plain sight like this, but there weren't any other options.

Analisa moaned softly, but it felt like a siren screaming an alarm. Jedrec quickly shifted her in his arms and wrapped a hand over her mouth.

I held my breath and prepared to be discovered.

We waited in the shadows while more men ran through the hallway. The only thing separating us from them was a thick curtain that had probably hung here for several hundred years. I wondered for a moment if we were the only ones that had taken shelter here when an enemy pursued them. But then, faster than I could keep up, I knew that we weren't. I knew others had hidden here before. Eden's parents. Delia and Justice. This wasn't the first time these drapes had kept innocents from evil hands.

Weird. The Psychic thing was starting to freak me out.

When the thump-thump-thump of boots faded away and the energy around us stilled again, we resumed our run to the ballroom.

I expected Sebastian to be waiting for us, casual as could be. I pictured him leaning against the doorframe, arms crossed, signature bored expression twisting his lips into an annoyed frown. "What took you so long?" he would ask.

But he wasn't there. Immediately my nerves jumpstarted with frenetic anxiety. Where was he? Why wasn't he here?

I helped Jedrec make sure Analisa wasn't too jostled from the trip to this part of the castle and then continued to scan the area for Sebastian. We couldn't exactly stand out here and wait patiently for him to show up.

We needed to hide or leave or just *not stand out in the open like this*.

Just as I started to truly panic, he appeared. And there was nothing quiet or subtle about his approach.

He ran at us like a stampede of bulls.

His arms flailed at his sides, motioning for us to move. His eyes were bug-eyed and frantic. I followed his orders without thinking, without questioning.

I turned around and sprinted through the ballroom. My bare feet slapped the polished floor, my breath wheezed in my chest.

Jedrec stayed at my back, even though I knew he could overpower me. *Always the bodyguard*. Sebastian shouted furious orders to *move faster, move faster, move faster!*

I pushed at the back doors. They were locked, of course. I tried Magic, but they would not budge. I panicked again. This close to the outside, and I couldn't get through the last obstacle.

"Duck!" Sebastian yelled.

I ducked. Jedrec followed me to a squat. Something heavy sailed over our heads and crashed through the large glass panes.

I let out an involuntary scream as shattered glass cascaded over me. Nothing cut or sliced, but the sensation of raining shards and shrapnel knocked the wind out of me.

"Let's go!" Sebastian yelled again.

The boots that we heard in the hallway followed us into this room. They were across the expansive space, guns drawn and triumphant smiles on their faces.

"Go, Sera! Now!"

I stood up and ignored the sharp debris cutting into my feet and jumped through the hole Sebastian made with an abandoned chair. My landing was not a pleasant one. I tried not to let the cuts to my feet debilitate me. And I wasn't the only one without shoes. Jedrec didn't have any either. We both had Magic though, enough to help ignore the pain to our feet.

I sprinted side-by-side with Sebastian, Jedrec on the other, straight to the balcony. As if we'd choreographed this exact moment, we all leaped to the thick stone railing and jumped off.

For a few seconds, I felt as though I could fly. My stomach lurched with the sensation and my body became weightless. Just as quickly as I'd registered the feeling the ground came up to meet us and I rolled on the hard, unforgiving ground.

I let out a moan of something crass. That really hurt.

My hand was tugged and then pulled and then my entire body lifted and set right again. I looked up at Sebastian and tried to shake of the foggy feeling of pain.

"We have to keep moving."

I nodded. He was right.

His Magic pulsed through mine with a healing shot of unity and I snapped awake. And then we were off again.

Our footsteps crunched against the white, pebbled gravel and then fell silent once we hit the grass. The bang of shots fired, the zipping whiz of bullets, the impact against stone or bush or branch filled the Romanian summer evening.

We ducked and ran hunched over. We made unpredictable side steps and pushed our bodies as fast as we could go.

We were almost there.

Almost.

Something hot seared across my shoulder, a burning sizzle that scorched my skin and punched the breath from my lungs. I gasped in a gulping breath and stumbled forward.

My mind registered that I'd been shot at the same time my arm went numb from the sting of extreme discomfort. My vision blurred and I tripped again. My other arm tangled in the wiry bush of the garden maze.

I felt my body fall and fall and fall, an unending catapult down into a bottomless hole. I was Alice in Wonderland without a destination. I was upside down in a right-side-up world. I was lost.

I was gone.

Chapter Nineteen

Sebastian

I held her tightly against my chest. So tightly my arms ached and my muscles felt stretched and overused.

We made it into the maze of tall hedge and narrow, winding pathways. I led the way with Seraphina against my heart, her head lolling from side to side, her mouth slightly slack from the depth of her unconsciousness.

Jedrec pushed against my back with my aunt cradled in much the same way.

We were handicapped men that would do anything to save these women in our arms. But we had such a long way to go.

I felt confident that we could lose Terletov's men in this maze. Analisa had designed her garden in a twisted pattern of confusion. This was somewhat of a cry for help a century ago.

The entire Kingdom knew the story of the fragile Queen's insistence that her garden be unkempt and difficult. She ordered that it be neglected. She chose plants that would grow in tangled knots and fight to gain ground. She wanted this place as unruly as her soul, as restless as her spirit.

And she had won her wish.

There were few in this Kingdom that could navigate these pathways confidently. More now than when Kiran and I were children. Back then, we were the only ones that knew our way around with the proficiency of bored, over-privileged children that had nothing else to do than memorize the secret passages of a mystical garden.

Even Analisa had never spent time in the monstrosity she'd created. This area of the Citadel had been left to the children. Talbott, Mimi, Kiran and I had spent days running these hedges.

And then one day we'd discovered the secret entrance along the back wall.

That same day we'd run into Amory in the ballroom. We'd been out past curfew. On Talbott's insistence, we'd returned to the castle and tried sneaking in through the balcony doors.

Amory had been waiting for us.

We had all jumped out of our skin when his tall, dignified silhouette came into view. We thought he would turn us over to my Uncle Lucan. Or at the very least spend the next hour lecturing our irresponsible behavior.

Instead, he'd looked at us in the dimness of the dark ballroom with the only light a long finger of golden glow reaching in through the open hallway door, and leveled us with his most serious expression.

"Never forget what you did tonight," he'd instructed. And that was all he'd said. He stared us down for a second longer and turned around and left.

We'd given each other big eyes and breathed a collective sigh of relief. Up until I turned seventeen and my uncle murdered that same man, I'd assumed he meant to teach us a lesson about disobeying curfew. I couldn't have guessed that his true meaning was for us to remember the back entrance of the Citadel wall because we would use it to unseat Lucan and run a Resistance I had no business being a part of.

And now it would save my life once more.

The zing of bullets still punctuated the urgency to flee. The bang of guns. The deadly explosion of branch and leaves as Terletov's men missed their targets.

The men couldn't see us, but they could hear our exodus. They knew we were somewhere in this jungle of sharp branches and invisibility.

By the time we reached the back gate I had panted with the heaviness of a human after a marathon. My lungs wheezed and my muscles burned with an unforgiving fire.

I stared at the heavy door for several moments, trying to decide what Magic still ran through its veins. I could put my hand to this handle and it could open.

Or Terletov could have changed the Magic during his takeover.

"Prince?" Jedrec breathed low and urgently behind me.

Did I have a choice?

I looked down at the face cradled in the crook of my arm. Shiny blonde hair, creamy skin, perfectly plump lips. The face of an angel. The face of perfection. My perfection.

No, I didn't have a choice.

The enemy closed in around us. It was through this gate or none at all.

I adjusted Seraphina in my arms and slid my hand forward until my palm hit warm brass. I closed my eyes and let the Magic inside of me pulse into the handle.

A breath of relief whooshed from me when the lock clicked open. I wasted no time turning the handle and pushing out onto the backside of the Citadel and the wild, untamed Romanian mountain I knew as my second home.

I waited for Jedrec to join me on the other side and then I shut the door. They shouldn't be able to follow this way.

If my Magic still worked, then the door should be as good as sealed.

And they shouldn't be able to go over the wall. I was sure Terletov wouldn't disable the Magic that covered the Citadel. For his own protection, he would keep all the wards in place.

That meant we had a few minutes to gain a head start.

And so that was what we did.

We ran and continued to run. The sun glinted over the western horizon. It would be dark soon. It must be late evening.

In the Citadel and during Terletov's interrogation, I had lost all concept of time. I had no idea how long we'd been separated from Kiran. Had hours passed? Days? Weeks? I had no idea.

Probably not weeks.

I hoped not weeks.

The air was still stiflingly hot, blanketing over my skin and compressing my lungs. My Magic stuttered and I willed it to be strong. Seraphina's flickered in and out, never staying around long enough to help give mine a boost, but never disappearing enough for me to panic that she wouldn't make it.

I took Jedrec around the lake and headed toward one of the mountain villages. This was the long way. We were on the opposite side of the Citadel from the underground tunnel. That would have been my preferred escape route.

But I couldn't complain now.

I wouldn't take us back around the Citadel, no matter how far we kept our distance. Besides, there was only one place in this part of the world I believed we would be truly safe.

And even then...

"It's going to be dark soon." Jedrec's voice cut through the bubble of isolation I'd started to believe we found.

There was nothing but the four of us, two pairs of feet shuffling through the rough terrain, accompanied only by the distant call of birds.

"We can't stop."

"We need to check on the women."

A dog howled ominously in the distance. I shared a look with the Titan. "We will. Just not yet."

Another dog joined the whinnying and my stomach turned slimy. Dogs roamed Romania in packs. Harmless strays that had nothing else to do besides follow pedestrians to bus stops and scrounge through whatever trash they could find. But far up the mountain... This deep in uncharted territory?

"Is it possible these hounds belong to Terletov?"

Jedrec gave a curt nod. "Quite."

"Then let's keep moving."

I cradled Seraphina closer. If Terletov had managed to turn hounds onto our hunt, we would be in trouble.

Neither Jedrec nor I was up to this chase, especially while we each carried a limp body in our arms. We were too weak. Too frustratingly impotent.

Damn.

We pushed our bodies to the absolute limit to keep a steady pace, even while the dogs and their howling grew steadily closer. The sun disappeared and somewhere overhead the moon shone brightly.

The canopy of trees clustered together and blocked out whatever natural light there would have been. The scent of wood fire drifted on a sultry breeze and soothed my rather frantically beating heart.

I started to believe we could make it.

Maybe Terletov would call off the search. Maybe he would give up for the night.

Maybe we would reach some kind of civilization and be able to borrow a car. Or steal one. I wasn't above looting at this point.

A crunching sound echoed through the night, a rumble of sound and warning. At first it came through my senses in a confused collection of possibilities. Swarm of deadly insects? Large forest beastie that planned to eat us for dinner? Aliens?

And then all at once it clicked. The hounds.

Their barking beat out a staccato rhythm that forced my heart to pound along with it. My nerves throbbed beneath my skin and my Magic jumped and jittered unpredictably.

The hounds were close. Too close.

And behind them would be Terletov's army.

"What should we do?" I panted. "Try to outrun them? Climb a tree?"

Jedrec's expression turned utterly desolate as he assessed our situation, which I found especially despairing. Jedrec was a Titan Guard. Out of the two of us, he knew how to read a conflict quickly and accurately. If he thought we had no hope, then we truly didn't have hope.

I glanced up at the large trees that stood witness to our pathetic escape. Could I stash Seraphina in one? Could I manage to convince

Terletov that she had disappeared and I was all he had left? Could Jedrec manage two bodies while I stalled the pursuing Immortals?

No. We needed to stay together. I needed to remain with Seraphina to make sure she stayed safe.

To make sure she woke up.

We ran across a dirt road just wide enough for one car to drive down. Well-worn tire tracks marked a path towards something, hopefully, habitable.

"This way," I called to Jedrec.

I kept us off the road and moving in the ditch. I knew the hounds could scent us no matter where we ran, but I didn't want to leave obvious footprints in the soft dirt.

A minute later an old house came into view. It looked completely abandoned without a single light on or car in the drive. The moonlight bathed the rundown structure in a yellow glow, making it appear more ominous than it should have been.

There was a barn behind the building with a partially collapsed roof. That was where I decided to take us.

It might turn out to be a bad decision, but I didn't have any other options. Besides, even if I was weakened as an Immortal, I was still infinitely stronger than a human. So if say, the house happened to be inhabited by a serial killer or sadist of some kind or the other, I should still be able to outmuscle them.

In theory.

I hadn't been up against many human serial killers prior to today, so I couldn't truly say.

But we'd run out of other options.

"Let's see if we can't take cover in the outbuilding," I suggested.

He looked around with a bleak expression forcing his eyebrows together before nodding his head slowly. "Fine."

The door was locked and even after I broke the lock with my Magic, it still struggled to open. Once inside the dark, damp place, I had to duck to avoid the thick mess of cobwebs and collapsed crossbeams.

I could see enough with my Magic to avoid the larger obstacles on the ground, but the rafters and balcony were almost completely collapsed in.

Jedrec shut the door behind us and followed after me as I picked my way through the debris and up to the roof. I held Seraphina carefully close to me lest I drop her.

Eventually, we made it through the tangle of debris and broken beams and propped ourselves in a flat section out of sight from the road. I set

Sera down and tugged my ripped and bloodied t-shirt off. Using what little Magic I had access to, I sent the t-shirt floating through the woods. I made sure it brushed against as many trees as I could and then at the very outskirts of where I could reach, I tossed the shirt up into the trees where it would be hidden well.

I picked Sera back up and kept her close to me. She was probably fine lying down by herself, but I was not.

I was not alright with losing any kind of touch after what we'd been through in the Citadel.

I vowed right then and there that I would spend the rest of my life making sure she never went through anything even close to this ever again. I felt violently ill when I thought about how close to death she was and how much pain and suffering Terletov had put her through.

And our troubles weren't over. We were not free and clear just yet.

I was the only person allowed to bother this woman. And I would never truly hurt her, not if I could help it.

The hounds came crashing across the road after our scent. The eight of them filled the yard and started barking in a wild frenzy. Soon enough, the men in charge of them followed after. They ran over the property, following the dogs as the animals tried to sniff out our scent.

Jedrec and I sat utterly still. I didn't even think that I breathed once; too afraid the hounds would catch the stale scent of my breath.

I felt the atmosphere shift when the dogs became confused. I had Magically pushed my shirt all around this property and sent it wildly through the woods. The animals couldn't figure out which direction we ran off in.

I couldn't tell if they were dogs that had been treated with Terletov's experimental Magic, but I could hear how vicious they were. Their growling and barking ripped through the otherwise quiet night, promising sharp teeth and a lack of free will. They would rip us to shreds and tear out our throats if given the command.

Honestly, I didn't think Terletov was capable of making an animal Immortal. More likely, he had found a great breed of hunting dogs and mistreated them until they were nothing but ruthless killers that could track any scent.

That theory made more sense to me, but rarely did Terletov do something that made any sense.

One dog broke from the pack and ran over to the barn. Jedrec and I pushed back into the shadows as best as we could, but the angry beast kept baring his teeth and snarling psychotically.

One of the men came over to investigate what caught his attention. The thug tried to pull the dog back to the main group, but the animal kept his strong opinion.

Jedrec stiffened next to me. I could feel his thoughts spin with options to save us. I leaned forward just enough to see how many we were up against.

Too many.

Way too many.

We would never get out of here alive if they found us.

The dog kept snarling and snapping at us while his friends seemed anxious to move on. Their handlers kept them in the yard, but they pushed against a Magical wall and bared their sharp teeth. They wanted to resume the hunt.

I wanted that too, but the fake hunt.

The man bent down to talk to the dog in a language I couldn't understand from up here. My ears perked up, but I couldn't make anything out over the other barking dogs and without as much Magic as I usually commanded.

The dog growled with intent and purpose until the man stopped fighting him. The dog took off toward the barn, ready to bite anything that stepped in front of him.

I waited impatiently as the creature circled the barn several times, barking up at us the entire time. The stupid animal knew exactly where we were, he just couldn't relay the info to his even dumber owner.

I dropped my head against the splintered wood behind me and hoped that was a good sign. At least these freakishly large dogs couldn't speak. That had to mean something.

Not that I expected them to, but you never knew with Terletov.

"Aster, let's go!" an American thug yelled at the confused man just twenty feet from us. "The dogs picked up the scent again!"

Aster did not seem to like that. He trusted his dog better than he trusted the other person.

In this Kingdom, and with their tyrannical leader, that was probably a good strategy.

Aster stood up, but other than that did not make any effort to move. His dog started growling low in the back of his throat. His nose pointed directly toward us. I stayed in the shadow, completely unmoving and hoped Seraphina didn't take this opportunity to wake up.

That would be disastrous but pretty on par with Sera's sense of timing.

Jedrec and I were tucked away in a section of the collapsed roof. We sat out of sight from the inside, if they were to search from there and also from the outside. We had a good view of the yard and the dog down below, but the overhang and supporting wall hopefully hid us from our pursuers.

Aster took a step toward the barn and I knew I would have to kill him if he found us. The rest of his party had taken off into the woods. The distant yapping of the hounds faded quickly.

He looked impatiently over his shoulder and then closely at the barn. I could see the indecision written all over his face and the angry dog made a pretty compelling argument. But he was alone now. I hoped that was enough to dissuade him from investigating further.

Finally, when one of the other dogs let out a loud howl as if he'd found something, Aster turned away from us. He called an order to the dog and took off in a sprint toward the rest of his hunting party.

The dog didn't immediately follow. He stayed growling and snarling at the barn more stubborn than ever.

Aster called him more firmly and the animal finally turned his mangy head and trotted after the rest of his pack.

I couldn't move my body. I wondered if I'd frozen myself with anxiety. Breath expelled from my lungs, but the rest of me couldn't work up enough courage or energy to relax.

"We should go," Jedrec suggested. There was a lazy thickness to his deep accent that made me concerned for his energy level as well.

If both of us were fading and the women were already gone, we needed to get somewhere safe as soon as possible.

My sense of direction was off without the full faculties of my Magic, but I had a guess which direction to go. First we needed to find a highway.

I sucked up my exhaustion and used Seraphina to motivate me to move. I staggered to my feet and brought her with me. With her still cradled in my arms, Jedrec, who also carried my aunt still, followed me back through the cluttered barn and out to the drive. We followed it for a long time until we found the highway that wound through these mountains.

Seraphina nuzzled against the bare skin of my chest and her breathing became more pronounced. If I could get to a phone, I could call Avalon and have him on the next plane to us. He should be able to borrow Eden's blue smoke long enough to wake Sera up.

And then the two of us, her and I, were going to have a nice long chat.

I just had to get to that phone first.

I turned in the opposite direction of the way the men had run after my phantom scent and started the long journey to the only safe place I could think of that was left in this entire damn country.

"Think we'll make it?" I asked Jedrec once I'd disclosed my plan.

"No," he said. "But then I didn't think we'd make it this far either. You're very resourceful, Your Highness."

"Er, I'm not, uh... People don't call me that anymore. My family gave up their titles when Eden took the throne."

The corner of his mouth kicked up. "Old habits are hard to break and the crown is in your blood. I'll always think of you as the Prince."

"I'm not sure if that's a bad thing or a good thing."

And then in his typical, subtle way, he said, "If it were Lucan's crown I was thinking of, it would be a very bad thing. But you've redeemed your family name. You've made it a very good thing."

"Thank you," I said humbly.

"I'll thank you too," he answered, "just as soon as you get us to safety."

"Right. I can do that. Or at least, I can try."

Chapter Twenty

Seraphina

I blinked awake and jumped to standing.

Which was a mistake for so many reasons.

The first was that I was practically naked.

The second was that I had no equilibrium and would have crashed back to the ground face first if two strong hands hadn't caught me.

My vision swam and my head spun for several long moments before I could focus again. Sebastian became a clear, real thing in front of me, his hands turned hot and gripping on my bare waist.

Cool air washed over my naked stomach and legs. I looked down at my body to find that I had been dressed in clean underwear and a sports bra. Who had done that?

Sebastian stepped closer to me so that I was forced to pay him attention.

I begged my mind to remember everything that I couldn't. For instance, how we got here together and how I ended up in barely any clothes.

The fight in the Citadel came back to me like a freight train. I remembered everything all at once, instead of in bits and pieces. I winced from the rust of it and then again when I remembered I'd been shot and forced out of commission.

"I'm okay?" I whispered.

Sebastian dipped his head until we could look at each other eye to eye. "You tell me."

"I mean the bullet. No permanent damage?"

He shook his head. "Avalon is pretty confident that you will be alright."

"Avalon?"

"Eden and Kiran didn't join us. They are on their way to Paris to meet Analisa and Jedrec. Kiran was anxious to see his mum. She hasn't woken up yet."

I nodded, struggling to absorb this information. "Analisa was alone in the room, other than Jedrec. Did he know what happened to Jericho's mom or dad?"

"Dead." Sebastian's voice became raw and pained. We knew they were traitors, but they were still our good friend's parents. "Terletov killed them both according to Jedrec. Right after Jericho took his father's Magic. Terletov considered them useless." I bit my lip but couldn't say I was surprised. "Jedrec had many things to say on the way here. He's lucky to be alive. And Analisa is nothing short of a miracle."

"Where exactly is here?" I tore my eyes away from Sebastian's concerned gaze and looked around the small... hut.

I was definitely in a hut. The walls were made of mud and the roof was thatched. There was a small wood stove next to the lumpy bed I'd been laying in that wasn't lit and a table against another wall that was piled with dishes and random treasures.

"The Gypsy camp."

My focus snapped back to Sebastian, who grinned at me proudly. "The Gypsy camp?" I thought of the old hag's words from before. She had been predicting that Sebastian and I would get back together. That we would have children together!

Which was crazy!

Also, Witch was crazy!!!

But I knew without a doubt that she would start meddling just as soon as she knew I wasn't on my deathbed.

I was surprised she wasn't already in here.

"So we're still in Romania?"

Sebastian nodded. "Yes."

I grunted and then swayed. I definitely wasn't up to full strength yet. My limbs trembled like vibrating Jell-O and my head seemed stuffed with cotton. I felt fuzzy all over.

"Are we going to leave soon?"

There was a heavy pause that made me instantly suspicious. Then he said, "You can leave very soon."

I pushed away from him and sat back down on the bed. It was narrow, so I didn't have to push back very far until my back rested against the wall. I pulled my knees to my chest and worked to find some balance and clear thoughts.

I was mostly healed from my fun time in the castle at Terletov's mercy, but my mind had trouble catching up and I was still obviously weak.

"What do you mean, *I* can leave soon?"

"I think you should head out, Sera. This mission has gotten incredibly dangerous. It would be safer for you to go back to Seattle and wait it out."

I didn't even know how to respond to that! Okay, that was a lie. I knew exactly how to respond to him, I just didn't know where to start. All of my quick retorts piled up on my tongue and created a mental traffic jam.

I took a breath to gather my thoughts and glared at him. "You're kicking me off the mission."

"I'm not," he answered quickly. "I'm sending you some place safer. I don't want you involved anymore."

"I thought you needed my Psychic abilities."

"I need you to stay alive more."

His words were like a punch in the heart, but I soldiered on, ignoring the sweetness he mixed with chauvinistic demands.

"Sebastian, I don't understand."

"It's complicated, Sera. There are lots of things between us that are complicated. But let me simplify at least this. I watched you nearly die. More than once. Terletov had his disgusting hands all over you. He inflicted unspeakable pain on you and there was nothing I could do about it. You also got shot. I carried you for only god knows how many hours because you were unconscious and unresponsive. I cannot... I *will not* go through that again. I thought I was going to lose you for good."

"You already lost me," I snapped. I was so irritated with him. I couldn't help it. I was angry that he thought he could protect me by sending me away. I was angry that he didn't think I could take care of myself. And I was really, really angry that he acted like he cared about me! Couldn't he just leave me alone?

That would be best for everyone involved! But mainly me.

Sebastian didn't hesitate to drop down to the bed with me. He fell on his knees and straddled my bare feet. His hands landed on my thighs where he pressed the lengths of his palms against my heated skin and dipped his head so we were only an inch apart.

"I didn't lose you like this. Not even close. We hurt each other before, Sera, but you didn't almost *die*. I didn't have to give you up because you were dead, or permanently unconscious. That, what happened at the Citadel and in the woods, will *never* happen to you again. I won't let it. So before you want to remind me that I lost you already, why don't you take a look around this room and remind yourself that you're alive."

"Thank you," I whispered.

He hadn't been expecting my quick turnaround. His eyes had clouded with confusion for a few moments before they were replaced with sincere affection. "For what?"

"For keeping me alive. For rescuing me. You didn't have to."

His thumb reached up and smoothed a path over my bottom lip. "And you didn't have to come with me to begin with. You could have avoided the whole mess."

"I could have." I probably should have... but I didn't. And so here we were.

Alone.

"Sebastian, I-"

"Sera, I think we should talk seriously about-"

"I'm not going home," I interrupted quickly. I didn't know what he planned to say, but I needed to clear this up quickly. "I'm not going to abandon this in the middle of it and I'm not going to let Terletov get away with anything else. I'm in this thing. You can't stop me."

At my defiant tone, Sebastian withdrew physically and emotionally. He slid away and landed on his feet. He was across the room in the next second with his hands tugging at the roots of his hair. "I don't want to stop you. I want to *protect* you. Why can't you understand that? Why am I the bad guy for wanting you to be safe?"

"Nobody ever said you were the bad guy. Why am I the weak female that can't take care of herself? If you didn't notice, I did just fine. And I would have kept doing just fine if that stupid bullet hadn't gotten in my way."

"But it did get in your way. It majorly disabled you. Seraphina, what if I wouldn't have been there to pick you up? What if the bullet would have found you inside the castle before we met back up? Do you realize what could have happened? How badly this could have gone?"

"Sebastian, there is always that chance! What would have happened to you if I would have been there to lend my Magic? You could have just as easily died. You could *still die*. It's unfair to send me away when you get to stay."

His voice rose as our argument escalated. "This isn't a competition! It's not you versus me. It's not how much I get to do against how little you do. This is about my need, my desire to keep you out of harm's way. I'm not a dictator, Sera. I'm just trying to keep you safe."

"I don't need you to keep me safe! That's what you're not getting. If something happens to me, it's not your fault. It would obviously suck, but I understand the consequences going in. I'm going in with eyes wide open and I'm okay with that. I'm sorry for your conscience if you can't accept that, but it's the truth. It's my fault entirely. You have nothing to do with it."

"Don't you understand? I have *everything* to do with it! I don't want you to leave so I can move on with a clear conscience. Damn it, Seraphina. *I care about you*. Do you understand that? I care about you more than I should. More than I ever have before. I care about you so much the thought of something happening to you again *kills* me. *It guts me*. I want you somewhere safe so that I can think about something else besides you.

I want you safe because the thought of you being in pain again or someone laying their hands on you makes me *murderous*. That's why I want to protect you. Are you happy? That's why!"

I opened my mouth to say something, but nothing came out.

Honestly, I couldn't think of a single thing to say.

He ran two hands over his face, clearly frustrated with our conversation and our tone. I had meant to diffuse our fowl moods with my apology, but then we both exploded.

That seemed to always happen to us. Our good intentions always got buried beneath volatile tempers and an inability to communicate clearly.

We were doomed in any capacity. Friends, lover, partners... it didn't matter. We just didn't mesh. At all.

The door opened and whatever was left to say between us turned to ash on the floor.

Avalon stuck his big head in the small house and looked back and forth between the two of us. He raised his eyebrows at my lack of dress and then studied Sebastian more carefully.

When Sebastian didn't offer an explanation, Avalon said, "We're meeting over some dinner to discuss our plan of attack if you want to join us."

"Your plan of attack?" I raised my eyebrows at the two boys.

"We're going after the Citadel," Sebastian explained quietly. "We're going to take it back."

That's why he wanted to send me home? The bastard! He wanted to get me out of the way so he could go right back into action!

I couldn't believe him!

"You're going back there? After we just escaped the damn place?"

He shared a sly look with Avalon. "I'm not going alone, Sera. And we're not going in blind."

"Just *nearly* blind. Sebastian we were barely conscious while we were there. There were guards everywhere. We barely escaped!"

"We have an army, Seraphina. We just didn't know what we were up against until now. I'm confident we can take the Citadel back," Avalon explained evenly.

I still wasn't convinced. We had an army, sure, but an army full of Immortals that were risking their lives for this half-cocked plan. "Let me guess, you're planning to use the back entrance and sneak in? Take them by surprise?"

Sebastian shared another look with Avalon. "Well..."

I jumped to my feet and I cut him off. "You don't think they'll be expecting that? We just escaped!"

Avalon snorted. "I hope they're expecting us. I want to end this, Seraphina. I want my Citadel back. And I want my Kingdom back. End of story."

"But think about the-"

Avalon swiped his hand impatiently through the air. "Enough. This is happening. Get ready. Two days ago, I should have been celebrating my new niece and nephew. Instead, this monster attacked them and kidnapped two of my closest friends. That same day, there were riots at the London property. A large portion of the Kingdom showed up to demand answers only hours after Terletov's men disappeared. The people wanted to know why their loved ones were being kidnapped and killed. And they wanted to know if the experiments would stop if we allowed Terletov to be King. They were willing to let this psychopath be King if it would protect them. I will not allow this to go on any longer. We're going back today. I know Sebastian wants you to go home, but you have my permission to stay. You can fight alongside us or you can get out of the way. You make the choice, but either way, that's enough."

And with that dramatic lecture, he spun around on his heel and slammed the door behind him.

I rolled my eyes. That was so typically Avalon.

The silence that followed Avalon's departure became heavy and uncomfortable. I didn't know what to say to Sebastian, so I chose not to say anything.

I realized that Avalon was right. We did need to reclaim the Citadel and the throne, but I didn't want to admit that I had been wrong. At the same time, there was no way in Hades I planned to abandon the mission now. If we were going to attack the Citadel, I wanted to be a part of it.

End of story.

"You're not going to go home, are you?" Sebastian broke the suffocating silence sounding painfully disappointed.

"No, I'm not."

He closed the space between us and took my hand gently in his. "What if I promise to come to you as soon as we're finished? I haven't seen your Seattle home. I'd like to."

I narrowed my eyes on him. "Why?"

He shrugged casually and swiped his thumb along the center of my palm. "It's something of yours I haven't seen. Touched. I want to do both."

I swallowed a cough. I didn't know if he meant his words to sound so sexual or not, but they did. I felt a slow heat sear through me, from the tips of my toes to the top of my head. Had I also hit my head during our escape?

"I don't think that's a good idea."

He took a step closer to me. "I didn't say that it was."

Heady butterflies soared through my belly and I had to look away from him. I eyed the door, knowing there was safety just on the other side of it. My friends would be out there. They could talk some sense into me.

I hoped.

"I'm not leaving, Bastian."

He let out a long sigh. I could feel his frustration and disappointment, but when he used his pointer finger to tilt my head toward him, I saw only heat and something deeper in his warm expression. "Then be prepared to get sick of me."

"Why?"

"I'm not letting you out of my sight. If you want to go with us, then so be it. But you're going to have to put up with me the entire time. That is non-negotiable."

"Maybe I'll call Andrei to join me."

The look he gave me should have scared me. It definitely should not have sent a shivering racing down my spine. "I thought we'd established his inability to keep you safe. He didn't even try to fend me off from a dance. He's a joke. He's a coward. And he has no place with you."

"He's-"

"Seraphina, I wouldn't push me on this if I were you."

I snapped my mouth shut. It had been an idle threat anyway. I hadn't even thought about Andrei since I called him in Italy. I just wanted to piss Sebastian off, but now that I'd succeeded, my victory didn't feel nearly as uncomplicated and petty as I thought it would.

Instead, my stomach felt fizzy and my pulse started racing.

"Why are you doing this? Why are you so protective of me?" My voice was a raspy whisper.

My heart stuttered in my chest and my stomach flipped again. This was what I wanted from him a year ago. I wanted his protection and I wanted his partnership.

What I hadn't wanted was to be left behind while he went on mission after mission. And now he planned to give me what I wanted. But it was too late, so why was he doing this to me?

What was the point now?

He answered my question a second later, when he said, "I know that you think I stopped caring for you when we broke up, but Sera, that isn't true. I will always care for you. I'll always want the best for you, even if you disagree with me about what that is."

I felt a prickling of paranoia raise the hairs on the back of my neck. He was being too sweet, too perfect. He was up to something; I just didn't know what it was. I wouldn't put it past him to lull me into a false sense of security and then have me tied up and shipped back to the States. Such was the true nature of his deviousness. "I can live with that as long as you know that I don't mind disagreeing with you. Actually, I kind of like it."

He grinned at my stubborn response. He leaned in until we were that tempting inch apart again. His nose brushed against mine and I closed my eyes out of instinct and overwhelming sensation. "I kind of like it too."

I swayed when he pulled away suddenly. I opened my eyes just in time to see him yank open the door and step through it. "Get dressed," he ordered. "Roxie's been almost worried about you. It's been traumatizing for her frozen heart."

The door slammed behind him and rattled the thin roof. I collapsed on the bed and dropped my face into my hands.

It was useless to fall for him again. We were over. We were so over.

And yet, I couldn't get my rapidly beating heart to agree.

How inconvenient.

Chapter Twenty-One

Sebastian

I fled.

I could admit that. I fled that room, that woman, that moment.

I'd made up my mind about her. Then there we were, alone, with her nearly naked and those beautiful blue eyes closed, her luscious mouth parted and expectant.

I could have kissed her. I could have pressed my mouth against hers and she would have been ready. But then she would have eventually come to her senses and pushed me away.

I had to force myself to wait until she was not just ready, but willing. When I kissed her again, I would make sure she fisted her hands in my shirt and pulled me closer. Not pushed me away.

Because when I say that I made up my mind about her, I meant that I made up my mind permanently. I wanted her.

I wanted her back.

I wanted her forever.

I had treated her poorly in the past, but not again. When I made her mine again, *and I would*, I wanted to do it right. I wanted to treat her the way she should be treated.

I wanted to make this permanent.

And I wanted to make myself permanent in every part of her life, heart and soul.

I hadn't lied to her when I told her I wanted to see her house in Seattle.

What I'd really like to do is make it my home too, but I couldn't tell her that just yet. I had a lot of time to think while she was unconscious and I was forced to wait for Avalon to come heal her.

It nearly drove me mad.

She'd been so sweet in her sleeping state. I hadn't been able to tear my eyes from her.

Jedrec and I had wandered for hours last night until we'd come upon a larger mountain village. We found a kind woman who had let us use her cell phone. She had taken one look at us and offered any kind of help we needed. We told her we were mugged and because we looked so dreadful, she believed us. I called Avalon first and told him to meet us at the Gypsy camp. He gave me Ileana's emergency number and I called her.

She'd been waiting for the call of course. The Gypsy Queen had answered with a terse, "What took you so long?"

I had no answer for that.

Then she went on to explain that transportation was on its way to pick us up.

We waited for another hour in the shadows of another rustic barn for our ride, which turned out to be a single horse and cart.

Gypsies.

We arrived at the Gypsy village near dawn. Avalon arrived two hours later.

During that time, I'd had a lot of time to think and marinate on the past, present and future. I'd had a lot of time to hold this stubborn, strong, gorgeous woman and think about her.

I'd come to a very important decision, one that would change my life and hers. I was done with our separation. I was done bickering with her about inane topics and struggling to stay away from her.

Seraphina was mine. She belonged to me. And I belonged to her. She owned my entire being, my soul, my Magic.

The time in Terletov's custody had proved that. The last year that I had to fight with all of my strength to keep from calling her, to keep from finding her, to keep from kissing her... had proved that.

I had been an idiot to try to live without her. A lonely, miserable idiot.

No longer.

When I convinced her to give us another try, and I would, I would do everything in my power to make it permanent and eternal between us. I wouldn't let her leave again. I wouldn't let us get in the way of this thing, this amazing, potentially epic thing, again.

While she was unconscious, I thought she might be receptive to the idea of trying one more time. I thought she had realized the same things I had while trapped in that room, tangled up in each other.

Apparently she hadn't.

After the last few minutes of arguing, I didn't think she was ready to admit any of her obvious feelings for me. She was still hurt from before and I couldn't blame her. But there was something undeniable between us and I wouldn't let her get away with ignoring it for much long. I would just have to take this slowly... carefully.

That didn't stop the surge of desire for her or the need to stake my claim over her and all of her things. I wanted to see her Seattle apartment and leave my mark, my touch, and my presence. Unlike her Omaha apartment that was saturated with me, this new home of hers didn't have anything Sebastian in it.

I wanted to change that.

Just like I wanted to do the same thing to her body. Her mind. Her soul.

She'd been without me for an entire year. I didn't know if she remembered how we were together, how I loved to play with the ends of her long hair, or stroke my fingers across the nape of her neck. I didn't know if she remembered the way we held each other through the night or gave each other long, seductive goodbye kisses, even if we were only going to be gone for an hour.

We were perfect for each other.

And I swore to myself that I would do everything it took to remind her of that.

The door to the house she'd been staying in opened and out she walked out in clothes Roxie had brought for her, black leggings and a black tank top. Apparently Roxie hadn't doubted that she would be part of this mission. I should have known better than to trust that woman.

Seraphina had pulled her hair up into a high ponytail and left her face clean and fresh. She was mission ready and should have looked practical and utilitarian. But I had never thought she was sexier than just now. The bottoms hugged her glorious ass and thighs and the tight top left little to the imagination.

I knew the thoughts running through her head were on the mission and killing a very deadly man.

But mine were decidedly different.

"You mess everything up."

The crackling voice ripped me out of my plans for Seraphina and back to the harsh plane of reality. I looked down at the Gypsy Queen and flashed my most charming smile. "My lady." I bowed my head regally.

She rolled her sharp, purple eyes. "That crap doesn't work with me." Her accent was thicker than usual and she seemed... tired. Very unusual for the Gypsy, who was usually feistier than any of my peers.

"What does work on you?" Schmoozing was my forte. Everyone knew that. Even Ileana. I should have predicted her sour attitude, but she was the Psychic, not me. "Apprise me of your preferences and I shall but do everything in my power to appease you, Your Royal Highness."

"Where is my cane when I need it? I should beat you like the others."

I suppressed my smile. Laughing at Avalon's misfortune would probably only make her angrier. She seemed cranky enough.

"Please don't," I pleaded gallantly. "I'm only trying to help."

"If you wanted to help me, you'd marry that girl by now. Your future is wearing on my nerves. I have other things to think about."

"I'm working on it," I muttered, effectively chastised. "She's not cooperating."

"She would have cooperated a year ago, you fool. Of course, she's not *now*. She's a complicated woman. And you're a donkey. I wouldn't cooperate with you either."

"Yes you would. You've always had a crush on me." I winked at her and watched her finally crack a smile.

"Maybe," she conceded.

We watched the courtyard full of Gypsies and Immortals as they prepared everything for dinner tonight. It would be a true feast, the celebration of a great battle to come.

"Are you here to tell me what to do with her?" I watched Seraphina track across the courtyard to Roxie. The two didn't bother hugging each other, neither girl was the affectionate type, but they cared for each other like only good friends could. Roxie put Seraphina to work with setting up the dinner and Sera dove right in.

She'd matured so much from our teenage years. I'd loved her even then, but now... Now there weren't adequate words to describe what I felt for her.

Ileana snorted, "No. You don't need me to tell you what to do. You're not nearly as dense as your King or the General. Thank goodness."

"Obviously."

"Obviously," she echoed with no small amount of awe for my arrogance. "There is much happening in your Kingdom, Prince. Enough to make this old woman feel it in her bones."

"What do you have to tell me?" Low pulses of fear surged through my Magic and put me on instant alert. This old woman could see the future. She had predicted enough for us to always take her word very seriously. And if she had sought me out specifically, then I would be involved.

"Tomorrow will not be the end."

"We won't win?"

"I cannot say whether the Citadel will be yours or not. I did not see that. I only know that whatever the outcome is tomorrow, win or lose, it will not be the end."

I felt her exhaustion spread to me, to my ribs and spine, to every part of me. "I've just decided to change that," I told her. "I'll make sure that tomorrow is, in fact, the very end."

She gave me a sad smile. "I would like you to try. But I can't help what I've seen. You will have other priorities tomorrow besides winning the day."

"What does that mean?" I demanded.

She didn't answer but simply went back to watching the activity around us. The sun burned orange near the horizon. Soon it would be dark and the heat of the day would sizzle away into a sticky night. The smell of campfire drifted on the warm summer breeze and the plucking of instruments warming up for the coming festivities mingled with laughter and light conversation.

Tomorrow could end badly for a lot of us. Tomorrow could mean death. So tonight would mean life. We would celebrate this day and the lives we still had and we would push off the fears and uncertainties that the morning would bring for as long as we could.

"Two new lives to watch. Two more lives to add to the thousands and thousands of strands that sift through my blood. They take a lot of work, you know. Those tiny Immortals that demand so much of my mind. They're so little but need so much." She had to be talking about the babies, but she sounded so sad. I immediately didn't like her tone and felt the need to defend them. She didn't give me the chance. "They won't be alone forever. One day there will be an entire generation of Immortals that they'll lead. Twins and twins and twins and twins and more. The Magic is back, Prince. You must protect it and then you must add to it."

Her words had become nothing but riddles now. I should have expected this, but I still raced to catch up with her. "Add to the Magic? How?"

Her smile turned devious. "I'm sure you'll figure it out," she said with a wink. "Now go to your woman before she forgets about you."

I didn't need to be told twice. It was impossible to tell if that was a real possibility or not. I didn't think Seraphina could forget about me. I didn't really think anyone could forget about me... but I also didn't think it was worth gambling on.

I leaned down and pressed a kiss to Ileana's wrinkled cheek. "You are a great woman. Thank you."

She reached up and patted my cheek with gnarled, rough fingers. The sentiment moved me somewhere deep in my chest. "And you are a great man, Sebastian Cartier, and a great prince. Go prove it to a woman that actually cares."

I walked away laughing. Only the Gypsy Queen could get away with disguising a pointed insult with such a sweet compliment.

"Good evening, Lovelies." I greeted the circle of women with all the false bravado I could work up. It was never easy walking into a company of women, more like a den of lionesses. These ones especially were intimidating enough on their own; each of them was a warrior and goddess in her own right, so together... whew. It took a brave man to face them together.

Thankfully, they all loved me.

"Bastian," Roxie murmured in greeting. "We were just talking about you."

That made me grin. Good. "I figured."

Seraphina stepped back a pinch, embarrassed that she'd been called out.

Roxie leaned in and in a conspiratorial tone said, "It was very valiant of you to carry Seraphina across an entire mountain range and save her life."

I looked across the circle and met Seraphina's frightened gaze. She looked like a wild animal trapped against the wall. She looked flighty. I held steady. "There was never another option, Rox. I will always do whatever it takes to *keep* Seraphina... alive." I played on the words purposefully and watched her big eyes grow even wider. She didn't know what to do with my seemingly abrupt change of heart.

I had to admit, I kind of liked keeping her guessing. She was adorably paranoid.

"But you would do that for any of us, right?" Roxie pushed.

I cut a glance at her and glowered. "I'm not sure I could lift you, Rox. You've got all that muscle. You need a bear of a man to handle you."

She glared back at me. "I don't need any man to handle me."

"Me either," Seraphina piped up.

I stepped into the middle of the circle, making my intentions clear. Olivia, Ophelia, and Roxie backed away. Liv patted me on the shoulder before she took her sister's hand and walked off. Roxie lingered for a few minutes later, clearly torn between Seraphina's beseeching silent plea and my clear intentions.

"Monaco," I said.

Roxie huffed a surprised breath. "Okay, but then that's it. You can't call it again."

"I know."

"Good. I'm glad to have that over with. You've been holding it over my head for far too long." And then she walked away.

I was finally alone with Seraphina. Again. But there had been at least a half hour since the last time.

Sera's eyes were on her friend. "What was that about? I've never seen Roxie agree to something so quickly."

I suppressed a smile. "She owed me a favor. I called it in."

"What favor?"

I looked back at Roxie too. She'd managed to make her way across the village and I doubted she'd looked back at us once. She was a very hard woman to crack, but I was the only soul on earth that truly knew what could undo her.

He just happened to be my closest mate and half-man, half-bear.

"We were in Monaco a few years back, just wasting time and spending money. Something happened that she didn't want anyone to know about. I told her I would keep her secret, but she owed me something in return."

Seraphina swung her incredulous gaze back to mine. Her blue eyes practically glowed in the twilight sky. Her cheeks flushed pink with outrage for her friend. "Where was I?"

"With your parents in Amsterdam."

"What happened?" her voice was a whisper of fear and suddenly I felt like the biggest arse.

"Nothing between me and her, Sera. God, nothing like that."

Her shoulders relaxed. "Then what?"

"She saw something she couldn't unsee. The rest of the night was spent in drunken debauchery in which she drove a Ferrari 911 into a fountain, froze three police officers to keep from getting arrested and robbed a casino."

"What?"

"It was not a good night for her. I, uh, helped her fix everything."

"That's so unlike Roxie!"

"I know. She knows. It was a bad night."

"What did she see? What could be so bad that would make her behave like that?"

I took a step closer and dropped my lips to her ear. "She watched Titus leave with another woman."

I felt the surprise and understanding ripple through her. She put her hands to my chest and I thought she might push me away, but she just held them there.

"I still can't imagine Roxie losing control like that."

"She's in love, Sera. People do crazy things when they're in love." I hadn't pulled away yet so I felt her full body shiver when I said the word "love." I leaned in just a touch more and let myself inhale the scent of her creamy skin. My lips grazed the curve of her neck when I said, "It wasn't that long ago that I threw you over my shoulder and kidnapped you from the date you were on. Love isn't exactly rational."

She cleared her throat. "I was in danger. I thought you said that didn't have anything to do with Andrei."

I smiled and bravely pressed a kiss to her throat. "Sure, that's why I did it."

This time her hands did push me away. "Sebastian, I need to go… I need to do something."

I lifted my head and met her stare. "What is it? I'll help."

She frowned. "No, I mean, I just, I… listen; tomorrow I realize I'm going to be stuck with you. I'd just like tonight to be Sebastian-free, alright? I need space."

Disappointment rang through me, but I gave her what she needed. I stepped back and separated myself from her. "Of course."

"Thank you."

"You're welcome."

She looked at the feast that had already begun, then back at me and then back at the feast. "I'll just, um, I'm hungry."

I held her gaze, "Me too."

Of course, I wanted to spend time with her and keep her close, but there was nothing like the satisfaction of watching her flee at those words.

Ileana was right; I just needed to make sure she didn't forget me. She couldn't deny this anymore than I could.

After tomorrow, I would throw everything into making her remember the good things about us, to making her think about nothing but me. I would keep myself near her until she couldn't deny this anymore.

She would be mine. And she would accept that I was hers.

And until then, I would just enjoy the chase.

Chapter Twenty-Two

Seraphina

The morning was cool despite the record hot summer we'd had. A thick fog settled over the rolling green hills of the mountain. The Citadel looked quiet and still from this distance.

It nestled into the hill and stood regally against the thick trees and majesty of the scenery. I had always loved this view. My family had made countless trips here during my lifetime. We'd pilgrimaged here for festivals and council meetings. My father had been Lucan's invited guest many times throughout my child, even though I hadn't officially met Kiran until he joined me at Kingsley. But I remembered cresting this hill every single time we'd visited and taking in the first breathtaking view of the capitol.

I would always breathe in a thick breath of relief and feel at home.

When I'd originally been made Kiran's fiancée, I couldn't wait for the moment that this castle would be mine. I imagined a lifetime of court held within these walls and the endless balls and parties I would throw.

When I lost Kiran to Eden, I had been less upset about losing the man than the Citadel.

I had hated Eden for taking this dream of mine away.

Obviously, I'd gotten over it and my greedy future aspirations. But I still felt the thrill and hope that came with this one stunning view.

The Immortal army Avalon had amassed joined me on the top of the hill. He'd called in Titans from everywhere, even from the places like St. Stephen's and Peru. It was a risky move to bring everyone here, but we wanted to throw all of our efforts into reclaiming this one place. And hopefully, *finally* take out Terletov for good.

But from here, things got a little tricky. Our cars and various vehicles of transportation lay abandoned on the side of the road. We would attack the Citadel on foot.

We were all equipped with swords and guns that could match any force Terletov and his men could throw at us. I wore black cargo pants and a long-sleeve black shirt to protect my skin.

Men and women fanned out to either side of the road with just as much love and respect for this place as I had.

The full Titan guard, save for the entourage that stayed with Eden, Kiran and the babies, made up most of our army, but not all. Those that had once been loyal to the Resistance also joined us. That's where the women came from. The Resistance had always been equal opportunity, unlike the Guard.

Sebastian put a heavy hand on my shoulder. "You could always wait for me here."

Or most of the Resistance had been equal opportunity...

I couldn't help but laugh a little. "I suppose you could do the same. I'm very worried about you. Better sit this one out so I feel better about myself."

He frowned at me. "Point taken."

I curtsied obnoxiously. "Thank you."

"You promised to stay with me."

"I didn't say I wouldn't. I just want you to get the idea that I would give this up out of your head. I'm doing this Sebastian. How did you put it? Oh, right. This is happening."

His lips twitched. "God, you're unbelievably sexy."

I felt my mouth drop open in surprise. My mind when blank and my stomach bubbled with excitement.

How did he do that so effortlessly?

Before I could make sense of his words or the look on his face, Avalon addressed the army with a shouting voice. "We take this back today! We will not put up with this treachery for a moment longer! This is ours by right! This is ours by law! The Magic has been freed and our people are free. We will not put up with Terletov and his tyranny for a moment longer! Join me friends and reclaim our capitol! Reclaim our freedom!"

I felt purpose and intent drive through my veins and electrify my Magic. I had needed yesterday to recover from Terletov's horrific torture, but I was ready today.

So ready.

We charged the hill as one legion. There were men stationed all around the wall when we finally reached it and the battle began immediately.

I didn't bother engaging with these minions. Sebastian and I were part of a select team. Our mission was to get the gates open and the rest of our people inside the city walls.

We veered off from the larger group and disappeared into the thick woods that bordered the Citadel. We ran along with Roxie, Jericho, Olivia, Ophelia, Titus, Xander, and Xavier. Avalon had hung back to fight with the army, even though I knew that this team was his home.

He had a hard time being anywhere else than with us.

The sounds of battle followed us as we went. I could have sworn I heard dogs barking and howling along with swords clashing and guns firing.

We stayed far enough inside the woods that we didn't run into any resistance until we emerged on the other side of the wall. And when we finally met the guards that stood sentinel against the back wall, we didn't hesitate.

We rushed them with no remorse and no fear. We raised our guns and started shooting.

They were jumpy and not focused on the attack. Their ears were turned toward the front of the Citadel where sounds of battle rang loudly through the forest.

They should have expected our attack, but these were not men bred for battle. These were just bad people that had signed up with the wrong guy. Terletov had trained them, but not well enough.

The Titans that fought alongside us had done nothing else with their lives except train for war. And the Resistance members had enough experience to put this pathetic insurgence to shame.

Sure, if they managed to surprise us, they could get the upper hand. But obviously not for long.

We took out our enemy in a few minutes. They put up a good fight, but in the end we opened the back door victoriously.

Sebastian had explained that his Magic had worked when we escaped. We went into this fight hoping it still would, but we didn't know what to expect. It was one of the reasons that we attacked so soon. We knew that Terletov would find the door once we went through it, but we hoped he hadn't had enough time to figure out how to change the Magic.

Sebastian put his hand to the handle and we waited with bated breath for the Magic to take hold.

The lock clicked over our rapid breathing and the door swung open. *Thank God.*

Our small team rushed into the brambly hedge. Right away there was more danger. I shot first and ducked when the bullet from my enemy whizzed by.

I'd just managed to get the guy in the stomach. He collapsed on the ground unconscious.

We used the same kinds of guns they did, only when we shot them they died. It was a consequence of their extreme strength and giving Terletov their loyalty. We might slip into a coma after a bullet, but they could not survive one.

I couldn't decide which fate I'd rather have if I were one of them. There ugly Magic was bound to kill them slowly. They were dead men either way.

Once the guy that shot at us was down, we moved forward a little more carefully. We took each corner with precision and intelligence.

By the time we got to the balcony, thirteen more men had been put out of commission.

At this point, we split up. Xander, Xavier, Roxie, and Titus ran along the wall toward the front gates, where they would, hopefully, overpower the men on the inside of the wall and let the army in. Olivia, Ophelia, Jericho, Sebastian and I would infiltrate through the ballroom and create a diversion big enough to give the rest of our team time to open the gates.

Easy.

We slinked up the balcony steps and climbed through the glass that hadn't been replaced since Sebastian and my escape. Our feet crunched on broken glass, signaling our arrival.

At least I had shoes on this time.

"Eden's going to kill me," Jericho whispered. He held a few sticks of dynamite in his hand.

It was amazing what the Gypsies kept in storage.

Amazing and also alarming.

"Are you sure we can't die?" Ophelia asked with wide eyes.

"Don't worry about it," Jericho assured her. "We'll be fine. The ballroom however... will not be."

"This is only the second time we've destroyed it," Olivia rushed to assure him. "Surely she will understand."

Sebastian gave her a dry look. "Eden understands accidentally blowing things up. Believe me. She has us all beat."

That was true. The Indian Palace for example.

I had loved that place too.

Sigh.

Sebastian, Ophelia and I took off running down the hallway to clear a path for Liv and Jericho. There were a few men that needed taking care of, but everything went as planned.

I felt the moment still, as if all of the air were sucked into the ballroom just before Jericho lit the long fuse. I heard Olivia and he start running and his forceful "Go!"

We took off sprinting again and this time didn't bother to stop and shoot bad guys. They didn't even know what to do with us when we ran by them. They stood dumbly confused until the first echoes of the foreboding boom finally hit them.

The dynamite detonated in a scream of destruction. We tried to outrun the explosion, but it was only seconds before I felt the pressure hit my back.

My feet stopped touching the ground and my arms flew back when the momentum threw me forward. My vision blurred and the air got knocked from my lungs completely.

I saw the wall in front of me, but there was nothing I could do to slow my impact with it. Luckily, the blast still followed behind me and the stone crumbled with me.

Pain shot through every bone and muscle in my body. White dots danced in my vision when I landed. My *Magic* felt damaged by the impact. Holy shit that hurt!

Someone should have been a little more upfront with me about the kind of ungodly pain I was going to go through in order to "create a diversion." They'd made it sound so simple.

Yeah right! Ouch!!!

Freaking ouch!

Strong arms wrapped around my waist and pulled me to my feet. "Did you survive?" Sebastian asked.

I winced, "No."

"Ready to leave?"

I smiled and finally his face stopped being three versions and funneled into one. "Not a chance. Besides, I'm already here."

"You're already here," he agreed.

He set me on my feet and moved on to help Ophelia. She wasn't as quick to shake off the blast. She still struggled to figure out her Magic. But as far as I could tell, the two human sisters were as strong and capable as any other Immortal I'd ever met.

Unlike the last time I was here, Magic rushed through my blood without faltering, without fading.

I felt incredibly resilient and capable. I felt invincible.

Which was a good thing, since I needed every ounce of stamina and strength I could muster.

The wall we collapsed led to what was once a guest room, but had been turned into a prison since Terletov took over. It looked a lot like the room Sebastian and I had been thrown into.

Dark drapes covered the long windows and all of the furniture had been removed. People lay scattered over the bare floor in various states of rags and nakedness. Their thin hands were bound behind their backs. They looked starved and sickly.

My stomach lurched at the sight of them and I felt murderous. How dare they be treated this way! How dare someone disrespect the gift of life like this.

I often teased Mimi for her humanitarian spirit. She was ridiculously bleeding-hearted. And I thought it was adorable that she cared so much for the human race who could only live a few decades on this earth anyway.

But seeing these people, sick, starved and mistreated, birthed a fiery revenge that burned hot and furious through my blood.

I could not accept this.

I *would* not.

Death would not be good enough for Terletov. I wanted to wrap my hands around his neck and make him pay for what he had done and for how many he had killed. I wanted to kill him, bring him back to life and then kill him again.

I wanted to put him through every last torturous procedure he'd used on his victims. I wanted him to scream in agony, cry in desperation, I wanted him to suffer in the purest, rawest sense of the word.

I covered my mouth and nose and tried not to gag on the stench and rot that filled this space. The people writhed and whimpered as we walked all the way into the room and stood over them.

I squatted down and tried to meet one of the women's eyes, but she turned her head and tensed in fear.

"I'm not going to hurt you," I promised in a gentle voice.

She didn't believe me.

I took out my sword and very carefully cut through the rough ropes that bound her hands. Her wrists were bloodied and completely raw. They flopped at her sides because she was too weak to lift them.

My stomach clenched in empathy and tears misted my eyes. I stood up abruptly, too overcome to face her. I turned to find Sebastian, hoping he could ease this for me. His haunted eyes met mine and I knew without a doubt that he felt the same upheaval of emotions I did.

"I'm going to eviscerate him," Sebastian declared.

Faraway shouting interrupted the quiet of this room. Our army had broken through the gates. The castle would be flooded with Titans any minute.

"Then let's go," I told Sebastian. "Let's hunt him down and make him pay for what he did to us. For what he did to them."

Sebastian turned to Jericho, but Jericho just waved him on.

"Go," Olivia ordered. "We'll see to them."

"Are you sure?" I asked her.

She leveled me with her steady gaze. "I'm positive. I've been here. I know what they're going through. We can handle it; just... just make sure he dies. Yeah?"

I nodded once. "Yeah."

Sebastian took my hand and pulled me back into the hallway. We took off running into the center of the castle. He seemed to know exactly where he wanted to go, so I let him.

"Where do you think he is?"

We turned the corner and started making our way down the hall, careful to listen out for any of Terletov's men. The hallways were dark. The torches had been put out and not even the emergency lights that lined the floor were turned on. The windows had been covered a long time ago and none of the daylight managed to sneak by. The blackness gave our mission an extra ominous feeling.

The hallways were also eerily quiet. Beyond the constant sounds of battle from the other side of the castle walls, not a footstep echoed. I didn't like that.

There should be more resistance. We should have to fight our way to Terletov.

It was way too easy.

"My gut is telling me the throne room. He's too arrogant to hide. And he believes he belongs there."

"Where is everyone?" I'd dropped my voice to a whisper, paranoid that someone could hear us. If there was anyone near, I couldn't see him.

My Magic made it possible to see through the darkness, but I wasn't omnipotent. I had limitations, even with my super skills.

We reached the main floor and still not a sound came from anywhere. We walked carefully down the corridor towards the throne room.

I clutched Sebastian's hand and vaguely wondered if we were stupid to attempt to kill Terletov on our own.

"Maybe we should wait for Avalon," I whispered.

His Magic reached out and pulsed through mine. It was the first time I'd realized our Magic had been connected since we were here last. I didn't know if he'd kept it purposefully subtle, or if he had forgotten to separate too. But we were definitely still connected.

It had to be the habit of it.

For so long this was my normal... that had to be why I didn't notice.

I cleared my throat and tried to figure out a polite way to pull it out now. Was that rude? Was there protocol for this? And we were just about to walk into a major conflict.

I decided to wait. We were stronger together anyway. We probably needed the extra strength during this battle. Once Terletov was dead, I would remove my Magic from Sebastian's permanently.

Something cold slithered through me at that thought.

I didn't like the idea of never being connected to Sebastian again. My Magic was warm and fuzzy right now, extra insulated and perfectly at peace. It hated being alone. And I was threatening to not only rip it away from the only connection it had ever known, but potentially leave it that way for the rest of my life.

"Are you alright?" Sebastian asked as we neared the throne room. "You seem... distracted."

I forced my mind to remember all of those humans on the floor of that room, packed together like discarded trash. It worked. I stopped thinking about all of the possibilities with Sebastian right then.

We had a battle to fight.

"I'm good," I told him. I put my hand on the door handle of the throne room. "Let's do this."

He nodded once and I pulled open the door.

"Finally," Terletov greeted us. He sat in the middle throne, Lucan's old seat. Alexi sat to his right. "I wondered what took you so long."

"We're here now," Sebastian growled.

"Then we can begin." Terletov nodded and that single, small gesture turned the room into a battlefield.

We were attacked from every side.

Chapter Twenty-Three

Sebastian

They came at us from all sides. The throne room... a rather sacred room for this Kingdom, even when Lucan ruled, became a war zone.

I used my gun until I ran out of bullets. Bang. Bang. Bang. The shots echoed deafeningly throughout the room. I deflected anything that came at me and at Sera.

I would probably catch hell for that later, but I couldn't watch her get hurt again. And so sure, I was the alpha jerk, but as long as she stayed alive and conscious, I didn't care.

Besides, our combined Magic seemed super-charged lately. Together we were so much stronger than ever before. We were faster, more agile and infinitely more prepared than these weak-Magicked minions.

They couldn't block bullets like we could, so they fell easily, whenever we hit our target. And unlike true Immortals that could only be made unconscious with a bullet wound, these imposters died instantly. Their sickly green energy would expel from their bodies immediately. Whatever Terletov did to them made them stronger, but their Magic so much weaker.

I would have felt sorry for them if they hadn't sold their soul to a monster and tried to take over a Kingdom I risked life and limb to build.

So, as it was, I felt no remorse when they fell dead at my feet.

Sera and I stood back to back in the center of the room, moving seamlessly and in sync. We had bonded our Magic in this same castle in an effort to stay alive and then on the run, I'd kept us connected just in case Sera needed my Magic. When Avalon pulled the bad Magic out of her, I had considered removing my Magic. I thought it might be the chivalrous thing to do.

But then I'd decided I didn't really care. I wanted us to be united forever, so why not start now? Besides, I was curious to see how long it would take her to notice.

I wasn't entirely sure if she had noticed yet. Surely she had to realize we were super-charged together. So now, I didn't know if she kept us connected because of the sheer power we could wield or for other reasons.

I preferred other reasons. But I couldn't exactly ask her.

My plan had entirely backfired.

We ran out of bullets at almost the exact same time. We both pulled swords from our belts and waved them at Terletov's men. They still had guns though, so it wasn't a very fair fight.

I would have to trust our Magic to continue deflecting.

"Are you here to get your revenge?" Terletov taunted from a casual position on a throne that did not belong to him. I could hear his smug grin and I wanted nothing more than to take my sword and plunge it into his guts and slice him open from navel to neck.

"Among other reasons," I growled.

"How precious. And you brought your girlfriend with you. That shows some foresight if I've ever seen it. Bravo for thinking ahead."

I thought about the army outside this door. I thought about all of the people that wanted this tyrant dead.

He had no idea what he was going to face today. So be it. He didn't deserve to know.

"And your plan is to hole up in here? A room without an exit? That is an equally golden idea." I risked a glance at him; he appeared unmoved by my words.

"I heard the people have started to riot."

Seraphina and I walked a slow circle, keeping our backs against each other's. The men paused their attack to let Terletov have his say, but I knew it was only a tactic to lure us into unpreparedness. I would not be taken off guard. He might as well give up now.

"They're afraid of you. As they should be. You would trade their life in a second to further your... study."

"That's very true, *my prince*. I'm pleased with how quickly you learn. But I don't agree with their fear. They simply have not learned to accept what is for the greater good. They need to embrace this new regime. They need to understand that I hold the keys to a better future. Their future."

My stomach turned at his disillusion. "I'm sure they would prefer their freedom and Magic left very much alone."

He snorted. "What Magic? The Magic has been stolen from us! I'm simply trying to reclaim our rightful inheritance."

I had never understood this argument of his. The Magic was stronger than ever. Seraphina alone proved this theory. Her amped up visions and increased powers were proof enough that the Magic beat stronger with every day that passed.

"You mean your Magic was stolen," I threw back at him. "*Your Magic* was stolen when our Queen was but a seventeen-year-old child. And now you've punished the entire Kingdom and half of humanity and are still no closer to reclaiming your Magic than you were all those years ago. It's pathetic really. It's contrived and desperate."

"And sick," Seraphina added. "It's so very sick. These men that you've *changed* are already dead and you don't even care. The blood on your hands has to be heavier than cement. And when you finally die, it will drop you straight to the pits of hell."

"I better not die then." He stood from his seat and bounded down the dais stairs. Alexi followed after him, his face grim and stoic. Dmitri stood a foot away from me and smiled. "Any idea where our lovely Queen is held up? I'd love to chat with her."

I glared at him. "You'll never find her. She's out of your reach."

"Do you know that when she took my Magic, I vowed to kill everyone that she loves before I sent her to the grave?" His cold eyes glittered with malice and I felt a chill of foreboding. "Every single creature that she holds dear. Or, I should say, every single creature that she holds *most* dear."

"You will not touch her." My body and Magic vibrated with fury. I would not let this psychopath leave here alive today. I would not let him anywhere near Eden or her family.

He smirked in a way I found unforgivably patronizing. "I don't want to touch her, at least not yet. I'd much prefer to meet the heirs to the throne first. I hear they are quite the cuties."

That word sounded wrong coming out of his mouth. Talking about the children did nothing to quell the building storm of revenge and rage building inside of me. I was finished with small talk. I wanted to move along to the main event.

I moved before he could spit out another twisted word. I swung the sword around and aimed for his chest. Before I could reach him, Alexi stepped between us, and our weapons clashed. I hadn't even realized he held a sword until we were in the middle of hand-to-hand combat.

I was not as proficient in hand-to-hand combat as I would have liked to have been, but my Magic would help. I had been practicing with the sword and the gun since this Terletov nightmare began, though. I hoped I could take out Alexi quickly and then move on to his older brother.

So that's what I set out to do. I glanced quickly over my shoulder to check on Sera. She seemed to be holding her own just fine.

Bullets continued to fire now that we were back to fighting, but I managed to deflect with my Magic each time. I also used my Magic against my opponent. I swung my sword out and hit his with jarring impact. I threw my Magic at him and knocked him back several steps.

I followed quickly after him and tried to angle myself toward Terletov. He had this talent of staying completely out of the conflict while hovering just around the edges. I decided that was because one forceful shove was likely to kill the man. He looked dreadfully frail these days. His skin had turned pallid and all around his eyes little black veins had started to snake out down his cheeks and up his forehead and temples.

He was a very sick man.

If we didn't kill him soon, he was likely to die of natural causes.

And his brother was not in any better shape.

But I needed to keep my eye on both of the Terletov men. If Dmitri planned to step in to save anybody, I believed the only person it would be was Alexi.

I feinted right at the same time I used my Magic to pull Alexi closer. His eyes had been just over my shoulder when I made my move. I took advantage of his fatal distraction and slid my sword through his kidneys before he even registered what had happened.

My blade was sharp and true. I felt the crush of flesh and bone beneath as I plunged the sword deep inside of him and then the explosion of green energy as it erupted from his wound.

I stepped back and took my weapon with me. I spun on one foot and swung out again. The room converged on me at once. I didn't even have time to gloat. Apparently nobody appreciated the fact that I'd taken out one of this Kingdom's two major problems.

This was going to be a long day.

An ungodly scream wrenched from Terletov and out of the corner of my eye, I watched him drop to his knees by his dead brother.

Men surrounded me from every direction. If I could just get through them, I could take out Terletov while he knelt on the floor, vulnerable.

I wondered what was taking Avalon so long. He should definitely have found us by now. But I worried he'd been held up outside. I could hear the battle still raging all around us.

I didn't know if that was a good thing or a bad thing.

Hopefully, it meant we were decimating Terletov's forces and there would be no one left to take up his torch once we'd ended him for good.

I kept Terletov in my sights at all times, even while taking on three and four men at a time. I expected my Magic to drain and for me to feel the effects of heavy fighting, but with Seraphina's linked to mine, my energy stayed at full-strength.

My body moved fluidly and expertly. My sword struck precisely. And my death toll had started to become epic.

If only I could get to Terletov.

Just as I laid waste to a particularly burly fellow, Sera's scream echoed through the room and caused panic to scrape through me. I whirled around and put my back to the far wall. I was readied to do whatever it took to help her. I didn't care who I had to kill or the lengths I had to go to make sure she survived; I would do whatever it took.

Without hesitation.

Terletov himself had managed to grab hold of her. I could hardly believe it. I had been watching him the entire time! How the hell had he done that?

He held her by the hair, tipping her head back so he could press a sword blade against her perfect throat.

"No," I breathed.

He flashed a sadistic grin. "You could save her if I just nicked her skin. You'd have your Queen use whatever bullshit she uses to patch her up. But not if I cut all the way through. How would you save her if I detached her head? How could your precious Queen save her then?"

I couldn't even think of a response. My throat and mouth had filled with such blind hate that no words could force their way through.

He yanked roughly on Sera's hair, causing her to jerk her head back at an unnatural angle, but she didn't make another sound. And now that I replayed her scream in my head with better clarity, I could recognize her sound as pure frustration rather than fear or pain.

This girl was so much stronger than I gave her credit for.

I was so very proud of her in this moment that I wanted nothing more than to rescue her so I could whisk her away to somewhere private where I could convince her to fall madly in love with me again.

And then we would stay there for days, weeks, maybe even months. Potentially years. However, long it took to make up for the last year of being apart.

I wasn't in any kind of hurry.

But first I had to save her.

"You killed my *brother*," Terletov snarled at me. "You're going to have to pay for that."

Crashing sounds worked their way from down the hallway. I could hear the pounding of footsteps running toward us, and voices shouting.

The cavalry. Just in time.

Terletov's brow furrowed as if he really didn't think there was a possibility that he'd lost. I wanted to smile, but it was too soon. I had to get Seraphina free first.

I met her wide eyes and tried to convey hope and trust. But it didn't seem to take. She looked part frightened and mostly pissed.

Of course, she wouldn't be so easy as to let us share a moment before her potential death. She would never let me have something so meaningful without working for it.

Just another reason why I loved her.

"Stop them," Terletov ordered his men. They left immediately and the sounds of battle began again just on the other side of the door.

Terletov backed toward the door with Seraphina still in his grasp. I met him stride for stride, trying to get as close to them as I could.

"Not so fast," he warned. "You have to pay for what you did. It is my *right* to kill her."

"Let her go," I growled. "It's time to accept that you lost."

"Never." He stood just at the door now. His men had closed it behind them. I wondered what he had planned. Titans filled the hallway and Avalon would surely be with them.

I had my answer in the next moment. He raised the sword as if to strike her, but the door behind him crashed open instead. Both Seraphina and he were knocked to the side.

In order to distract me, he shoved her in my direction and I instinctively caught her. But at the same time, Terletov spun around and plunged his sword into the first person through the door.

Avalon.

Avalon gripped the hilt of the blade embedded in his midsection and fell to his knees. Terletov looked down at him with a satisfied grin and then ran from the room. I yelled some incoherent instructions at the Titans fighting in the hallway, but I had no idea if they heard me or understood anything.

Seraphina pushed me. "Go!" she yelled.

I made sure she could stand on her own and then I ran to Avalon. He had fallen over and lay awkwardly on his side.

I glanced at the hallway and then back at my friend. *Shit!* What should I do?

"Go after him!" Avalon wheezed. He coughed and blood sputtered from his mouth.

Shite! I couldn't leave him.

"I'm not leaving you." I fell to my knees and grabbed the heavy hilt. "This is going to hurt."

"Just leave it in," Avalon begged. "I'd rather you left it in."

I looked up to find Mimi on her knees behind him. I hadn't even noticed her with Avalon bleeding out on the floor.

"Get it out of him," she pleaded. Tears slipped from her eyes and wet her flushed cheeks.

I couldn't let my sister see this any longer. I had to do something.

"I'm serious, Bastian," Avalon whimpered. "It's going to hurt. Leave it in."

"You're such a baby!" I could not believe him. "It already hurts! I can see your bloody intestines!"

He clutched at the hilt as if he could hold it in forever. I rolled my eyes because he was seconds from passing out. If we were going to play the waiting game, I was obviously going to win.

"I'll do it quickly," I promised him. "You won't even feel it."

He made a noise that I couldn't define other than agonized. I gripped the hilt, spread my knees to get some kind of leverage and amped up my Magic.

I had imagined the blade just slipping right out, the same way it had gone into him.

That was not what happened.

It took quite a bit of effort, even with Magic aiding me. By the time the sword came free, I had a fine sheen of sweat covering my brow.

Avalon's hands covered his still bleeding midsection where Magic seeped out of him. He closed his eyes and tilted his head back. Mimi cupped his jaw immediately and pressed a gentle kiss to his dry lips.

"I'll be fine," he whispered. "I already feel the Magic working. I just have to wait it out."

"Good," I grunted while my sister started crying harder.

"Did you get him?" Avalon wheezed.

"Get who?"

"Terletov?"

Was he serious? "Obviously not. He ran off right after he stabbed you."

Avalon opened his eyes to scowl at me. "I told you I was fine! You should have gone after him."

I staggered to my feet and turned around. Sera had collapsed on the ground and sat there shaking and shell-shocked. Mimi wasn't the only one deeply affected by the image of Avalon's guts spilled open all over the floor.

I bent over and picked her up, cradling her in my arms once again.

"I can walk," she whispered.

Reluctantly I set her back on her feet but kept her pressed against me. "Can you at least tell me my fears were validated?" I beseeched her.

A small smile tugged at her lips, but she ignored my question. "I can't believe we didn't get him."

"We got his army though," I reminded her. "And the Citadel. It wasn't an entirely unproductive day."

Avalon groaned dramatically. I rolled my eyes. Seraphina sighed.

"He'll be fine."

"Sebastian!" My sister sounded aghast with my nonchalance.

I shot her a cheeky grin. "I'll have some of the Titans prepare your room, Your Highness."

"I... you don't understand what that was like for me. I can't watch that again," Mimi whispered.

I looked down at Seraphina and understood exactly. "I know what you mean, sister dearest." I cupped Seraphina's face and let her see the undisguised adoration I felt for her. She didn't look away, but her face flashed with a myriad of confused emotions. "Stay with him, Mimi. I'll see if I can find out what happened to Terletov. I'll send someone in to help with your husband and have your room or at least a room prepared for you. Just stay with him. I'll take care of everything else for you."

She smiled weakly at me. "Kiran was right to put you in charge, Bastian. You're good at this."

I winked at her. "I'm good at everything."

Before she could disagree, I grabbed Sera's hand and led her from the room.

"I should go check on those humans we found. I should see if there are any more rooms filled with abused people."

"We can do that together. This day isn't over, Sera. Don't even think about leaving my side."

"If we split up, we could go fast-"

"No," I said firmly.

"Sebastian-"

"Sera, did you see that look of horror on my sister's face when her husband was stabbed and bleeding?"

"Yes."

"Well, I might not be able to pull off her theatrics, but that's how I feel about you and about what could happen to you. Do you understand? Do you understand why I don't want to let you out of my sight?"

She looked at me like she couldn't believe I admitted that. Honestly, I couldn't believe it either. But I was at the point where I would do anything to keep her with me, even if that meant telling her the whole truth for once.

"Okay."

I smiled gently at her. "Thank you."

She shrugged and that was the end of the conversation. She stayed with me the entire rest of the day as we tried to make sense of the Citadel and what happened to Terletov. He seemed to have just disappeared.

We might have dismantled his army and taken away his base of operations, but I knew without a doubt that we hadn't seen the last of Dmitri Terletov.

Chapter Twenty-Four

Seraphina

"Can you walk?" I looked down at the emaciated woman that I'd helped sit up. Olivia handed her a bottle of water and urged her to drink slowly.

When she finished with the water, Liv and I each took her under the arms and helped her to her feet. We tried to steady her, but she had no strength to hold her body up.

A Titan watched us struggle for less than thirty seconds before he came over to take her from us. We passed her off with instructions to carry her to the medical wing Sylvia had set up before Terletov took over the Citadel.

There had been a team of Titans, supervised by Ophelia and Xander, working all day and night to set the wing to rights again. The rest of the Titans had been dispersed throughout the castle to open every single door and search for displaced humans and Immortals. Bedrooms were searched, closets, kitchens, secret passages we hadn't even known existed. Basically, we had people scouring every single inch of this structure and surrounding town in case there were any more victims.

So far, we had found seventy-six bodies. Not all of them had survived Terletov's reign.

I felt bile bubble up in my stomach. It had been a tough twenty-four hours, to put it mildly.

I didn't think I would ever recover from the horrors I'd seen and experienced. The smell alone could have knocked me on my ass.

We had been working constantly, ever since we chased Terletov from the castle. I shivered at the memory that he was still out there, still terrorizing this planet with his sick and twisted ways.

We needed to find him pronto. And of course that was a major priority. But we also had to take care of these people and return our Citadel to the pristine, noble seat where our Kings and Queens ruled.

Another riot had broken out in London two days ago, even though the royal family had fled the house. And then yesterday, there had been rioting in Paris where Sebastian's parents lived.

Sebastian had been shocked that the Kingdom still associated his family with the Monarchy. I had tried to hide my eye roll. As if people just forgot that Bianca was Lucan's sister. Or that Sebastian had once been a prince and second in line to the throne.

The Paris riot had been awful. Immortals had attacked the Cartier Residence with nasty aggression and threatened to burn it to the ground. The incident had made the news in Paris, although the human media couldn't quite explain the conflict.

Jedrec had taken Analisa there to heal, and so Bianca had been forced to call the local authorities. Kiran and Eden were there too in order to be with his mom, who had finally, and thankfully, woken up. We all hoped the riots would be put to a stop now that the Citadel was back in our control.

But it would take some serious work to gain the Kingdom's full trust again.

And who could blame them? Terletov had wreaked havoc on this people all across the globe. And he was still alive. We still hadn't managed to end him once and for all.

But at least we had our home back.

"I'm exhausted," Liv sighed once we saw the Titan and the broken Immortal woman through the door.

"You're Magic should help," I told her. I knew how hard it was for Eden to remember her Magic. Olivia probably had the same issue.

Obviously, that was not a problem I could relate to in any way.

She leaned against the doorframe and looked at me, really looked at me. I saw it in her face then, exhaustion and something deeper, a tiredness that transcended the physical.

"I think this is something not even Magic can help," she sighed. "It's more like weariness. I'm world-weary. It's a bone-deep kind of thing, you know?"

My heart clenched. Now this was something I could relate to. "I do know. How's Jericho? How is he dealing with the news about his parents?"

"He's dealing," she sighed. "It obviously wasn't easy news, but he's been grieving them for a while. If anything, I think the confirmation that they're dead might have given him closure."

"I could see that."

She crossed her arms and looked down at her feet. "You know, I hated this world at first. Your Magic and your way of life. I blamed you for ruining me. Well, not you specifically, but your people as a whole." I nodded, showing her I understood. "But then I guess you all kind of grew on me and I adapted to the Magic and... Jericho." She cleared her throat and smiled adoringly at her tennis shoes. She was either super in love with Nike or Jericho, and she was in that annoying honeymoon phase.

"But it's so hard here. I mean, my normal life had its ups and downs too, but this is *insanity*. All of these people! And the killings and Terletov! I can barely wrap my head around the destruction. I don't know how you survive the heartache."

I looked at the once-glamorous room. The silk curtains were tattered and filthy. The polished floor was covered in a thick layer of ash and filth. The rich furniture had been removed and replaced with rubble. This castle that used to smell like promise and excitement had turned rank and bitter. My chest squeezed again.

"I don't know either," I admitted. "Maybe because it's never been roses and rainbows. To an extent this Kingdom has only known suffering and death. We had a few years of reprieve between the old regime and Terletov, but when you live as long as we do, that's hardly anything."

Olivia's expression saddened. "That does not sell me on this whole Immortal thing."

I chuckled a little at her bleak outlook. "It's not all bad," I promised. "There have been bad men that try to destroy us, but if anything it's made us stronger as a people. We survived Lucan and we'll survive Terletov too. And after we get rid of him, we'll piece ourselves back together and crawl out of the fire a brighter, beautifully refined Kingdom. I'm not saying that our trials are good things or that I wanted them to happen, but we are resilient and we're usually smart enough to learn from these experiences and grow."

"How can you possibly grow from this?"

I thought about Lilly and Talbott, and how afraid to get married Lilly had been. She hadn't wanted to be a spectacle or gossip fodder for the Kingdom. I thought about Avalon's push to make the nation a democracy and abolish the Monarchy forever. "The Kingdom has been notoriously slow to change," I explained. "I think this will be a boost in the right direction. Hopefully."

"I suppose there will always be evil in the world." She sighed. "Humanity obviously has their fair share of tragedy and catastrophe."

"It's what we do to counteract the evil that matters, right? I learned that lesson the hard way a long time ago."

"What do you mean?" She stood up straight and cocked an eyebrow at me.

I couldn't help the embarrassed smile or the faint blush of red to my cheeks. I wasn't the blushing kind of girl usually, but my past was the one thing in my life that could bring me to my knees with humiliation. I had just been so... wrong. So very wrong.

"I used to *be* the evil in the world, Liv. I mean, I wasn't exactly the Wicked Witch of the West, but I had my fair share of villainy."

"Seraphina the reformed bad girl? I never would have guessed."

I laughed along with her. "I know what you're thinking; I'm just so sweet and innocent. It's hard so hard to picture me doing deeds of destruction."

Her smile turned more thoughtful. "No, it's not that you're so innocent or anything. It's just that... well, I know Sebastian and you were so serious for so long. And I trust Sebastian to make smart decisions with whom he falls in love. I have a hard time believing he would go for someone evil."

"I wasn't exactly evil. I was mostly spoiled. And I was engaged to Kiran when Eden came into our lives. I didn't exactly play nice."

"Ah," Olivia said with understanding. "Love makes us do crazy things."

"Except I was never in love with Kiran. It was just, well mostly a status thing. Kingdom politics and what not."

She gave me a look that said she could care less about Kingdom politics. I just loved that about her.

"I figured it out though," I reassured her. "I realized there was more to life than being a princess and more to my heart than an unfeeling contract, neither of us wanted to be a part of. I need love and trust."

"Truth." She winked at me. "Sebastian showed you that?"

"He did." My voice was a forced whisper. It was hard to admit that was true. He had also shown me what it meant not to trust someone and what it meant to lose someone. My chest already felt tight, but with the reminder of how much I'd loved Sebastian and how much I'd lost when we ended things, my heart fissured into a thousand different cracks and splinters.

"Can I ask what happened between you two?" I must have looked slightly horrified because she quickly explained, "It's just that when you talk about him, it's like you had this fairytale romance. But you're not together now. I'm just trying to understand."

I didn't answer right away. I didn't know how to answer right away. The words tumbled around in my head, but they felt empty and inadequate. Finally, I said, "We wanted different things. And neither of us was willing to compromise."

"You said that before. I just... I can't believe that's all. I mean, seriously, that's it?"

Her simple response jarred me. "Yes. I mean... yes." I shifted on my heels and looked around the room, needing something to do with my hands. Her response left me uneasy and restless. What did she mean *that's it*? Of course, that was it! We both wanted different things. How is there a future in that? Finally, I couldn't take it anymore. "What do you mean by that?"

She gave me a patient smile. "Well, I thought you guys loved each other."

"We do! Er, I mean we did!"

"Then who cares if you want different things? Figure out a way to make it work. Or to give each other what you wanted. Who cares what those different things are. If you love each other, you stick together and make it work. Isn't it better to be together than apart?"

"I don't know about that." I felt as uncertain as I sounded. "It was hard to be together. We just didn't... there were big issues there. He wanted one thing and I wanted another and it caused this major conflict between us. It wasn't something either of us could move past. Obviously. I mean, we broke up because of it."

She squinted at me, seeming to try to completely understand me. Good luck to her, because honestly, I didn't even know how to understand me these days. My excuses for not being with Sebastian were still as present as ever, but her words made sense too.

If I had stuck with him, would we have eventually figured it out? If I would have gotten over my own narcissistic need to be the center of his world and have everything lined up in perfect little rows with perfect little bows, would we have found a way to be together and still met both of our needs?

"It's always going to be hard to be with someone, Sera. Love is hard. Sure it's easy at first, but the long-term stuff is hard. It's hard to compromise and be unselfish enough to meet someone else's needs and desires. It's hard to give up yourself and what you want when there is someone else to think about. But that doesn't mean it's not worth the effort. In fact, I think it makes everything so much better. You guys might fight and you might disagree, but you also love each other deeply. There is so much good mingled with the hard. I would argue more good than hard. So yeah, you have to truly work for it to be good and stay good, but that's how everything is in life. You can be lazy and give up, but then you're just alone."

I balked at her straightforward tone. "Geez, Woman! Why don't you just make me feel like the worst!"

She tossed her head back and laughed. Her blonde bob bounced around her chin and I felt a bonding between us. We were becoming friends, real friends. Even after all of these years, I wasn't used to the concept. I had kept fake people around me for so long that I was always a bit baffled when people genuinely wanted to be friends with me.

It was actually kind of pathetic.

A new wave of Titans carting limp bodies walked by and both of us sobered. We watched the casualties of this war move by us with unmoving limbs and a desolate lifelessness in their eyes. If nothing else, this conflict with Terletov had put this life I led into sharp focus.

We had this alleged Immortality attached to us, yet even Mimi had been terrified when the threat of death reached her husband.

I thought back to Sebastian and how awful it had been to watch him fight Terletov. I couldn't deny that I still had feelings for him.

Okay, I could deny it. And I did deny it a lot.

What I really meant was that I couldn't ignore them anymore.

I loved him. I had loved him for a long time and the intensity of my feelings had never disappeared.

Sure, for a while, it turned to something ugly and hateful. But when we were together and the emotion between us was as pure and blissful as it was intended to be, I couldn't hate that. I couldn't hate him.

It was time to stop lying to myself and lying to him.

I flexed my Magic that was still intertwined with his, even though we worked on opposite ends of the castle currently. I hadn't been able to talk myself into removing it.

It felt so natural to be connected to him, so familiar... so right. So much like home.

When we fought Terletov and his men, I couldn't bring myself to pull away from him. I needed him. As much bravado as I liked to strut around with, storming the Citadel had been pretty terrifying.

And then the whole near death experience... Yeah, I needed Sebastian and his Magic more than ever.

I just didn't know what to do with it.

And I didn't know how he felt.

Sure, there were times when I thought he was seconds away from jumping my bones, but that could just be habit for him. He had always been attracted to me. I had never doubted that, no matter how vain it sounded.

But was there still something deeper between us?

I didn't know.

"You're not so bad, Olivia." I pushed off the wall and moved into the hallway. "For a human."

I felt her elbow in my ribs as she kept pace with me. "Yeah, and you're not so bad for an *Immortal*."

It was my turn to laugh. "It really is amazing how disgusting you can make that word sound. We've survived for thousands of years on elitism and prejudice against humans and then you show up."

She grinned at me as we walked down the hall. "Just in time."

"Just in time," I repeated. "I'm glad Jericho has you. He deserves someone like you."

"You know what? I hear that a lot."

We moved to a different wing of the castle. We had been working over there all through the night and that was the last room we had to clear. Now we needed to check back in the throne room for more orders.

Sebastian was in charge while Mimi kept Avalon locked in a bedroom until he was back to perfect health again. Jericho had called Talbott earlier this morning and reported all of the disturbing details. Lilly and he planned to fly in sometime tonight. They had avoided the majority of the conflict for some time, but they were anxious to get back to the Kingdom. Now that Terletov's forces had been shrunk to just him, Talbott felt like Lilly could be safe here.

Eden and Kiran decided to stay with his mother for a while longer. Eventually, they would bring her back here, but they wanted her condition to stabilize first.

We walked into the throne room and dodged the chaos that buzzed through every inch of the space. Titans came and went with urgent information. Humans and Immortals that hadn't been incapacitated by Terletov roamed restlessly, waiting to be cleared and sent home. Castle employees had started to come back to the Citadel once the word was out that we'd reclaimed our capitol, along with several other Immortals seeking refuge until Terletov could be pronounced dead.

The labs and experiments Terletov had set up here had all been destroyed.

It was a wonderful feeling to know those things were taken care of. Even if Terletov was still out there. His death was just housekeeping at this point.

Sebastian stood in the middle of the room directing traffic and listening to all kinds of complaints and information. He looked completely in his element, utterly in charge.

I leaned against the back wall and watched him for a few minutes. I knew he could already feel me in the room, but he hadn't had the opportunity to acknowledge me yet.

I felt his Magic jump to attention when I walked in though and I had to take that as a good sign.

Wait. What? Was I really thinking about this seriously? Sebastian and me again? It seemed so crazy. And I couldn't believe that I'd let Olivia talk to me for ten minutes and then give up all of my convictions and heartache.

Except it wasn't exactly Olivia's advice that had me thinking this way. If I were honest with myself, I had been bending this way for a while. Slowly. Surely. Incrementally.

Maybe I had never not been leaning this way. Maybe I had always hoped Sebastian would come to his senses and sweep me back into his arms. But maybe not.

It seemed like ever since Lilly's wedding, there had been something different about him. There had been something that captured my attention and didn't let go.

He wasn't the same boy I dated. Well, he was... but that boy had become a man in the year we spent apart. He had matured in ways I never thought possible. He had become this giving, unselfish, incredible leader.

People stood straighter when he walked into the room. People listened to him when he had something to say.

I listened to him. I stood straighter. And the longer I listened and the longer I stood in his presence, the more I realized I couldn't fight this attraction between us. And more, I couldn't stop falling for him all over again.

Finally, he lifted his eyes from the Titan that was in the middle of some lengthy report. Our gazes crashed together from across the room and a crooked smile lifted the corner of his mouth. I felt the slow pulse of his Magic ripple through the room until it surged over me, a hot tingle that started in my toes and floated to my head, leaving me dizzy and lightheaded.

He mouthed a, "Hey," at me and lifted his hand in a cute little wave.

"Hey," I mouthed back.

His attention went back to the Titan that had continued talking despite Sebastian's distraction. I smiled at how serious Sebastian's expression turned the minute his eyes left me. I could still feel the heat of his Magic and the intensity of his gaze as it lingered over me.

I continued to watch him, oblivious to everything else in the room. I couldn't stop. I suddenly felt panicked that I had forgotten some of his features in the time we spent apart. I followed the curve of his masculine jaw and the lines of his strong nose. I watched his hazel eyes burn with intensity and intelligence. His dark blonde hair had been pulled on and tugged as he worked throughout the night, and it stood in unkempt tufts all over his gorgeous head. His broad shoulders stood perfectly at attention and his hands rested on his trim waist.

He was the most gorgeous man I had ever seen. And only part of that was because of his good looks. When I let myself move beyond the hurt of our breakup, I could admit that most of his beauty came from inside of him.

He had a tendency to be selfish in the past, but now he seemed to think only of others. He was a great big brother to Mimi. He was protective and loyal, but teasing and tough enough not to spoil her. And I supposed he had been the same with me only in a different way.

I had been spoiled my whole life by parents that were too busy to acknowledge me. They had thrown money at me since the day I was born. I did the job of carrying on the family legacy, and looked just pretty enough to feed their ego, but I was not worthy of their time and affection. They had bigger, better pursuits to clamor after.

Sebastian had known that, but never felt sorry for me. I supposed for a large part of his life, he could relate. Instead, he had treated me delicately in some ways and sternly in others. He never let me get away with my snobbishness or prejudice, but always made sure I knew how much he loved me and wanted to spend time with me.

A sick churning burned through my stomach. I had made a mistake breaking up with him.

A colossal mistake.

And now it might be too late to do anything about it.

The Titan nodded his head at Sebastian and then marched from the room. Sebastian's eyes found mine again and they warmed significantly.

He closed the distance between us in long, confident strides. "Let's get out of here."

My heart jumped at his sudden directive. "Don't they need you?"

He threw a quick glance over his shoulder before looking back at me. "They'll be fine for a while. I have something more important to do."

"More important than this?" I gestured at the busy room.

"Much." He took my open palm and tucked it into his.

"And you want me to come with you?" This was confusing. By the looks he had been giving me, I hadn't been expecting him to be thinking about Kingdom business. Disappointment added to the acid in my stomach and for a second I thought I might be sick.

"You have to come with me, Sera," he murmured, dragging me from the room.

"Why?"

"Because it's about us."

Chapter Twenty-Five

Sebastian

Seraphina stared at me for long, unending moments. I couldn't read her thoughts, even though our Magic still floated around our bodies connected as tightly as when we dated. It was frustrating. I was supposed to be half-Witch, half-Psychic and how convenient would it be to read all those thoughts flitting through her complicated mind? But alas, Kendricks notoriously favored the Witch side of our heritage.

And at the very root of my gene pool, I was a Kendrick.

Also, I was in love with Seraphina.

Had I said that yet?

So in love. So very in love.

I might have realized this slowly if life went as it should. But it didn't. We found ourselves in war after war, fighting sadistic dictator after sadistic dictator.

And so, when I saw Seraphina in that room, at the mercy of one Dmitri Terletov, I snapped. I lost all sense and reason. And when I emerged, it was reinforced that I loved this girl.

Not only did I love her, but I wanted to spend the rest of my life with her.

I had been a fool before. I had been selfish and shortsighted.

I had been restless with youth and still angry from losing an uncle I had both loved and hated. My early relationship had been confusing. Seraphina had struggled with a lifetime of privilege and prejudice.

We were two kids that had been rocked to the core form a Rebellion neither of us belonged in. And then as we struggled to re-identify ourselves and come up with a lifestyle that catered to our new beliefs at the same time fit our old stereotypes, we clashed constantly with each other.

And then there was peace in the Kingdom, which made us both fidgety. Maybe our destruction had been inevitable.

But so was this moment.

When I made her mine again.

I knew we had both grown and matured over the last year. And maybe that's what we needed. We had spent the last of our teenage years wrapped up in each other and when adulthood hit us, we had no idea how we were supposed to act or what it meant for us to grow up apart from each other.

Well, we got our chance. But I was done with finding myself without Seraphina now. I needed her. I wanted her. I couldn't breathe without her close and I certainly couldn't feel unless it was her touch on me.

We were made for each other.

We were soul mates.

And now she needed to believe this too.

I took her hand and led her down the long corridor. She didn't fight me, and that small act of nonviolence spurred my hope. Her Magic gave nothing away, but she hadn't pulled it either.

I glanced at her out of the corner of my eye and she returned the gesture with the same exact look.

Damn, if this girl wasn't going to drive me mad.

I took her to the room I had claimed as mine. I needed privacy for the impending conversation. I had been working for twenty-four hours straight. I needed a break. And I needed to talk to Sera.

I could not continue to run this renovation and take care of all of these people that needed me until I had a conversation with Sera.

I had been trying to appear put together and in charge, but my thoughts had been invaded by this woman. My blood ran hot. And my attention span was nothing but a joke.

This had to happen.

And now.

I opened the door and gestured for her to go first. She gave me an adorably confused expression but walked into the dark room.

I followed quickly behind her and switched on the light just before I closed the door behind us.

She had walked to the center of the sparse space. When the light came on, she spun around on her heel trying to make out the furniture that indisputably made up a bedroom: a dresser, a rather large bed, and a small sitting area.

I tried to suppress my smile.

Truly, I tried.

She turned back to me with eyes wide. "I expected a meeting of some kind."

"This is not a meeting."

"I can see that."

I took three steps forward until we were toe to toe. "I should never have let you walk away from me."

She didn't seem to comprehend my words. She stared at me while her eyes only continued to grow. I wanted to smooth the worry lines that had bunched together on her forehead, but I refrained. I doubted that would aid my cause.

"Sebastian," she whispered.

I had to close my eyes against the sensation my name breathed on her sweet lips caused to riot inside of me. My name had come softly and devastatingly out of her perfect mouth. She had wrecked me with just those three syllables in her drawling American accent.

I wanted to devour her right then and there. I wanted to press my mouth to hers and consume every inch of her. I wanted to remind her that she was mine and that I was hers.

But I knew I had to explain myself first or she would run. She would never trust me again unless I earned it.

"Sera, I shouldn't have let you end things. We should never have ended. I love you. I've loved you since I was eighteen and we had no idea what we were doing or who we would be. I loved you the day you left me so much that it killed me to watch you go. I never recovered from that. Never. I've tried to bury my feelings for you and pretend they don't exist. I've tried to punish you for making me hurt. And I've tried to pretend that what we had wasn't as intense as it was. But I can't do any of that anymore. I can't stop myself from wanting to be with you, from wanting to touch you... from wanting to be in your life."

"What are you saying, Bastian?"

"I was stupid to let you go. And I'm tired of paying for that mistake. I want to be with you again. For real. Forever. I'm tired of skirting around the issue and ignoring the chemistry between us. I'm tired of going to bed alone and erasing text messages I want to send you and emails that beg for your forgiveness. We belong together, Sera. I know you believe it too."

"And if I don't?"

"I feel your Magic, Darling."

She cleared her throat and took two steps back. I hated the distance between us. I hated that she didn't fall immediately into my arms, weeping with joy.

Alright, maybe I'm being a little melodramatic.

She cleared her throat again. I could tell she was nervous and I hated that. I wanted to comfort her. I wanted to wrap my arms around her and draw her to me, holding her against my chest until her heartbeat slowed and her pulse returned to normal.

And then I wanted to speed it up again for different reasons.

"We were a disaster together."

"We weren't."

"We were explosive."

"We were passionate."

"We fought all the time."

"We were scared of how deeply we felt for each other."

"We were immature."

"We were young."

"We couldn't compromise."

"We didn't know how good compromising could be."

"So what exactly are you saying?"

"I'm saying we made a lot of mistakes before, Sera. But that's what they were... mistakes. We've learned. We've grown. We've spent the last year trying to stay apart from each other and it's just not working. We belong together."

"We belong together?"

I could hear the fear lacing each of her words. Her hands trembled at her sides and her body seemed violently nervous. I hated watching her doubt what I knew would be the answer for both of us.

What I knew would be our salvation.

"I tried to live without you. I tried to remove myself from your life and pretend that it didn't tear me apart every single day. I can't do it any longer. I'm exhausted trying to keep my distance from you. I want you, Sera. I want to be with you always. I want to make a life with you, a future. I want to put this behind us and acknowledge that we love each other."

She put a hand over her eyes and shook out her glorious mane of blonde hair. "I can't believe you dragged me in here to have this conversation."

I closed the distance between us. I couldn't stand it. I had to touch her.

My chest brushed up against hers. She jumped from the contact and pulled her hand away from her face. She squeaked seeing me so close to her and stepped backward.

I matched her stride for stride until her back pressed against the bedpost. Her eyes grew huge when she realized where she'd put herself. Her hands flailed at her side until the stretched behind her to grab the post for stability.

She looked so vulnerable standing there in front of me. Her slender neck was extended so that she could look up at me while simultaneously looking down at me through her practiced snobbery. Her lips pressed into a pout that made me want to lick the seam of those perfect lips until she opened them and gave me what I wanted. Her arms were folded behind her back as if I'd bound her just like that.

And her eyes...

Those beautiful blue sapphires glittered like the most priceless gems. She was one part furious, another part scared and a significant part excited.

I liked my odds.

"What happens when I get pushed to the back seat again? What happens when you find another priority?"

"That won't happen." I traced the curve of her jaw with my knuckles and enjoyed watching her shiver from my touch.

That didn't stop her sarcastic, "Oh, you just sound so confident. I should just believe you, right? It should just be that simple?"

"I didn't say it would be simple. It's never been simple between us. You're a difficult woman. And you like to make things even more difficult. If I had to promise one thing, it would be that this isn't simple and that it will never be easy."

Her eyes narrowed and I watched a hundred filthy words flicker over her tongue. She couldn't decide which to use first. She probably wanted to call me all of the names.

"It's adorable how cute you think you are."

I couldn't help but chuckle. "It's adorable how hard you're trying to fight this. You're mine, Sera. You've always been mine." I dropped my hand to her waist and slid my fingers beneath the hem of her t-shirt.

The pads of my fingers settled against the silky heat of her skin and I let out a sigh of contentment. This was where I belonged.

She was where I belonged.

"And I'm yours," I swore to her.

I watched her work to swallow and then struggle to find the right words. Finally, she whispered the truth. "I'm scared."

"Me too."

"What if this is a mistake?"

"What if it's not?"

Her hand flicked out and slapped my chest. "Can you just give me an answer? Just one! None of this rhetorical question bullshit?"

"So feisty..." My attention had fallen to her lips. I needed to kiss her. That might help her along.

"Sebastian, I'm serious. I need something substantial here. I need something real."

My focus flipped back to her eyes and I knew she was right. I needed to give her something that would draw her to me and keep her there. I needed to be completely honest.

Bare.

I needed to show her how desperately I needed her.

"Sera, I never intended to leave you behind all those months ago. I just wanted to protect you. I wanted to keep you safe from a monster I thought could destroy you. But what happened instead was that I destroyed us. You recognized what I was doing before it ever crossed my mind. I didn't intend to suffocate you or mislead you. And I certainly never intended to postpone our permanent future with you. I thought I was doing what was best for us. It seemed like the worst time to ask you to marry me. And when I looked around at our friends, especially at Talbott, who had lost Lilly just after they became engaged, well, honestly, to ask you to marry me then felt incredibly selfish and insensitive. Of course, I should have expressed my feelings to you verbally. I should have said these things out loud. I thought... I don't know what I thought. I guess I assumed you would just read my mind and figure it out for yourself. These things seemed obvious to me. It was honestly a little shocking to me that you hadn't thought of them on your own." I watched with a small amount of amusement as her face heated with fury and her body stiffened beneath me. But I wasn't finished. "And then you left me and I realized who the real fool was... me. I realized how much of an idiot I had been. With some space between now and then, I have a little more perspective. I pushed marriage away to protect us. And you pushed for marriage to protect us from other people, aka Terletov. We both wanted the same thing, but our applications of what we wanted were executed poorly."

"That's an interesting way to look at things," she murmured thoughtfully.

"It is," I agreed.

"When did you figure all this out?"

I grinned at her, "Yesterday."

She hit me again. "For real?"

"No, not yesterday. But it took me much longer than it should have."

"So that's it? You just decided we love each other and we should be together now? That's like an executive order and I just have to step in line?"

I dropped a kiss to the tip of her nose and then brushed one across her parted lips. God, she was so very beautiful and she just had no idea how much she owned me. She had no idea that she was the one in charge.

I couldn't compete with her complete authority.

"Tell me you don't love me."

"Sebastian..."

"Tell me, Sera. Tell me that I'm imagining this thing between us. Tell me that I haven't felt your Magic wrapped up in mine for days now. Tell me that you can move on from me and that you can imagine being with anyone other than me."

Waiting for her to answer was the most torturous few moments of my life, worse than anything Terletov had put me through. The idea that she could even think about being in love with someone else cut through me and ripped the separate halves of my soul to pieces.

I thought back to Lilly's wedding and the hours I'd been subjected to watching her dance with her date. I wanted to kill the Russian with my bare hands.

This woman before me was my past, present, and future.

We belonged together.

Her cheeks turned a rosy pink and she lifted her beautiful blue eyes to mine. Usually, I compared them to ice because they were so crystal-like and clear. But at this moment they were much too hot to be considered ice. They burned with her response, sizzled with the heat of her feelings for me.

I held back my victory smile out of respect for the Russian.

Yeah, right. I held back nothing.

"You know I love you," she grumbled. "You know I never stopped loving you. Isn't that why you brought me here? Isn't that why you threw that huge speech at me?"

I leaned down and captured her smart mouth with mine. I didn't wait for us to warm up or remember what we were doing. I dove right in and plunged my tongue into her mouth.

We'd done this often enough that I figured we'd remember the logistics quickly enough.

I had been right.

My other hand moved to her waist too and I yanked her to me. Her hands shot to my shirt and clutched at it frantically. I pressed my body into hers, forcing her back against the bedpost again.

Our mouths moved in hungry synchronization. We kissed, licked and bit at each other, desperate to taste and reclaim as much as we could, as fast as we could. This was something as familiar as breathing to both of us.

And I relished it... Worshiped this moment.

It was like coming home. It was like finding my center after a lifetime of being off-balance.

"Sera," I breathed.

She wrapped her arms around my neck and clung to me. That was the only encouragement I needed.

I picked her up and tossed her onto the bed, following her down before she even settled on the mattress. Her hands reached for my chest immediately, smoothing them out against my heart.

I was about to dive in for more kisses when her words stopped me. "I want to be with you again, Bastian. I want this to work."

"It will work," I swore to her. And I believed that it would. I would do anything it took to make this work.

I would not give up on us ever again.

"How do you know?"

"Because it never stopped working, Sera. We just gave up before we got to the good stuff."

A small smile touched her lips and I leaned down to kiss the corner of her mouth. I had to keep touching her… tasting her. I wanted to spend the next thousand years in this bed.

I wanted to spend the next ten thousand years with this woman.

"This is the good stuff?" she laughed lightly.

"This is just the beginning of the good stuff. There is so much left to get to with you." I propped myself up with one hand and used the other to trace a line from the hollow of her throat to her navel. "I love you, you beautiful, stubborn, strong-willed woman. And I am sorry I let you think differently. I'm sorry that it took me so long to come fetch you."

"Fetch me?" she laughed.

"Fetch you," I confirmed and then sobered. "You should never have felt as though I didn't want you. That was never true. I have always wanted you. And I always will want you. I was just… I was just stupid. There is no other word for my behavior and poor decisions than stupid."

"I was just as much to blame. You don't have to be so hard on yourself."

"It doesn't matter now," I murmured. "We both know better now."

"We do."

I dropped down to give her slow, sensual kisses that I hoped reinforced my words. I knew I had a long way to go to make up for the trust I destroyed, but it was my number one priority. I would earn back her trust and every bit of her love no matter how long it took. And then I would spend the rest of my life keeping it.

In the last few days I had been told that I was redeemed for my family's misdeeds, for the selfishness I flaunted.

But it was only because of this woman. She redeemed me.

She was my redemption.

After several long, blissful minutes, she pulled back and hit me with a very serious expression. I swallowed a sudden lump in my throat and waited for her to deliver the blow.

"I'm happy we had this discussion," she said glibly. I nodded, trying to smile. I could feel the qualifier coming a mile away. I just wanted it over. Not that it would stop me from keeping her. I would just have to try more unconventional ways. Like kidnapping. "But," she continued. See? I knew it was coming. "But, I don't want you to feel pressured or rushed or anything. I think we just need to take this slow and see where things go. It's sweet that we think we love each other, but we've watched this dissolve once before. It's taking a lot of strength on my part not to doubt this entire endeavor. I just... I just can't be hurt like that again, Bastian. I want to take this slow."

I nodded like I understood, like those were the exact same thoughts I had been having.

They were in fact, the opposite thoughts I had been having.

"Sure," I croaked. "We can take this slow."

"It's just that... I know I had been pushing for marriage like crazy before we broke up and I just... I just don't want you to think I'm still like that. We could never get married and I would still be happy. It's not important to me like it was back then. So if you could just, er, forget I was ever like that... that would be great."

I continued to nod. I probably resembled one of those idiotic bobble head toys, but I couldn't seem to put two words together.

"I love you," I told her just to get her to say it back.

"I love you too." Her words were balm to a suddenly aching heart. I needed to hear the conviction in her voice, the truth in those words.

I relaxed some after she said them, but not enough.

I had run from the idea of marriage before, but the excuses I gave myself before weren't an option anymore. Lilly and Talbott were married. The twins had been safely delivered. Terletov's army had been completely dismantled and it was only a matter of time before we caught up to him.

And I had nearly lost this woman.

More than once.

If I had been opposed to marriage before, I was now adamantly an advocate.

Except, now Seraphina had decided to slam on the breaks.

So I decided to do something I promised myself I would never do. I promised myself that I would go into this conversation with an open mind and be completely flexible to Seraphina's wishes.

I also promised to be perfectly honest.

So, when I told Seraphina that she had nothing to worry about and that I wasn't thinking about marriage either and that she could relax... I broke every single one of my promises and lied straight to her face.

She didn't seem quite convinced, but I erased the rest of her worry with another talent of mine... kissing.

And I didn't stop. I couldn't.

I had been deprived of this for much too long. My lips knew exactly how to tease her into a lusty frenzy. And her tongue knew exactly how to bend me to her complete and utter will.

We were lost to each other, just the way we should be.

Just the way we were supposed to be together.

Chapter Twenty-Six

Seraphina

I watch a gnarled hand reach down and pick up an infant by the throat. His fingers curl maliciously around the tiny neck and squeeze. The sharp, yellowed nails dig into the soft flesh of the baby.

My heart leaps to my throat and my lungs freeze. No!

"You've taken everything from me," the monster hisses maliciously. He hovers near a bottomless pit, dangling the baby over the edge.

The mother screams out for her newborn son, promising whatever the monster wants. But it's too late. He's wanted revenge for too long to make placating deals. Now he just wants to hurt and harm.

Now he just wants to kill.

I'm so afraid for the baby boy that it takes me several long moments to realize he's also holding a tiny little girl. She's just as small as the boy, but her raging scream pierces louder than the boy who bleats angrily. She is pissed and if she had teeth I know she would have turned the monster's knotted hand into a bloody stump by now.

It makes me proud of the little thing. I love her spunk. I love her outrage. She is so like her mother.

Those thoughts create a well of sadness inside me. I love these children and I am going to watch them die.

The cavern is filled with shouts and threats, but the monster has leverage while he holds the children. How did he find them?

"You're next," the monster grins at the mother. "But maybe you'll follow them willingly." A horrific silence pauses all time and thought. And then in one swift thrust, the monster flings the screaming babies into an abyss so deep and dark that I know without a doubt they are lost forever.

The mother screams a ragged, broken sound and dives in after them.

And then we all go. The entire Kingdom jumps into the pit to be swallowed up in darkness forever.

I jolted awake, trembling and shaken to my core.

Sebastian sat up with me, stirred by my sudden panic. His arms reached around my waist without question and he tugged me against his chest. His whispered words soothed against my hair, but my mind refused to comprehend them.

"The twins, Bastian."

I felt him still next to me. His body turned to stone with the words on my lips. "What are you talking about?"

"A vision." My voice was a tattered rasp. Fear and despair had wrapped around my throat and threatened to choke me to death. "I dreamt... I dreamt that Terletov found the babies."

"Sera..." The opposite of mine, Sebastian's tone was a harsh warning that reminded me of how dangerous he could be when provoked. I felt hysterical terror. He felt the call to action and decisive planning. "Tell me."

"In my dream, Terletov had the children. And he killed them, Sebastian. In front of all of us."

"I love you," he whispered gently against my temple. His tone and words were at such contrast from the rigidness of his body that I jerked. He pressed a sweet kiss against my skin and then jumped out of bed.

He thrust his legs into jeans and yanked on a t-shirt. He grabbed his phone off the nightstand and punched in a number. The phone rang against his ear for a long time. Nobody picked up. He pulled the phone away, looked at it and dialed again. After three times of this, he must have given up on that caller and dialed a new one.

"Talbott," he demanded once the other end picked up. "Are you in the castle? Don't come here then. We think the twins are in danger. Wait for orders and you can meet us." He hung up and dialed another number. "Meet us in Avalon's room in three minutes." He hung up again and dialed a third number. "Mimi, we're coming up in two minutes... all of us... well get him dressed... It's an emergency, Little Sister. Get ready... No time. I'll explain when we get there."

I had been watching him partly stunned from the bed. When he hung up on his sister, he whirled around to face me. His hard gaze softened when he found me still rumpled in bed, but I could feel the desperation to get moving radiate from his body.

"Get dressed, Sera. We're going after Kiran and his family."

"What if it was just a dream?"

"Was it?"

My stomach clenched with nerves and a sick feeling washed over me. "No," I confirmed.

"Neither Eden nor Kiran will pick up. The team sent after Terletov has not been able to locate him. I think your dream tracked him down."

His words spurred me into action. I jumped from bed and threw on the same clothes I'd been wearing since the Gypsy village. I shoved my feet into my shoes and threw my hair up into a high ponytail.

"Sebastian, in my vision, the twins-"

"No, Sera. We won't let it happen. *I* won't let it happen. Let's go."

I hurried after him as he ran down the hallway and up the stairs to Avalon's room. Jericho and Olivia were just coming from the opposite way when we reached the propped open door. Sebastian and Jericho shared a grave look and then we all entered the dark room.

Avalon sat at the edge of his bed with his face buried in his hands. When the four of us entered, he looked up with fear plastered all over his face. "It's Eden."

"Seraphina had a vision," Sebastian explained quietly.

"He got to them. I feel it. She is blocking me for some reason, but I can still vaguely feel what's going on." Avalon rose to his feet and cursed viciously. "I don't think it's her though. I don't think she's intentionally blocking me. I can feel her fear and... something is very wrong. But I can't get through to her."

"Why not?" I demanded. This was my one hope. Avalon was supposed to know where she was. He was supposed to be able to locate her immediately.

"I don't know!" He picked up a chair and threw it across the room. It crashed into the wall and splintered to pieces. Amelia threw her arms around his waist and he crumpled against her.

"She's near a Source," Sebastian said, snapping his fingers. "She has to be."

Avalon's head popped up with understanding. "That's right. We've always lost contact near one. India... the prison here. Morocco. It makes sense."

"So which one?" Jericho demanded.

"One that's still active," Amelia said. "If it's blocking your connection then it still has to be working. And she would have had to travel there quickly. It's only been thirty-six hours since we lost him and he would have had to go all the way to Paris, figure out a way to get to them and then forced them to move."

"He has the twins," I offered. "That's how he got their cooperation." A stiff silence moved through us as my words settled over our small group. "He couldn't have moved very far with all of them in toe."

"What if he went back to St. Stephens?" Sebastian suggested. "The Source in Peru was still active, but changed. Whenever Eden and Avalon have dealt with one, they've, for lack of a better word, absorbed it. But the one in Vienna didn't die either; it became something else, something significantly darker."

I perked up. "That would make sense. We watched it turn. Terletov obviously had more plans for it."

Avalon winced and pressed his fingers to his temple. "It's a gamble," he finally said. "I have no way of confirming this theory."

A cell phone rang, shaking us out of our thoughtful quiet. Avalon grabbed his phone and stabbed at it until it obeyed. "Hello?" he demanded into the phone. He listened for a moment and then said, "Analisa, we know. We've been brainstorming for the last twenty minutes." He listened some more while all of us strained to hear what was said on the other end. Our Immortal hearing could pick up Analisa's panicked demands to find her son and grandchildren, but it wasn't an easy conversation to eavesdrop on. The woman had recently been through hell and now the same lunatic that had terrorized her had taken the only family she had left. I felt a strong wave of empathy for Analisa.

Avalon stayed patient as long as he could, but after a few more minutes of listening to her, he said, "Ana, I understand that you're scared. But you need to know that we're going to find them. All of them. And we're going to bring them home alive. I need to let you go now though. We have a lot of logistics to work out. Is B there with you? Good. I'll call you the second I know more." And then he hung up.

For a moment I just blinked at Avalon. Those women, Analisa and Bianca, were these huge matriarchs of the old regime. I had grown up with a healthy fear of them. And now... now Avalon gave them nicknames and hung up on them.

I... Honestly, I didn't even know what to do with that.

I decided to just move on. That would be best for me.

"Should we split up?" Jericho asked in a measured tone.

Nobody wanted to split up.

"What other Sources still exist?" Sebastian put an arm around me and pulled me tightly to his side. I rested my head on his shoulder and wrapped two arms around his middle. I needed his strength right now. I needed him to center me.

Amelia, Jericho and Avalon all did double takes at the same time. They seemed completely perplexed by our behavior. In fact, the only person in the room who didn't seem surprised was Olivia.

But I guessed she could probably see this one coming after our earlier conversation.

"What's going on?" Amelia demanded as if it was something nefarious. Avalon suppressed a smile and tugged his wife back to his side. His hand settled on the back of her neck and she shot him a disgruntled look. "What?" she snapped. "This is not normal!"

"We've worked through some things, Mims. Sera and I are... we're-"

"We're trying this again," I finished for him.

He snorted a laugh. "No, we're not trying anything. We're back together. For good this time."

My stomach flipped. I cast a cautious glance at him from the corner of my eye. He did not seem to be joking.

"It better be for good this time," Mimi all but growled.

"Look how happy they are." The way Avalon said that made it sound like he was making fun of us. "At least they'll stop trying to murder each other."

"Maybe," I allowed.

"Hopefully," Sebastian shrugged.

"Congratulations?" Jericho put in. Olivia nudged him with her elbow in his ribs. He squirmed but schooled his expression into an encouraging mask of confidence.

Yeah, yeah, Jericho. Like you're such a love guru.

Avalon cleared his throat and tried to refocus the conversation. People could place their bets on this relationship at another time and place. "Known Source Magic... West Africa. Maybe more over there... There's still one somewhere in Siberia. Rumors of something in Mongolia." He shrugged helplessly. "None of those places are pinpointed though. Unless Dmitri knows something not even Lucan did, then he would have to locate them before he could use them."

"It has to be Vienna," I announced. "It has to be. Where else would he take them?"

We looked at each other and waited for the answer to fall from the sky. It didn't.

I closed my eyes and searched through my Magic. I was Psychic, damn it. I should be able to take some of the guesswork out of this.

My blood tingled with electricity as my senses perused the vast stores of my Magic. I reached for an answer, for some clear indication of where we were supposed to go.

With Sebastian's Magic intertwined with mine, I felt immeasurably stronger. Our Magics worked together seamlessly. They fueled each other; his Magic made mine more powerful and vice versa.

It was incredible.

I had forgotten the rush that came with this kind of energy. And when we were together before, I wasn't even half this adept.

I stretched my senses and let the Magic speak to me. I had hoped for a clarifying vision or something credible, but all I got was an intense sense of direction.

But I supposed that was better than nothing.

"Vienna," I finally shared. "They have to be in Vienna."

Avalon narrowed his bright green eyes on me and frowned. "How do you know?"

"Because I'm Psychic."

"Me too."

"Yeah, but I'm really Psychic. And only Psychic. Also, Ileana alluded to this happening earlier." Avalon quirked a brow at me, and Sebastian squeezed my shoulder to encourage me to keep going. "Listen, I had a vision. I saw Terletov with the twins. And I saw what happened if he got to do what he wants to do to them. Just so you know... it's not good. I need you to trust me on this one." My words came out confidently and decisively, but inside I quaked with anxiety.

What if I was wrong?

What if I led them on a wild goose chase while Terletov murdered my friends and their infant children?

My heart beat frantically in my chest. I could not let that happen.

I could not plunge this Kingdom into a darkness thicker and deadlier than even Lucan.

Terletov had to die. *And soon.*

"I trust you, Sera." Sebastian's clipped voice seemed to shout through the room. His clear trust in my ability moved me at some profound level. Yes, I loved him.

I would always love him.

And this moment was just one of the thousands upon thousands of reasons.

"Sebastian, you realize what's at stake." Avalon eyed us like we'd both lost our minds.

"I know that we have no other leads. And I know that we wouldn't even know Kiran and Eden were in trouble if it weren't for Sera. Furthermore, I know that if we don't move now, we're going to be too late. We have to go, Avalon. And this is the only lead we have. Plus, it makes sense. We know Terletov has something planned for St. Stephens. We just don't know what it is. And we know that it's close enough to Paris that he could have driven there within the time frame we're working with."

Avalon stood up and nodded. "Alright. St. Stephens. Bastian, organize two-thirds of the Guard here. Jericho, get on the phone with Talbott and apprise him of the situation. He is welcome to meet us there if he wants, but tell him we won't wait for him to move."

We moved into motion and didn't stop. There were all kinds of details to organize and coordinate in the castle. Then we were on a plane and I was breathless and quiet for the entire ride into Austria. I stayed tucked to Sebastian's side while we waited in anxious agony to get back on the ground and move again.

Once we landed in one of the Kingdom's private, out-of-the-way hangers, we piled into stored cars and sped off into the early dawn hours. We'd brought an army of Titans with us, as well as the usual team with the addition of Olivia and Ophelia.

Talbott and Lilly were en route, but we didn't expect them before we stormed the church.

This would be a tricky attack. Speed was at the top of our list. There was an urgency chasing us like hellhounds at our heels. Our entire crew felt the earnestness to get to Eden and Kiran. But at the same time, we couldn't draw human attention to ourselves.

Usually our conflicts took place out of the way of humanity. The Citadel for example. St. Stephens was smack dab in the capitol of Austria. So... human contact would probably be unavoidable.

This mission called for an insane amount of Magic to pull off. And hopefully we wouldn't miss any loose ends. We were all anxious to murder Terletov and not one of us wanted to answer to a human judicial system for what we would consider justice.

Plus there were so many of us.

We had divided off into waves. We hoped that Terletov was alone, but there was no way to know that for sure.

Avalon had decided his team would be split into the first two attacks and the Titan Guard would trickle in behind us, either to clean up our mess or rescue us.

By the time we reached St. Stephens, the still sleeping city was quiet, but dawn broke on the horizon. Pockets of life emerged around us along the soon-to-be-busy street.

The tall, antique buildings rose over the gray streets. The tram zipped around with lonely passengers. A few vendors trudged to work and lifted gates or unlocked doors, their busy days starting as soon as they walked off the street and into their place of work.

Vienna had the cleanest streets I'd ever seen in Europe, but today they were painted with an ominous brush. I felt the prickles of foreboding as I prepared my mind and body to engage with the most evil thing I had ever known.

These humans were preparing to start their very normal, very mortal days.

I prepared to go to war.

Sebastian squeezed my hand. I looked up at him and met those deep hazel eyes I could read so clearly now. "I love you," he said. I felt his words punch through me.

He did love me. I could feel just how much.

I could feel his love pulse through our Magic. I could feel it beat with my heart and breathe with my lungs. I could feel it fuse with my blood and wrap around my soul so tightly I knew I would never be the same.

"I love you too," I promised him.

His eyes softened some, but not much. "Survive this, yeah?"

I couldn't help but smile. "I was planning on it."

Intensity seemed to snap inside him. "I'm serious, Sera. I need you to survive this."

"Alright. But I'm going to need you to promise the same thing."

He flashed me a cheeky grin. "Nothing could stop me from being with you. Not even this psychopath. I'll survive, Baby. And then you won't have any reason not to stay with me from this day forward."

"Well, at least you have incentive."

"Believe it."

He squeezed my hand one more time and then let go. It was time to enter the cathedral. The witching hour had come.

Terletov was going to die.

Chapter Twenty-Seven

Sebastian

I kept a tight hold on Seraphina's hand as we slipped through a side door into the darkened cathedral. Soft light filtered in through the stained glass windows. The sanctuary smelled like candle wax and incense. I breathed in deeply hoping to steady my rapidly beating heart.

I was wound tight with nerves, anxious to start this battle and anxious to end it. I hated that Sera was with me. I wanted her somewhere safe. I wanted her anywhere away from Terletov and the evil he could create.

But I was desperate to keep her near me at the same time.

I knew she could handle herself and I wasn't about to let anything happen to her. But there were too many variables to completely trust the outcome of this confrontation.

Avalon led the way with Mimi tucked to his side. There was another woman I wished would have stayed at home.

But women never listen to me.

It was rather obnoxious.

Jericho and Olivia followed behind us. In a few more minutes the rest of our "team" would join us. Titus, Xander, Xavier, Roxie, and Ophelia. And then the Titans would come. We spread ourselves out in ten-minute waves.

I wanted Terletov dead before the Guard ever showed up, but that might be wishful thinking.

We used Magic to keep any human suspicion averted from us. It wasn't hard if you knew how to manipulate gently. And most of us did. Olivia wasn't allowed to try, but only because of how *gently* we'd seen Eden act with her new Magic.

Poor Olivia and Ophelia. So much of the way we treated them stemmed from how Eden had behaved. Which wasn't fair to them because obviously they were very different from Eden in her teens. Better to error on the side of caution though.

We quietly crept through the sanctuary, sticking close to the walls. The floor vibrated beneath my feet, a ripple of Magic pulsing through the ancient stone. I snapped my head up to catch Avalon's eyes. Terletov was either here or the source Magic beneath the church was close to collapse.

A renewed sense of urgency rushed through my blood, heating it to a rapid boil. I felt the primal call to war sing through my being, a feral awakening that promised a deadly, gruesome end for my enemy. This unrest, this beast of rebellion would end today.

I would see to it.

The stairs leading to the catacombs were hidden behind the locked iron gate. Avalon used his Magic to unlock it and we walked through without anyone the wiser.

We carried no weapons. We'd left guns and swords behind, favoring our powerful Magic instead. We had Eden's blue smoke and enough promised revenge to defeat a thousand Terletovs.

The air turned stale and cool as we moved further into the earth. The dead slept on either side of us as we continued to creep silently through the tombs.

The rumbling increased with our progress. The ground trembled and rocks and gravel trickled from the ceiling. The silence lessened the further down we traveled and a crackling in the distance, like electricity at an exaggerated level sparked.

Seraphina looked up at me with an ashen face.

The last time we were down here, I had been the one afraid of the unknown. But today we both felt the sickening crush of fear for what was to come. Gone were my irrational phobias of ghosts and skeletons. And in their place a gnawing, gaping abyss of worry for my cousin and his family expanded and gathered strength inside of me.

All of our thoughts revolved around the children and Terletov's plans for them.

On the trip over, Sera had explained her dream to me. I had gotten chills listening to the darkness that would descend on our Kingdom if the twins died. If Kiran and Eden went with them.

That could not be allowed to happen.

We descended into the second layer of catacombs. A heaving quake shifted the ground beneath our feet and the entire church overhead shifted violently. I grabbed hold of Seraphina's waist to keep her from toppling over as we slid one direction and then the other.

Avalon and Jericho both shot a look my way. Were we walking into a trap? Suicide? Would we be able to stop Terletov without becoming victims ourselves?

The corridors narrowed until we had to move in a single file line. Eventually, we couldn't even walk straight on. We turned to the side and slid through passages that were not meant for visitors.

The light up ahead had been blue the first time we were here, but now it glowed a cloying pale green. I could feel the malevolence radiating from the ancient Source, pulsing its way through the stone and dirt, threatening to crumble this entire structure on our heads.

Avalon was first into the room. The bad Magic crackled and sizzled in the middle of the circular space. We filed in along the wall and watched the Magic expand and retract as if it had to take ragged, painful breaths.

We simultaneously gasped and jumped back when a long finger of rogue electricity whipped out and hit the wall. The Magic bruised the wall, leaving a charred smudge that would have burned anything organic. Nobody was hurt, but it was a close call.

I looked at the curved walls and noticed long slices of Magical black marks all over them. The Magic seemed completely unstable, lashing out at any random moment.

What was happening to the Magic was definitely concerning, but not more so than the absence of Terletov.

We glanced at each other. Avalon held up five fingers that showed how much time was left before the next wave of Immortals would join us.

I felt the pressure to find Terletov before they arrived. Not because I didn't want their help, but suddenly it seemed important to be extra cautious. We didn't want to set him off unnecessarily. Or spook him into doing something drastic with the babes.

Seraphina unlinked our hands and started to slide around the room, keeping her back against the wall. I wanted to believe we were strong enough to withstand a stroke of that Magic, but I remembered what happened when Terletov's goons had thrown their bodies into it. They had been obliterated.

I was mildly against that happening to Sera.

"Where are you going?" I asked her as I followed right behind her.

She stopped suddenly, pausing just in time to avoid getting electrocuted by another wayward strand of aggressive Magic.

"There's a crack in the wall. Over there." She pointed to the opposite side of the room. She was right. A narrow fissure split the wall from floor to ceiling, just big enough for a person to slip through.

How hadn't we noticed this before?

Maybe it hadn't been here before...

Avalon and Mimi started to move around the room the same style we were, but going in the opposite direction. It was a gamble to try to predict the Magic in the middle of the room, but one we had to take. Jericho and Olivia followed Avalon.

The next spit of Magic came faster than before. We jumped at the cracking sound of it, but thankfully it hit the ceiling instead of one of us.

Seraphina picked up her pace and I raced behind her. We reached the split before Avalon and without pausing to wait Seraphina pushed her way through, leaving me to follow after her.

I did. And then ran straight into her back. Her hands were raised at her side, her body taut with tension.

I lifted my head and peered over her shoulder.

There he stood. The man of the hour. Dmitri Terletov. He held one baby over the side of a large, seemingly endless pit, just like Seraphina had predicted. The other infant lay haphazardly at his feet in the dirt. She was dressed in something adorably pink but her face was red from screaming and her feet kicked riotously in the air as if she could take out this evil man all by herself.

I smiled at her spunk. Only Eden could create something this wild from birth.

"Don't move," Terletov snarled with a thicker-than-usual accent. He looked exhausted. His shoulders sagged and his arm shook from where he held out the infant.

Gavriel's head hung awkwardly from his neck and he too bleated out angry protests. Eden and Kiran sat huddled in the corner, bloodied and beaten. Their hands were bound together and something chained them by the neck to the dirt wall at their backs.

Eden's eyes were as black and furious as I'd ever seen her. Her entire body radiated with rage. Her Magic surged in pulsing waves outwardly and I wondered if that was the reason for the volatile Magic in the other room. Even I could feel the sheer power emanating from her. It bounced around the room like steel boomerangs, returning to her and then shooting off again in search of a place to land.

"Eden?" I lifted an eyebrow her direction.

"No," she hissed. "I can't use it."

Kiran shot me a sharp look. We had been speaking with our expressions for the better part of our lives. I read everything I needed to in just that one glance. They couldn't access their Magic. They couldn't get out of their restraints.

And if I didn't save their children the entire world would burn to the ground.

"Silence!" Terletov shouted at us. His hand faltered and I prepared my body to jump into the dark pit after the child. He righted the infant and flashed a sick smile at the new parents. "They are finally listening," he told Seraphina and me. "They are finally listening to the things that I have to say."

"And what things are those?" Seraphina asked with a measured lilt.

I could feel her Magic spread out through the room. It crawled along the floor and over the walls as if casting a careful net over her prey.

Avalon pushed at my back, but I knew he felt the atmosphere of this room. He knew not to push too hard.

"I had you both, didn't I?" Terletov narrowed his eyes and swayed toward us. "You are the reason my empire fell, yes? You are the reason my brother is not at my side. *You* are the reason I have no army."

"And no Magic," Eden growled. "Don't forget that."

"Silence, Witch!" he screamed at her, spittle flying from his lips. "I lost everything because of you! I was set to overthrow Lucan. Did you know? First I would take you, take your Magic. Then I would storm the Citadel and take my rightful place on the throne. You would have died at my hands and all would have been right. But instead you forced me to find creative ways to reclaim my Magic. I crawled out of the pits of that prison *on my own*. I learned how to use Magic again *on my own*. And I built an army, an army of followers that hate you and everything you stand for, *on my own*. You took my Magic and my future and my brother from me. And now you've taken my empire."

"You're bloody mad," Kiran growled. "You would have been free had you not tried to overturn the Kingdom. We would have never known that you were alive, let alone killed your brother! You did this to yourself!"

Terletov snarled something ugly at Kiran before stepping closer to the edge of the pit. I couldn't see how far down it went from here, but if this was the image from Sera's dream then I didn't have to see it to know it didn't end. It was a passageway straight to hell.

Or maybe it was only that way metaphorically. Either way I knew that no one would survive the outcome of losing the twins or our King and Queen.

"Fools!" Terletov shouted. "You are fools!"

Seraphina's Magic continued to creep around the room. Her strength was stealth and she seemed to pull this off perfectly. I knew the only reason I was aware of what she was doing was because our Magics were connected.

And they would always be connected. No matter what happened today.

"I'm going to take everything from you," Terletov swore. "I'm going to do it slowly. I'm going to make you watch as every last thing is taken away from you. I'm going to make you relive the pain of losing everything you loved over and over and over. And when you've lost everything, then I'm going to take your Kingdom. The only thing I'm not going to take is your lives. Oh, no. I want you alive for all of this. I want you to watch on for eternity as I destroy everything you've touched."

Kiran fought against his restraints. I felt Eden's Magic building. It was a force that pressed against my skin and pushed the boundaries of the physical world. Nothing could restrain her, not even Terletov's reinforced metal.

"I'll never let that happen." Kiran jerked his head and the chains clanked against the wall. Stone crumbled from the ceiling, showing off how much strength he still had. "You still can't beat us. Not even when we're tied up and Magic-less."

I shifted to the side, out of the way of the entrance. We needed Avalon in here now. Eden might not have access to her Magic, but Avalon and Mimi still did.

It was just the baby in his arm and at his feet that kept us from jumping him and ending this already.

"I've already beaten you." Terletov slid baby Amari to the edge of the pit with the toe of his loafer.

His wrinkled suit hung off his thin frame, boasting of a once stronger man. His thin hair hung in limp, greasy strands across his forehead and his skin had turned a pasty yellow. My nose started to wrinkle as his disgusting scent permeated the damp room. The babies continued to scream and Eden and Kiran continued to fight their restraints.

Seraphina lunged forward, apparently tired of waiting on Terletov to do something. I felt her same impatience, but my gut kicked when I watched her get thrown back against the wall from a sweep of Terletov's Magic.

I got clipped in the side with it. It pushed us apart. I flew to one side of the crack in the wall, closer to Kiran. And Seraphina flew to the other, closer to the abyss than I was comfortable with. She pushed herself up, but I could see how shaky she was. She had gotten hit straight on. My heart hurt inside my chest. I wanted to crawl over to her and pull her into my arms. I wanted to pick her up and run with her, never looking back.

But there were too many other people that needed us.

And I was afraid that if I made a move to her, I would only make things worse.

I hated how powerless I felt.

"Don't test me!" Terletov shouted. "I will end you. And I will end these children." The children screamed louder, their faces bright red and their voices hoarse from their impatience.

A bubbling rage built inside of me. I would kill this man before he could hurt anyone I loved.

"If you hurt those children I will murder you," I snarled. "You will be dead."

Terletov scoffed at my threat, but Eden cut through his arrogance with her own ominous warning. "He's already dead, Sebastian. Can't you see that? Look at how sick he is. He won't last through the night."

"Give me back my Magic!" His shout rattled through the room at the same time another tremor of Magic shook the walls. I could hear the zapping of electricity as it struck in the other room. It lasted for longer than before, zinging up and down the wall.

Eden tilted her chin with defiance. "I've never been able to give you your Magic, Dmitri. That power has always lain solely with you. That's the secret to returning Magic. The owner must reclaim it. The owner must fight to take it back. I could never give it to you. It was never in my power and always in yours."

Terletov's eyes shone with hope for the first time maybe ever. He took a step away from the pit and moved toward Eden.

She wasn't finished with her verbal slaying. "But you're too weak now. Don't you see? You waited too long and now your body isn't strong enough to survive."

Rage twisted his face into a monstrous mask. He held out his free hand to her and made a gnarled fist. I could see the exertion he put forth from his red, sweaty face, but I could also see that nothing happened.

He really wasn't strong enough to reclaim his Magic. He'd destroyed his chances when he stole someone else's energy and turned it into a sick, rotten thing inside of him.

"No," he gasped, the deadly realization dawning on his drawn face.

And then three things happened at once.

First, Terletov stumbled back to the pit and thrust baby Gavriel directly over it. Second, Avalon shoved into the room and lashed out with his Magic. It burst in a bright, hot wave directly at Terletov, slamming him against the far wall.

And third, Seraphina jumped to her feet and dove into the black pit where Terletov had loosed his grip on the babe and let go.

Chapter Twenty-Eight

Seraphina

I was weightless for about three seconds before I hit the hard ground, burning my back from the rock debris and dirt I landed on.

I had Time-Slowed just in time. I had the nagging sensation that this baby boy was going to get dropped and so I had done my best to prepare for the moment it happened.

I dove after him, slowing him down long enough for me to catch him, cradle him next to my body, turn over and land on a ledge thirty feet into the pit.

Some kind of scary Magic buzzed below. I could feel it licking at my skin and burning straight through my clothes. I pulled myself to my feet and held the baby tighter to my chest.

He had calmed down some, but his body still stretched out uncomfortably and his whimpers had not stopped.

"Shh," I cooed to him. "Auntie Sera has you now. Shh..."

I could hear the sounds of fighting overhead. The smacking of a body against a hard surface, the clanking of chains and shouts from my friends. The baby and I were pretty much submerged into darkness. The faint light from the surface glowed overhead, but we had been plunged into thick blackness.

The Magic beneath me rumbled hungrily. It seemed to sense living beings above it. The unseen force whipped out at my calves and ankles, making me jump and wince from sharp, shooting pain.

Residual electricity crackled over every place the weird Magic touched. Panic pooled in my belly and started to rise up my chest like floodwaters.

I had heard Eden tell the story of what it was like for her to face the Source Magic in India. I had witnessed what it was like for Avalon in Morocco.

I was not like them. I wouldn't survive a confrontation with real, true, Source Magic. The baby had a better chance of surviving this than I did.

I tucked him into the crook of my elbow and held him tightly against my body with my left arm. With my right, I reached upward and searched for a place to hold onto. Something immensely powerful made this hole I'd fallen into like it had dug straight down into it. The walls were not smooth and held hope that I might be able to climb out.

Using as much Magic as I could gather, even pulling some from Sebastian, I set about climbing out of the hole with one hand. And I swear, I held my breath the entire time.

I shoved my feet into narrow spaces, only to have the dirt fall away underneath and make me grapple for any kind of holding just to keep from tumbling backward into the terrifying unknown. The baby cried and trembled in my arms, only adding to my anxiety.

"Shh, little one," I sang. "I'm taking you to Mommy."

I let out a scream and clutched the wall desperately with just my fingertips when suddenly the entire foundation of this place shook violently. Magic surged from beneath me and chased my heels. I shut my eyes so tightly that tears squeezed from the corners.

Only a little bit further, I promised myself.

When the ground stopped moving again, the bottom of this pit groaned a long yawning sound. I imagined a huge mouth waiting to swallow me up as soon as my precarious grip slipped. I kept my body pressed against the wall, but it was nearly impossible to keep climbing with only one hand.

Rocks kicked over the side of ledge from above and hit me in the head. I leaned over Gavriel, trying to protect him as best as I could. He screamed bloody murder in my face.

"I'm just trying to help," I told him. He screamed at me some more.

I could hear his sister crying out overhead. The sounds of fighting continued on. I wondered for how much longer though. There were so many of us against just one of him.

I prayed that Amari was safe somewhere and that Terletov hadn't managed to grab her.

"Sera!"

I looked up, desperate for more of that voice. "Sebastian." My voice was a whisper, but I knew he heard me.

He looked absolutely startled to find me climbing the wall, baby in toe.

Okay, maybe it was a little farfetched that I'd caught the baby, but I didn't have many talents. Time-slowing just happened to be something I excelled at.

"You're alive!" He still seemed unable to make sense of my climb.

"I am," I squeaked.

"And the baby is alive!"

"Of course, the baby's alive." Obviously, I didn't jump into the pit for the fun of it.

The walls rumbled more aggressively and I had to smash Gavriel against my chest and the wall and reach out with both hands to hold on. I looked down and prayed the baby would survive this ascent.

He was so tiny in my arms, so very fragile. Theoretically I knew that he was an Immortal, but he was still a newborn! Just a few days old.

He had been born into a very scary world. But hopefully we were about to fix that for him.

"Come on, Sera!" Sebastian called after me and I responded.

I had to.

I wanted to.

That man... That man that had never let me go, that had followed after me and brought me back to him. I loved him. I had never stopped loving him.

I would never stop loving him.

I couldn't.

And so I climbed. I used all of my Magic and all of my strength. I found handholds in places that I shouldn't have been able to hold onto, and my feet found a place to go with every step. I miraculously kept the baby safely tucked to my side.

He was angry, but he was alive.

Someone held onto Sebastian's legs and he reached down into the pit. His fingers dangled above me and his hazel eyes pierced right through me. As the ground shifted and trembled around us, I climbed to where Sebastian could reach the baby and held Gavriel out to him.

Holding the baby carefully, with two hands, he looked at me with this infinite well of love and kissed my sweaty forehead. "I'm coming back for you, Sera. *Hold on*."

I nodded, too out of breath to respond. He shouted for whoever held onto him to pull him up and they did. My breath stalled in my chest as I watched Sebastian hold the baby away from the wall and over the deep abyss as they dragged his body back onto solid ground.

Once Sebastian and Gavriel disappeared, I resumed my climb, anxious to get to the top now that I had two hands to work with.

The yawning sounded again, something like a great beast groaning for sustenance. I felt the prickles of urgency raise the hairs on my neck and moved with renewed purpose.

The dirt walls around me began to vibrate aggressively. I let out a squeak of panic and moved my hand over the rocky surface, struggling to find a better hold. The ground beneath my feet began to shift and disappear. A cracking sound caught my attention and I looked down just in time to see the ledge I'd landed on earlier break off and crumble into the ominous black hole.

I was losing my hold and I had nowhere to go.

I could Time-Slow, but that would only prolong my death if I fell.

That same dangerous, superheated Magic bubbled up from below like a volcano burping lava. It hit my back, stunning me completely with shock and stinging pain. I felt my hands release their grasp, but I had no strength to do anything about it.

I watched in horror as I started to fall backward, slowly at first, but I knew my momentum would pick up. I could swear I felt the abyss below lick its savage lips in anticipation for my fall.

My heart felt like it would burst in my chest and I couldn't work out a coherent thought in my head. There was nothing up there but raw, unfiltered panic.

But then I wasn't falling.

Something grabbed both of my wrists and in the next second my body slammed against the rock wall. The breath left my lungs at the same time I was yanked upwards.

Grateful tears came next.

"I've got you, Sera. You're not getting away from me that easily," Sebastian exclaimed. He leaned over the ledge again, straining for me.

I closed my eyes and let him pull me up. My body shook and my spirit soared. I had been sure I was on my way to meet my end. Positive of it.

And then I wasn't. Life waited for me instead of death. Love instead of the aching loneliness of that hole.

The Magic below did not like that its meal had been snatched from its claws. The cavern shook violently, debris falling from the ceiling.

Sebastian hauled me over the edge and we lay together, head to head with our bodies stretched in opposite directions for several long moments. I could feel and hear the commotion around me, but I needed this minute to savor my rescue, to breathe in the man I loved with all of me.

I felt the stabbing punctures of the Magic from below and jumped back into action. I crawled to my feet and Sebastian was there to catch me when I staggered to the side.

At the same time, we looked over at where Terletov was cornered, more furious than ever. Which made him as dangerous as ever.

Someone had freed Kiran and Eden. Kiran held Amari in his hands and Olivia stood next to him with Gavriel in hers.

Eden trembled with rage, too violent to even hold her child.

Avalon and Jericho hovered aggressively over Terletov, ready to deliver their final judgment.

"You deserve this," Eden declared. Her voice shook and her Magic pulsed so strongly we could all feel it. The rest of our team had filtered into this room. We were an army against this one, horrible man. "You tried to take my Kingdom, my loved ones, and my children from me. You tried to destroy the few things I would risk my life for over and over again. You could not defeat me when I was seventeen and you will not defeat me now. I wish you had to live with your defeat, but I cannot stomach the idea of you existing in the same world as me."

Terletov's angry expression transformed to something purely savage. He pushed off the wall and lunged for her. His stolen Magic gushed out from his hands in a dark green explosion. I sucked in a gasp and felt my feet move before I even registered planning to intervene.

It was for nothing though. Eden was ready for him.

She threw out her hands and met him, Magic against Magic. Only hers was infinitely stronger. And she had a hell of a lot of friends on her side. In the next second, her husband, her brother, Jericho, and Sebastian stood with her. Together they thrust Terletov back, overpowering his pathetic Magic with sheer might and force.

His feet slid on the smooth dirt floor, his arms flailed wildly. And just as the walls shook and large rocks began to fall down on top of us, just as the Magic below bellowed out a hungry groan of warning, just as Terletov's eyes glinted with promised victory, they gave him one, final push and he disappeared over the ledge.

His scream followed him down, shaking the still volatile atmosphere.

"Duck!" Eden screamed.

It wasn't over yet.

I dropped to the ground, Sebastian landed on top of me, shielding me with his body. I slammed my eyes shut when the whitest light invaded this dim room. Electricity crackled at an ear-splitting level and I could feel the hot tendrils of it swoop down and burn the back of my legs and head. Sebastian covered the rest of me, so I knew he took the worst of it.

I worried about the babies, but I had to believe their parents would keep them safe.

For long minutes the Magic from the other room flooded this space and with one last scream and Magical maneuvering from Eden, she thrust the tainted Magic into the pit. Because even with Terletov's tampering, even though he had managed to turn this Magic dark and evil, Eden still controlled it. She was still linked to its very core. And when she commanded it to do something, the Magic obeyed.

Terletov's final screams echoed up to us. The Magic groaned a more pleasant sound and finally the ground stopped shivering.

In the wake of all that action and excitement, silence fell on us heavier than ever.

It was over.

Sebastian eased his weight from me and I rolled over to take inventory of my friends and make sure they all survived. He held out his hand to me and pulled me to my feet.

I watched Olivia and Roxie hand over the two babies to their desperate parents. Both Eden and Kiran fell to their knees, cradling their beloved children against their faces and hearts. Avalon and Mimi followed after them, wrapping their arms around the couple and little ones.

I couldn't stay away. Screw family moments. I loved these people too.

I jumped on top of them, careful of the babies. But I was too anxious to touch them all and reassure myself we had all survived, so I couldn't stay away.

Sebastian's chest pressed into my back and his arms wrapped around my stomach. We all stayed like that a long time. Just holding each other. Just taking in the moment.

Finally, Sebastian pulled back and announced, "I'm officially retired. If this happens again, count me out."

We broke into adrenaline-filled laughter.

"You can't quit now," Avalon told him. "You finally made yourself useful. If anyone sits out next time, it's Talbott. A whole lot of good he did this time around. I thought he had oaths and all that crap."

"I did have oaths, but between high school and this, I quit. I'm too old for this crap." Talbott's voice boomed from the crack in the wall and we all looked up to see a very healthy looking Lilly tucked into a very relieved looking Talbott.

"Sorry, we're late," Lilly said sweetly.

We all laughed some more and stood to our feet. "You haven't even seen your godchildren yet," Kiran tsked. "We're going to revoke your godparent privileges."

Talbott grinned at them. "Do that and we'll ask Avalon to take over responsibilities of our little one," he threatened.

There was a long pause while we all absorbed that information. I broke the silence with a very intelligent "Nu-uh!"

Lilly beamed at me and placed her hands on her stomach. "Yes," she confirmed.

We rushed her all at once, and then realized where we were and decided it was probably better to take this conversation to the surface and away from Terletov's dead body and the destruction around us.

The babies still bleated their complaints on the way to the surface, but soon they would have the comfort they wanted and all of their needs fulfilled. We chatted animatedly as we went, all of us excited to have finally won this long sought after victory.

In the catacombs, Sebastian tugged on my hand and held me back from the happy crowd of our friends anxious to get someplace they could talk.

I stayed with him, drinking in the sight of his gorgeous body and his warm hands on mine. I was transfixed by the look of absolute adoration he showed me.

"I'm glad you didn't die," he told me once we were alone.

I looked around this crypt that I knew he hated and smiled at him. If he were this desperate for some alone time with me, I could play nice and give him what he wanted. "I'm glad you didn't die, too."

He leaned in and placed a gritty, dirty, very seductive kiss on my lips. He tasted like sweat, earth, and blood, but also like him. I hummed my approval.

When he pulled back, his eyes had darkened with desire and his Magic vibrated with something heavier than love, deeper than eternity. "I thought I'd lost you," he confessed.

"You won't lose me again," I promised him. "This is it, Bastian. I'm yours forever."

"Marry me," he sighed. I didn't respond. I couldn't. My eyebrows had shot to my forehead and my heart had stopped beating.

"What?"

"Marry me." It wasn't the love-struck plea I had imagined all of my life. Instead, his words came out a forceful command that would not be argued with or ignored. "Sera, I can't stand the idea of us being apart again. And I refuse to entertain the idea that you don't think I'm committed to you like before. I want to be with you, from this day on. I love you. I've always loved you. You keep me in line; you keep me alive. You challenge me. You accept me. You see through me, but you also see me. I have never met a more loving, beautiful soul than yours. And I would be nothing without you. Marry me, Sweetheart. Let's make this official."

I couldn't see for all of my blissful happiness. Oh, and because of the stupid tears. I threw my arms around his neck and pressed my body into the safety of his.

"Yes," I told him and I hiccupped again, "Yes!"

His arms squeezed around me, becoming a stronghold that kept me standing. "I love you, Sera."

"I love you too, Bastian."

Endless minutes passed as we basked in each other's happiness and shared secret kisses that were a preview of what more was to come.

"Ready?" After a long time of just being with each other, present in this incredible moment, Sebastian took my hand and started leading me to the surface.

"I am."

"Good," he sighed. "Because Kiran already has two children and now Talbott is going to have one of his own. I don't want to pressure you, but we can't let them win."

I looked at him and tried to gauge if he was joking or not.

I was shocked to find that for the first time in Sebastian's life, he was completely and utterly serious.

Oh, my.

Epilogue

Another Year Later
Sebastian

I plopped onto the couch, cake in hand, birthday hat tightly strapped to my head. The tiny string cut into the underside of my jaw and I wanted to throw the damn thing on the floor and stomp on it. But since it seemed to make the little savages in the highchairs happy, I kept it on.

"They're adorable," Seraphina cooed next to me.

"They're very messy," I informed her. She slapped my arm with the back of her hand. I wiggled closer to her and enjoyed the press of her side against mine. Sylvia's seating was the extra stuffy kind and we sunk together in a delicious tangle. Our Magic bounced around the room in happy union and buzzed with all the vibrancy of true love.

Somehow, despite our stubborn personalities and equally selfish tendencies, we'd managed to put ourselves aside and find our true love bliss.

And I had to say, it was worth all the trouble to get to this point. I had never been this happy, this peaceful... This settled.

"They're one," Seraphina reminded me. "It's their first cake. I think they're supposed to be messy. That's the whole point."

"They're royalty. Shouldn't they know how to use a spoon by now?" I raised a challenging eyebrow. Surely, I had used silver by the time I turned one. "Is it too much to ask for some civility?"

She snorted. Actually snorted. "You're such a snob."

I kissed the tip of her nose, making it sticky with my frosting-coated lips. "It's why you love me so much."

She didn't object. In fact, some might say she encouraged my behavior by moving her lips to mine and showing just how much she loved me. She tasted like sugar and everything sweet and I could have easily never stopped worshipping her perfect mouth.

"Enough, you two! Get a room." Avalon's grumpy voice cut through the lust-induced haze Seraphina had encouraged with just some minor kissing.

"Someone's cranky," I sniped at him, while I reluctantly pulled myself from my beautiful fiancée. That's right, fiancée. I had made it official as soon as I'd had the time to design her rather large ring. My sister might have a moral issue with diamonds, but my lovely bride-to-be did not. I'd asked her after a lovely meal made in her Seattle condo. No grand gesture. No fireworks or big hoorah. Just the two of us over a candlelight dinner in a place where no one in the Kingdom bothered to look for us. So much of our relationship had been tied up in our friends and Kingdom business. But when we decided to share the rest of our forever together, I had wanted it to be just the two of us.

She said yes. I didn't even have to kidnap her.

Seraphina sighed at my departure, as she should. But then she saw who hovered over us and shoved her plate of birthday cake in my lap. "Give me, give me, give me!" She wiggled her greedy fingers at my sister and her whole body came alive.

"Thank god!" Mimi cried and shoved another bleating thing at us. "I need a break!"

"They keep us up all night," Avalon whined, trying to pawn off another one on me. I reluctantly set the cake to the side table and looked at the red-faced troll that was apparently my nephew.

Seraphina settled back against the couch and drew her legs up so she could cradle the little beast in her lap. I looked over at the girl and thought she definitely had the better looks of the two. Although, since both resembled me to some degree, they were obviously stunning creatures.

"Ajax won't go to sleep and Bea won't stay asleep. It's been h-e-l-l," Avalon explained. "There is not enough Magic in the world to get me through this."

My nephew Ajax, whose name meant "strong warrior" and was named after his stand-in grandmother, Angelica, and his grandfather Justice, and my niece, Bea, short for Beatrix, who's name meant "blessed," were as feisty and strong-willed as their parents.

I loved watching the King and Queen suffer, just as much as I enjoyed watching my cousin and his bride suffer. Ah, parenting.

"Don't look at me like that, Bastian," Mimi snapped. "One day this will be you!"

The two month old in my arms gurgled his approval. And with that angelic sound, I looked to Seraphina and realized that I couldn't wait.

The other set of parents walked into the room and collapsed onto the sofa. Talbott and Lilly had their hands filled with a set of five-month-old twins. The two girls were named Eliza, after Lilly's middle name and her deceased grandmother Elizabetta, and her identical sister Vera.

Ileana's words replayed in my head, "Twins and twins and twins and twins."

We were missing a set. I didn't have to be Psychic to know that Seraphina and I would be joining the parenting ranks soon after our next-month wedding.

"I can't wait," I told Mimi with a genuine smile.

She smiled back at me and fell into conversation with Lilly about feeding schedules. Avalon closed his eyes and appeared to fall asleep while standing and Talbott sat by his wife's side, a place he rarely moved from, and simply watched her with rapt fascination.

Kiran and Eden hovered over their cake-covered children, snapping pictures and talking with the animated women that filled the rolls of grandmothers, Angelica, Sylvia, Annalisa and my own mother.

Titus, Xander, Xavier, Roxie, Jericho, Olivia and Ophelia laughed together as they filled plates with delicious food Eden had set out.

My friends. My loved ones.

We were all together under this one roof in Omaha, Nebraska, sharing life and relishing peace. The last year had been spent rebuilding the Kingdom and salvaging our world from the destruction Terletov had wrought.

It had been an exhausting year, filled with heartache, healing and hope. It had been a wonderful year, filled with new life, a happiness I hadn't imagined I would ever experience, and peace.

The road to get here had been a painful battle that cost us much, but gave us much in return. It seemed only right that we would end this journey in the place that it began.

"I can't wait to add our own to this party," I whispered to Seraphina while we both gazed at these adorable creatures that had captured our hearts along with all of their peers.

"Me either."

"I love you," I promised her.

She leaned forward and pressed her forehead against mine. "I love you too, Bastian. Forever."

And when she said forever, she really meant it. The Magic was restored. Fully. Completely.

Universally.

So, at this point, there was only one thing left to do. I leaned forward and kissed her. It was the start of forever, but the end of this chapter.

And from that moment on, we lived happily ever after.

Because after all, this is a love story.

The end?

I hope you enjoyed the conclusion of the Star-Crossed Series. I started writing this series in 2009. Reckless Magic was the first book I published and the book that began this self-publishing journey. I am sad to leave this world behind, but excited for my future projects. I couldn't have left this world with a better love story than Sebastian and Seraphina. They are one of my favorite couples of all time. I hope you fell in love with them as deeply as I did.

Keep reading for a sneak peek at my next adventure, Adult Contemporary Romance.

Please enjoy an excerpt from The Five Stages of Falling in Love, available now.

Acknowledgments

To my God. Thank you for this opportunity, for this passion... for this drive that will not stop. Thank you for teaching me to rely solely on you. Thank you for showing me the beautiful in everything and in every word.

To Zach, thank you for everything you do so that I can work. You take care of the kids, you clean the house, you make meals and you remind me to focus. You remind me to walk away. You make me laugh and you make me want to be better. You are the reason I published Reckless Magic to begin with and the only reason I've been successful. You have encouraged, supported and laughed with me during this entire journey and I know I am the luckiest woman in the world to have a man that cares so very much. I believe in this dream, but you make it happen. You are the very best man I know and I am so blessed to be in love with you. Sarcasm is the new sexy.

To my kiddos. You guys are it. The reason I do this. The reason I work so hard. The reason I will always work hard. Thank you for loving me anyway.

To my mom, thank you for always being there for me and encouraging me when I am down and cannot find the point. Thank you for encouraging me when everything is right. Thank you for loving this series from the very beginning. Thank you for pushing it on everyone you meet and know. Thank you for the incredible number of babysitting hours you gave me so I could write the Star-Crossed Series from beginning to end. You are the most wonderful mom and nana. I am blessed by you.

To Kylee, Ashley, Diana, Bridget, Brooke, Candice and all the guys from Greenlife for taking a chance on this series. You were the first people I knew that read the Star-Crossed Series. You made me hope that this could be real. You made me believe that I could be an author. And you supported me when nobody knew who I was. Thank you. Your support, encouragement and excitement mean more to me than you'll ever know.

To Lindsay, thank you for being such a great friend. Thank you for never reading a single word I've written, but for supporting me anyway. Thank you for convincing so many people to read my work. Thank you for never hugging me.

To Pat, thank you for designing such amazing, memorable covers that have become so synonymous with the Star-Crossed Series. Thank you for working for free. Thank you for believing in me enough to create something unbelievably beautiful and eye-catching. Thank you Sarah Hansen, from Okay Creations, for designing covers five and six. You're one of the best in the business and I was so fortunate to get to work with you.

Thank you Caedus Design Co. for designing The Redeemable Prince cover. You took my concept and turned it into one of the most beautiful covers I've ever had. You are so talented. Thank you for sharing that with me.

Thank you, Jennifer Nunez, for editing the first five books. Thank you for putting up with all of the crazy capitalization and adding phone numbers. Thank you for loving these characters and reaching out to me. Thank you for being such a great friend.

To Carolyn, thank you for taking on the monumental task of editing for me. From the very beginning I have been a work in progress. You have taught me so very much over the years. You made my words make sense and you made them better. Thank you for your patience, your critical eye and your constant devotion to not just correcting something, but helping me understand the whys of it. I have grown as a writer with your help. And I thank you for that.

To my Hellcats, Amy Bartol, Angeline Kace, Shelly Crane, Quinn Loftis, Georgia Cates, Lila Felix and Samantha Young. Thank you girls for becoming a support system I could not live without. You are there for all of the great moments and the really, really hard moments. You've become so much more than peers, you've become some of my closest, dearest friends. Thank you for all of your music, your laughter and those moments I know I couldn't do this without your perspective and insight. You're some of the best authors in this industry and I'm just lucky to be a part of this group and to count each of you as friends.

To my Panel. Girls. Who knew you would become such incredible friends? I could never have anticipated the kind of community we've developed. Thank you for your encouragement and words of wisdom.

Thank you for your perspective. You are invaluable to me. Thank you for that. And thank you for loving my characters and worlds as much as I do.

To the Reckless Rebels, thank you for devoting so many hours to promoting me. Thank you for loving my stories and loving my heroes even more! You girls work so hard and I am so blessed by everything that you do. Thank you for giving up your time to help and support me.

And finally, to the readers. Reckless Magic was the very first book I self-published. I had spent two years working on getting it published traditionally and being rejected. I had no idea what self-publishing would do for me or that it would turn into a career and then my dream job. I couldn't imagine someone picking up my books out of the thousands upon thousands of other books out there. And I really couldn't imagine someone reading my book and actually enjoying it! But you did. And not only that, but you stayed with me to the very end. And you went even beyond that. I have treasured your emails, posts, messages, comments, tweets, phone calls and absolute enthusiasm for these characters and this world. Thank you for sharing your love for this story with your friends and families, with strangers and your co-workers. You are the best marketing system a girl could ask for. Without you there wouldn't have been a second part to this series. Without you I wouldn't be where I am today. You are the greatest, loveliest readers in the world. I am convinced of that. Thank you for taking this journey with me. Thank you for following the characters to the very end of their story. I am struggling to let this story go, but I cannot wait for what is to come in the future. I hope you enjoyed the final book of the Star-Crossed Series. Thank you for reading.

About the Author

Rachel Higginson was born and raised in Nebraska, but spent her college years traveling the world. She fell in love with Eastern Europe, Paris, Indian Food and the beautiful beaches of Sri Lanka, but came back home to marry her high school sweetheart. Now she spends her days raising their growing family. She is obsessed with bad reality TV and any and all Young Adult Fiction.

Other books by Rachel to be released early 2015 are The Five Stages of Falling in Love, an adult contemporary romance, The Heart, the third and final installment of The Siren Series and Bet on Me, an NA contemporary romance.

Other Books Out Now by Rachel Higginson:

Love and Decay, Season One
Love and Decay, Volume One (Episodes One-Six, Season One)
Love and Decay, Volume Two (Episodes Seven-Twelve, Season One)
Love and Decay, Season Two
Love and Decay, Volume Three (Episodes One-Four, Season Two)
Love and Decay, Volume Four (Episodes Five-Eight, Season Two)
Love and Decay, Volume Five (Episodes Nine-Twelve, Season Two)
Love and Decay, Season Three, Episode One

Reckless Magic (The Star-Crossed Series, Book 1)
Hopeless Magic (The Star-Crossed Series, Book 2)
Fearless Magic (The Star-Crossed Series, Book 3)
Endless Magic (The Star-Crossed Series, Book 4)
The Reluctant King (The Star-Crossed Series, Book 5)
The Relentless Warrior (The Star-Crossed Series, Book 6)
Breathless Magic (The Star-Crossed Series, Book 6.5)
The Redeemable Prince (The Star-Crossed Series, Book 7)

Heir of Skies (The Starbright Series, Book 1)
Heir of Darkness (The Starbright Series, Book 2)
Heir of Secrets (The Starbright Series, Book 3)

The Rush (The Siren Series, Book 1)
The Fall (The Siren Series, Book 2)

The Heart (The Siren Series, Book 3) coming February, 2015

Bet on Us (An NA Contemporary Romance)
Bet on Me (An NA Contemporary Romance) coming Spring 2015

Follow Rachel on her blog at:
www.rachelhigginson.com

Or on Twitter:
@mywritesdntbite

Or on her Facebook page:
Rachel Higginson

Please enjoy an excerpt of The Five Stages of Falling in Love, coming January 27th, 2015.
Pre-order available now wherever eBooks are sold.

Prologue

"Hey, there she is," Grady looked up at me from his bed, his eyes smiling even while his mouth barely mimicked the emotion.

"Hey, you," I called back. The lights had been dimmed after the last nurse checked his vitals and the TV was on, but muted. "Where are the kiddos? I was only in the cafeteria for ten minutes."

Grady winked at me playfully, "My mother took them." I melted a little at his roguish expression. It was the same look that made me agree to a date with him our junior year of college, it was the same look that made me fall in love with him- the same one that made me agree to have our second baby boy when I would have been just fine to stop after Blake, Abby and Lucy.

"Oh, yeah?" I walked over to the hospital bed and sat down next to him. He immediately reached for me, pulling me against him with weak arms. I snuggled back into him, so that my head rested on his thin shoulder and our bodies fit side by side on the narrow bed. One of my legs didn't make it and hung off awkwardly. But I didn't mind. It was just perfect to lie next to the love of my life, my husband.

"Oh, yeah," he growled suggestively. "You know what that means?" He walked his free hand up my arm and gave my breast a wicked squeeze. "When the kids are away, the grownups get to play..."

"You are so bad," I swatted him- or at least made the motion of swatting at him, since I was too afraid to hurt him.

"God, I don't remember the last time I got laid," he groaned next to me and I felt the rumble of his words against my side.

"Tell me about it, sport," I sighed. "I could use a nice, hard-"

"Elizabeth Carlson," he cut in on a surprised laugh. "When did you get such a dirty mouth?"

"I think you've known about my dirty mouth for quite some time, Grady," I flirted back. We'd been serious for so long it was nice to flirt with him, to remember that we didn't just love each other, but we liked each other too.

He grunted in satisfaction. "That I have. I think your dirty mouth had something to do with Lucy's conception."

I blushed. Even after all these years, he knew exactly what to say to me. "Maybe," I conceded.

"Probably," he chuckled, his breath hot on my ear.

We laid there in silence for a while, enjoying the feel of each other, watching the silent TV screen flicker in front of our eyes. It was perfect- or as close to perfect as we had felt in a long time.

"Dance with me, Lizzy," Grady whispered after a while. I'd thought maybe he fell asleep; the drugs were so hard on his system that he was usually in and out of consciousness. This was actually the most coherent he'd been in a month.

"Okay," I agreed. "It's the first thing we'll do when you get out. We'll have your mom come over and babysit, you can take me to dinner at Pazio's and we'll go dancing after."

"Mmm, that sounds nice," he agreed. "You love Pazio's. That's a guaranteed get-lucky night for me."

"Baby," I crooned. "As soon as I get you back home, you're going to have guaranteed get-lucky nights for at least a month, maybe two."

"I don't want to wait. I'm tired of waiting. Dance with me now, Lizzy," Grady pressed, this time sounding serious.

"Babe, after your treatment this morning, you can barely stand up right now. Honestly, how are you going to put all those sweet moves on me?" I teased, wondering where this sudden urge to dance- of all things- was coming from.

"Lizzy, I am a sick man. I haven't slept in my own bed in four months, I haven't seen my wife naked in just as long, and I am tired of lying in this bed. I want to dance with you. Will you please, pretty please, dance with me?"

I nodded at first because I was incapable of speech. He was right. I hated that he was right, but I hated that he was sick even more.

"Alright, Grady, I'll dance with you," I finally whispered.

"I knew I'd get my way," he croaked smugly.

I slipped off the bed and turned around to face my husband and help him to his feet. His once full head of auburn hair was now bald, reflecting the pallid color of his skin. His face was haggard, dark black circles under his eyes, chapped lips and pale cheeks. He was still as tall as he'd ever been, but instead of the toned muscles and thick frame he once boasted, he was depressingly skinny and weak, his shoulders perpetually slumped.

The only thing that remained the same was his eyes; they were the same dark green eyes I'd fallen in love with ten years ago. They were still full of life, even when his body wasn't, still full of mischief while the rest of him was tired and exhausted from fighting this stupid sickness.

"You always get your way," I grumbled while I helped him up from the bed.

"Only with you," he shot back on a pant after successfully standing. "And only because you love me."

"That I do," I agreed. Grady's hands slipped around my waist and he clutched my sides in an effort to stay standing.

I slipped my arms around his neck, but didn't allow any weight to press down on him. We maneuvered our bodies around his IV and monitors. It was awkward, but we managed.

"What should we listen to?" I asked, while I pulled out my cell phone and turned it to my iTunes app.

"You know what song. There is no other song when we're dancing," he reminded me on a faint smile.

"You must be horny," I laughed. "You're getting awfully romantic."

"Just trying to keep this fire alive, Babe," he pulled me closer and I held back the flood of tears that threatened to spill over.

I turned on The Way You Look Tonight- the Frank Sinatra version- and we swayed slowly back and forth. Frank sang the soft, beautiful lyrics with the help of a full band, the music drifting around us over the constant beeping and whirring of medical machines. This was the song we thought of as ours, the first song we'd danced to at our wedding, the song he still made the band at Pazio's play on our anniversary each year.

"This fire is very much alive," I informed him sternly. I lay my forehead against his shoulder and inhaled him. He didn't smell like himself anymore, he was full of chemo drugs and smelled like hospital soap and detergent, but he was still Grady. And even though he barely resembled himself anymore, he still felt like Grady.

He was still *my* Grady.

"It is, isn't it?" He whispered. I could feel how weak he was growing, how tired this was making him, but still he clung to me, held me close. When my favorite verse came on, he leaned his head down and whispered in a broken voice along with Frank, "There is nothing for me, but to love you. And the way you look tonight."

Silent tears streamed down my face with truths I wasn't ready to admit to myself and fears that were too horrifying to even think. This was the man I loved with every fiber of my being- the only man I'd ever loved. The only man I'd *ever love*.

He'd made me fall in love with him before I was old enough to drink legally, then he'd convinced me to marry him before I even graduated college. He knocked me up a year later, and didn't stop until we had four wild rug rats that all had his red hair and his emerald green eyes. He'd encouraged me to finish my undergrad degree, and then to continue on to grad school while I was pregnant, nursing and then pregnant again. He went to bed every night with socks on and then took them off sometime in the middle of the night, leaving them obnoxiously tucked in between our sheets. He could never find his wallet, or his keys, and when there was hair to grow he always forgot to shave.

And he drove me crazy most of the time.

But he was mine.

He was my husband.

And now he was sick.

"I do love you, Lizzy," he murmured against my hair. "I'll always love you, even when I'm dead and gone."

"Which won't be for a very long time," I reminded him on a sob.

He ignored me, "You love me back, don't you?"

"Yes, I love you back," I whispered with so much emotion the words felt stuck in my throat. "But you already knew that."

"Maybe," he conceded gently. "But I will never, ever get tired of hearing it."

I sniffled against him, staining his hospital gown with my mascara and eye liner. "That's a good thing, because you're going to be hearing it for a very long time."

He didn't respond, just kept swaying with me back and forth until the song ended. He asked me to play it again and I did, three more times. By the end of the fourth time, he was too tired to stand. I laid him back in bed and helped him adjust the IV and monitor again so that it didn't bother him, then pulled the sheet over his cold toes.

His eyes were closed and I thought he'd fallen asleep, so I bent down to kiss his forehead. He stirred at my touch and reached out to cup my face with his un-needled arm. I looked down into his depthless green eyes and fell in love with him all over again.

It was as simple as that.

It had always been that simple for him to get me to fall in love with him.

"You are the most beautiful thing that ever happened to me, Lizzy." His voice was broken and scratchy and a tear slid out from the corner of each of his eyes.

My chin trembled at his words because I knew what he was doing and I hated it, I hated every part of it. I shook my head, trying to get him to stop but he held my gaze and just kept going.

"You are. And you have made my life good, and worth living. You have made me love more than any man has ever known how to love. I didn't know this kind of happiness existed in real life, Liz, and you're the one that gave it to me. I couldn't be more thankful for the life we've shared together. I couldn't be more thankful for you."

"Oh, Grady, please-"

"Lizzy," he said in his most stern voice that he only ever used when I'd maxed out a credit card. "Whatever happens, whatever happens to me, I want you to keep giving this gift to other people." I opened my mouth to vehemently object to everything he was saying but he silenced me with a cold finger on my lips. "I didn't say go marry the first man you find. Hell, I'm not even talking about another man. But I don't want this light to die with me. I don't want you to forget how happy you make other people just because you might not feel happy. Even if I don't, Lizzy, I want you to go on living. Promise me that."

But I shook my head, "no." I wasn't going to promise him that. I couldn't make myself. And it was unfair of him to ask me that.

"Please, Sweetheart, for me?" His deep, green eyes glossed over with emotion and I could physically feel how painful this was for him to ask me. He didn't want this anymore than I did.

I found myself nodding, while I sniffled back a stream of tears. "Okay," I whispered. "I promise."

He broke out into a genuine smile then, his thumb rubbing back and forth along my jaw. "Now tell me you love me, one more time."

"I love you, Grady," I murmured, leaning into his touch and savoring this moment with him.

"And I will always, always love you, Lizzy," he promised.

His eyes finally fluttered shut and his hand dropped from my face. His vitals remained the same, so I knew he was just sleeping. I crawled into bed with him, gently shifting him so that I could lie on my side, in the nook of his arm and lay my hand on his chest. I did this often; I liked to feel the beat of his heart underneath my hand. It had stopped too many times before, for me to trust its reliability. My husband was a very sick man, and had been for a while now.

Tonight was different though. Tonight, Grady was lucid and coherent, he'd found enough energy to stand up and dance with me, to tell me he loved me. Tonight could have been a turn for the better.

But it wasn't- because only a few hours later, Grady's heart stopped for the fourth time during his adult life, and this time it never restarted.

Stage One: Denial

Not every story has a happy ending. Some only hold a happy beginning.

This is my story. I'd already met my soul mate, fallen in love with him and lived our happily ever after.

This story is not about me falling in love.

This story is about me learning to live again after love left my life.

Research shows there are five stages of grief. I don't know what this means for me, as I was stuck, nice and hard, in step one.

Denial.

I knew, acutely, that I was still in stage one.

I knew this because every time I walked in the house, I wandered around aimlessly looking for Grady. Because I still picked up my phone to check if he texted or called throughout the day. Because I looked for him in a crowded room, got the urge to call him from the grocery store just to make sure I had everything he needed, and reached for him in the middle of the night.

Acceptance- the last stage of grief- was firmly and forever out of my reach, and I often looked forward to it with longing. Why? Because Denial was a *son of a bitch* and it hurt more than *anything* when I realized he wasn't in the house, wouldn't be calling me, wasn't where I wanted him to be, didn't need anything from the store and would never lie next to me in bed again. The grief would cascade over me, fresh and suffocating and I was forced to suffer through the unbearable pain of losing my husband all over again.

Denial *sucked*.

But it was where I was right now. I was living in Denial.

Chapter One

Six Months after Grady died.

I snuggled back into the cradle of his body while his arms wrapped around me tightly. He buried his scruffy face against the nape of my neck and I sighed contentedly. We fit perfectly together, but then again we always had- his big spoon nestled up against my little spoon.

"It's your turn," he rumbled against my skin with that deep morning voice I would always drink in.

"No," I argued half-heartedly. "It's always my turn."

"But you're so good at it," he teased.

I giggled, "It's one of my many talents, pouring cereal into bowls, making juice cups. I might just take this show on the road."

He laughed behind me and his chest shook with the movement. I pushed back into him, loving the feel of his hard, firm chest against my back. He was so hot first thing in the morning, his whole body radiating warmth.

His hand splayed out across my belly possessively and he pressed a kiss just below my ear. I could feel his lips through my tangle of hair and the tickle of his breath which wasn't all that pleasant first thing in the morning, but it was Grady and it was familiar.

"It's probably time we had another one, don't you think?" His hand rubbed a circle around my stomach and I could feel him vibrating happily with the thought.

"Grady, we already have three," I reminded him on a laugh. "If we have another one, people are going to start thinking we're weird."

"No, they won't," he soothed. "They might get an idea of how fertile you are, but they won't think we're weird."

I snorted a laugh. "They already think we're weird."

"Then we don't want to disappoint them," he murmured. His hand slid up my chest and cupped my breast, giving it a gentle squeeze.

"You are obsessed with those things," I grinned.

"Definitely," he agreed quickly, while continuing to fondle me. "What do you think, Lizzy? Will you give me another baby?"

I was getting wrapped up in the way he was touching me, the way he was caressing me with so much love I thought I would burst. "I'll think about it," I finally conceded, knowing he would get his way- knowing I always let him have his way.

"While you're mulling it over, we should probably practice. I mean, we want to get this right when the time comes." Grady trailed kisses down the column of my throat and I moaned my consent.

I rolled over to kiss him on the mouth.

But he wasn't there.

My arm swung wide and hit cold, empty mattress.

I opened my eyes and stared at the slow moving ceiling fan over my head. The early morning light streamed in through cracks in my closed blinds and I let the silent tears fall.

I hated waking up like this; thinking he was there, next to me, still able to support me, love me- hold me. And unfortunately it happened more often than it didn't.

The fresh pain clawed and cut at my heart and I thought I would die just from sheer heartbreak. My chin quivered and I sniffled, trying desperately to wrestle my emotions under control. But the pain was too much, too consuming.

"Mom!" Blake called from the kitchen, ripping me away from my peaceful grief. "Moooooom!"

That was a distressed cry, and I was up out of my bed and racing downstairs immediately. I grabbed my silk robe on the way and threw it over my black cami and plaid pajama bottoms. When the kids were younger I wouldn't have bothered, but Blake was eight now and he'd been traumatized enough in life- I wasn't going to add to that by walking around bra-less first thing in the morning.

He continued to yell at me, while I barreled into the kitchen still wiping at the fresh tears. I found him at the bay windows, staring out in horror.

"Mom, Abby went swimming," he explained in a rush of words.

A sick feeling knotted my stomach and I looked around wild-eyed at what his words could possibly mean. "What do you mean, Abby *went swimming*?" I gasped, a little out of breath.

"There," he pointed to the neighbor's backyard with a shaky finger.

I followed the direction of his outstretched hand and from the elevated vantage point of our kitchen I could see that the neighbor's pool was filled with water, and my six-year-old daughter was swimming morning laps like she was on a regulated workout routine.

"What the f-" I started and then stopped, shooting a glance down at Blake who was looking up at me with more exaggerated shock than he'd given his sister.

I watched her for point one more second and sprinted for the front door. "Keep an eye on the other ones," I shouted at Blake as I pushed open our heavy red door.

It was just early fall in rural Connecticut; the grass was still green, the mornings foggy but mostly still warm. The house next to us had been empty for almost a year. The owner had been asking too much for it in this economy, but I understood why- it was a beautiful, stately colonial with cream stucco siding and black decorative shutters. Big oak trees offered shade and character in the sprawling front yard and in the back, an in-ground pool was the drool-worthy envy of my children.

I raced down my yard and into my new neighbors. I hadn't noticed the house had sold, but that didn't surprise me. I wasn't the most observant person these days. Vaguely I noted a moving truck parked in the long drive.

The backyard gate must have been left open, because even though Abby had taught herself how to swim at the age of four- all by herself, the end result giving me several gray hairs- there was no way she could reach the flip lock at the top of the tall, iron fence.

I rounded the corner and hopped/ran to the edge of the pool, the gravel of the patio cutting into my bare feet. I took a steadying breath and focused my panic-flooded mind, long enough to assess whether Abby was still breathing or not.

She was, and happily swimming in circles *in the deep end.*

Fear and dread quickly turned to blinding anger and I took a step closer to the edge of the pool while I threw my silk robe on the ground.

"Abigail Elizabeth, you get out of there right this minute!" I shouted loud enough to wake up the entire neighborhood.

She popped her head up out of the water, acknowledged me by sticking out her tongue, and promptly went back to swimming. *That little brat.*

"Abigail, I am *not* joking. Get out of the pool. *Now*!" I hollered again. And was ignored- again. "Abby, if I have to come in there and get you, you will rue the day you were born!"

She poked her head back up out of the water, shooting me a confused look. Her light green eyebrows drew together, just like her father's used to, and her little freckled nose wrinkled at something I said. I was smart enough or experienced enough to know that she was not on the verge of obeying, just because I'd threatened her.

"Mommy?" she asked, somehow making her little body tread water in a red polka dot bikini my sister picked up from Gap last summer- it was too small which for some reason made me *more* angry. "What does *rue* mean?"

"It means you're grounded from the iPad, your Leapster and the Wii for the next two years of your life," I threatened. "Now get out of that pool right now before I come in there and get you myself."

She giggled in reply, not believing me for one second and resumed her play.

"Damn it, Abigail," I growled under my breath- not that I was surprised by her behavior. She was naturally an adventurous child. Since she could walk, she'd been climbing to the highest point of anything she could, swinging precariously from branches, light fixtures and aisles at the grocery store. She was a daredevil and there were moments when I absolutely adored her "the world is my playground" attitude about life. But then there were moments like this, when every mom instinct in me screamed she was in danger and her little, rotten life flashed before my eyes.

Those moments happened more and more often. She tested me, pushing every limit and boundary I'd set. She had been reckless before Grady died, now she was just wild. And I didn't know what to do about it.

I didn't know how to tame my uncontrollable child- how to be both parents to a little girl who desperately missed her daddy.

I focused on my outrage, pushing those tragic thoughts down, into the abyss of my soul. I was pissed, I didn't have time for this first thing in the morning and no doubt we were going to be late for school- again.

I slipped off my pajama pants, hoping whomever had moved into the house, if they were watching, would be more concerned with the little girl on the verge of drowning than me flashing my black, bikini briefs at them over morning coffee. I said a few more choice curses and dove into the barely warm water after my second born.

I surfaced, sputtering water and shivering from the cool morning air pebbling my skin. "Abigail, when I get you out of this pool, you are going to be in *so* much trouble."

"Okay," she agreed happily. "But first you have to catch me."

She proceeded to swim around me in circles while I reached out helplessly for her. First thing I was doing when I got out of this pool was throwing away every electronic device in our house just to teach her a lesson. Then I was going to sign her up for a swim team- because the little hellion was very, very fast.

We struggled like this for a few more minutes. Well, I struggled. She splashed at me and laughed at my efforts to wrangle her.

I was aware of a presence hovering by the edge of the pool but I was equally too embarrassed as I was too preoccupied to look. Images of walking my children into school late *again*, kept looping through my head and I cringed at the dirty looks I was bound to get from teachers and other parents alike.

"You look hungry," a deep masculine voice announced from above me.

I whipped my head around to find an incredibly tall man standing by my discarded pajama pants holding two beach towels and a box of Pop-Tarts in one arm, while he munched casually on said Pop-Tarts with the other.

"I look hungry?" I screeched in hysterical anger.

His eyes flickered down at me for just a second, "No, you look mad." He pointed at Abby, who had come to a stop next to me, treading water again with her short child-sized limbs waving wildly in the water. "*She* looks hungry." He grinned at me, his mouth full of food, and looked back at Abby. "Want a Pop-Tart? They're brown sugar."

Abby nodded excitedly and swam to the edge of the pool. Not even using the ladder, she heaved herself out of the water and ran over to the stranger holding out his breakfast to her. He handed her a towel and she hastily draped it around her shoulders and took the offered Pop-Tart.

A million warnings about taking food from strangers ran through my head, but in the end I decided getting us out of his pool was probably more important to him than offing his brand new neighbors with poisoned Pop-Tarts.

With a defeated sigh, I swam over to the ladder closest to my pants and robe, and pulled myself from the water. I was a dripping, limp mess and I was frozen to the bone after my body adjusted to the temperature of the water.

Abby took her Pop-Tart and plopped down on one of the loungers that were still stacked on top of two others and wrapped in plastic. She began munching on it happily, grinning at me like she'd just won the lottery.

She was in *so* much trouble.

I walked over to the stranger, eying him skeptically. He held out his remaining beach towel to me and after realizing I stood before him in just a soaking wet tank top and bikini briefs, I took it quickly and wrapped it around my body. I shivered violently, and my dark blonde hair dripped down my face and back. But I didn't dare adjust the towel, afraid I'd give him more of a show than he'd paid for.

"Good morning," he laughed at me.

"Good morning," I replied slowly, carefully.

Up close, he wasn't the giant I'd originally thought. Now that we were both ground level, I could see that while he was tall, at least six inches taller than me, he wasn't freakishly tall- which relieved some of my concerns. He still wore his pajamas: blue cotton pants and a white t-shirt that had been stretched out from sleep. He had almost black hair that appeared still mussed and disheveled, but swept over to the side in what could be a trendy style if he brushed it. He seemed to be a few years older than me- if I had to guess thirty-five or thirty-six- and he had dark, intelligent eyes that crinkled in the corners with amusement. He was tanned, and muscular, and imposing. And I hated that he was laughing at me.

"Sorry about the gate," he shrugged. "I didn't realize there were kids around."

"You moved into a neighborhood," I pointed out dryly. "There's bound to be kids around."

His eyes narrowed at the insult but he swallowed his Pop-Tart and agreed, "Fair enough. I'll keep the gate locked from now on."

I wasn't finished with berating him though. His pool caused all kinds of problems for me this morning and since I could only take out so much anger on my six-year-old, I had to vent the rest somewhere. "Who fills their pool the first week of September anyway? You've been to New England in the winter, haven't you?"

He cleared his throat and the last laugh lines around his eyes disappeared. "My real estate agent," he explained. "It was kind of like a 'thank you' present for buying the house. He thought he was doing something nice for me."

I snorted at that, thinking how my little girl could have... No, I couldn't go there; physically, I was not emotionally capable of thinking that thought through.

"I really am sorry," he offered genuinely, his dark eyes flashing with true emotion. "I got in late last night, and passed out on the couch. I didn't even know the pool was full or the gate was open until I heard you screaming out here."

Guilt settled in my stomach like acid, and I regretted my harsh tone with him. This wasn't his fault. I just wanted to blame someone else.

"Look, I'm sorry I was snappish about the pool. I just, I was just worried about Abby. I took it out on you," I relented, but wouldn't look him in the eye. I'd always been terrible at apologies. When Grady and I would fight, I could never bring myself to tell him I felt sorry. Eventually, he'd just look at me and say, "I forgive you, Lizzy. Now come here and make it up to me." With anyone else my pride would have refused to let me give in; but with Grady, the way he smoothed over my stubbornness and let me get away with keeping my dignity, worked every single time.

"It's alright, I can understand that," my new neighbor agreed.

We stood there awkwardly for a few more moments, before I swooped down to pick up my plaid pants and discarded robe. "Alright, well I need to go get the kids ready for school. Thanks for convincing her to get out. Who knows how long we would have been stuck there playing *Finding Nemo*."

He chuckled but his eyes were confused. "Is that like Marco Polo?"

I shot him a questioning glance, wondering if he was serious or not. "No kids?" I asked.

He laughed again. "Nope, life-long bachelor." He waved the box of Pop-Tarts and realization dawned on me. He hadn't really seemed like a father before now, but in my world- my four kids, soccer mom, neighborhood watch secretary, active member of the PTO world- it was almost unfathomable to me that someone his age could not have kids.

I cleared my throat, "It's uh, a little kid movie. Disney," I explained and understanding lit his expression. "Um, thanks again." I turned to Abby who was finishing up her breakfast, "Let's go, Abs, you're making us late for school."

"I'm Ben by the way," he called out to my back. "Ben Tyler."

I snorted to myself at the two first names- it somehow seemed appropriate for the handsome life-long bachelor, but ridiculous all the same.

"Liz Carson," I called over my shoulder. "Welcome to the neighborhood."

"Uh, the towels?" he shouted after me when we'd reached the gate.

I turned around with a dropped mouth, thinking a hundred different vile things about my new neighbor. "Can't we... I..." I glanced down helplessly at my bare legs poking out of the bottom of the towel he'd just lent me.

"Liz," he laughed familiarly, and I tried not to resent him. "I'm just teasing. Bring them back whenever."

I growled something unintelligible that I hope sounded like "thank you" and spun on my heel, shooing Abby onto the lawn between our houses.

"Nice to meet you, neighbor," he called out over the fence.

"You too," I mumbled, not even turning my head to look back at him.

Obviously he was single and unattached. He was way too smug for his own good. I just hoped he would keep his gate locked and loud parties few and far between. He seemed like the type to throw frat party-like keggers and hire strippers for the weekend. I had a family to raise, a family that was quickly falling apart while I floundered to hold us together with tired arms and a broken spirit. I didn't need a nosy neighbor handing out Pop-Tarts and sarcasm interfering with my life.